THIS BOY

THIS BOY

A Novel By
F. Mark Granato

All rights reserved

F. Mark Granato
fmgranato@aol.com
Fmarkgranato.com
www.facebook.com at Author F. Mark Granato

F
GRANATO
F. MARK

THIS BOY

A Novel by

F. Mark Granato

..

Also by F. Mark Granato

Titanic: The Final Voyage

Beneath His Wings:
The Plot to Murder Lindbergh

Of Winds and Rage

Finding David

The Barn Find

Out of Reach:
The Day Hartford Hospital Burned

UNLEASHED

To my wife,
as we near our 40th anniversary:
It was your smile
that stole my heart as a boy,
but your extraordinary spirit
as a woman
that has filled my life.

THIS BOY

That boy took my love away
Oh, he'll regret it someday
But this boy wants you back again

That boy isn't good for you
Thought he may want you too
This boy wants you back again

Oh, and this boy would be happy
Just to love you, but oh my
That boy won't be happy
Till he's seen you cry

This boy wouldn't mind the pain
Would always feels the same
If this boy gets you back again

Authors Note

When I began *This Boy*, my intent was to write a love story from the perspective of a young man growing up in the South End of Hartford in the tumultuous mid 1960's and early 70's — a period of immense upheaval and tragedy in American history.

But as I got deeper into the story, the events of this most amazing period in America began to jar me. At first I thought it was just the pain of dredging up dreadful and often heartbreaking memories. Then it hit me. What were bothering me were the glaring parallels I suddenly saw of the 60's and 70's to the early years of this new century.

But more than anything, it was the pain of recognizing that America never seems to learn from it past mistakes.

Much of *This Boy* recounts the divisive agony of the Vietnam War, a conflict that grew out of control through government deceit. The Gulf of Tonkin incident in 1964 resulted in Congress giving the U.S. President nearly unlimited authority to wage war in Southeast Asia. In fact, the Gulf of Tonkin never happened, as history has proven, but was a shameless excuse to escalate the conflict. More than 50,000 American boys died while two Presidents pursued an aimless war with Vietnam so we would have "Peace with Honor" and their presidencies would not be tagged with the loss of an American conflict. Move the clock forward 50 years and a new President launched a war in the Middle East with the same authority citing the grave threat of "Weapons of Mass Destruction," which, of course, were never found because they never existed. We were fooled, again, and thousands more American troops died for no reason.

This Boy also traces the destructive force of racial bigotry that nearly burned America to the ground in the 1960's. Hundred's died in dozens of riots protesting inequality and divided America as never before. Legislation was enacted ensuring equality of all races, creeds and colors as the Constitution had intended. But 50 years later, do we have equality? America of 2016 is as close to a race war as it was in 1966.

The parallels are countless, as are the lessons never learned. For example, billions are spent on weapons while pennies are committed to medical research. Education is woefully underfunded across America. And our elected leaders do not represent our country, but serve only to get their fill at the Pork Barrel buffet.

The lessons of the 60's and 70's were painful and should be bad memories. But instead, we waste the knowledge we should have gained from them by committing the same ignorant mistakes over and over again. Our mistakes of the past exist only as reminders of how little we have learned from them.

And the beat goes on.

F. Mark Granato
November 6, 2016

Fenwick

~~~ ❡ ~~~

August 16, 1980

It was sunset and the light had dimmed to where I could just make out her shape lying on a wicker chaise at the end of the veranda. I waited for the brass wall lanterns to snap on, signaling the end of another summer's day. Right on cue, the soft lights washed the porch in a dusky glow that was just enough to let me study her. She appeared to be resting peacefully, her body so thin now that it barely indented the thick cushions of her chair. But in the diffuse light I couldn't tell if she was sleeping or perhaps just staring out over the fading horizon.

My heart hurt. I needed to know everything in these precious minutes.

It occurred to me as I stared in silence, that the ache I felt was the same I had experienced the very first time I saw her so long ago on a mid-August day, when I had fallen instantly in love with the teenage girl with her sun bleached hair and ocean green eyes. So much had changed since then, except for the one thing that never would. My love for her was still as deep and unconditional as ever.

But now we were no longer teenagers. And it wasn't only love that made my chest ache. It was fear, too.

The air had chilled, abruptly and unexpectedly in the minutes before the sun set over Long Island Sound, perhaps an ominous warning of what I dreaded would happen this night. But it had been a glorious day, full of angel hair clouds floating against an azure blue sky, the sun's rays warming beachcombers and swimmers right up until late afternoon. An orange glow still appeared on the horizon as the final seconds of daylight slowly faded.

The ocean–facing porch on the old mansion in Fenwick, a tiny but very wealthy borough of Old Saybrook, Connecticut had given us a stage from which to view the day's end that was more beautiful and enchanting than any I had ever witnessed before. The sunset was almost like a Monet coming to life with a pallet of brilliant colors that slowly muted into the darkness.

On most summer nights we would sit on the private beach below the mansion at the foot of the giant sea wall that protected it and watch the sunset. But not tonight. She was much too weak to make her way down the winding, weathered staircase that would bring us to the still warm sand and near the ebbing tide lapping at the shoreline.

"Are you cold?" I whispered as I walked closer to her side, worried that she might be dozing and I would awaken her. Sleep was so difficult for her now.

She opened her tired eyes and smiled up at me, always intent upon putting my worries to rest.

"Maybe just a little," she responded softly.

I smiled, but hearing her unnerved me. Her voice had always been so full of energy. Not loud but assured in an elegant sort of way. When she spoke people listened not only because she was extremely articulate and entertaining, but also because the sound that came off her lips was so pleasantly melodious. It wasn't hard to fall in love with the sound of her voice before you even came to know her. The rest was inevitable.

But now, one had to lean close to hear her. Her voice had become weak and faint, with just the slightest hint of gravel.

"Then let me get you into the house," I said quickly, leaping up like Sir Galahad to scoop her up out of the chaise lounge on which she lay. From experience I knew I would have no trouble lifting what was left of her ravaged body.

"No, don't, please no..." she resisted, looking into my eyes while she gently pushed my hands away. "I want to stay, enjoy the smell of the ocean and watch the stars come out."

"Then let me get you a blanket at least," I insisted with as much cheer as I could feign and hurried into the living room to fetch the throw off one of the two, oversized off-white salon couches that flanked the huge stone fireplace running up the center of the house. This would be a good night to light a fire, I thought, then hesitated for a moment as I often did, taking in the room. I loved this space, perhaps because she had decorated it herself. I could see her in every detail of the room.

3

It had once been a cavernous, dark, dreary great room that I had detested for being cold and austere. In many ways it had reflected the personality of her mother who had been given the house as a wedding present from her doting husband, a man who adored her for reasons I never came to appreciate. Built after the Great New England Hurricane of 1938 had destroyed the previous home sitting on the same four-acre parcel, the Victorian style mansion had survived several hurricanes since. But even more impressive was that it had withstood the fury of the late Betty Hanson.

Back then, the overabundance of mahogany trim, wainscoting and deeply stained floors combined to create an overwhelmingly heavy and oppressive ambience. It mirrored the former owner's mostly bleak outlook on life even when she was young and fabulously wealthy. Most of the floor area was covered in deep maroon and ink blue oriental rugs, apparently an effort to add some color to the pallet. But even though these 19th century pieces were worth a fortune even then, their muted shades did little to add any relief to the milieu. The floor to ceiling windows that lined both sides of the room were hidden behind heavy brown velvet drapes that were always pulled closed, robbing the room of natural light. The whole effect was just depressing. I always felt that with a little moisture, it would have been the perfect environment in which to grow mushrooms.

But when her daughter had finally inherited the house after the death of her parents some years before, in a flurry of energy she had transformed the gloomy, lifeless environment into the most inviting world, a place shining with anticipation of hope and happiness.

She wasted no time in tearing down the drapes allowing the huge expanse of windows to bathe the room in soft, unfettered sunlight during the day, which produced the unexpected bonus of making the space appear even larger, yet somehow cozy. Exposed bleached oak floors, white painted moldings and the addition of the two oversized salon couches infused an air of "summer cottage" into the 15,000 square foot mansion.

Now the room was a reflection of what she had been. Always the antithesis of her mother, full of life and vitality, a bit wild, but inevitably so inviting. Only I knew that this room had served as a kind of painting to her — a canvas meant to cover the hurt that had broken her heart. The hurt that boy...

I stopped myself. There were no longer "boys" fighting over a girl. Yet I couldn't stop remembering him as, "That boy." I wanted to laugh, but I couldn't. The pain of the struggle to win her, the long, agonizing years alone, and now the finiteness of her health that would rob us of a future together for which I was so desperate, was very real. And while forgiveness was in my heart, it was reserved only for her.

Perhaps it was because "This boy" had finally made the song come true, and I intended to live up to the terms of its promise. It still amazed me that a song that we had sung together long ago, a poignant but amusing way of articulating what she knew to be my feelings, had really come to be a synopsis of my life. A life spent in pursuit of the woman I never believed would love me again.

The lyrics, never far from my lips, came back to me as I returned to her carrying the blanket.

"That boy, took my love away..."

5

But she was mine again. Forever. What was excruciating was knowing that so little of "forever" would be of this world.

I intentionally stepped heavily back onto the veranda so she would hear me return.

"Hey, what took you so long?" she said. "A girl could freeze around here..." she laughed, her thin lips easing into a smile.

"Sorry..." I said, regretting my dawdling in the great room. It bothered me to disappoint her in any way.

"Oh, don't be silly," she said and patted the side of her chair.

"Sit with me, please?"

"Sure, best invitation I've had in a long time." I moved some pillows around so my weight wouldn't hurt her. She was so frail now.

"What's today?" she asked, as I cozied up alongside her.

"It's the... 16th," I said. The summer was flying by as fast as our lives together. "August 16th."

"Do you know where we were 15 years ago last night?" she continued.

I laughed out loud.

"I can't remember where I put my car keys."

She smiled.

"Silly. Really. Do you remember?"

I wasted no more of the precious memory.

"With you. On the best date of my entire life."

"I remember telling you that you'd remember it that way," I replied in mock indignity.

"Where?" she asked, delighting in the game. She coughed and held her ribs from the pain, but quickly came back for more.

"Where for heaven's sake!" she demanded.

For a moment, my mind imagined that the grey hair she now wore pulled back off her face into a simple twist had transformed again into the shoulder length, sun bleached locks that had framed her beautiful face so perfectly at 17 and her cloudy green eyes sparkled once more with the mischief that was part of her mystery. She had always been my Mona Lisa.

"Let me see. The year was 1965, the date was August 15th and we were at Shea Stadium for a concert on our very first date. I had known you less than 24 hours and we were together in the most exciting, most unbelievable place on earth. We had a pair of the most sought after tickets in the world to see..." I purposely let the final words dangle.

My heart skipped at the sight of her delight in being invited to say the magic words that had begun such a profoundly complex relationship.

She waited until she could summon up enough air to yell out the answer.

"The Beatles!" she squealed, for an instant sounding just like one of the screaming, love struck teenaged girls that had all but sabotaged the Fab Four's valiant efforts to perform that night in front of more than 55,000 screaming fans. I was partially deaf for days after.

The game continued.

"Opening Act?" I asked.

"We missed King Curtis and Cannibal and the Headhunters but we did catch Brenda Holloway and Sounds Incorporated," she replied instantly, her voice drifting off as she became winded from the excitement of the memory.

"Impressive. Are you all right? Can I get you a cup of tea?" I asked, sorry now that I had started this.

"I'm fine," she lied. "More."

"First song."

"Twist and Shout. John Lennon." She smiled, knowing she was invincible.

And still so lovely. I fought back an urge to cry. Instead I leaned down and kissed her forehead. She was feverish.

"You are incorrigible," I said. "What a memory."

"You forgot the best part," she said. I thought she was being mischievous, but the tone of her voice was sad.

"And that was?" I asked, puzzled.

"I was with you. Best night of my entire life. The one I will never forget."

I swallowed hard.

"Interesting," I replied.

"What do you mean?"

"Most of that night is a blur to me. I mean the part about seeing the most famous rock n' roll band in the world up close, about being part of that scene. It isn't what I remember most."

"What do you remember most?"

"Being with you."

She caught her breath like a schoolgirl hearing the words "I love you" said to her for the first time.

"Really?"

"I remember every second of being with you, of holding your hand when we ran to catch the subway, of kissing you goodnight. Of knowing that I was helplessly, hopelessly in love with you and... "

"And what?" she prodded me. "Don't stop now. You only got to second base that night. No telling where the end of this story might lead you." She snuggled back into the crook of my arm.

"And that I didn't have a chance in the world of making you mine. Of the sudden understanding that we were from two different planets and there was a lot more

8

than just 50 miles between the South End of Hartford and Fenwick."

The smile fell from her face.

"I have never felt more excited, more alive or more in love than I did that night, nor more despondent about my future and any chance of happiness," I continued. "Because I knew you couldn't be a part of my life. It was if the roles of Cinderella had been reversed. You were the princess in the castle, and I was the poor boy without hope."

She was quiet as I finished.

"I'm sorry," she finally said. "It wasn't fair... to either of us."

"No. It wasn't."

I suddenly realized I had gone and killed the fleeting happiness with which we'd begun our evening. It wasn't the first time.

"Oh, nonsense," I said, desperately backpedaling. "We'll have many more nights together. I promise. With no one or anything in our way."

"Not sure," she whispered, looking away.

I searched for something to say. How long could we continue to avoid the truth...

"There's one!" she suddenly said, pointing up to the first star of the night. I saw it. Just a tiny pinprick of light, but enough to change the subject. She was an expert at the art. Thank God.

"Let's get you inside, it's getting colder."

"No!" she barked at me and coughed from the effort. "Please... let me stay, just a few more minutes."

"Darling, you're already feverish..."

"I don't care. I want to be here... with the ocean and the sky... and in your arms. I haven't had enough of any of them..."

9

She paused and turned to look up at me. Her eyes were sad.

"Especially not nearly enough of you," she said. A single tear rolled down her cheek.

The crack in my heart grew another quarter inch.

"You've owned me since I was 18," I managed to whisper, trying to hide the breaking of my voice. "Every minute of every day, even if I wasn't here, even when you didn't love me."

She squeezed my arm, her manicured nails digging into my skin.

"I just didn't know I loved you. But I did. In the end, he was only here while I waited for you."

I tried to force a smile to my face, but it would not come.

"That boy…"

She reached up and put a finger to my lips, hushing me.

"Kiss me, please?" It wasn't a request. It was a need. I didn't wait for a second invitation.

I pressed my lips to hers, remembering to be gentle and poured my passion into a tender kiss. When I tried to break off, she held me, prolonging it.

We held the kiss even as I picked her up to carry her inside to the warmth of the fireplace.

I began to walk very slowly back to the great room with her in my arms, then abruptly stopped, carrying her to the edge of the porch. It had struck me that she may not see the stars or hear the ocean waves breaking on the shore ever again.

I turned my head to the sky.

"Look, sweetie, more stars. And if you listen, the surf is picking up with the wind. Can you smell the ocean?"

She leaned her head back and stared up at me.

10

"What?" I asked, my voice about to crack again.

"Favorite Beatles song?"

"Oh...

"C'mon..." she demanded.

"But you already know," I pleaded. "Don't you?"

"Yes... I do."

"Then why...?" I asked.

"Because I need to hear you say it...so I can believe it." She choked up.

"This Boy."

She smiled. Another tear.

"Is it true?" she begged me.

"Yes," I said without hesitation. "Nothing before now matters. You were always in my mind and heart. I always have and always will love you."

She brought her face to mine, and hugged me as hard as she was able, then hid her face again in the crook of my arm.

"Take me inside now, love," she said. "Thank you for the stars and the waves and the ocean. Now I need one more thing from you."

"Now what could that be? Riches? Treasure? Precious baubles? Whatever could you want? Your wish is my..."

"Yes, treasure."

I cocked an eye, unsure of what she wanted.

"I want you to tell me the story of us...so I can take it with me..."

I couldn't stop the tears that wet my face as I carried her into the house, no more than I could prevent my heart from slowly shattering into a million pieces.

But on this night, perhaps our last together, I would share with her, again, the story of us.

No matter how much it hurt.

11

One

~~~ ❧ ~~~

Saturday, August 14, 1965

With a throaty, ear-splitting roar, the primer-black 1957 Chevy convertible's front wheels crossed the solid double yellow traffic lines and swung recklessly into the oncoming lane as its impatient driver floored the hot rod. An elderly couple turned to watch from the front seat of their vintage Rambler, frightened by the sudden appearance and denture-rattling exhaust racket of the passing car.

"Get a friggin' horse, old man!" the car's front seat passenger yelled at the white-haired gentleman behind the wheel of the slow moving car. "There oughta be a law..." he added, flipping off the driver with a one finger salute.

"Cool it," the Chevy's driver shouted to his passenger above the din of wind whipping through the open car. "Don't you have grandparents you moron? They're old. They drive slowly. What's the big deal?" he asked while smoothly pulling the Chevy back into the southbound lane but lifting only slightly off the throttle.

The small block V-8 nestled in the engine bay of the late model car had been modified with the best of a shade tree mechanic's know-how to eek out another 30 or so horsepower. With an open exhaust system tricked out with "dump" pipes just below the manifolds, the car sounded more powerful than it actually was. But that was just fine for its teenaged owner. The sound was music to his ears.

The dash-mounted AM radio blared out rock n' roll music to add to the cacophony of noise that jarred residents of rural Haddam on Route 81 as the car and it's five high school seniors sped towards the shoreline.

The boys all worked summer jobs at Carducci's Ristorante, a fancy Italian eatery in Hartford's South End owned by their high school football coach. It was about the best summer job a kid could hope for and they all had great respect for owner Paul Carducci, a former high school football star himself who'd come up the hard way and made good. Paul enjoyed taking care of kids who had to fight their way through life like he had, starting from nothing. He occasionally did catering and tonight a regular customer who also happened to be a millionaire had asked him to serve a lavish party he was hosting at his mansion in the tiny, exclusive borough of Old Saybrook known as Fenwick.

Carducci handpicked the five teens that he had coached during their high school years. They were a tight knit group and he knew they'd watch each other's backs. The boys were all strangers to wealth, but he was counting on their respect for him to put them on their best behavior and tolerate the aristocratic behavior he knew was intuitive to the Fenwick set. Besides, they'd each earn $100 for the night, more than a week's pay. That ought to be some incentive to walk the line.

"Hey, turn that up will ya?" one of the back seat passengers yelled as a record was introduced by WDRC radio disc jockey Dickie Robinson, an idol of nearly every teen in the Hartford area and a major influence on the local rock n' roll scene.

"Turn up that dial, guys and gals. It's that time again!" Robinson teased his vast listening audience that was growing bigger by the day. "Here we go. You know how it works. The fourth person to call me here at 'Big D' 1360 radio will win two tickets to Shea Stadium for the opening concert tomorrow night of the Beatles US tour! That's right — you'll win two of the hottest tickets in America if you're the fourth person to call in 522-1360, that's 522-1360! Get ready, get set… dial that number!" he instructed frantic teens all over the Greater Hartford listening area.

"Shit!" the five teens in the speeding Chevy hollered almost simultaneously. "Danny, pull over, fast, into the gas station!" the tall boy in the front passenger seat named "Chickie" yelled to the driver, Danny Logan, his best friend since the first grade.

Logan saw the gas station at the last second and didn't have to be told twice, swerving the big Chevy into the lot just as they were about to pass by.

He slammed on the brakes and all five teens jumped out of the car almost before it stopped rolling, desperate to find a payphone.

"There," Logan screamed and pointed. "On the wall inside, behind the register." He was first through

14

the door and nearly knocked over the attendant who was sitting behind a counter browsing through a magazine.

"What the..." he hollered as Danny nearly knocked him off his stool to get to the phone.

"Sorry, buddy," he said unashamedly while fishing a dime out of his pocket and depositing it into the payphone. Urgently he dialed the number and was shocked a minute later to get a connection rather than the busy signal he expected after playing the game for the last three weeks. There was a pause, silence and then a voice came on the phone and said, "Hold, please."

In the background, Logan heard Robinson on the air announce, "We have a winner! That's right, we have a winner! Let's find out who it is."

Logan looked around at his buddies in confusion.

"Don't do anything. Don't even breath, Danny!" Chickie yelled.

Suddenly, the voice came back to him.

"WDRC, Big D 1360 here," Logan heard. It was Dickie Robinson. "And to whom do I have the pleasure of speaking with?"

Danny Logan almost couldn't get the words out.

"Crap, Danny, say something!" Chickie screamed out for fear Robinson would think he had a bad line and hang up. "Tell him your name!"

"Uh, Dan! Danny Logan!" the boy finally spit into the telephone.

"Where you from, Dan?" the disc jockey asked. His voice echoed out of the car radio in the background.

"Uh... Hartford, sir...yah, Hartford. Broad Street..."

"Well, Danny Logan from Broad Street in Hartford, guess what the Big D 1360 Radio has for you?" Robinson asked like a circus ringmaster.

15

"Tick... tickets?" Logan nearly screeched into the telephone.

"That's right, son. Two tickets for tomorrow nights' concert at Shea Stadium in New York to see those fabulous mop heads from Liverpool. The Beatles!"

"Holy..."

Robinson quickly cut him off before Logan could utter the expletive that was on the tip of his tongue.

"And who's the lucky lady who will be joining you, Danny?" Robinson pried, milking the moment for every drop of PR he could wring out of the boy.

Logan was caught completely off guard by the question.

"Uh, well, I, uh..."

Probably got a dozen young ladies in mind, hey Danny?" Robinson said, letting him off the hook. "Whoever she is, have a blast on the Big D, WDRC 1360 on your radio dial, Dan, the tickets will be waiting for you at the "Will Call" booth at Shea Stadium. And now, let's hear from them!" Immediately, the sound of John Lennon singing *"Help! I need someone..."* filled the air from the Chevy's radio as Logan took the phone from his ear and stared at it, in shock.

"Holy shit!" Eddie, Tony and Mike, the trio from the back seat of the Chevy screamed nearly in unison.

"You frigging did it, Danny! You did it!" Eddie said, slapping his long time friend on the back. "I don't believe it!"

"Who you gonna take, Dan, who?" Mike, the freckled face redhead asked, getting right to the point. You wanna sell the ticket? How much? How much?"

They were all crowding around him, slapping him on the back and pummeling him with questions.

"Get off me, you guys," he yelled. "Shit, I don't know what I'm going to do with it. I sure as hell ain't selling it to you, Mike. You want to be my date, fer cryin' out loud?"

"Well... who you gonna give the ticket to?" Eddie Graziano asked. The six-foot, 175- pound Logan glared at him, but carefully. Graziano had been the center on their conference winning football team and weighed in at six foot five and nearly 300 pounds. When he asked a question, most people gave an answer.

"Sorry to disappoint you, Eddie, but it ain't going to be you either. "

"Aw, c'mon, Logan, you gotta at least give us a shot at it... like we could draw straws or something. Man, this is a once in a lifetime deal here," Tony, a slight, whiny kid who was the team kicker complained.

"Forget it, Tony."

"Oh man..." Chickie protested for the group. "That's bullshit. You don't even have a girlfriend."

"Yah... well, neither do you, hotshot..."

"Hey man, I'm just saying."

"Well... I gotta think about what I'm going to do," Logan said. "C'mon, we gotta get to work."

The five teens piled back into the hot rod and made their way along the winding Route 81 until they reached Clinton. Then they headed north along Old Boston Post Road towards Old Saybrook, situated at the outlet of the Connecticut River into Long Island Sound.

There was silence in the car, each of its passengers pouting over how close they'd come to witnessing rock n' roll history. All except Danny Logan, whose head was spinning with excitement... and confusion.

He really didn't have any idea of what to do with the ticket, not having a steady girlfriend or even someone he'd like to date. Logan had only one brief brush with what he would consider a serious relationship. It was a several weeks long affair that ended with him being humiliated by a girl who only wanted to be seen with him during the football season. The experience had made him leery of getting involved again.

At the time, he licked his wounds by rejoining his buddies in Goodwin Park on weekends where they hid in the wooded area by their high school and got drunk on cheap beer. It was the way teenage boys handled disappointment bordering on heartbreak. They went right back to doing what they did best. Hanging together, working on their beat up old cars, hitting the beaches and playing pick up games of tackle football. Life went on.

So what would he do with the precious ticket?

He had a younger cousin who came to mind, a cute kid two years younger, but he couldn't imagine the grief he would get at school for taking her to the concert. He might as well take his mother, but she was usually drunk by that time of night.

As they approached Old Saybrook he forced himself to stop thinking about it. Worse case, he'd make arrangements with Chickie to secretly meet him there under the threat of murder if he shared the news with anyone else. But the thought of wasting the greatest date night ticket ever on a guy he drank beer with made his stomach churn.

"Ya know, we can't screw this up tonight," Logan said, desperate to change the subject. "Carducci's counting on us," he yelled out to his passengers as he reached over and turned the radio down.

"Somebody's gonna give us shit though, you know that, right Dan? You can be sure there's gonna be some rich kid there that's just going to have to shoot his mouth off," Chickie said as a matter of fact.

"Yah," Mike chimed in. "It's gonna happen, sure as shit."

Eddie Graziano scowled at the thought of a confrontation. He didn't back down from anyone. Neither did he want to let down his coach who'd been as much of a father to him as his own.

"Tell ya what," Graziano said after a few minutes of contemplating the problem. "If anyone runs off at the lip, just let me know. I'll put the stare on the guy. Shuts 'em up every time."

There was laughter in the car. Each of them knew the "Graziano stare." It would stop a charging bull with a full head of steam dead in his tracks. He'd bailed them out of more than one situation where they'd been outgunned or outnumbered.

"Deal?" Graziano asked.

Logan laughed first. "Yah, deal, Eddie. But who's going to stop you if you lose it?"

"Shit, we'd have to call in the frigging Marines," Tony said.

"Better make that a whole division of Marines," the oversized Graziano responded, prompting more laughter. "But I ain't gonna lose it. Out of respect for Paul. You all better do the same."

"Right you are, Eddie," Logan said.

Old Boston Post Road abruptly ended in the center of Old Saybrook.

"Where did Paul say we'd find this burgh?" Chickie asked.

"We're supposed to find Bridge Street. It's a long causeway over the water that brings us right to it," Logan replied.

"Over the water? The water?" Tony squeaked, his panic getting the best of his vocal chords.

"What, you can't swim, pansy?" Graziano laughed at the slighter boy, always the one to voice the concern everyone else had but didn't want to be the first one to mention.

"Relax… it's only a couple miles towards the water and a causeway is a bridge, you brick heads. We'll be high and dry, guys," the driver said.

They came to a stop sign at the end of Main Street. Ahead was the ocean.

"No signs for Bridge Street," Tony said.

"But there is a hot dog stand to the left, so if we can't find it we'll survive," Graziano said so seriously that they all burst into laughter.

"Is food the only thing you think about?" Chickie said to his overweight friend.

"No…" Graziano said, feigning hurt feelings. "Well… maybe…"

Logan spotted the causeway ahead. It was an extremely narrow, two-lane blacktop built on a stone foundation with only a frail looking guardrail between traffic and the ocean. He stopped to let a car approaching from the other direction finish the crossing. The car had been hugging the double yellow traffic lines the entire distance, perhaps a half a mile across. There didn't appear to be room for two cars.

"Man, what I wouldn't do for a Volkswagen right about now," Tony said from the back of the car.

"Aw hell, piece of cake," Logan said, and with that, floored the big Chevy, spinning the tires and laying down rubber to show they'd been there. For teenage boys it was the equivalent of a dog marking his territory.

A road sign ahead said the speed limit was 25 miles per hour. Logan flew by it at 60.

"Screw it," Mike said. "If we're going to die, it might as well be in a way they'll be talking about for a while!"

Ahead, Logan came upon a slow moving car with a couple of old sightseers inside. He didn't slow the hot rod Chevy but began edging the car into the next lane.

Chickie visibly moved up in his seat when he saw what Logan was about to do.

"Danny! You're not going to do what I think you are..."

"Well..." Logan said, a kind of grin coming to his face that only a teenager with a wild streak would recognize.

Before the others could react, Logan had the Chevy nearly up against the guardrail in the other lane and was beside the slower car, its occupants pale with fright. He was by in a flash and swerved back into the right lane, nearly brushing the Chevy's right side tail fin off the guardrail as the rear tires of the big car lost traction and fishtailed.

"Holy shit!" Eddie yelled as the others began slapping the back seat in hysterics at the sheer recklessness of Logan's action. It was not unlike the way they lived. They were fearless.

It was a bravado that wasn't prompted by a desire to attract attention, but rather a statement that they didn't think much of their futures. They were about to graduate from high school, only a couple of them had plans to go to college, and in the back of everyone's mind was the news of a military action in Vietnam that seemed to be getting bigger by the day. The draft was something they didn't talk about, but it was always there.

"I'll be damned," Chickie yelled as the end of the causeway approached. "There's a sign. 'Fenwick.' Jesus Christ, the frigging place does exist."

Logan pulled to a stop and waited for traffic to pass, then made a left hand turn by the elaborate carved wooden sign, centered on a landscaped island and surrounded by well-manicured shrubs and flowers. A flagpole stood behind it with the Stars and Stripes flying proudly above. Below it hung the Connecticut state flag.

"Man, there's a memorial at the entrance," Mike said out loud. "People live here? It looks more like the gateway to a cemetery."

It was hard to tell. The entranceway effectively blocked any visibility into what lay beyond.

"Look, Carducci said Fenwick, four o'clock. That's where we are and..." He glanced at his wristwatch. "Right. That's what time it is. Can't imagine that flag is there to mark a garbage dump."

Logan gunned the Chevy around the small island and drove slowly down the narrow road ahead. The only road, from what he could see. To the left was the ocean they had just crossed over on the causeway. To the right, there was nothing but acres of gently rolling, sharply cut grass. A solitary man was walking across it about 50 yards ahead carrying something over his shoulder. Then he happened to see it, just a faint swatch of red flapping in the breeze coming off the ocean. It was a flagstick. The kind one found on a golf course.

"What the..." he began in surprise. Eddie finished the sentence.

"It's a friggin' golf course. We're driving through a golf course."

"Jesus, how rich did Paul say his friend was? He has his own golf course?" Chickie piped in.

22

Silence enveloped the car, still moving at an unaccustomed leisurely pace. Only the drone of it's open exhaust pipes interrupted the natural chorus of the gentle breeze and the sound of ocean waves crashing somewhere ahead. They were all somewhat intimidated just by the grounds.

Logan took a right turn when the road abruptly cut across the golf course. That's when the mansions came into view.

Chickie let out an admiring whistle.

"Man..." Eddie followed from the back seat. "We ain't on South Street anymore," he said, taking in the huge, cedar shingled "cottages" of the very wealthy that summered or lived year-round at Fenwick. Logan was so struck by the sight that he brought the car to a halt and just stared.

"Are those houses — or hotels?" Tony stuttered, standing up in the back seat of the convertible, awed by the sight.

"I didn't know there was a Disneyland in Connecticut..." Mike mumbled, slowly rising from his seat in the back. "Holy shit."

To their right, the boys could peer down two streets lined with the outlandishly large homes, at once nearly breathtaking in their beauty and sinful in their excess. They had never seen anything quite like it.

"Man," Eddie whispered. "It's a long way from bussing tables to living here."

"Yah," Chickie answered. "But I don't think the owners did much sweating to afford these places. Playing golf doesn't count."

Logan didn't like their attitudes.

"Hey you guys, knock it off. There's the 'haves' and the 'have nots', right? We don't get a choice in life. You gotta make your own way. A hundred bucks for

23

one nights' work is a good way to begin. Let's not get pissed off before we even start the job."

Graziano let out a deep breath.

"You're the boss. Danny, but you got to admit, life ain't fair. Having said that, guess we all owe Paul enough to swallow a bitter pill…"

Logan pulled the car slowly forward to a street sign that read Pettipaug Avenue. Beneath it was a sign painted by a calligrapher's elegant hand announcing "The Hanson Party."

"This be the place, chumps," Logan called out and turned down the road that was paved in hard packed gravel that added to the elegance of the setting. Slowly they drove past a half dozen or so of the stately mansions, all positioned to look out over Long Island Sound above the protection of a great concrete seawall. The sun was low in the cloudless sky and they were able to take in the exquisite details of the summer cottages with their weathered shingles and oversized windows. A pair of storm shutters flanked each window, at the ready in case of the fierce storms that could come racing across the Sound with little warning. Such a storm — the Great Hurricane of 1938 — had walloped the tiny village without warning, but many of the structures had survived because of the seawall that dropped nearly 30 feet to the private beaches below. Actress Katherine Hepburn's family home, at the very tip of Fenwick had been lost.

Logan stopped in front of the mansion. Three stories high looking right out over the ocean, it was covered in weathered shingles with white painted trim. There was a garage in the back that could hold at least six cars, a tennis court and an in-ground pool with a surrounding concrete patio that looked like it could seat a hundred people. He thought for a moment that the owner must have borrowed the landscaping from Elizabeth Park back home in Hartford. It was if a thousand rose bushes and dogwood trees had been laid out in a pattern of gardens and pathways to transform the back of the summer cottage into a lush playground worthy of the White House. Just for a second he allowed himself the fantasy of taking his breakfast by the pool. It was an oasis of wonder for a boy who had only known paved streets and three-story tenement buildings his whole life.

There was a chorus of slurs and four letter words from the car.

"Cool it," Danny yelled. "They hear us and we're out of a job before we start." He pulled the car farther down the road as Paul Carducci had instructed him then swung the Chevy on to a dirt path that appeared to be an entrance for delivery trucks. The hot rod was now hidden from the mansion, which Logan surmised was the reason Paul had given him explicit instructions on where to park to begin with. He felt better when he spied his boss' Cadillac parked in the same place he was headed, next to the restaurant's catering trucks.

He pulled in and killed the engine. The air was suddenly quiet and for the first time, they could actually hear the sound of the waves from Long Island Sound just yards away.

Chickie popped opened the door and spread his arms, sucking in the crisp ocean air.

"Man, have you ever tasted anything sweeter?" he asked.

"Yah, a cold Budweiser after washing dishes for four hours," Eddie laughed.

"No, he's right," Logan said. "Smell that air. Look at this place. Man, have we died and gone to heaven?"

25

"Ask me that after the party," Tony said skeptically.

Carducci suddenly appeared at the back door landing, a flight of steps above them. From the upper railing he gave them a mock blessing as if greeting his admirers in St. Peter's Square.

"My boys, my boys..." he smiled. "Good to see you." He looked around, feigning concern. "I don't hear any sirens, no blue lights... you mean to tell me you came all the way here without breaking a single law?"

"Well..." Logan began.

"Well what?" Paul responded, not knowing he was the butt end of his own joke.

"Yah, we were good boys, Mr. Carducci. Didn't pluck a single rose out of the garden or kidnap any debutantes. But we were tempted," Graziano teased.

"I'll give you a debutante, you juvenile delinquent," Carducci shot back with a smile. "C'mon, let's get to work before our customer catches us slacking off first thing."

"That would be Mr. Hanson, I take it?" Danny asked.

"Yup, a dear old Marine Corps buddy. A while back, we spent some time together on a couple of very rocky islands in the Pacific while the Japanese took turns trying to kill us. Needless to say, they weren't successful and we came home on the same troop ship. Been friends ever since."

"You guys got something in common, Mr. Carducci," Chickie said.

"What's that, Chick?"

"Besides being rich, you both got good luck. My dad visited some of those same islands. Doesn't like to talk about it much."

26

"You'd be right about that, son. Don Hanson and I both left some friends behind... it's not something we talk much about either. We talk business, mostly. And on that note, we'd better get to it. Come on up here and let's get to work shucking some oysters."

The five teens scurried up the wooden stairwell into the kitchen just as two trucks pulled in with tables and chairs to be set up around the pool.

"Logan, you and Chickie go help those guys with the tables and chairs," Paul Carduci instructed. "They'll need your muscle," he grinned. "And remember, if you run into any of the local natives — it's best behavior. Got it?"

"Got it," the two boys echoed, hurrying back down the stairs.

An hour later the two trucks were emptied and tables and chairs now decorated the area around the pool and tennis court. The owner came out and introduced himself to the boys.

"Hey, boys, I'm Don Hanson, thanks for helping me out tonight," he said warmly, shaking their hands.

"Big party tonight, I'll tell ya," My daughter's 17th birthday. She'll be leaving for Radcliffe College in a couple of weeks so I want this to be an extra special night for her. She's the love of my life, that little girl. C'mon over here and let me show you what I bought her. Damn, I hope she likes it," he said, barely able to conceal his excitement.

"She's been after me since before she got her license a year ago to buy her one of these. I'll be damned if I know what she sees in it. I can't even get in the damn thing. But what the hell. If it makes my little girl happy..."

They stopped in front of the first set of garage doors and Hanson unlocked them, swinging them wide

27

open. Inside was a large object, obviously a car, with a canvas tarp over it and a gigantic bow adorning the hood. But it wasn't just any car.

"Oh, man," Danny Logan was first to comment.

"Way too small and sleek to be a Chevy, that's for sure," Chickie added.

"It's English... I'll bet it is," Danny said, a secret admirer of the British Leyland products coming out of England.

"You know your cars, son," Hanson said while carefully removing the ribbon. "Here, give me a hand with the tarp. Didn't want it to get dusty."

The two boys peeled back the canvas protection to reveal the car. Logan was right. The British Racing Green paint, polished to a diamond gloss, leapt at them as the late afternoon sun flooded the garage.

"I knew it," Logan said. "It's an Austin Healey 3000 BJ8 Mark III. A 2+2 convertible. Damn thing looks like its going a hundred miles an hour even parked."

"Whoa..." Chickie mumbled, not sure he had ever seen the model before.

"She's pretty, hey boys?" Hanson said. "Get a load of the white piping on the leather seats. Think she'll like it?"

"Like it?" Logan laughed. "What's not to like?"

"Is that a four-speed transmission?" Chickie asked, drawing a frown from his high school buddy.

"Of course, man. Can you imagine this thing with a stupid GM turbo-hydramatic? It's the 4-speed manual gearbox and the high revving motor that makes this thing fly and handle like nothing— I mean nothing — you can imagine. This car has raced at LeMans, Sebring..."

"You really do know your cars, son," Hanson marveled. "Hope you'll talk with my daughter about it later. Above all, please tell her to drive it slowwwwly, if you will."

"Easier said than done, Mr. Hanson. This car will bring out the worst in a..." he began before catching the look of horror on Hanson's face.

"You had to go and tell me that," Hanson grimaced. "Like I said, just try talking some sense into her, will you, for me?"

"Sure thing."

"Help me cover her up again, will ya boys? My little girl will be down here snooping around before long."

They made it by minutes. Just as the three arrived back at the pool, Elina Hanson, wearing a long terry cloth robe tightly cinched at the waist was just about to take a dip before the party. Shaded by the late afternoon sun above and behind her, the girl's features were hidden as she walked down the stone stairway, it's brick sustaining walls lined with luscious green ivy, leading to the pool.

"Hi Daddy," she waved to her father, ignoring the two boys.

"Hello sweetheart," Hanson yelled back, a wide grin spontaneously breaking over his face. The man's affection for her was obvious. "Come here and meet my friends, will ya?"

She smiled, shyly, seeming to be embarrassed by the awkward moment. But then, inexplicably, the tall, statuesque girl reached down and loosened the belt from her robe and casually shrugged it off her shoulders. It dropped to the ground exposing the stark white, two-piece bikini she wore beneath it. Logan's eyes widened in surprise and he desperately tried to hide a grin. Chickie swallowed so hard it was audible.

As Elina brazenly turned and walked barefoot out of the shade towards them, the low riding bikini bottom tied at the hips plainly argued her womanhood and also accentuated her toned, bare midriff. But it was the bandeau style top, drawn together by a silver rhinestone clip between her full breasts that left little to the hormone-driven imaginations of the two boys. She was deeply tanned after weeks of cavorting beneath the summer sun, causing the white swimsuit to almost glow against her honey colored skin. The overall effect was simply breathtaking. With her long, shapely, silky smooth legs she reached them in several strides and hugged her father, kissing him lightly on the cheek.

He lovingly cupped her face with his hands and kissed her on the forehead. She reached up and hung to his wrists, her nails flawlessly manicured, and flashed a perfect set of teeth and a sparkle in her ocean-green eyes that left no doubt she was as full of the devil as she was beautiful.

"Happy birthday, darling," Don Hanson said to his daughter. "It's hard to believe you're 17 already. I hope tonight will be everything you dreamed it would be."

"Oh, Daddy," she responded to her beaming father, "I know it will be perfect." Abruptly she turned to the boys, hardly oblivious to their silent paralysis but coyly ignored it. Elina Hanson might have been young, but she was already well aware of the magic of her charms if not yet her innate seductive powers. The freedom of college would no doubt enlighten her.

Nonchalantly she used her fingers to tuck her shoulder length blonde hair behind her ears. It was naturally bleached and highlighted by the sun. She wore little makeup, just a bit of eye shadow and a pink shade of lipstick. Around her neck hung a thin, gold necklace

framing the word "Elina" in a graceful script. Her whole presentation was exceedingly simple and elegant, yet beneath her coolness was a smoldering sexuality that Logan and his buddy could almost smell. Strangely, her father seemed unconscious of it.

She turned to Danny Logan, her eyes sweeping past Chickie without even a hesitation. "Aren't you going to introduce me to your friends?" she said to her father.

"Of course, sweetheart," he said, still taking in his daughter's beauty. "This here is Danny, a friend of Paul Carducci. And his buddy, uh... I forgot your name son..." he apologized.

"My friends call me 'Chickie', but my name is Charlie... I mean, Charles... Anderson." Elina and the overwhelming surroundings had quickly impressed upon Chickie that South Street was indeed a very long ways away. Not that his attempt to put on some polish seemed to have any effect on his employer's daughter. She seemed to have eyes only for his best friend.

"I'm Danny Logan," the six-foot-two, sandy haired boy introduced himself to Elina. She smiled, just parting her lips enough to let Logan know she was interested. No wonder. Logan was handsome by any stretch and was blessed with brown eyes that radiated kindness.

What she didn't know yet was that he was a whole lot meaner than he looked, having grown up in a vastly different world than she knew. He carried himself with a bit of a tough guy edge that had been handed down to him by his father and his father before him.

Logan had a slightly mysterious aura, sort of an aloofness that was hard to pin down. It made him popular in school with both the guys and girls. But he was in no hurry to be tied to a steady romance and

31

preferred the company of his buddies. It wasn't that he didn't have an interest. He was smart enough to know that drinking beer and drag racing with the guys was only going to hold his interest so long. The truth was he had yet to find a girl he felt he could trust and who could sustain his interest. He wasn't about to make the same mistakes that made his life at home in a falling down three-family tenement on Broad Street in Hartford a living hell. He had plans to attend the University of Connecticut in the fall, at least as long as he could get student loans to finance it. But his heart wasn't really in it. In truth, the future was a mystery to him.

"Hi, Danny Logan, I'm Elina. You can wish me Happy Birthday if you like," she teased, gently biting her lower lip with her teeth. Logan was caught off guard by her blatant flirting and was embarrassed for her father. But still, Hanson didn't seem to notice.

"Elina," a raspy voice suddenly called from the staircase. A slightly built woman wearing large, dark sun glasses stood on the stairs, one hand on the railing to steady herself, her other hand holding what appeared to be an afternoon cocktail. She took a last sip from the glass and handed it to a passing waiter. She wasn't smiling.

"Betty," Don Hanson called to her in genuine delight. "So glad you decided to come and check out the preparations. Did you enjoy your nap?" he asked pleasantly. The well-coiffed brunette, wearing a Chanel sailor's striped jersey and loose silk shorts, held herself with a model's posture on the staircase and merely glanced at her husband. She ignored his question.

Hanson didn't appear to be put off by the snub, rather he walked to the staircase and extended his hand to her.

"Come and meet a couple of the boys who'll be helping us tonight, dear," he asked.

"In due time, Donald," she snapped. "In the meantime, perhaps you might ask your daughter to put some clothes on before the help is unable to concentrate on the work ahead. Apparently she has yet to understand the best advice a woman can follow. A girl should be two things: classy and fabulous."

Elina spun to face her mother, fire in her eyes.

"No, I have not ignored your advice mother, even if you insist upon claiming ownership of it. As we both know, that is a quote from your idol, Coco Chanel, who you may recall also said the following.

The older woman visibly stiffened at the rebuke from her daughter.

"And that would be...?"

"It is always better to be slightly underdressed."

The woman shook her head in disgust. She reached into her pants pocket and retrieved a gold cigarette case, opening it in silence. Her husband stepped forward to light the cigarette she put to her lips.

"Ah, my Elina. You have so much to learn," she said, shrugging her shoulders. "But let's not fight, especially in front of our guests. Hello boys," she smiled. "I'm Mrs. Hanson, if you haven't already guessed." She walked the few steps to meet them, a noticeable stagger in her gait. The boys hurried to greet her, recognizing the telltale sign from their own family situations. Both awkwardly took her extended hand as if they were meeting royalty.

"It's very nice to meet you, Mrs. Hanson," Logan said first. Chickie shook his head in agreement.

"I trust your work here is nearly done, boys?" she asked.

"Yes, ma'am," they answered in unison.

33

"Good," she replied, turning back towards the stairs.

"Then perhaps you would be good enough to allow Elina the privacy her wardrobe demands and she can take her swim without an audience."

"Betty..." Don Hanson interrupted calmly. "There's no call to be rude. Let's go boys. We do have work to finish," he said.

"Yes, sir," Logan responded, embarrassed. "C'mon, Chickie. Let's follow the boss." They turned and walked away, ignoring the splash behind them.

Hanson led them away in silence, back to the safety of the garage.

"Sorry about that, boys. I'm afraid two spoiled women in one house is at least one too many," he laughed.

There was an awkward silence among the three.

"Uh, yah, Mr. Hanson, don't worry about it," Logan finally said, eager to drop the subject. "No big deal."

"Your daughter is sure beautiful, Mr. Hanson," Chickie added, then quickly wished he hadn't said anything.

Don Hanson's fists clenched and his eyes burned a hole in the boys face.

"I guess I shouldn't have expected any more from a couple of street rats, now should I?" he retorted, flashing anger. "Just keep your eyes on the work, boys, ok?"

They were silent.

"You two park cars tonight. I don't want you near my guests," he said, his warm demeanor towards them completely gone 'When that's done, I want you on the beach clearing tables and cleaning trash. Am I understood?"

"Mr. Hanson, I didn't mean... I mean, we..." Chickie tried to apologize, although he was a bit bewildered by the man's reaction.

"Leave it, boy." Hanson turned and walked away, heading for the kitchen.

When he was out of earshot, Chickie looked at Logan who was busy studying his sneakers.

"What the fuck did I say?" he asked his friend.

"It's not what you said, Chickie, it's that you said it. We're just the help, 'boy,' and don't forget it. And with that, let's do as we're told and get back to work. The less time we spend near either one of those broads, the safer we'll be," Logan answered. "C'mon, let's get into the duds Paul brought for us. There'll be people pulling up fairly soon," he said glancing at his watch. They began walking back to the Chevy.

"Beats the shit out of me," Chickie said. "I just said she was beautiful, that's all."

"He heard you, trust me. Now forget it."

"Well, one thing's for sure."

"What's that, buddy?" Logan bit.

"That's one chick who won't be seeing the Beatles tomorrow night!"

Logan laughed. He had forgotten all about his windfall and what he was going to do about it. "Yah, for sure. But what I wouldn't do to get to know her a little..."

"Take your own advice, Danny," Chickie said. "We don't belong in this world. And it don't make any sense to get close to anyone who lives in it."

"Mind you remember that when you join her in Cambridge next month, Chickie," Logan chided his friend. "If I'm not mistaken, Radcliffe is just a couple of bus stops from MIT... 'boy'."

"Look, pal, my head don't turn just for a well stuffed white bikini," Anderson said, slightly miffed at his friend. The moniker "Chickie," a playground nickname derived from his eye for the girls that had stuck to him since the beginning of high school, was misleading. He may have had a weakness for skirts, but Charles Anderson was class valedictorian and headed for MIT's Sloan School of Management in the fall to study economics on a full academic scholarship. He did his best to hide his sharp intellect around his peers, preferring to be recognized as cool rather than smart.

"Yah, your head didn't turn, but your eyes sure bugged out of it. Man, you couldn't have been more obvious."

"No!" Chickie protested. "I'm way too cool for that."

"Yah, no question pal, you were cool," Logan jabbed his friend again. "Good thing Hanson wasn't packing or you'd be missing a couple of kneecaps," he laughed.

A look of horror flashed on Anderson's face.

"The guy's not connected, is he?"

Logan turned and faced his friend, a deadly serious look on his face.

"You mean Carducci didn't tell you who this guy is? The New York connection... you really didn't realize who you were screwing with? Jesus, Chickie...he's a 'Made Guy' for crying out loud!"

"Oh God, no..." Chickie said, closing his eyes.

Logan couldn't hold back anymore. He burst out laughing at his friend.

"You prick!" Anderson yelled, lunging at Logan who was already running away from him. The banter wasn't that unusual for the two who had been best friends since before elementary school. They were alike

36

in many ways, unlike in others. Anderson was a brilliant student with big plans for the future, Danny Logan was an outstanding athlete void of aspiration. But the one thing they shared in the absolute was loyalty.

They were inseparable as friends and confidants. More importantly, Hanson hadn't been far off base when he referred to them as street rats. Both the offspring of drunken, abusive parents, they'd found strength in each other's pain. They'd never had the chance to be real children and they grew up fast on the streets, each never losing sight of the other's back. College loomed as a real test of their ability to walk alone. It wasn't something they talked about.

They reached the car, out of breath but still laughing. Logan popped the trunk of the Chevy and threw a white shirt and black bow tie to his friend.

"Here. Put these on. Consider it a dry run for your future," Danny Logan said.

"Maybe the white shirt, 'boy,' but save the tie for your own neck," he responded, tossing it back. "I'll be needing a valet some day when I'm living in a penthouse not far from Wall Street," Chickie shot back. "Think you can handle the truth?"

"Does the job come with a room?" Logan laughed.

A half hour later, Hanson's guests began arriving at the oceanfront mansion and the two teens were hustling cars off to an adjoining property. They were run ragged by the pace but the tips were good and they were enjoying the added bonus of spending a few minutes behind cars they'd only dreamed of owning. Cadillacs, Lincolns, Jaguars, Ferraris, Porsches, even a Rolls here and there. Every time they slid behind the wheel of a car, they got a taste of a fantasy fulfilled. It was like getting a peck on the cheek from the prettiest girl at the prom. But still there was a bitterness to the kiss. Most of the cars were driven by teens their own age.

By 8 p.m., the flow of arrivals had stopped and the two boys headed for the beach as Hanson had directed. They passed by Mike, Tony and Eddie who were bussing tables, but only nodded at them. A live band was doing rock and roll covers for the mob of kids in the pool, most of who were drinking from champagne glasses. There wasn't an adult in sight. Logan would have liked to stop and look for Elina but didn't dare.

He was nearly to the sea wall when he realized he was alone. Chickie had stopped at the pool to gaze upon the bevy of bikini-clad teens partying with the birthday girl. Logan ran back and grabbed him, pulling Anderson away back towards the beach.

"Are you crazy? Hanson will kick your ass if he sees you gawking at those broads. What the hell, Chickie, use your brains."

"Yah, yah. Just looking, that's all," Anderson admitted reluctantly.

They made their way down the steep, winding wooden staircase that brought them to the beach and started cleaning tables and picking up trash. There was a large group of partyers gathered around a roaring driftwood bonfire that lit up a section of the beach. They were loud and obviously very drunk. A couple of guys with guitars were there to take requests but were mostly ignored by the crowd. Danny could see the shadows of several couples further down the beach making out in the sand, but ignored it and kept to his business.

Around 11 p.m., Paul Carducci came down to check on them with Mike and Eddie in tow.

"I have a feeling the rest of the party is going to be moving down here pretty soon," he warned them.

"Brought you some backup." He didn't mention anything about their run in with Hanson earlier in the day.

"Where's Tony?" Logan asked.

"Poor bastard is in the kitchen doing dishes. He's going to earn his money tonight," Carducci laughed.

"Yah," Danny answered, but nodded his head towards the staircase, which was suddenly full of young, drunken partyers making their way down to the beach. "But he'll be safer than we will," he laughed. "Get a load of this group."

Carducci raised an eye. "You know, the Hanson's went to bed. I don't think there's another adult in this whole place. Not smart. Watch your P's and Q's, boys. I don't like this."

"Jesus, look at her," Chickie pointed to the staircase. They watched as Elina Hanson was literally carried to the beach by a couple of good-sized guys dressed only in swim trunks. Elina was still wearing her white bikini, but her hair was wet and wild. She'd had way too much to drink.

"Uh, oh," Carducci said. "Guess I owe it to my buddy to make sure she's alright," he said and began walking towards the group.

"Careful, Mr. Carducci. They're pretty well liquored up," Eddie warned.

"I got this," Carducci answered. He began walking toward the three. The two boys were leading the inebriated girl farther down the beach into the darkness. Paul yelled for them to stop as they were almost out of sight, but one of their friends got up and challenged him. Danny Logan watched as the two had words and then the teen pushed the older man to the ground and kicked him in the ribs.

"Stay down you old fuck and mind your own business," the punk said loudly enough for anyone on the beach to hear.

"That was a mistake," Logan said to himself. He was off in a shot, rushing to Carducci's aid. Chickie, Mike and Eddie were right behind him.

"Check Paul," he hollered to them, "I'll get these assholes."

"I can't see them," Chickie hollered, running beside his friend.

"I think they pulled her up into the tall grass on the right," he said through clenched teeth. He heard Chickie fall hard to the ground behind him. He had tripped over a large piece of driftwood hidden in the darkness. Logan pushed on and suddenly was on them.

The two guys had Elina pinned to the ground and she was screaming and squirming to escape. Her top of her bathing suit had been torn off and she was lying nearly naked on the sand, hidden in the high grass. Logan had no question of what her "friends" were planning to do next.

He closed within six feet and leapt at the first of the two who had just pulled his swim trunks down around his ankles. Logan hit him like a defensive tackle with a clear shot at sacking an undefended quarterback, burying his head and shoulder into the guy's chest. His target went down like a large sack of potatoes, falling heavily to the ground.

"What the fuck," the boy moaned, "I'll frigging kill you asshole."

His partner had already released Elina's hands and jumped up to pound Logan, who sprang to his feet and ducked the first round house punch the punk threw at him. Before he could swing again, Chickie appeared out of nowhere and tackled him the to the ground. He

40

sat on the boy's chest and punched him twice in the face before Logan stopped him.

"Jesus, Chickie, don't kill him," he said. "It ain't worth it. They'll take his side."

He turned to the two teens and screamed at them to take off.

"I'm calling the cops man, you dig? Get out of here while you can!" Neither boy protested, scrambling to their feet and ran into the night.

Elina was still on the ground, weeping hysterically as Mike and Eddie caught up to them with Paul Carducci a few feet behind. Logan pulled off his shirt and put it around her shoulders to cover her nakedness.

"Oh, shit, man," Eddie said, realizing the situation. "Stop right there guys, let's just turn around and make sure there's no one else coming over here with any ideas. Mike and Paul turned their backs, staring back at the bonfire.

"Did you get that one who kicked Mr. Carducci?" Logan demanded.

"All taken care of," Mike responded, holding up a hand with bloodied knuckles. Paul smiled. "Hope the bastard knows an orthodontist."

Chickie was sitting with Elina trying to calm her but not having much luck. Logan sat down next to her and wrapped his arms around her shoulders hugging her. She sobbed into his arms.

"It's alright, Elina, it's ok, it's all over," he said to her. "C'mon, party's over. Let's get you home." He helped the girl to her feet and held her as they walked back to the staircase and climbed the seawall back to the protection of the mansion. Down below, Carducci got a bucket of water from the shallows and doused the bonfire.

"Party's over folks, time to head home. Guys, get these folks back to their cars and out of here. If anyone's too wasted to drive, call their parents to pick them up. Anyone gives you a hard time, let me know and I'll call the police to handle the situation. Got it?" Mike, Eddie and Chickie nodded and headed for the staircase.

"Chickie? Before you do that, spring Tony from the kitchen. The Hanson's can do their own goddamn dishes. I'm going to see my friend Don right now to let him know what went on here tonight."

Quietly, Danny Logan had helped Elina back to the house and up to her bedroom. He was so intent upon helping her that he didn't even notice the huge proportions and luxury inside the mansion. If he had, he would have seen that Elina's bedroom alone was bigger than the entire apartment he lived in with his parents. But he was more concerned with the young girl's well being at that moment. He sat with her until she had composed herself and was about to leave when the door to her room swung open. It was Don Hanson.

"God damn you boy! Didn't I tell you to stay away from my daughter? What the hell are you doing here? Did you touch her?" She was still wearing his shirt and Logan was bare chested.

He leapt to his feet as Hanson charged into the room.

"Mr. Hanson, you don't understand," Logan said.

"Daddy, stop! You don't know... he saved me!" Elina cried to her father.

"I will beat you to death you white trash son of a bitch," Hanson yelled and advanced towards the boy who put up his hands to defend himself.

Suddenly, Paul Carducci was in the doorway.

42

"Hanson, you clown. Stop where you are or I'll drop you myself, you understand? I can still do it, old friend."

"What...?" Hanson began, totally confused. "What the hell are you all doing in my daughter's bedroom? And why is she wearing this punk's shirt?"

"That 'punk' just saved your daughter from being raped! Or worse..." Carducci said, shaking his head. "By her rich 'friends.' She can tell you who they were, I'm sure. But it was Danny here who took on the two guys who planned to have a good time with her. Why is she wearing his shirt? Because he took his off to replace the bathing suit her 'friends' ripped off of her."

Hanson went pale and looked as if he might be sick. He went to his daughter and wrapped his arms around her.

"Oh my God, I'm so sorry, I should have been out there... your mother... she was in a bad way... I had to get her inside..."

A voice shrieked out of a room down the hall from Elina's bedroom. It was Betty Hanson, obviously very drunk.

"Don," she called out, slurring her husband's name. "Donald, Donald, God damn it, I need you, I got sick in the bed..." she said.

"Oh, Jesus," Paul said. "You know Don, for all your money, I wouldn't trade places with you if God himself begged me to. Good night. I'll send you my bill. C'mon Danny, let's get out of here."

Hanson shook his head in embarrassment and rushed out of the room to his wife.

Logan looked at his boss and shrugged his shoulders. Then he sat back down next to Elina who was crying.

"I'll be with you in a minute, Coach, just give me a second here."

"Ok, kid," Carducci replied. "Don't do anything stupid." He winked.

"Yah, gotcha."

The older man left, closing the door behind him. The room was lit by a single lamp on a small table next to her bed. Logan saw their shadows bouncing off the walls and ceiling and only then realized the enormity of her bedroom.

"What is this, some kind of castle?" he blurted out.

"What?" she looked up at him in surprise, still sobbing.

"Nothing."

They were silent for a few minutes. He reached over and took one of her hands and squeezed it. She leaned forward and put her head on his shoulder.

"Lousy way for your birthday to end, Elina. I'm sorry," he said.

"You're sweet, Danny. It's ok. Thank you for..." she hesitated, not sure what to say.

"It's alright."

She lifted her head and stared into his eyes.

"I can't believe they did that to me."

"Yah. Some guys..."

"But not you... or your friends. You're special," she said.

Logan laughed. "Now that's not a word many people would call us. I come from a different world, Elina. Your father's not too far off base..."

"I'm sorry he said that..."

"Yah. No problem. Not the first time I've heard it."

44

She put her head back down on his shoulder and they were quiet.

"Really sorry about your birthday." An idea came into his head as the words left his mouth.

"I wish there was some special thing I could do for you to make up for it..." He was afraid to go any further. She was out of his league. Out of his universe, for that matter.

"This is pretty special, Danny..."

He went for it.

"You know, a funny thing happened while we were driving here tonight," he said.

She lifted her head again, and looked at him, wondering. God, she's so beautiful he thought to himself. Do it. Do it.

"I... I won a couple of tickets. From the radio. WDRC. Tomorrow night..."

She jumped up off the bed.

"The Beatles? At Shea Stadium? Are you kidding me?" she said, her mouth agape, her eyes wide with excitement.

"Uh... no, I'm not kidding. And, you see, I don't have anyone..."

"Yes! Yes! Yes! I'll go with you! Oh my God, are you kidding me? That's the best birthday present ever!"

"Ha," he laughed. "Better than what's in the garage?"

"A thousand times! The Beatles! I can't believe it... I begged my father," she said.

"Uh, oh... that's bad."

"He'll never know. I'll meet you in New Haven and we'll take the train in to New York and take a taxi to Shea. I know how to do it," she said, bubbling with excitement.

"I've never been to New York..." he said sheepishly. "Or anywhere else for that matter..."

"I have... just meet me at the train station in New Haven... can you do that? The Beatles! I can't believe this!" She leapt at him, still sitting on the side of the bed and kissed him on the mouth. He was so surprised he never closed his eyes.

She broke it off quickly, not even realizing what she had done. Danny stood up to leave and wasn't sure his legs were connected to his body. He couldn't believe she was going to go out with him.

"The train station, yah, ok. What time?"

"Be there at four o'clock, ok? We'll have plenty of time. Ok? Oh jeez, what am I going to wear? The Beatles! Danny, the Beatles!"

She hugged him and kissed him again.

"You are so special, Danny... I don't know your last name."

"Uh... Logan. Yah, Logan," he said without much certainty in his voice.

"Goodnight, Danny Logan," Elina said. "I can't wait to see you tomorrow."

"Now that's not exactly something I expected to hear tonight," he said, shyly.

He waved at her awkwardly and made his way out of the house without running into Hanson. The guys were waiting for him outside. He grabbed a spare T-shirt out of the trunk and slipped it on.

"Let's get out of this joint," Chickie said.

"Yah, enough excitement for one night," Eddie added in disgust.

"Where's Paul?"

"He already blew out of here. Pretty pissed," Mike said.

46

They climbed into the Chevy and the small block engine roared to life. Danny goosed the gas pedal and spun the rear wheels on the way out of the driveway.

"Well, at least they'll know we were here," he said, knowing he had left a cloud of smoke and dirt behind him.

"Yah. Don't imagine we'll be back," Tony said.

"I dunno about that,' Chickie said. "I got plans. Wouldn't mind owning a place like this some day. Or having a girl like Elina to call mine."

"Hit the radio, will ya Danny?"

"Sure." He flipped the dial and immediately a Beatles cut from their first album came blaring out over the speakers he had strategically located in the car.

"It won't be long yah, yah, till I belong to you..."

A grin broke out on Danny Logan's face that lasted the next 50 miles. It was only when he pulled up in front of the tenement he called home on Broad Street that the smile faded.

He leaned his head against the steering wheel.

"What in hell am I doing?" he asked himself as the sound of his drunken father cursing his mother reverberated from the house.

Two

~~~ ℘ ~~~

Sunday, August 15, 1965

Scientists measure the power of sound in decibels, or dB's. Human speech registers about 25 decibels and any noise above 85 dB's can cause pain to the human ear. A jet engine will generate as much as 120 dB's 100 yards away.

"Holy shit," an ashen-faced cop standing before the hysterical Shea Stadium audience shouted, grabbing his ears as the Beatles ran onto the field at precisely 9:17 p.m. on Sunday night, August 15, 1965. An explosion of sound rocked him on his feet the instant the four young men from Liverpool had captured the horde unaware and they stepped out of an innocuous armored car and on to the field. The policeman, who was not unaccustomed to loud crowd noise as he moonlighted as

48

a security guard for sporting events at Shea, Yankee Stadium and Madison Square Garden, instinctively looked up into the night in horror expecting to see a Boeing 727 about to crash into the field. But the sky was empty. Simultaneously, at the nearby Lamont-Doherty Earth Observatory of Columbia University, a scientist stared in confusion as the needle-like pen of the seismograph he was monitoring jumped with the sound, indicating the occurrence of a small earthquake.

The cop looked back into the crowd of teenagers filling the stadium and realized the source of the bedlam was not a jet from nearby LaGuardia Airport as he feared. It was only the 55,600 frenzied kids all screaming hysterically at once.

Despite the overwhelming din, the police officer, along with 2,000 of his colleagues moved forward to hold wooden barricades in place as thousands of ticketed fans began to rush the field and thousands more without tickets attempted to scale the walls surrounding the park. Panicking, he yelled to a fellow officer, less than an arms length away.

"This is nuts," he screamed. "Pandemonium. We'll need the National Guard to keep these kids off the field." The other cop looked at him and shook his head, unable to make out what his partner was saying. No matter. It was a sentiment shared by every police officer pulling overtime that night to somehow retain order at Shea Stadium. Most of them were scared for their lives.

Somehow, the police and the traffic barricades held the crowd back as the foursome ran out on the field to a rickety plywood stage erected over second base that seemed hopelessly minimalist and out of place considering the magnitude of the historical event. But for the band, it was the final destination of a head-spinning trip that had begun at 7 p.m. that evening at the Warwick Hotel on West 54th Street near 6th Avenue.

There, sneakily avoiding more than 1,000 fans who had been waiting for hours just to catch a glimpse of the musical phenoms by escaping out a hotel service door, the four members of the Beatles climbed into a stretched Lincoln Continental Limousine with heavily tinted glass and drove to the Wall Street heliport on the East River. Having escaped the luxurious prison where fans had held the Liverpool musicians captive for more than 30 hours, they excitedly boarded a waiting Boeing Vertol 107-II helicopter. It was their first flight in a helicopter and they begged for a few minutes of sightseeing from their secure vantage point.

The group was flown around the Statue of Liberty and then briefly over New York City before the nose of the helicopter was pointed towards Queens, the site of the 1964 World's Fair adjacent to Shea Stadium. There they landed on the Port Authority heliport and were led into the basement where they were met by another limousine of sorts: an armored car provided by Wells Fargo that drove them slowly to the Stadium. The Wells Fargo guards presented each of the band members with a company badge that the good-natured group pinned on to their tan, custom tailored worsted wool serge jackets, designed in a military theme with epaulets, pleated breast pockets and Nehru collar.

The truck lurched to a stop just before reaching the entrance to the field. Inside, the Beatles were still debating the order of the song list they intended to play that night. Finally, after a 20-minute wait inside the armored car, the signal was given to open the doors. As first Paul McCartney, then Ringo Starr, John Lennon and finally George Harrison jumped from the armored truck, they stopped and took in the massive audience that had been waiting as long as seven hours for their arrival. Simultaneously, tens of thousands of flashbulbs detonated from every point in the stadium. It was if a solar flare had erupted in the middle of Queens, a light so bright that the pilots of a passing jetliner flying 30,000 feet above the stadium thought there had been a catastrophic blast at the World's Fair.

Wide-eyed, the four mop-topped musicians hesitated for a moment, overwhelmed by the reception of the largest stadium crowd the world had ever seen. Their instructions were to wait for the "really big" introduction from the man who had brought them to America for the first time the year before. On cue, the King of television variety shows, Ed Sullivan stepped up to a microphone at home plate and began speaking, almost completely drowned out by the continuing roar of fans.

"Now…ladies and gentlemen," he screamed into the microphone, "honored by their country, decorated by their Queen, loved here in America… here are The Beatles!"

All over Manhattan, the Bronx and Queens, people stopped and gazed upwards into the clear skies, wondering where on earth the sudden thunder-like rumbling was coming from.

The four lads began to jog towards the stage, then broke into a full tilt run as they realized that hundreds of crazed fans had broken through the police barricade and were chasing them towards the relative "safety" of the hapless stage at the edge of the infield. It was at least an island of refuge, cordoned off by several hundred more police assigned to protect them.

Danny Logan was there in the midst of this bedlam, but didn't see or hear any of it. It was as if he was alone in a world of his own where only one thing existed to occupy his attention. He had eyes and ears for only the 17-year old blonde beauty sitting next to him in Section 31, Row A, Seat 16, Gate D. He was in Seat 17. The numbers would remain etched in his memory forever.

Unfortunately, the attention was one way and he knew his good luck in winning the tickets was a mixed blessing. He couldn't get her attention.

Their seats, located in the Metro Boxes on the first base line, were beyond his wildest expectations. "From a radio contest?" he thought. He must have apologized to Elina a 100 times on the train coming in, anticipating nosebleed grandstand seats. But for once in Danny Logan's life, good fortune had fallen into his lap. They were still a good distance from the band, but just above ground level with a view right over the top of the sea of uniformed cops guarding them. The only thing that worried Danny was a sudden mad crush from behind that would spill the two of them onto the field where they could be trampled. Elina was oblivious to their precarious situation.

She was screaming as loud as every other teenaged girl in the arena and completely awestruck by the scene. It had taken them four hours to get to Shea but her fascination with the band was such that the excitement had nearly erased the nightmare of what had happened the night before.

She'd been waiting for Logan as he pulled into Union station in New Haven at 4 p.m. that afternoon and nearly leapt off the bench she was sitting on when she spied him in the beat up Chevy.

He swallowed hard. Elina Hanson, a stunningly beautiful future social debutante, Radcliffe freshman and heir to a fortune he could only imagine, was waiting for him, Danny Logan. A Hartford street rat with only the money in his pockets, no foreseeable future and a past he only wanted to hide. Before he could even blink away the mind-numbing dichotomy, she had reached the car and was wrapping her arms around his neck.

"You came, you came! I'm so excited!" she said.

He laughed off the attention out of a mixture of confusion and embarrassment, and smiled.

"Well, if you don't let me park the car, some cop is going to get excited too," he laughed.

"But it's true!" she answered. "I'm going to see the Beatles! I still can't believe it!" she yelled into his ear then kissed him on the lips. Danny Logan just about melted, and for a moment at least, he forgot about the question that had nagged him all night and day.

"What are you doing, Danny? She's out of your league and you know it. Stop kidding yourself. It's a one night fling." Even with the excitement of seeing her, the knot in the pit of his stomach tightened even more. He'd only shared the news with Chickie, his best friend, that morning.

"Man, you gotta know this is gonna hurt eventually," Chickie said. "But for now, go for it man. Have a hell of a time and get a little taste of life on the high side," Chickie encouraged him. It was actually those words that had given Logan the courage to drive to New Haven. He kept telling himself not to be disappointed if she didn't show.

"Her father will never let her," he figured. "Go out with a 'boy' from nowhere and nothing? Yah. Sure."

He swallowed hard when he saw her waiting on the bench. It wasn't a dream. She had pulled her long blond hair into a ponytail and was wearing a sleeveless white cotton blouse, cut off jeans and sandals. The girl was exquisite, even dressed so casually. He couldn't take his eyes off her.

The money he'd hard earned the night before had come in handy as he bought the train tickets, despite Elina's objections. There was no way she was paying the fare. He was going to do this right or go down in flames.

They took seats in a forward coach on a Metro-North train into Grand Central Station and Elina talked all the way to New York about the Beatles. But when they arrived, it was his turn to be in awe. He couldn't stop staring at the majesty of the building, completely overcome by its colossal atrium. He felt like a hillbilly who'd come out of the country for the first time in his life. It wasn't far from the truth. But Elina knew her way around, thanks to numerous shopping and Broadway trips with her mother and even catching an occasional Yankees, Mets or Knicks game with her father.

She dragged him to the subway where they boarded the Queens-bound #7 train to Willest Point-Shea Stadium. His jaw dropped when he finally saw Shea, magnificent in its blue and orange painted ramps that wrapped around the stadium providing access to the various levels of the facility. It was incredible, the size alone taking his breath away. But then again, the boy from the South End of Hartford had only one sporting arena to compare it to: Dillon Stadium in Hartford's Colt Park, a 10,000 seat field that mostly hosted high school football games. He was in awe the first time he had seen Dillon and played there. It had been the biggest moment of his life. Shea was beyond anything he had ever imagined.

By the time they reached the stadium, it dawned on Logan that he didn't know anything more about his date than what he had learned the night before. Elina was completely preoccupied with the Beatles. But she still completely mesmerized Danny Logan. Even hours after meeting up with her, he was still certain it was all a dream. But when she grabbed his hand and pulled him to the "Will Call" window where a ticket agent handed over the two passes that Logan had won, she made it real.

The girl who had it all, quite literally everything, pulled him out of line, put her hands on either side of his face and looked into his wide eyes.

"Danny," she said softly, "I know you think I'm just a spoiled brat who gets everything she wants. But it isn't all you might think it is." She hesitated, her eyes filling with tears. "You saw that last night. I just wanted you to know that this is the sweetest thing that anyone has every done for me, and I'm so glad I met you. Not just for the tickets... but for making me feel really special." Then she kissed him gently on the lips.

He was stunned again. "Elina, I..." She interrupted him.

"No, not now. We have so much time to talk and really get to know all about each other. Not now," she begged. "Let's just go and find our seats and go crazy. Please?"

He laughed with relief, his anxiety of being with her, of trying to hide how much of a simpleton he felt like, evaporated.

"Your wish is my command, my lady," he said, bowing at the waist and waving his hand. "Let us find our waiting thrones!"

She giggled with excitement and ran off with him in pursuit, ignoring his warnings one last time about how bad he feared the seats would be.

And then they were there, less than 75 yards away from the stage. It was an almost perfect vantage point in the most imperfect setting imaginable. But none of it mattered. They were there to see the Beatles.

It was past eight o'clock by the time they took their seats and the stadium was already more than 90 percent full. The couple had missed opening acts "King Curtis" and "Cannibal and the Headhunters," but like most others waiting for the main show, they half listened to the next couple of warm up artists. Motown's Brenda Holloway would have brought the house down if she were on any other stage in the world this night as she belted out her soulful renditions of *I'll Always Love You* and *Every Little Bit Hurts,* and Sound Incorporated's huge hits, *Spanish Harlem* and *Rinky Dink* got little more than nodding attention. Promoter Shel Silverstein had mixed in a little bit of everything to build crowd excitement. But not even Elvis Presley himself could have held this crowd's attention for very long.

The 55,600 waiting fans had come to see the most amazing act to hit the music world in history and no one or nothing else would satisfy them. In America, the Beatles already had a cult-like following and had suddenly and profoundly redirected the evolution of music virtually overnight. Their music was also a catalyst for young people who were bursting with energy and ideas but stymied by parents who were in a post-war malaise and still shattered by the assassination of President John F. Kennedy less than two years before. All they wanted was peace and quiet.

It wasn't to be. For even as Shea Stadium was filling to capacity for a night of musical celebration, the news media was reporting that 21 people had died the previous day in race riots that had torn Los Angeles apart, Chicago was being policed by 2,000 National Guardsmen because of similar unrest and President Lyndon Johnson had ordered 6,400 more Marines to South Vietnam that very morning. Peacetime in America was unraveling quickly. Tonight, America's young were

56

oblivious to the challenges the next decade would bring to their generation and that their enthusiasm and energy would sour. However, they were keenly aware of the less ominous sociological revolution that was spreading like wildfire from coast to coast. Peaceful rebellion, too, was in the air this night and the excitement was palpable. "Flower Power" was germinating in the world's biggest garden in Queens, New York. And the four young men from Liverpool were innocently planting the seeds.

Then the moment was upon them. Elina grabbed Danny's arm when she saw the Wells Fargo truck slowly pull into the stadium. When the doors flung open and the Fab Four appeared she was on her feet in an instant, screaming until her lungs hurt, waving her arms frantically trying to get the attention of any one of the Beatles who were racing for their lives to the stage.

Afterwards, he wasn't sure how or why the question had come to him at that moment, but Danny Logan turned to Elina and asked: "Who's picking you up at the train station? What time did you tell them?"

She turned to him, quickly, a little awkwardly and smiled.

"No one's picking me up, silly. I thought you'd bring me home."

"To Fenwick?"

"Yah..." She turned back to the field and watched as Paul McCartney hoisted his trademark, left handed 1962 Hofner Violin hollow body bass guitar over his shoulders and stepped to the microphone.

"How'd you get to New Haven?" Danny probed, an uneasiness making the back of his neck tingle.

"My girlfriend dropped me off. It's no problem, is it?"

He looked at her. She turned away.

57

"You mean... your mom and dad don't know you're here... with me?"

With that, a look that could have passed for a statement of Elina's own revolution came over her face and she smiled wickedly. Then she turned back to the stage, drifting into another world, oblivious to the anxious boy sitting next to her.

McCartney stepped up to the microphone, laughing out loud like his other mates at the lunacy of what was happening around them. Not even they were prepared for this greeting and hadn't realized that they were the guests of honor at the biggest coming out party in New York history. The handsome young bass player and brilliant songwriter hollered a greeting to the audience into his microphone but it was all but inaudible. The specially built 100 watt amplified speakers behind him and a ring of tall, yellow speakers that were supplementing the Shea Stadium sound system was hopelessly outmatched by the audience roar. So much so that McCartney couldn't hear himself. Nor could his band mates hear him. Each of the musicians also picked up on a sound delay that made the situation even worse. Paul looked at John Lennon and George Harrison almost with a plea, knowing the quality of their performance would be awful and there wasn't a "bloody" thing they could do about it. John, Paul and George gathered at center stage then looked up at Ringo, sitting on a raised platform with his drum kit. The drummer shrugged his shoulders, twirled his drumsticks and rolled off a few licks on his snare. It was if to say, "Let's get on with it." But years of playing in smaller venues where the sound was so intense and piercing that it would give them headaches for days and endless hours of rehearsals would save them.

In typical, boyish, "It is what it is" fashion, McCartney stepped fearlessly back up to the microphone and the crowd watched him mouth, "One, two, three, four..." then instantly launched into the opening bass guitar stanza's of the group's opening number. The screaming, gravel edged voice of John Lennon somehow broke through the uproar as he sang the words, *"Well shake it up baby, now"* and McCartney and Harrison leaned together and harmonized the lyrics to *"Twist and Shout."*

For the thousands of teens who had waited hours for this moment, the earth shifted on its axis. The noise around the stadium that was already nearly unbearable impossibly doubled in volume. Girls fainted and peed themselves. They cried, and in the hot summer air did the most un-lady like thing: they perspired, their hair matting to their foreheads. Hundreds simply couldn't deal with the rush of adrenalin and pushed towards the field, desperately trying to reach their idols. The cops would have none of it, determined to hold their ground. The nervous Beatles would yell to the police immediately protecting them and point to groups encroaching on their frail grasp of safety on an island of plywood.

Danny Logan took it all in and just shook his head. He might as well enjoy it, he thought and make sure Elina enjoyed the best night of her life because it was probably the last night of his. Her father was sure to kill him.

Without a breath in between songs, Lennon finished *"Twist and Shout"* and McCartney launched his golden voice, with its pitch and timbre capable of bringing teenage girls to weeping in seconds, into the high-pitched *"She's A Woman,"* one of eleven number one singles the group had recorded the previous year.

Logan could barely make out the song let alone the lyrics, but he knew the group's litany of work by heart. And in the middle of the song, it was if McCartney spoke to him directly.

"I know that she's no peasant," he sang, the lyrics shooting a chord through Logan's heart. The ballad, written by McCartney, made him anxious again. He couldn't get comfortable knowing the girl next to him came from a world of wealth and privilege he couldn't even imagine. Or, that her parents would be livid if they knew she was in his company.

And so it went for the next 30 minutes, a mere blink of an eye for the rabid fans who had such high expectations of the concert. But in that half hour, the Beatles knocked out a dozen rock n' roll hits that kept Elina and every teenage girl in Shea Stadium screaming. But while she was completely mesmerized by their music and the extraordinary environment, Danny Logan couldn't help but internalize the group's song set. It was if every song was aimed directly at him and his very confused emotions.

The massive crowd roared approval when the group performed *"I Feel Fine."* The lyrics swam through Logan's head as John Lennon sang, once again causing him to perseverate on what side of the tracks he was born.

"She's so glad,
she's telling all the world
that her baby buys her things you know,
he buys her diamond rings you know, she said so...
she's in love with me and I feel fine."

"Dizzy Miss Lizzy" followed, the crowd by now whipped into an absolute frenzy. It made no difference

if they could actually hear the group perform the song. If the fans picked up enough of the tune to identify it, they knew the lyrics by heart and sang along.

Danny Logan laughed to himself as he sang with John Lennon, the lyrics so aptly describing the confusion that Elina had brought to his world. She grabbed his hand and pulled him to his feet to join hundreds of kids dancing in the aisles to *"Ticket to Ride"* and *"Everybody's Trying To Be My Baby"* then mercifully took her seat again to concentrate on Paul McCartney's rendition of *"Can't Buy Me Love."* Logan loved the song, but never had related to its message, which now, sitting next to a girl beyond his dreams in every way, plunged him into despair.

> *"I'll buy you a diamond ring my friend*
> *if it makes you feel alright,*
> *I'll get you anything my friend*
> *if it makes you feel alright*
> *Cause I don't care too much for money,*
> *money can't buy me love..."*

He barely heard the rest of the set. *"Baby's in Black," "Act Naturally," "A Hard Day's Night,"* and finally, *"I'm Down"* brought the concert to an abrupt end and the Beatles scurried off the stage and ran for their lives to the safety of the Wells Fargo truck that drove them out of Shea.

Elina sat down in her seat after watching until the taillights of the truck had disappeared from view, emotionally exhausted. She looked up at Danny with tears streaming down her cheeks and kept repeating, "I can't believe it, I can't believe..." over and over. Danny draped his arm over her shoulder and held her close. The same scene was being repeated all over the Stadium

61

as a sense of shock descended over Shea. For nearly an hour, almost no one left the arena, as fans hugged and cried so overwhelmed were they by the performance. There was a sense amongst the crowd that they had not only just witnessed history in the making, they had participated in it.

"Oh, Danny," Elina finally sighed, breaking her silence after leaning against his shoulder for over an hour, watching the crowd and sponging up every last second of the night. "I can't thank you enough, this was so special, so incredible... I mean, just so unbelievable. It makes me sad that I'll never be able to share with anyone how I really felt tonight. There's no way I could explain it." And then she reached up and pulled his head down to her waiting mouth, kissing him long and hard. He felt the tip of her tongue slide between his lips. It was the most unnerving yet delicious intimacy he had ever experienced.

She broke it off, slowly, then hugged him. Danny Logan was speechless. Then reality bit.

"Oh, man, I gotta get you home..." he said, panicking. The night air was still hot and he felt beads of perspiration rolling down his light shirt. "Your father is going to kill me. He doesn't even know where you are, Elina."

"Relax, Danny," she said, pulling him closer. "My parents think I'm at a girlfriend's house for the night. They thought it would do me good to be with a friend after what happened at my party." A smile came to her face. "They were right. I've never felt so good."

He stared at her, puzzled. It was if the events of the night before had never happened.

"You mean you didn't do anything about it, like report the guys who attacked you?" he asked. Logan had half expected to be called by the police to give a statement.

She waved her hand away as if it was a nuisance she didn't want to be bothered with.

"No, I convinced my dad to let it go. I was stupid, got drunk. It was my own fault. That's what boys do."

"What?" Logan stammered pushing her away from him so he could face her. "Elina, where I come from, 'boys' don't go around trying to rape girls and get away with it."

She hung her head.

"I don't want to make a big fuss about it," she answered. "My mother said it would get into the newspaper."

Logan was pissed. "Yah, it might get into the paper. She's right. Better to let them get away with it than to sully the family name."

"Danny…" she whined.

"Forget it. It's not who I am, Elina. Or where I come from. It's not how we do things."

They were still sitting in their stadium seats. The crowd began slowly moving out. They were in no hurry. The silence between them was awkward.

"Where *do* you come from, Danny?"

He looked into her eyes, wondering why it had taken her so long to ask the question.

"I live in the South End of Hartford," he answered without hesitation, as if being so direct made him somehow courageous. "I doubt that you've ever been there."

"I went to the Wadsworth Atheneum once, and I've been to the Mark Twain House," she replied, hopefully. "Are they near where you live?"

He grinned, amused by her naiveté, but aggravated by it, too.

"Yes," he said sarcastically. "But I wouldn't say those places are especially 'representative' of where I live."

"What do you mean?"

It was his turn to hang his head and when he spoke he looked away from her.

"What I mean is that I live in a three family dump infested with rats with a leaky roof and rotting plumbing. Your father would probably call it a slum. And my mother and father are drunks and they fight all the time. I'm home as little as possible. It means I hate who and what I am and where I come from."

She looked at him, startled.

"That about do it?" he asked, turning to face her, his voice dripping with disdain and embarrassment more than anger. He looked away again.

Elina was silent. Having grown up as sheltered and pampered as she had, Logan's confession was difficult to understand.

"It can't be that bad, Danny, you sure have good friends," she said.

"Yah. You could say we all have shared similar challenges." He was getting more angry by the minute for allowing himself to get into this situation. He knew it had been hopeless from the start.

"Look. It makes no difference," he said in defeat. "This could never happen, probably never should have happened.

"Even one date?" Elina asked, startled.

"Is that what this is?" Logan challenged her. "I mean, was I a date... or a chance to see the Beatles?"

She saw the look of hurt in his eyes.

"Well... I guess it was both. I wouldn't have come with you — even to see the Beatles — if I didn't like you," she said.

"Yah. And cows can fly, sister," he said in ridicule.

"I don't deserve that..."

Logan saw that her eyes were welling with tears. Oh, shit he thought. It wasn't what he wanted to happen.

"It's not my fault that my parents are rich. Or that yours drink and fight. If it makes you feel any better, my mother is the biggest bitch on the planet. And a drunk. She hates me. My life isn't perfect, Danny Logan."

"Pretty damned close." He said in a staccato tone. The words were out of his mouth before he could stop himself.

She stood up and stared at him, rage in her eyes. He hadn't realized just how beautiful a shade of green they were. The tears made them that much brighter. Logan was so fixated on her face, he never saw the hand coming at him that slapped him across his own.

"You don't know... you just don't know," she said, tears now rolling down her cheeks. But there was fire in her eyes.

"Elina, I'm sorry..." he began, feeling terrible that he had started this. He rubbed his cheek. She'd really belted him.

"You hide behind your miserable life like it's some kind of badge of courage... like it gives you the right to look down on people like me. People who have stuff, do you hear me? It's just stuff!"

She wiped her eyes, furious that she was so emotional.

"Yah, I have stuff, and we live in a big house on the ocean and I'm probably what you would call a spoiled brat. But there are some things missing in my life just like yours, Danny Logan."

His eyes narrowed. What could she possibly want?

"Like what?" he couldn't help but ask.

The look on her face said she could tear his eyes out for being so stupid.

"Like people who really care about me... love me..." she replied, her voice dropping off. "All I am to my mother is another piece of artwork to show off. And to my father...let's just say I'm a distraction from the pain of living with his drunken, miserable wife."

Logan was silent.

"That about do it?" she mocked him. Seats a couple of rows away had emptied. She walked over and sat down in one, leaving Logan alone, his mouth agape.

He shook his head in frustration and had no idea of what to do next. He knew that he hadn't been able to keep his own self-loathing in check, and perhaps had blown any chance of getting to know this girl better. But as he stared at Elina sitting alone, the truth descended upon him without even a second to consider or debate it. Danny Logan was already in love with her. It had happened the moment he had met her by the deceptively welcoming pure blue waters of her pool at the great mansion in Fenwick, a world that was actually as cruel and alien to him as Mars and just as frightfully inhospitable. He was an infection that Elina's parents and the caste of society to which they belonged, simply would not tolerate.

It was so clear to him. But suddenly so were the consequences of saying goodbye to Elina without ever having tried to win her love. He was smart enough to know that it would haunt him forever.

He walked down the stairs and plopped down in a seat next to her. She didn't acknowledge his presence.

"Ya know, when I was driving to New Haven, I thought a lot about how this night might go," he began speaking, his eyes locked straight ahead.

She didn't respond.

"First, I figured there was a good chance you wouldn't show at all. In which case I would have given the tickets to the first two girls I saw and driven home."

Elina remained silent.

"Then I wondered what to do if by some miracle you did meet me in New Haven? What would I do? How would the night go?"

Silence.

"I came to the conclusion that there would be three parts to our time together. The first would be the pure joy of being with you and listening to you talk non-stop about the Beatles."

She turned and looked at him, still silent. He continued to gaze ahead.

"Check. And then I figured that at some point during the night, I would begin to feel sorry for myself about being with a girl that I couldn't have. I would recognize that it was all sort of a mean joke on me, and I would get angry and say stupid things and probably ruin our date and your memory of the greatest concert ever."

Now she stared at him, her ocean green eyes pleading with him to finish the story the way she desperately wanted.

"Check? In fact, double check. But then I thought about how I might salvage the disaster of my own creation by making our trip home as much fun and as full of the 'consequences be damned' attitude that got us here." He reached for her hand.

"Betcha the hot dog stands are still open. Buy you dinner, beautiful girl?" he pleaded, turning towards her and locking on to her eyes, hoping her tears had dried.

She remained silent for a moment longer, then leaned forward and touched her forehead against his.

"Even if the hot dog stands are closed, can we still hold hands?" she replied.

Logan pulled her close and pressed his lips against hers in a gentle kiss thanking her for forgiveness.

"What time do your folks expect you tomorrow morning?" he asked.

"Mid morning, no earlier."

"Then the night is young and has just begun," Logan replied. "Hey, that sounds like a song. Maybe I could be the fifth Beatle."

She laughed out loud. It was the best music Danny Logan had heard all night. They raced out of the stadium, wolfed down a hot dog and ran back to the subway station to catch the last train back to Grand Central Station.

It was nearly three in the morning when the train pulled into New Haven. Elina had been sleeping against Danny's shoulder for over an hour.

"Wake up, sleepy head..." he said, gently nudging her awake.

"Are we here?"

"New Haven. Gotta ways to go, beautiful."

"Beautiful?" That woke her up. "I must look awful..." she whined.

"You couldn't if you tried," Danny Logan said, slowly learning the art of being a gentleman.

'I'll bet you say that to all the girls," she said, punching him playfully on the shoulder.

"There are no other girls, Elina."

Her eyes widened in surprise. "None?"

"None."

She sighed.

"Well, that does it," she said.

"Huh?"

"I claim you as my boyfriend."

His heart sank.

"Now don't be kidding around about stuff like that. Some of us guys actually take it seriously," he replied. His stomach started to hurt.

"I've never had a boyfriend," she said. "There have been boys... but not like you, Danny Logan. You are Grade A, Class 1 boyfriend stock. The kind girls like to keep around. Forever."

He was speechless. Until he had to say it.

"What about..."

She shook her head. "They don't matter. It's my life. I'll love who I want to love."

Danny Logan closed his eyes as the train pulled to a complete stop. He was afraid to open them for fear it would all be a dream. But no, the beautiful blonde girl was still holding his hand. In fact, her other hand was tenderly rubbing his chest.

"Beat you to the car," she laughed and jumped out of her seat. "We can talk there." Elina was out of the train and running down the platform before Danny had even gotten out of his seat.

Love?

He closed his eyes again and felt fear. Not physical fear. He'd take on anyone, anytime to fight for something he believed in. It was fear of losing her to something he couldn't control that frightened him.

Fear of destiny.

But that would have to wait because she was already in the Chevy honking the horn. Not a good idea at 3 a.m. in New Haven. He bolted from his seat and raced to the car.

"Are you crazy?" he laughed at her, jumping into the drivers seat and fumbled around trying to find the ignition in the darkness. Only a dim glow from a street light 50 yards away illuminated the car. Finally he felt the key slip into the ignition and the engine roared to life.

"Yes, Danny," she said. "Crazy about you."

Wordlessly, she reached over and turned the key off, killing the motor, and slid across the front seat towards him.

"What are you..." Danny began. But her lips got in the way. She kissed him hard on the mouth, pushing him back against the driver's door and climbed on top of him, forcing him beneath her. In an instant they were lying prone across the front seat, locked in an embrace that was making Logan's head spin.

"Elina..." he whispered, trying to slow her down.

"Shh..." she said.

Straddling him, she rose upright and while looking into his wide eyes, slowly unbuttoned her blouse, finally pulling it off her shoulders. Then she reached up and released the center clasp of her bra, allowing it to fall from her body. In the dim light he could just make out the swell of her full, naked breasts, which she made no effort to cover. For a moment, she stayed like that, allowing him to look at her. It was an image that burned into his memory, at once so innocent, beautiful and powerful that it would stay with him all his life.

"Touch me, Danny, please? I want you so much," she whispered taking both his hands and placing them on her breasts. He gently caressed her, luxuriating in the exquisite feel of her creamy smooth skin interrupted only by the hardness of her tiny nipples. Her hands urged him on and she closed her eyes, lost in ecstasy. But as he stared up at her, his heart about to explode from emotions he had never felt for another girl, something told him to fight for control, and a wave of uncertainty made him hesitate then pull his hands away. He knew that they were about to pass the point of no return and they weren't ready for this.

She opened her eyes, startled to her senses by the abruptness with which he had stopped and reached down searching for his hands again.

"Danny, it's all right, I want this," she said, leaning down to kiss him and moving his hands back to her chest. She sighed deeply at his touch. Danny Logan wasn't completely inexperienced, but he had never been confronted by such eagerness. Especially by a girl he really cared for.

He grazed the sides of her breasts with his fingertips, careful to be gentle while his lips found her neck and shoulders. He was losing control again, adrift in the pleasures of her taste and natural fragrance. It was now or never.

With his last breath of restraint, he took her face in his hands and held her.

"Elina… we…"

She tried to kiss him, gyrating against his body and longing for his touch.

"It's ok, Danny," she pleaded again. "I love you… I want this.

Love? There was that word again.

He put his hands on her shoulders and gently pushed her back. She was disoriented and looked at him as if he were crazy.

"Elina... you're not going to believe this... I don't even believe I'm doing this... but we have to stop." He put his hands on her face again and kissed her deeply but slowly trying to ease the sexual tension between them.

He grabbed the steering wheel and pulled himself up in the seat, then held Elina close while gently raining kisses on her neck and face.

"I don't understand," she finally said, her blouse still open. He reached to pull it closed. "Don't you want me?"

"Yes, I want you, and that's the problem. I know you don't understand," he said.

"I'm confused, Danny, I'm not like this with other boys..."

Great, he thought. He was giving her all the wrong messages. There was only one that could make sense of it all.

"Elina, my heart is about to burst because I'm so in love with you. I've never felt this way before," he began. "But I don't want this to be a one night thing. I want to know you, for you to know me. I want you to know that you really love me, not only when I'm nice, but when I'm an idiot, when I'm a fool, and when you have to fight to love me because I'm not from your world."

"Whoa..." she whispered. Her beautiful eyes filled with tears again.

"No one has ever said they loved me before, Danny Logan. No one."

He hesitated for a moment.

"Well... what's it feel like? I can't tell you I'm on very familiar ground either," he said.

"Does it mean that you'll want to see me tomorrow and the next day, that you'll want to be with me and hold me all the time? And put up with me?" she asked.

"Yah, I'm pretty sure it means all that, Elina... and more."

He looked into her eyes again and kissed her, reaching down to caress her one last time. She shuddered with delight but pulled away."

"But I thought...?"

"That's the 'more' I meant. When the time is right." He kissed her again. She smiled.

"Danny Logan... I think I do love you."

He had that strange feeling in his chest again. It was an ache for something he'd been without for so long.

He reached for her hand and brought it to his lips, planting a kiss on her fingers.

"Ya know what? Forget the Beatles. What you just said to me is the best love song I've ever heard." He paused, staring into her eyes.

"I love you, Elina. No matter what happens, always remember that."

He started the Chevy again and slowly pulled out of the Union Station parking lot. It was after four in the morning. The sun wouldn't be up for another hour or so.

"The first thing a really good boyfriend does is keep his woman well fed," Logan said in a serious tone, setting Elina into gales of laughter.

"It's gonna be like that, huh?" she said.

"Yah, girl, you're not going to be able to live without me."

"Then let's head for Saybrook and we can stop at an all night diner I know and have breakfast," she said. "It will probably be faster than you pulling off the road somewhere and having to hunt something for us to eat," she laughed.

"You mock me girl..." he smiled, so glad that he had averted a disaster.

They drove a few miles in silence, Elina sitting close to Danny in the front seat of the old Chevy. They pulled up to a stop light on Chapel Street and stole a kiss.

"Someday, Elina Hanson, you're going to remember this as the greatest date you ever had," Logan said.

"You may be right," she said and squeezed his hand. Then she reached for the radio dial and turned up the volume.

The voice of the late night DJ came over the air from WDRC.

"Got another treat for all you early risers or late night hell raisers," the voice said. "Our all night Beatles play continues after what can only be called an epic concert at Shea Stadium last night. Man what a show! Let's welcome in the daybreak with one of my favorite cuts off the *Meet The Beatles* album from 1964. Boys and girls, cuddle up real close for this one." Suddenly the air was filled with the sound of acoustic guitar and the voices of the Beatles singing "This Boy" in harmony.

> *"That boy took my love away*
> *Oh, he'll regret it someday*
> *But this boy wants you back again"*

Spontaneously, they began to sing along to the sad ballad as they drove.

"I love this song, it's so beautiful," Elina said.

"So sad," Danny replied.

"Nothing to worry about tiger, there's no "That Boy" in my picture. "

"So it's just 'This Boy?'"

"'This Boy' will do fine, forever," she said, holding his arm.

"You never know, do you," Danny answered. But it's like the song says." He sang the final stanza to her.

"This boy wouldn't mind the pain
Would always feel the same
If this boy gets you back again"

"Like I said, Danny Logan, 'This Boy' will do fine," Elina laughed.

"I hope so," he replied.

"Because I'll be here forever."

Three

~~~ ℘ ~~~

Elina called him late the next afternoon from a pay phone.

"They still think I was at my girlfriend's, Danny. My father asked only if I was feeling better after what happened at my birthday party. Frankly, I don't think my mother really cared where I was one way or another."

Logan was using the kitchen phone at Paul Carducci's restaurant. He didn't dare give her his home phone number. His mother would be blind drunk this late in the day and his father had already parked himself on a stool at the First and Last Tavern for the night.

"Thank god, I wouldn't want you to catch hell because of me," he responded.

"Well, being only 17 and out with a boy all night is one thing, I suppose," she laughed. "But the only

76

reason they'd be mad is because they're bigots, Danny. Let's forget about it."

"Forget about it? How can I forget about it? I've been going nuts all day thinking about you. Can I see you tonight? Can you get away?"

"Yah, I'll tell the 'wardens' that I'm taking one of my friends out for a ride in my new car, ok? Where can we meet?"

"Nowhere we might get spotted, that's for sure. But I've got an idea. You know, I bet you've never been to a real beach."

"A real beach? I have one in my front yard," she said, quizzically.

"No. I mean a public beach, where other people actually have a right to go. The kind of place my friends and I go to all the time."

"Oh."

"There's nothing to be afraid of." He wished he hadn't said it. It made him a snob, too.

"I'm not afraid."

"Forget it. You know we only have about two weeks until you leave for Boston..." Logan said. He couldn't get it off his mind.

"I know," she said, her voice breaking. "But that doesn't change anything. You can come up on weekends and..."

"Elina," he interrupted her. He couldn't think about tomorrow let alone what would become of their relationship after she enrolled in Radcliffe after Labor Day. Why had she come into his life now? Just as she was about to leave? Was this some sort of hateful game destiny was playing with him? The question was one of several that had been festering in his mind the entire day.

"Let's make the most of the time we have now, please? After that... what will be, will be." He barely got the words out.

"You're right... so, what beach?" She sniffled, giving away the tears that were rolling down her cheeks. "Is it near here?" It would be so much easier if she could just tell him to come to Fenwick. But that would be a disaster, she knew. Inside, she realized that it was only a matter of time before her parents found out and tried to kill their relationship.

"It's called Hammonassett, right off Old Boston Post Road near Madison. We can meet at Meigs Point, there's a parking lot there... bring your bathing suit. We'll go for a sunset swim."

"It sounds romantic..."

"Wait till you see it. Miles of beach. We can walk and talk... and maybe hide in the tall grass in the dunes for a while..." he said, remembering how close they had come last night to what would have been a very awkward morning after. But he was determined to have a real relationship with this girl. They had so many obstacles to overcome. Sex would only complicate matters. For the time being, "first base" was their limit.

"Meet you there at 6:30, ok?" Logan said. "I'll leave right after work. It'll take me about 45 minutes to get there. I can't wait to see you."

"Ditto, bub." She paused.

"Danny?"

"Yah?"

"I think I love you..."

In the kitchen of an Italian restaurant some 50 miles away, set in the South End of a small city filled with two family tenements and mostly poor and low income families representing a dozen different cultures, Danny Logan felt his heart skip. It was the words of an angel that caused the palpitation. An angel who had never seen the world in which he lived let alone experienced, who woke up in the morning to the sound of ocean waves breaking at her front door and sunlight streaming on to her own, very private beach. Her neighbors were white and wealthy and lived in their own mansions acres away.

Yet, despite the irreconcilable gulf of society that existed between them, the boy responded with his heart rather than his brain.

"And... I love you, Elina."

He stared at the phone as the line went dead, wondering again what he could possibly be thinking of. But out of the mass of confusion that was twirling through his brain at that moment emerged a calming, if not ironic thought.

It came to him that the struggle he'd waged to pass a required class in Shakespearean Literature might have paid off, if only because of a phrase he now remembered from *Romeo and Juliet*. The author had described the young protagonists as "a pair of star-cross'd lovers." But it was Romeo's response that had buried itself, unknowingly, in Danny's heart.

"I defy you, stars."

The words had planted the first seeds of ambition in the teenager and defined the girl of his dreams. For if she were his true love, then she would instinctively embrace them as he had.

"Sometimes, you just gotta fight for it, Danny," Coach Paul Carducci had once told him in a tight game. "The odds may suck, but if you want it, you gotta go get it." It wasn't exactly "Shakespearean," Logan thought, but Carducci's words rang as true now as they had then.

At 6:30 on the button, just as the waning sunlight had turned to that warm, golden shade that signals the beginning of dusk, Logan heard the approach of the powerful but mellow exhaust he had been waiting for and smiled. A moment later he watched the new British Racing Green Austin Healy wind its way into the parking lot of Meigs Point at Hammonassett Beach. The young blonde behind the wheel, her hair whipping devilishly behind her in the nimble convertible, expertly downshifted the sports car to a stop next to his hulking Chevy. It was a small thing and just "stuff," as Elina put it, but the disparity between the cars was just another example of the divide between them.

"I defy you, stars," Logan whispered as the anxiety that seemed inherent in being with her crept up his neck.

He opened the door of the roadster and took her into his arms. They kissed, long and tenderly.

"It feels like I haven't seen you in a year, Danny Logan, and it's only been a few hours. How are we going to deal with..."

He interrupted her. "Time for that later. C'mon, let me show you a big piece of the ocean with a beach to go with it," he said. He looked around the parking lot. There were only a couple dozen cars left. "And pretty soon, we'll have it all to ourselves."

Holding hands they raced across the parking lot to a pathway that had been carved deeply through the sand dunes and tall coastal grass by thousands of visitors over many decades. It was a canyon of sorts that rose to the beach, the walls of which were nearly to the top of Elina's head.

The ocean was invisible until suddenly, as she emerged from the path, there it was in all its vastness and mystery and she caught her breath at the isolated beauty of it. Miles of unhindered sandy beach led in both directions and just faintly in the far off distance, she saw the thin line of land that marked Long Island. It was the first time she had seen the Sound from the perspective of nature, rather than the porch of a mansion at Fenwick.

It took her a moment to take it in.

"Oh, Danny, you are so right. It's beautiful. And the sun is beginning to set. We have to watch it!"

"Absolutely, but the right way to do it is to be in the water! Are you wearing your suit?" he asked.

She reached down to her waist with both hands and pulled her striped jersey off over her head, revealing a black bikini top. Her cut off jeans were next to fall.

"Fully prepared, sailor," she laughed.

"My god, you are beautiful, Elina," he said, startled again by the seductive powers of her young body.

He pulled off his tee shirt before the stirring in his loins became any more unnerving and grabbed her hand again.

"Last one in the water…" he laughed.

She squealed in delight, alive with the sense of freedom Danny Logan awoke in her. At that moment, they were equals in every way. And very much in love.

The tide was going out as the sun began it's plunge over the western horizon, and they ran across 50 feet of a sand bar before being able to dive into the water. Danny, a strong swimmer, emerged ten yards ahead of her then quickly swam back to embrace Elina. He grabbed her around the waist and held her to him, walking backwards until the water was at his neck. She clung to his neck and wrapped her dangling legs around his waist.

"Now, this is the best part," he said to her, turning them to face the setting sun.

"We've got the best seat in the house to see the most amazing spectacle on earth," he told her, the suns rays streaming towards them like a spotlight on their beaming faces, filled with happiness, radiating above the dark waters of the Sound.

It was perfect.

Because no one could see them.

Four

~~~ ❧ ~~~

Labor Day, 1965

Chickie wouldn't take no for an answer.

"Listen, man, you can't keep hiding this. It's stupid," he lectured Logan, his best friend. "You have to stand up to her parents or the whole thing is a waste of time."

"You just don't get it, Chickie," Danny replied. "Have you forgotten how they treated us the night of Elina's birthday party? We are nothing but trailer trash to those people. If I surface anywhere near her, they're going to put her in chains. After they shoot me."

The lifelong friends were sitting in Danny's car in the parking lot of Carducci's Ristorante after work, sharing a six-pack. It was the first time the two had spent any time together since the "Fenwick Fiasco," as they had come to call it. Danny had been spending every spare moment with Elina before she left for school the next day. Chickie would be leaving for Boston as well to begin his first year at MIT and Danny would be enrolling at UCONN in Storrs the following day.

Chickie wasn't happy that his best friend had essentially disappeared during their last couple of weeks together in Hartford, but envied him.

"Man, if I was as hot for any girl as you are for Elina, there's no way I'd let her parents scare me off. I tell ya, Danny, her father is going to think you're a pushover once he finds out about this. And it's only a matter of time before he does. And the battle axe, too."

"Yah, well it's not what Elina wants either, pal," Logan said and drained his second beer. "But I don't want to cause a scene before she leaves for Boston. I'm laying low for now."

"Shit," Chickie responded. "I feel for you, buddy."

They sat in silence. Logan opened another beer.

"When are you leaving for Boston?" he asked Chickie.

"Tomorrow, same as Elina. Got to enroll, then I think classes begin the next day. I'll miss ya, buddy, but it's sure going to be nice to say goodbye to Hartford for a while."

"Yah, there hasn't been much here for us." Logan was on the verge of saying something about how much their friendship had meant to him, but the words wouldn't come. Chickie was having similar emotions.

"I think I'm going to dump the 'Chickie' handle when I get to school," he said out of the blue.

"Huh?"

"Don't think I want to find myself applying for jobs in a few years as Chickie Anderson. I'm going to intro myself as 'Charles.'"

"Not 'Charlie?'" Logan asked

"No. Time to start getting serious about life, Danny. Hell, that's what you're doing with Elina, isn't it? I mean... this isn't just a fling, is it?"

"No fling. Never felt this way before. Doubt that I ever will again."

"Well, since we're each the only person in the world the other can trust, I'll make you a promise to watch out for her in Boston. Sloan is only a few blocks from Radcliffe. I'll stay close for you," Chickie said.

"I appreciate that... but if you show up at her dorm and announce that 'Charles' Anderson is here to visit, you think she might mistake you for somebody selling encyclopedia's door to door?" Logan asked with a straight face.

Chickie sprayed a mouthful of beer in amusement. "You asshole. Just for that, I take it back. She's on her own."

"I think I'm actually more comfortable with that," Danny kidded his best friend. "You sure about that trust thing?

"Like I said..."

Logan stuck out his bottle and tapped it on Chickie's.

"No kidding. Friends forever. No matter what happens or where life takes us. Agree?"

"It didn't need to be said, Danny. What do the Marines call it?"

"Semper Fidelis."

"Yah, Semper Fi. Always faithful."

They were quiet again, finishing their beers before Danny left to sneak in a visit with Elina near Fenwick.

"Ya know, I've got an idea," Anderson said.

"What?"

"For after we graduate."

"What? I'm all ears."

"I say we start a business. I'll be a Wall Street wiz by then so we can open our own investment house. You know, start a fund."

"I'm not sure what my major's going to be yet, but what role do you see me playing in this investment firm of ours, 'Charles?'" Logan bit.

"Well... actually, I was thinking you could be my dog. Three meals a day, a warm place to sleep..."

"Get out of the car, 'Charles'," Logan laughed, leaning forward to turn the ignition.

"What? Something I said old pal?"

"No. It's just that I keep looking over at the passenger seat and I see your ugly puss. And if I dump you then I can fill said seat with the world's most beautiful blonde."

They both laughed.

"Let it never be said that you lacked for brains, Danny. Roll slow, bud. Say hi to 'our girl' for me." Chickie jumped out of the car before Logan could swing at him.

"What?" Chickie laughed again, feigning innocence. He needed to take a piss and was afraid he was going to wet his pants from laughing.

The Chevy pulled out of the lot and turned down Franklin Avenue. Out the driver's side window shot a message to 'Charles.' It was a one-finger salute.

Logan laughed to himself as he drove, remembering the good times he had shared with his

86

friend. This was one of the conversations he'd probably never forget.

He was right.

Never.

An hour later, he met Elina on the beach at Cornfield Point, a small summer cottage community adjacent to Fenwick. The houses were tiny here, worth only a fraction of the neighboring mansions. The comparisons didn't stop there.

Working people owned these cottages, many passed down through several generations of family. They were summer retreats only, with no insulation or heating furnaces to offer much shelter in the dead cold of winter. But these tiny bungalows were the pride of their middle class owners, many who hailed from Hartford, New Haven or other southern Connecticut cities and towns. Before discovering Fenwick, Cornfield Point was a small slice of heaven to Danny Logan, representing wealth and success he could only dream of. He often had to remind himself that the people here weren't better off than his own parents. They were just people who wanted more out of life than the inside of a bottle.

He spotted her car, purposely parked some distance from the nearest streetlight, hidden in the darkness. He pulled the Chevy behind the new Austin Healey and scanned the beach.

It took him a few minutes but he finally saw Elina sitting on the beach below a stone seawall at the water's edge, leaning against one of the several wooden jetties that had been erected along the coastline to slow erosion. In her dark sweatshirt and bluejeans, she blended into the night, only the moon's reflection off the water casting shadows that might betray her presence. But it would take searching eyes to spot them.

The ebbing tide revealed glistening salt flats as Danny got out of the car. Instantly a salt-filled breeze whipped his face and he sucked in a deep breath of the invigorating air. He had always loved the ocean, and found Cornfield Point, Hammonassett and the few public beaches along the Connecticut shoreline an escape from the squalor, noise and heat of Hartford. But even in winter, he would drive to the beach to clear his head of his family's depressing apartment and the constant arguing that filled it with sadness. Here, he could always breath and fill his ears with the soothing rush of the ocean.

Danny met her with his arms extended and they embraced. He kissed her long and hard, knowing that they had only hours left together. The ocean breeze, the far off crash of the surf's receding tide and the moonlit night combined as a symphony behind their kiss. They were oblivious to everything but their passion for each other. Slowly, they sank to the sand, holding the kiss.

Finally, Danny spoke.

"It doesn't matter what they think," he told her, his hands caressing her face and hair. "I'm not going to be a loser forever. I'll earn their respect, I promise you."

Elina kissed him once more, her passion building again quickly. She would not be denied on this night.

"Do you hear, me Elina?" Logan asked, desperate for a commitment from her that would sustain him during the lonely weeks and months he knew lay ahead.

"Yes, Danny," she whispered to him. "But I don't care what they think…"

"I do," he said, tired of hiding from her parents and those who would judge him without even a sense of the man he would become.

"Boston is not that far away. I won't have a car at UCONN, at least until next year. But I'll find a way to see you, maybe in October. Until then, you have to write to me… every day… and I'll do the same. At least in my heart, I'll be as close to you as I am now."

They kissed again, two shadows in the sand.

"I promise, Danny, and then it will be Thanksgiving and Christmas in no time… oh, I can't believe these last few weeks have gone by so fast. My stomach hurts just thinking you won't be there tomorrow."

"But I will, Elina, I will… not a day will go by that I won't think of you, of being with you. And then, when college is done, we can be together forever…"

She abruptly reached up and put a finger to his lips. "No, not so fast. We have to focus on one day at a time. It's going to be so hard, Danny, I'm so afraid."

He held her, silently, his face buried in her neck. He didn't want her to see his own fear.

"I won't lose you, Elina, I won't, no matter what," he whispered to her. She pulled back, staring at him with tear filled eyes. His heart was breaking.

"The Beatles…" he managed to say, his voice quivering. "Our favorite song…"

She smiled, knowingly.

"This Boy…" she whispered softly.

"Do you remember the promise?"

A tear trickled down her beautiful face.

"*Would always feel the same,*" she sang, quoting the last lyrics of the ballad. They were the words Danny Logan pledged to her.

"Don't ever forget…" he said, wiping away her tear.

She wrapped both her arms around his neck and dragged him to the sand, wanting, needing his touch.

"Now Danny, please, now…" she begged.

Five

~~~ ໑ ~~~

December, 1965

It would begin almost the instant he thought about the walk to the student union.

Danny Logan would feel the first crawly twinges of anxiety begin to work up his spine. His legs would go weak. He would sweat despite the December cold and his heart raced.

Yet each afternoon, he forced himself to walk across campus to the student union where inside was the post office and a mailbox assigned to his name.

He would stand in front of the small rectangular metal door, holding his key. He knew there would be no letter waiting for him, just like there wasn't one the day before or in the days before that. What had begun as a torrent of letters, sometimes several in a day, had slowly trickled to perhaps two a week, then one, and finally, nothing.

Still, he would insert the key, turn the lock and look inside. The mailbox would be empty, as he knew it would. With that knowledge would come a crushing sense of loneliness and a pain in his heart he could not make go away.

Then mindlessly, as he had every day for the past week, he would walk a couple of miles off campus to the nearest liquor store and buy a bottle of cheap Irish whiskey. Ironically, it was the same rotgut he'd watched his father pour down his gullet for years.

He was desperate not to think of Elina, of what had happened, but his heart broke a little more with each step. So every day became a race to get numbed, to get so inebriated that he couldn't remember why his heart hurt so much. But before he could taste that first swallow of amber anesthesia and his brain slowly addled from the alcohol, he focused on memories of his father. Of all people, he thought, it was his father who had come to mind when the full brunt of his loss had hit him. That mean, drunken old fool. It took quite a few walks to the liquor store before he understood why.

Danny Logan had never come to grips with why his father seemed to live to be drunk. It never made sense to him that anyone would want to go through life blurry eyed, impaired, barely able to walk after drinking all day and into the night. He guessed that it made him happy somehow. But now he saw that he had misunderstood him.

The first time the answer came to him was like being punched in the face. And instantly he felt an emotion for his father that he never had before, or ever thought he would. It was sadness.

It came to him that his father drank to ease the pain of living his life as it passed him by. The lifetime that fate had dealt him. The endless hours and days he had to endure the misery and disappointment of knowing that his dreams had died and that his love had been wasted on a woman who could not love him in return. The time before death would call to claim the scraps of his soul that were left to scavenge.

Logan would get drunk off that bottle while he walked back to campus and slowly the pain in his heart would numb. Eventually, just before the alcohol prevented him from reasoning at all, he would have one last thought. There was nothing ironic about the Irish whiskey swilling in his own guts now. The depth of his misery was as bottomless as his father's, a man whose fate he would share.

Sometimes he would make it to his dorm room before passing out, more often than not he would fall by the roadside and sleep it off. It was a wonder he didn't freeze to death or get hit by a car.

Logan would awaken before dawn, confused only by where he was. Why he had gotten drunk wasn't a question at all.

There was no letter in the box.

He had no scented sheets of stationary to read and re-read to help him imagine that the words of love she once wrote had been real. There was only an empty space that he filled with memories of a girl, and what might have been, but predictably was not to be.

The question that haunted him as he struggled back to consciousness was not why she had abandoned him.

But why the only two people in the world he cared for had betrayed him.

* * * * *

It wasn't meant to happen. It just did. At least that was how Elina had pathetically tried to explain it to him.

The weeks after classes began were a busy time for each of them. But Elina and Danny never failed to find the time to pen a letter to each other every day. Even Chickie, now "Charles," found time to send Logan a note.

"All's well here, chum," Charles wrote. "The course load is a bit more than I had expected, but I'll live. Happily there are plenty of longhaired, mini-skirted diversions to keep me occupied during my few hours of freedom on weekends. If you weren't so stuck on old what's her face, I could probably set you up for a wild weekend."

Danny read the letter from his friend with amusement. It was just like him. Charles had a wild side that was as much a part of his personality as his gifted intellect. He was determined to sow his oats and not let a single opportunity pass. Danny would never admit it, but a part of him almost wished he could be so laissez-faire about relationships. He often puzzled that the two of them could think so differently about women because they shared such painfully similar experiences growing up. But although they were both the products of dysfunctional, alcoholic parents, Danny longed for the security of a long-term, monogamous relationship, while Charles only had time for "love 'em and lose 'em" encounters.

Elina's letters filled Danny with a contentment he'd not felt before. She never failed to share her love or her dreams for their future together. For the first time in his life, Logan became a student, applying himself in the classroom with an energy he had had not exhibited at any time in his schooling. He chose to major in English, a choice he made in a spur of the moment decision, perhaps influenced by the Shakespearean Literature course with which he'd had some success. On the inside cover of his first textbook he inscribed the words Shakespeare had written in Romeo and Juliet that had given him courage after meeting Elina: "I defy you, stars." He was actually beginning to think he had a future ahead of him and that someday he could fulfill the pledge he had made to Elina to earn her parent's blessing.

"I'm not going to be a loser forever. I'll earn their respect, I promise you."

He missed his Chevy, parked at home because freshman weren't allowed to have cars on campus. It robbed him of the ability to drive to Boston to see Elina. He knew it was for the best because the temptation to see her would be constant and he'd never be able to concentrate on school. They made plans to meet in Boston on the Columbus Day holiday weekend.

Two days before he was going to hitchhike to Radcliffe to see her, he retrieved her daily letter from his mailbox and slid to the floor to tear it open. To his surprise, Elina wrote that one of her professor's had unexpectedly assigned a complicated paper due on the first day back to classes. Their weekend was blown.

"I'm so sorry and disappointed, Danny," she wrote, "I was so looking forward to seeing you. Please try to understand."

"Shit," he muttered to himself, so disappointed despite his best attempts to stay upbeat. He crumpled the letter into a ball and threw it into a wastebasket.

He began walking back to his dorm when he was suddenly struck with an urge he couldn't control.

94

"Hell. I can't wait anymore." Less than an hour later he was standing by the roadside of the Wilbur Cross Highway with his thumb out. Destination: Boston.

An older couple that was travelling to see their son, a student at Holy Cross College in Worcester, almost immediately picked him up. Other than introducing himself as a freshman at UCONN, he never got another word in to the monologue the mother insisted upon having about her boy's many "extraordinary" qualities. After well over an hour of politely listening Logan was ready to scream. He was glad when they let him off in Auburn on the Massachusetts Turnpike. Thanks to the babbling mother, he had formed an extreme dislike for a young guy he'd never met. Danny Logan wondered what it would be like to have parents who cared about him as he stuck his thumb back out. He shook off what he knew was just jealousy and tried to focus on surprising Elina.

It took him a while on the frigidly cold Mass Pike to get another ride. Darkness had fallen and he was hard to see. A hundred cars flew past. Finally, a Harvard professor making his way back from a conference at Trinity College in Hartford spotted him and pulled over. Luck was with him. He was headed for his apartment, which was no more than a few blocks from Elina's dormitory.

The professor was a quiet man who introduced himself only by his first name, George, and wasn't much for conversation. They drove the first 20 miles in his vintage Volvo mostly in silence. Then he innocently asked Danny if he enjoyed sports and that led to conversations about the Celtics and the Red Sox that lasted right into Boston. The professor began pointing out historical landmarks as they made there way toward

Cambridge. They passed by the Massachusetts State House as they drove through the Beacon Hill neighborhood.

"Ever been to Boston, Dan?" the professor asked.

"No sir. Can't say that I have."

"Lot of history here, son.

Logan was more interested in all the young people he saw on the streets. Clearly this was a college city. He was a long way from Storrs.

"Sure are a lot of people my age..." he said.

"Oh, yah. Must be nearly 60 colleges and universities in Boston. Where did you say your girl was attending?"

"Radcliffe," he responded just as the professor pulled his car into Harvard Square.

"What dorm?"

"Uh... Bertram Hall," Danny remembered.

"Sure, that's one of the South Houses in the Radcliffe Quad," the professor said. "I know it well from my younger days," he laughed.

"Uh..."

"Sounds difficult, Danny, but it's actually only a couple of blocks northwest. It's no more than a ten-minute walk across campus. Good luck finding her. And stick with those Red Sox, hey? Another couple of years... you never know."

"Never say never, professor, especially when it comes to the Sox," Danny laughed and thanked him for the lift. He lit out into Harvard Yard, busting with emotion knowing that he would finally see his Elina after weeks of being separated.

He asked a few strangers for directions and quickly found himself in front of Bertram Hall. Logan recognized the address he had memorized from all his letters: 51 Cambridge Street. But never in all his imagination had he realized the dormitory was such a palace. Built in 1901, the neo-Georgian brick building oozed wealth. He was immediately intimidated. But he'd come this far and wasn't about to turn back now. It was just after 10:30 p.m. Surely Elina would still be up. He took two steps towards the front door when it burst open.

Charles Anderson emerged from inside wrapping a scarf around his neck.

The two made eye contact immediately. Charles was instantly flustered and awkwardly turned to go back inside before realizing it was too late.

"Chickie, old buddy!" Danny yelled in genuine surprise and delight at seeing his friend. He rushed forward and gave him a bear hug. "Sorry, I meant to say 'Charles.'"

"Danny, what the hell are you doing here?" Charles stammered, ignoring the comment.

"Well, that's some greeting for your best friend. I haven't seen you since frigging Labor Day."

"It's just that... I didn't expect to see you, that's all."

"I wanted to surprise Elina, she sent me a letter saying she couldn't take any time over Columbus Day weekend like we planned," Danny explained. "I hitchhiked all the way here from Storrs."

"Oh. Well, she's..."

"What are you doing here?" Danny asked. "Checking up on my girl?" he said in jest.

Charles hesitated before responding and turned away from his friend. "Uh, yah... I guess we've, uh... sort of gotten to be good friends," Charles answered, his voice strained.

"Friends? I hope that's all," Danny laughed. "What's her room number, bud? I can't wait to see her."

"Uh... I think she's probably gone to bed, Dan. Why don't you come hang with me tonight and you can see her tomorrow? C'mon, let's grab a beer," Anderson said.

"No way man. I love ya brother, but I need to see her now. I'll catch up with you tomorrow, ok?" he answered and pushed by Charles.

"Danny, don't..." Anderson said but Logan ignored him and went inside. Charles watched as he stopped at the reception desk and inquired of Elina's room number and with a grin on his face hurried off to find her.

Anderson shook his head, ashamed of what he knew was about to happen. Then he turned and ran into the darkness of the Quad.

Inside, Danny took the stairs two at a time to reach Elina's third floor dorm room which she occupied alone. He was in awe of the building, unconsciously comparing it to the four-man room he shared at UCONN. The dorm had more of a luxury hotel feel to it than college housing.

He knocked on her door. A moment passed before he heard the rattle of a chain lock being slid across its brass retainer. Before the door opened, he heard her speak.

"Charles, you are such a devil. Back for more?" she giggled. "I told you I've got an early class tomorrow. You are insatiable. Save it for the weekend, please? You know I told Danny..." She opened the door before finishing the sentence and her mouth dropped in disbelief.

"Danny..." she said, panicked. "I meant... I mean... what are you doing..." She was naked.

His knees buckled and he backed away from the door as she closed it quickly. "Let me put something on," she said from inside, the sound of her voice full of strain as her mind raced to find an escape from being caught.

With her boyfriend's best friend.

She threw on a robe and flung open the door again, then grabbed Danny by the arm and pulled him inside, hugging him as the door closed behind them.

"I was sleeping, you surprised me, Danny," she said, burying her face in his chest so he couldn't see her. He pushed her away, gently, staring at her bed, the sheets disheveled. There were two pillows, side by side. It was obvious.

"Guess I should have called," he said, his voice a whisper. He was in shock. "Didn't expect you to have... company." It didn't take a genius to understand what he had walked in on.

"Danny... there was no one here," she lied, "just me... I was sleeping..."

"Chickie... I saw him downstairs."

She said nothing but tried to embrace him again.

"My best friend..." he mumbled. "How...?"

She said nothing.

"Why?" His eyes were full of tears. He felt sick to his stomach.

"Why, Elina?" he asked again, begging her for a reasonable answer.

She didn't have one. Elina was frantic, searching for anything to say that would make this go away. It wasn't possible.

"I... I was so lonely, Danny... he just started coming by to see me. I don't know how it happened..."

"Your letters."

She hung her head.

"You said you loved me."

"But you were so far away..."

99

Then there was silence as the world seemed to stop for Danny Logan. He was oblivious to everything but the pain piercing his heart.

Long moments passed. Elina sat on the edge of the bed and cried, desperately hoping Danny would come and wrap his arms around her. It wasn't going to happen. The boy walked to the oversized window of her dorm room and pulled open the closed, floral patterned chintz curtains. They were obscenely bright and cheery given the moment and he fought the urge to tear them down. Instead, he out over the Radcliffe Quad with its dozen exquisite dormitories, all filled with privileged beauty queens like Elina who hailed from wealthy families. One more time, he was reminded that he was a visitor to a place where he didn't belong. In the distance, he thought he could make out the features of Charles Anderson looking up at the window. It didn't matter. He felt no anger towards him. Only betrayal. That hurt more.

Finally he turned to the girl who had shaken his world the very moment he met her. A girl who had convinced him that he could be loved and that perhaps the future was not so bleak as his past. But that was all gone now.

"They were right, you know," he said.

"Who," Elina sobbed.

"Your parents."

"How?"

"I am a loser, way over my head," he said, his voice breaking.

"No Danny, don't say that," she cried, jumping up from the bed and reaching for him. He shook off her touch.

"I wasn't born to this, I don't deserve to have you. I've just been kidding myself."

100

He turned and walked to the door, stopping before he opened it, his heart desperate to find words that would fix this, but his better judgment telling him to call it a day.

"Goodbye, Elina," he said softly.

She pleaded. "Danny, no, please don't go, let's talk about this... oh please," she cried. "Danny, wait... remember our song?" she asked in desperation.

He laughed quietly.

"This Boy."

She sensed him hesitating, but it was only the absurdity overwhelming him. "It's just a song," he said to himself.

"I remember, Elina. I remember a lot of things. Especially your promise."

"We can make it better, Danny, we can," she begged him, tears of regret falling from her eyes. "Charles doesn't mean anything to me."

He turned back to her, his eyes flashing anger for the first time.

"He doesn't mean anything to you? He was my best friend. My best friend..." he repeated, slowly pronouncing each word. It was such a hollow phrase now.

"And I loved you. Did that mean anything to you?" he asked her. "Did you think of that when you were..." He didn't finish the thought, the image it conjured up was too painful. Elina was silent. She looked away in shame.

"You know, I thought this only happened in books... and silly love songs," he said to her.

Danny Logan turned back to the door and opened it.

"Funny," he said before walking out.

"There really is a 'That Boy.'"

* * * * *

Even years later, Logan couldn't recall how he managed to get back to Storrs. What he could remember was going to his mailbox several days later in a fog and checking it for a letter. To his surprise, there was a single envelope in the box, and with no other motivation than curiosity, he opened it and pulled out the single sheet of stationary inside. His hands shook.

"Dear Danny,
I'm so, so sorry that I've hurt you. I never intended for this to happen and can only hope that you can forgive..."

Logan shook his head in disgust. He couldn't bear her words and shredded the letter without reading more. Then he carried the scraps of paper outside with him, back to his dormitory. He walked around to the back of the building, knelt down and with his bare hands, ripped through the grass and into the soil, digging out a small hole. He dropped the torn paper into the grave and then stopped, wondering if he should say something as a priest would over a dead body. Instead, he spit into the hole, filled it in with the dirt and grass and walked away.

After a two week bender and numerous nights spent passed out in the woods or on the roadside back to his dormitory, he had just enough strength left to save himself.

Two days before Christmas, so hung over he could barely think, Logan walked to the registrar's office and quit school. A secretary there asked if there was something she could do, noting that his grades were excellent for the first few months of classes, then inexplicably he had failed everything.

"Perhaps we could arrange for tutors," Mr. Logan. "I would be happy…"

"That's very kind of you, but I'm just not cut out for this," Logan lied.

"You shouldn't give up so easily, young man," she said.

"Perhaps you're right, ma'am. But I've learned something recently."

"What's that?"

"About dreams." He hesitated, not anticipating that admitting the truth would hurt so much.

"Sometimes they're nothing more that. Just fantasies not worth chasing."

"Are you sure?" she asked.

"Sure?" he answered. "Only of one thing."

"What?"

"The stars won."

She stared at him, perplexed by his odd response. He turned and walked out, wondering where in the world he belonged.

Six

~~~ ❧ ~~~

April, 1967

Logan scanned the newsroom and leaned back in his well-worn desk chair. There'd been a lot of backsides sitting in it before his, but now it was his seat of honor. For the first time in his life, he felt like he was somewhere he fit.

The vast newsroom was alive with activity. Hundreds of people were scurrying around like rats in a maze doing a myriad of jobs. But the dozens of reporters who were either banging away at a manual typewriter or on the telephone or juggling both owned the most coveted of assignments. Some had a phone to their ear, cradled tightly between cheek and shoulder while they carried on typically intense conversations and typed simultaneously. Their fingers moved with lightening speed over the keys, feeding sheets of white paper with letters that became words, then sentences, then whole paragraphs that ultimately became news stories.

Logan had come to believe that it was a kind of magic that created a newspaper every day, a miracle of talking, listening, probing, analyzing and summarizing facts and information that was boiled in ink, rolled on to news print and presto! A newspaper was born.

It was at once the most exciting and intellectually invigorating environment he'd ever been in, even if it was a little rough around the edges. The cavernous room was grey with smoke from hundreds of cigarettes and cigars all burning at the same time and reeked of tobacco and coffee. To a newspaperman, it was a kind of stale but reassuring fragrance, not unlike the comforting scent of one's own home. But the endless cacophonous clamor was such that one had to develop an internal switch to shut off the noise.

Logan had avoided the cigarette habit thus far in his career, despite the many role models surrounding him who worked their typewriters with a lit butt or stogie hanging from their lips. But, like most of the reporters, he had developed an addiction to coffee. Nearly every writer in the news "bullpen" had at least a half emptied cup of coffee next to his typewriter at all times. Most of the time it was cold. They drank it anyway.

Logan had been promoted to the City Desk as a reporter less than six months before after nearly a year as a runner, fact checker, proofreader, copy editor — just about any job that had to do with putting out an afternoon newspaper with the exception of writing the news. He'd worked hard at thankless assignments before the Managing Editor Jim Greaves finally gave him a shot at actually covering the news as a full time reporter.

Danny Logan had practically crawled into The Hartford Times just after Christmas in 1965, begging for work at the country's oldest afternoon paper with a circulation of nearly 215,000. Only weeks after dropping out of college, he was broke, broken hearted and sleeping on his high school friend Eddie Graziano's couch. But he had stopped drinking and was slowly but shakily getting back on his feet with his buddy's help. It was Graziano who had suggested The Times. He had an uncle who worked in circulation who offered to put a good word in for Logan if he was interested, figuring that the semester studying English at UCONN might at least get the kid an interview.

"I appreciate your uncle's offer, Eddie, but I don't know if I can write. I mean, I only took a few classes," Logan said, afraid of embarrassing himself. He'd done enough of that for a while.

"Hell, who's talking about 'writing', Danny? From what my uncle says, you'll be lucky to get a job as a gopher at that place. But it would be a start. Man, you're smart enough to learn how to write. I mean, if you get the chance."

With that half-hearted encouragement, Logan borrowed a jacket and tie from his friend, sucked up his courage and marched up the granite steps of The Hartford Times building at 10 Prospect Street. With its imposing façade of six massive green granite columns and Beaux-Arts architectural style, there wasn't a more impressive or intimidating building in all of Hartford.

"Where you from and what's your education?" the personnel manager asked pointedly. Logan guessed the man to be in his late fifties with thinning hair, thick glasses and little time for small talk. Danny knew his

106

name was 'Holcombe' only because there was a placard on his desk. He hadn't taken time to introduce himself.

"Uh, born in Hartford, graduated high school, then spent a semester at UCONN, sir," Danny replied as politely as possible.

The personnel guy's glasses slipped down to the end of his nose as he dropped his head at the response and raised his eyes level to Logan's.

"One semester?"

"Yes, sir."

"Why did you bother?" Holcombe replied, unable to avoid the question despite its inherent sarcasm.

Logan looked away, uncomfortable already. It occurred to him that he might not belong here either.

"Just wasn't for me," he lied.

The interviewer shook his head. "Oh," he said, unimpressed.

"Major?"

"English, sir."

"Well, that answers that," said Holcombe.

"Answers what, sir?"

""English major. That's why you think The Times would be a good fit."

"Well, I, uh…"

"Listen, kid," Holcombe said, pushing back his chair. Logan thought he was about to get tossed out on his ear.

"English has about as much to do with reporting the news as the color of my shorts. Nothing. There are a lot of newsmen here who never finished high school, let alone had the privilege of attending college even for a semester. You wanna be a newspaper man, you gotta have a nose for news, ink in your blood and like the taste of newsprint for breakfast."

He stopped and stared at the young man in front of him and sized him up, incorrectly, as it turned out. But for now he concluded that he had another dreamer in front of him, a kid who probably dreamt about a Pulitzer. He should thank him for stopping by and show him the door. But for some reason he didn't. Yet.

"One semester? Didn't fit? Bullshit," he said.

Logan's eyes widened.

"There's a broad in this equation, right? And if you lie to me I'm going to boot your ass out the door right now."

For a fleeting moment, Logan had a thought to stand up and smack the guy for being an asshole. Paul Carducci had told him a hundred times to count to ten before he did or said anything when he was angry. At nine, Logan figured there was no denying the truth.

"Yes, sir."

"Over it?"

"No, sir."

"Well, you get points for honesty if not brains. Here," he said handing him a sheet of lined paper and a pencil. "Take this, go out to the desk in front of my office and give me a take on the weather outside. You got ten minutes."

Logan panicked and looked confused.

"I was hoping for a different response," Holcombe said sarcastically.

"A take?" Logan repeated.

"Yah. One take."

"What's a 'take,' sir?"

"A page, for Christ's sake. Get out of here."

Logan nearly tripped getting up from his chair and sat quickly at the desk trying desperately to remember what the weather had been when he entered the building. He was so nervous he couldn't remember.

Exactly ten minutes later, Holcombe raised his hand behind the glass window of his office and snapped his fingers, beckoning for the copy. Danny hurried in and handed it to him. It wasn't quite one full page.

The personnel manager scanned the paper, his red pencil rapidly marking it with corrections and edits. Logan thought he was dead. Holcombe smiled.

"Not a one. Damn it, not a single one."

"One what, sir? I think it was raining but I'm not sure..."

"Not one misspelling. That says you care, and maybe even that you're smart. You passed. Start tomorrow as a runner. Report to my secretary at 8 a.m. Tie, no jacket. Sneakers. She'll tell you what being a runner means then. Now, get out."

"Yes sir," Danny said in shock. "Yes, sir and thank you sir. I'll do my best, I promise..."

"Now..." he repeated, pointing to the door.

"Yes, sir." He got up and made it as far as the door when Holcombe stopped him.

"Kid," he said. "Take some advice. Get over the broad. She already took college away from you. You're a newspaperman now. Don't let her take that, too."

Logan smiled. "Yes..."

"Go." He pointed again. The young man didn't need any further encouragement.

And now, less than a year and half later, after taking on any job Holcombe threw at him without complaint, he was a reporter for one of the best newspapers in the country. Holcombe had been right about his potential. Danny Logan was like a sponge as he absorbed the workings of a newsroom. And to his own surprise, he found that he did indeed have ink in his veins and a bloodhound's sense for sniffing out a story. He not only had a natural gift for writing, he could smell news.

But Elina was hardly a distant memory. Despite his determination to put their aborted fling behind him, not a day passed that he didn't think of her. She had torn a huge hole in his heart that would never heal completely. He had no interest in meeting anyone else, in fact resisted the many attempts of friends and colleagues to find him the perfect girl. In his heartbreak, Logan was certain he had already met her. There would never be another woman who touched him as deeply as Elina. So, the Hartford Times became his mistress.

Now a junior at Radcliffe, Elina wrote to him occasionally. Although her letters were filled with trivia about life at school and living in Cambridge, he sensed that the words were nothing more than something to fill the vacuum between them. It was if she had thrown their relationship away, but could not completely let go. He typically scanned her letters then threw them in his desk drawer to be forgotten. He'd only answered her once, when she mentioned that Charles, now her roommate in an apartment they shared in Cambridge, was wondering if they could get together some time and "make peace."

"It's good to hear that you're well, Elina and happy with Charles," he wrote, swallowing hard at the thought of them being together. *"But please tell him that there's no need to make peace with me. A man needs only to make peace with himself."* That was about the most polite way he could think of to tell his former best friend that he had no interest in ever seeing him again. He thought about signing the letter "This Boy," but settled for his name. There was only room to be cute with Elina if there was hope. He had none, and continually reminded himself

that he didn't belong in her world. Somehow, that took the sting out of the hurt that still burned inside him.

But he had precious little time to think of her or her roommate. Jim Greaves, his editor, had gone out on a limb for him to get the desk on the city side and he was working hard to prove himself. At that moment, he was working on two very difficult stories that he sensed were intertwined in some way. He just hadn't found the link yet.

The first was the growing anti-Vietnam war sentiment that was creeping up all over the country and lately, in Hartford as well. City politicians hadn't seen it coming and for a long while maintained that it wouldn't happen in New England, which was decidedly JFK and Lyndon Johnson country.

The second was the also growing racial discontent in Hartford that was largely being ignored, much to the chagrin of minority leaders in the city who were warning there was trouble ahead. In the last ten years the city's minority population had more than doubled and whites were moving out of Hartford into the suburbs at an alarming pace. The Black and Puerto Rican communities were fighting wretched housing conditions, widespread poverty, little or no health care and high unemployment. But the story was taking a back seat to Vietnam and the page one photographs of local young men killed in action. For the seventh wealthiest state in the Union, its capital city was rapidly becoming an embarrassment — and a time bomb.

Logan was having more success in covering the anti-war movement largely because of the growing countrywide crusade. Already he had placed page one, lead stories with his byline on the tens of thousands of protestors who had turned out in Central Park in March and an equally large group in San Francisco in April.

He was working with the representatives of the Hartford-based chapter of the Students For A Democratic Society, a mushrooming youth anti-war protest group that was springing up all over the country. Known as SDS, the organization had been formed in 1960, but its stance on the Vietnam War had made it a household name as a student activist protest organization. But now, as the story Logan was writing would clearly point out, the SDS focus had turned from protest to radical resistance and often, violent demonstrations at colleges and university's across the country. The local SDS chapter had promised that Connecticut campuses were among the organization's targets and tensions were already beginning to grow at UCONN, the University of Hartford and Yale among others.

He quickly stopped his daydreaming and went back to work, polishing his story that was slated to run in the next Saturday edition. He had to turn his copy in to Greaves by the end of day.

Logan was deep in thought editing his work when he felt a presence hovering over his desk. He turned to find Charles Holcombe, the personnel manager.

"Oh, sorry Mr. Holcombe, didn't know you were standing there," he apologized.

"Yah. That's how most people react to me," the always-intense man replied, as close to an attempt at humor that he was capable of. He was known in the newsroom as a guy who had the personality of a newspaper left in the rain: impossible to read. His thoughts were as hidden as the words on wet newsprint. Logan liked the man, primarily because he had given him a shot at a job, but as much because he got right to the point and didn't waste time bullshitting.

"Here," Holcombe said to him, handing him a sheaf of forms with a University of Hartford letterhead at the top. "Fill these out."

"Why? Remember, I told you that college wasn't..."

"For you," the personnel manager interrupted. "Yah, I remember. Still not over the broad, huh? Well, you might want to rethink this college thing."

"Why, Mr. Holcombe?" Logan asked, puzzled.

"Because, as you may have noticed, there's a war going on and we have something called a 'Draft' in this country, managed by community draft boards. These are comprised of citizens who volunteer their time with the intent to 'volunteer' your time to get shot at in a foreign land," he said sarcastically. "The process is murky at best, and truthfully, if you have friends on a draft board, it's not to difficult to duck the call. But, if you so happen to piss off one or more of its members, you should expect them to look favorably on selecting you to learn how to shoot a gun and relocate to the sweltering jungles of Southeast Asia to kill Viet Cong. And don't expect an explanation as to why you are being invited on this all expenses paid but sometimes one-way vacation. The government hasn't had much luck explaining the mission as of yet."

"Doesn't sound like much of a democratic process," Logan responded, suddenly recognizing his vulnerability.

"Truly," he responded with unmistakable disgust. "And not even celebrity or a valid objection like refusal to serve because of religious beliefs can get you out of it if you have a target on your back. Not even the Heavyweight Champion of the World. Muhammed Ali. Can you believe it? The story will appear in tonight's paper. Greatest boxer in history found guilty of draft

evasion by a kangaroo court and stripped of his title. He
may never fight again." Holcombe closed his eyes for a
moment before continuing.

"My oldest son elected not to go on to college and
has since been 'volunteered' to fight with the U.S. Army
somewhere outside of Khe Sanh in Vietnam. I have no
doubt that the fact   I work for a newspaper that has
publicly stated its lack of support for the war played a
role in his being drafted. He has 10 months to go on his
tour. My wife prays a lot." Holcombe was on the verge
of losing it. Logan noticed that he suddenly looked very
pale.

"I, on the underhand have chosen to enable my
newspaper to seek the truth about this conflict... and its
victims... by making sure bright young men are
available to report the news." He hesitated for a
moment, knowing that he had exposed himself and his
emotions. It was not something he did often.

"That being said, you've been flying under the
radar since you dropped out of college. No telling why.
But with the story you're working on, I think it's a safe
bet to say you will definitely piss off the wrong person
one of these days. Might even be somebody from the
FBI. Big brother tends to start files on reporters writing
stories that have anything to do with the anti-war
movement."

Logan, who had developed his own views on
Vietnam and had to work very hard to keep his personal
opinions separate from his work, flinched at the word
"FBI."

He raised his brow. "You have my attention, Mr.
Holcombe. But I don't understand the University of
Hartford connection..."

"You need to get a deferment quickly, Danny,
and unless you've been keeping it from us that you're

married with children, a member of the clergy, a conscientious objector, physically handicapped or homosexual, you only have one chance at getting one," Holcombe responded. "Go back to college immediately so you can apply for a 'II-S' classification. It's more commonly known as a student deferment."

"So I have to quit my job and go back to school?" he asked in alarm.

"No, U of H has an evening school program that will qualify you for the deferment. But you'll have to carry nearly a full load."

"Shit," Logan said.

"Shit nothing, Logan. Better to work your ass off then get it shot off. And besides, you need that degree. You're a smart kid."

The compliment was a surprise. Holcombe wasn't known for spontaneous praise. Logan looked down at the wad of papers in his hand. Clearly he needed to take this seriously.

"Thank you, sir..." he stammered, "I'll get..."

"I know the admissions dean there, I'll give him a call. See to it that you get those forms to him immediately and then get your butt down to the Selective Service Office and apply for the deferment. Got it?"

He shook his head. "Thanks..."

Holcombe ignored him. "Oh yah, about the broad," he added. "She's waiting in my office. Asked to see you. We don't allow visitors without business in the newsroom. Follow me and do what you will." He didn't offer any apology for making her wait.

"Elina? Here?" Logan stammered in surprise.

"Save it," Holcombe replied. "Just get her out of my office," he said and walked away. Logan followed.

115

"Great looking broad, Logan," Holcombe offered as they walked. "Not worth blowing off college, though," he mumbled. "Unless you married her and had children right away." Danny barely heard him.

Elina was sitting at the desk outside Holcombe's office and a huge grin appeared on her face as she saw her former boyfriend walking towards her. Logan's heart pounded in his chest at the sight of her. It was the first time he had seen her since the night his world caved in 18 months ago. A lot had happened since.

She looked the part of a Radcliffe student, if not a drop dead gorgeous high fashion model, dressed in a form fitting designer label dress with high heels. It was if she was going to a fancy restaurant rather than classes. Just that thought reminded him again that she was out of his reach. Until that moment he was confident that he'd come to terms with his place in life.

"Danny, look at you! A reporter for the Hartford Times! It must be so exciting..." she said, her voice trailing off as she saw that he wasn't smiling.

"Elina, what are you doing here?" he demanded, gruffly. "I'm working." He thought for a moment. "Are you ok?" he asked, knowing he should have asked that first.

"I'm fine..." she said, somewhat shaken by his greeting. "Just in Hartford to have lunch with my dad." Don Hanson was Chairman and CEO of one of the major companies in the city. Logan couldn't remember which one. Didn't matter much.

"Oh. Good. Give him my regards, we were so close," he said sarcastically, but immediately regretted it.

"Danny... don't be like that," she said, looking sad. "I just wanted to say hello and see what 'This Boy' was up to."

116

He thought later that a sharp stick in the eye wouldn't have hurt as much as those two words. But he pretended not to hear them.

"Well, it's good to see you, Elina, but now I have to get back to work. I seem to have misplaced my trust fund." He couldn't help himself. Hurting her felt good.

She smiled away his comment. "No time for coffee?" Elina asked with a look in her eyes telling him it was important to her.

"No..."

"Sure he does," Holcombe suddenly piped in. "Take your lunch early, Logan. Get out of here."

"But..." Danny began to protest.

"I think you know I'm not keen on saying things twice, Logan," Holcombe said.

"Please, Danny... just coffee. Maybe you have a cafeteria here?" Elina begged.

"Sorry, no waiters and only paper napkins," he snapped. The smile disappeared from her face.

He caught Holcombe staring at him. One minute the guy was telling him what a fool he was, the next trying to play matchmaker.

"Jesus Christ," Logan said in frustration. "C'mon, Elina. Coffee. 15 minutes. I'm on deadline," he said sharply.

"Deadline! That sounds so impressive," she said, the smile returning to her face.

Holcombe rolled his eyes.

Danny took Elina's hand and walked quickly to the nearest elevator without a word. The cafeteria was in the basement. He didn't speak to her on the way down.

"You gotta pour your own," he said pointing to the counter where coffee, hot meals and sandwiches were available around the clock.

117

"I can handle that," she said.

He grabbed a cup for himself and walked ahead of her to pay for both, then found a table against a wall far from any other employees. Logan watched her as she awkwardly made her way through the line and then stopped to scan the room looking for him. He didn't try to attract her attention.

She finally saw him and sat down and immediately started in again about how impressed she was with his job.

"Save it, Elina. It's a job. That's it. It's not going to make me rich so you can tell your parents they don't have to worry about me moving into the neighborhood. What's on your mind?" He was angry.

"I..." she started to say but Logan suddenly lost his temper again and pushed away from the table.

"Do you know how fucking long it took me to get over you? And not only for breaking my heart. For screwing my best friend! What do you want from me?"

She immediately became teary-eyed. Elina wasn't used to this kind of confrontation.

"I was hoping..." she began and then abruptly stopped, unable to get the words out.

"What? Spit it out. I really don't have time for this."

"That... you could forgive me," she blurted out.

His jaw dropped.

"Forgive you?" he said, slowly repeating the words in astonishment. "Did Charles put you up to this? So that we can go through life like the three Musketeers or something?"

"No..." Tears were rolling down her face. "He's not like that. This is about you... and me. About being friends."

118

"Friends." He called upon Paul Carducci's advice again and began counting to ten. He made it to five.

"You think I could be your friend?"

She reached for his hand and squeezed it. Her touch was still so familiar. He pulled his hand away.

"I want us to be friends. So much. And for you to forgive me. Things will never be right between Charles and I unless you forgive me... and be my friend," she said.

His eyes widened. So this was about her relationship with Charles.

He said it louder than he intended.

"I don't care about how things are between you and Charles, Elina. And frankly, I wouldn't care if he was hit by a bus. But more importantly, I can't be your friend, Elina."

"Why not?"

He laughed softly and shook his head, not in ridicule but only at the ridiculousness of the question. She was still so god damned beautiful, he thought. But naïve. It was so hard not to just give in to the spoiled child in her, to give her anything she wanted if only to make her smile. But he couldn't.

"You never did understand, did you?" he asked.

"Understand what, Danny?" she sobbed.

"How much I loved you." Her ocean green eyes had never looked more incredible.

She dropped her head. "I guess I didn't. I was young, maybe a little crazy..."

"You were young? It was only a year and a half ago that you threw me away like so much trash, Elina. If you were grown up you'd know that you couldn't ask me to be your friend. You'd know that you broke my heart. Smashed it! You'd know that I'll never get over it. You'd know why I can't ever be any part of your life."

"Danny, please... " she said, desperation in her voice. He wondered why.

"Remember our silly song? That night on the beach? You said that you..."

"*Would always feel the same,*" he interrupted her, reciting the lyrics that had meant so much to him.

"No matter what, you said." She was pleading.

He stared into his coffee cup for a moment before responding.

"Elina, that's the problem."

She looked into his eyes trying to understand.

"I still feel the same. I always will."

He stood up from the table without taking his eyes off her, knowing he might not ever see Elina again.

"That's why I can't be your friend."

Then he walked away and didn't look back.

Seven

~~~ ℘ ~~~

Fall, 1967

Through the long, hot summer and fall of 1967, Logan's reputation as a news reporter grew as rapidly as his experience increased covering the violence that flared across the U. S., spurred by racial unrest and widespread anti-Vietnam War sentiment.

Long simmering racial tensions exploded in 159 sweltering inner cities of America as frustrations boiled over. In the Cincinnati suburb of Avondale, Martin Luther King Jr. preached a message of non-violence at the Zion Baptist Church on June 11, but his efforts to calm the brewing anger had the opposite effect. For the next three days, rioters smashed, burned and looted hundreds of stores, buildings and cars in the business district and 700 National Guardsmen were called up to

121

quell the disturbance. The match had been lit. Before the end of June, protestors wreaked havoc on city streets in Atlanta, Boston, Buffalo and Tampa.

The tensions worsened in July as civil unrest spread like wildfire across the country. In Birmingham, Chicago, Rochester, Minneapolis, Plainfield and Newark, New Jersey, angry words quickly turned to smashed storefronts, looting, burning buildings and overturned cars. The flames of discontent reached new heights when Detroit exploded with violence, killing 43 people and wiping out more than 1,400 buildings. Only the presence of the National Guard and mandatory curfews finally quelled the mobs.

Danny Logan's assignment was to report on the violence as it tore across America and to stay in touch with the mood in Hartford. He had learned to keep his ear to the ground and to maintain contacts not only with minority leaders in the beleaguered neighborhoods of falling down tenements in the city's North End, but also with those in power at City Hall.

"What's your bet, Danny," Managing Editor Jim Greaves asked the young man, "When is Hartford going to blow? And when's the last time you got some sleep?"

The two were in Greaves' office and the news veteran was reviewing Logan's story on the Newark riots scheduled to lead the first edition that afternoon. It was good stuff. It had better be, he thought. He was betting the store on his star, 21-year old reporter. No more than a kid.

With less than 18 months experience, Logan was the lead reporter the Hartford Times had on the hottest story of the summer. And it was about to get hotter. But Greaves had a hunch about Danny the day he'd promoted him to reporter. The boy was hungry, not only to do a good job, but to make something of himself. You could feel his passion for the work, but more importantly, smell his desire for respect. Greaves had confidence in him. He reminded him of his own early days at the paper, when he got snake bit by the news business. He never had been able to shake it off. You wouldn't get rich writing a newspaper, but you knew you had done a job worth doing at the end of a day, everyday. A man couldn't ask for much more.

For his part, Logan was nearly living in the newsroom. Between the racial unrest and a nation divided over the Vietnam War, he was constantly reporting on the biggest news of the day. And even to a young man who'd just become old enough to vote, it was obvious that the stories he was writing added up to a country deep in crisis.

"Ah, I'm ok Mr. Greaves. There's so much going on I'm afraid if I take time to sleep I'll miss something," he responded to his editor. Greaves just smiled. The news game did that to you.

"To answer your question, I'm afraid Hartford's a pressure cooker ready to blow. It will probably take just one little thing, something overblown or taken out of context, just a cop or a politician saying the wrong thing to light up the streets. There's an awful lot of pissed off people in the North End, and City Hall has been painfully reticent about stepping up to fix some of the issues that might let off some steam. Honestly, I think it's too late. Hartford, as you say, is going to blow. And probably not just once."

"How the hell did we get here, Danny?" Greaves asked. "This used to be a nice, quiet city. And aren't they calling this America's 'Summer of Love' out on the West Coast? What's going so wrong in Hartford?"

Logan was silent for a moment, thinking carefully about the answer to his boss' question.

"Well, I don't come from much, Mr. Greaves, the South End isn't exactly a rich man's paradise," he replied. "But you drive down Barbour or Garden Street… hell, even Albany Avenue and take a hard look. People are living like animals in our city, in homes that are ready to fall down and their kids are starving and don't have adequate medical care. The businesses are all run by white men who won't hire anyone that's not. And they price gouge. The poorest people in the city pay more for everything. Black kids can't get jobs even though the Mayor promised he'd work to make it happen. The Unions are blocking young people from even getting into the apprentice programs to learn a skill." He shook his head.

"In the ten years from 1955 to 1965, the population of the North End went from 25 to 75 percent black. And 90 percent of the white population moved out. Almost the entire Jewish Community moved out of the North and West ends. Two entire cultures have almost disappeared from Hartford. Unbelievably, no one at City Hall seems to have noticed or cares that the culture and needs of their city have completely changed. They still don't, in my opinion. We ought to be ashamed."

He hesitated, afraid he had already gone too far and there was still more he wanted to say.

Greaves was stunned by the depth of his answer. But Logan wasn't finished.

"And by the way, Mr. Greaves, take a look around the newsroom. You see anyone here who looks different from you and me?"

"Well…" Greaves started.

"The guys with the mops and brooms don't count, sir. There's not a black or Puerto Rican writer in the room."

Greaves looked long and hard at Danny Logan, wondering how much guts it took for him to look his boss in the eye and tell him the truth. He could only shake his head in response.

"Yah. America is changing, Danny. And it's going to hurt like hell. But you made your point. Guess I have some work to do in my own backyard," he said in agreement.

Two days later, Danny Logan led the paper again when riots broke out in the North End of Hartford after a black teenager was arrested for allegedly swearing at a white waitress. Four nights of unrest followed with the smell of tear gas hanging heavily over the city. Arson, looting, bottle and rock throwing, smashed fire hydrants and assaults followed the pattern that had swept the U.S. that summer. But Mayor James Kinsella's new promises to making sweeping changes in the impoverished areas of the city brought a temporary calm. A mandatory curfew also helped.

It wouldn't last.

Logan had walked the streets those nights, at more than a little risk, getting a first hand look at the violence and interviewing victims and perpetrators. His balanced coverage of the news brought praise from minority leaders, but outrage from City Hall that insisted on blaming the disturbances on "outside agitators." Logan's reporting included an interview with Connecticut Senator Abe Ribicoff, the highly respected politician, who said he believed that "the cause of the riots stem from 100 years of neglect of the black community's needs. Black Americans are now presenting the consequences of that neglect to the nation." But given an opportunity to comment, senior Connecticut Senator Tom Dodd insisted to Logan that the Hartford riots were a "civil war targeting the whites and are the work of extremists controlled by Red China and Fidel Castro."

Hartford leadership was aghast at the chasm of opinion and action between their representatives and two of the most respected members of the Senate. But both promised action in congress to address the urgent situation.

Before that could happen, reporter Danny Logan witnessed and almost became embroiled in what could have been a full-scale civil war on the streets of Hartford.

On September 18, with anger running white hot, a small group of Blacks and Puerto Ricans gathered in the North End and began a protest march toward the largely Italian South End. By the time they reached the downtown business area, the invisible no man's land that divided the minority and white sections of the city, the crowd had grown to more than 200 angry people.

But waiting in the South End were more than 300 white businessmen and homeowners who weren't about to let the protestors cross the corner of Franklin Avenue — known as the main thruway for Hartford's "Little Italy" — and Barker Street.

Walking with the marchers, Danny Logan watched ahead as more than 250 riot-geared police appeared at the order of Mayor Kinsella to try to prevent the looming confrontation. He also saw local priests appealing to the white crowd to go home.

But what ultimately stopped the protestors from pushing through the line was the sight of Italian residents brandishing shotguns from the porches and windows of their businesses and homes. There was no doubt that bloodshed was imminent. Logan moved closer to the front of the marchers to hear what was happening.

The Sergeant in charge of the riot police quickly sought out the leader of the march, a young black man with fire in his eyes and clenched fists.

"Son, hear me out for a minute," the cop said. "I want you to know that it's not my guys you have to worry about, but if you look to your right and to your left and scan those buildings, you will see an awful lot of firepower aimed directly at your heads. You fellas have made your point. I suggest you turn around and go back to where you came from before this turns into a really, really bad situation. Catch my drift?" The young man took a look around him and nodded.

Hartford police then moved quickly to head off the bloodbath by arresting many of the protestors and dispersing both groups. The battle had been averted, Logan wrote later, but there was no doubt that war had been openly declared.

Black youth took to the streets of the North End that night setting fires, looting and throwing rocks and bottles at police cars. Gunshots rang out in the darkness. Kinsella labeled the young rioters "hoodlums," which incited even more anger in the Black community. Police cracked down hard with a curfew and an uneasy peace settled over the City.

"You've got a target on your back now, Dan," Greaves said to him after Kinsella's press conference announcing his plan to revitalize the North End to head off new violence.

"Hell, Mr. Greaves, I only wrote the truth. I reported what I saw with my own eyes and what I heard from the people who live on those streets. There were no 'outside agitators' that I saw. That's just more paranoid conspiracy crap like the stuff that's coming out of the Johnson White House. Besides, it doesn't matter who the instigators were. Did you read the Martin Luther King quote I used in last night's piece?"

"A riot is the language of the unheard," Greaves recounted. "The man can twist a phrase and your conscience with it. Quite a gift."

"But he's on the money."

"You may be right, Dan, just be careful. Those guys in City Hall have long memories."

Logan shrugged his shoulders.

"So do I, Mr. Greaves. If Kinsella and his bunch don't come through with their promises, they're going to be a lot unhappier with my stories, because there's going to be a lot more to write about," Logan promised. "And frankly, this is my life now. I really don't care if I'm anyone's target."

Days later Senators Ribicoff and Dodd announced their individual plans. Ribicoff planned to submit a $1 trillion spending bill for housing and full time employment programs, arguing that part of the problem was the $30 billion a year that was being wasted on Vietnam at the expense of American cities. Shockingly, Senator Dodd announced that he would submit legislation that would make crossing a state line to incite a riot a Federal Crime punishable by a 20-year prison term. The editorial Board of The Hartford Times was flabbergasted by the almost contradictory approaches of the states' two esteemed Senators and said as much. Confusion reigned throughout the city and state at every level of government and with local protest leaders. Even more alarming, the Black Panthers, a black revolutionary organization once defined by FBI Director J. Edgar Hoover as "the greatest threat to the internal security of the country," saw Hartford as a fertile breeding ground for more violence.

Hartford's unrest was hardly the end of racially motivated violence in the "Summer of Love." Milwaukee's racial tensions boiled over on July 30, and violence lasted nearly ten days. Riots spread to the nation's Capital on August 1, but then unexpectedly quieted over the next few months. The press turned its attention to the broadening conflict in Southeast Asia and the growing divide over support for the Vietnam War at home. Danny Logan, while taking night school classes at the University of Hartford, was quietly attending meetings of the local chapter of the Students for a Democratic Society, keeping a pulse on student views on the issue. Tensions were high within the SDS membership.

On an early October afternoon, Logan, sleep deprived as always was working on a story about rumors of a major push in Vietnam's Que Son Valley in the Quang Nam and Quang Tim provinces. The news had leaked out of Washington enraging the Pentagon and the White House. It was a Marine operation that was going to go hot in a matter of days, rumors had it, but facts were sketchy other than that the operation represented a major escalation of the war. Simultaneously, he was scanning the wire services looking for news of an antiwar protest that had shocked Washington D.C. earlier in the day when nearly 100,000 students marched on the White House and the Pentagon. LBJ was in real trouble, Danny thought as he read wire copy on the developing story. Polls taken during the summer had indicated that American support for the war had fallen below 50 percent for the first time. A protest of this magnitude would be a real blow to Johnson's presidency.

He went back to his desk, intent on knocking out what could be two major stories that afternoon. With luck, the paper would likely carry both stories on its front page in the evening edition. But his concentration was temporarily interrupted when he was surprised by a battle of another sort.

It was near 1 p.m., midday but perilously close to his deadline when he was suddenly aware of Charles Holcombe's presence over his desk. The personnel manager had an unnerving habit of staring at the subject of his visit and standing silently until his presence was acknowledged. Logan had to continually remind himself that the guy had done him a good turn and had earned his patience.

"Yes, Mr. Holcombe. To what do I owe your visit? Has my former girlfriend dropped by with cookies for her favorite matchmaker?" he chided.

"No, but her father is in my office," Holcomb replied snidely.

Logan's jaw dropped.

"Don Hanson? The Chairman of, uh…"

"Mutual Insurance Company, only the State's largest employer."

"Yah, right, Mutual. He's here to see me?" Logan asked in amazement.

"Yes. And he has an escort. A preppie type about your age. Says he's your best friend."

Logan winced.

"I don't have a best friend," he snapped.

"Yes, you do, Logan. You're typing at it," Holcomb laughed. "Follow me, or would you rather entertain your guests in the 'privacy' of the newsroom?" he laughed.

What in hell was this about, Logan thought. Hanson? And… Chickie?

Hard as he tried, Logan could not change the look of disgust he knew was painted on his face as he entered Holcombe's office to greet Hanson and his 'best friend,' Charles Anderson.   Anderson, wearing an expensive dark suit off the rack at Brooks Brothers and looking every bit like a corporate wannabe, stuck out his hand. Danny ignored it and turned to Hanson.

"It's been a while, Mr. Hanson," he said with little warmth. "What can I do for you and..." He stopped and turned to Charles, staring into his eyes.

"Why exactly is he here?" Logan couldn't get past his surprise.

"Well, that's two questions in one, isn't it, Danny? Do you have time for a chat?" Hanson asked, pleasantly enough.

"Not really. But I'm sure you don't like hearing the word 'no.' You and I can talk." He pointed a finger at Charles. "But I have nothing to say to him."

"Now, now, Danny. It takes a big man to be gracious in defeat. Give it a try."

Logan's hands instinctively balled into fists. It took all he had not to punch the rich bastard in the mouth before he pummeled Anderson into the next world.

"Gentlemen, let's move this discussion into the conference room please," Holcomb interrupted, sensing animosity that he had not expected.

"C'mon Danny, just hear him out, will ya? You and I can talk later," Charles pleaded.

"Fuck you," Danny swore as he followed Holcombe into the conference room.

He wasted no time.

"Mr. Hanson, given our brief and unpleasant introduction a few years ago, I haven't the faintest idea what you're thinking in coming here. Especially with this piece of trash." He looked directly at Charles as he said it.

131

"Well, have it as you like it, Danny. I'll be direct," Hanson said, taking a seat.

"Please do so, and be brief."

Hanson's face was turning red. He wasn't used to being spoken to in this manner.

"This has nothing to do with my daughter or her relationship with Charles," Hanson said.

"I would hope not. I'd hate to think I could have less respect for you."

Hanson paused for a moment to keep his own anger in check. He sighed. This was not what he was here for. Charles sat quietly. He didn't recognize the brazen, self-assured guy confronting them. Where had Danny Logan the aimless wise guy gone?

"Listen Danny, I'm not here for this. I apologize. Actually I came because I've come to respect you for what you've done, what you represent here at The Times. "

Logan did not respond. He wasn't about to let this guy off the hook so easily.

"What is it you want?"

"Your support."

"Not if it cured cancer," Logan shot back.

"Wait a minute, Dan, hear him out," Charles Holcombe interrupted. "Please remember you are representing The Hartford Times."

Logan began counting.

"Ok, spit it out. But I'm on deadline."

"Thank you," Hanson said, composed again.

For a moment at least, the two men, one born in Hartford's version of Hell's Kitchen, the other to a life of privilege, became equals despite their inherent distrust of each other.

"Have you ever heard of the 'Bishops' Danny?" Hanson asked.

132

"Yah, I've heard of him. We're not close."

Hanson laughed. "No, not the Catholic Bishop of the Archdioceses of Hartford. I'm talking about the Bishops of the city. The business Bishops."

"You mean the big shots like you who run the insurance companies and essentially call all the shots at City Hall?" Logan responded knowingly. "Yah, I've heard of you. You really wouldn't want to know what I've heard."

"Oh, come now. Power always attracts critics. But we 'Bishops' like to think we are a powerbase that can make things happen in Hartford," Hanson responded calmly.

"Oh... sort of like city fathers," the reporter responded sarcastically. "Odd, I thought we had a Mayor and a City Council and department heads, etc., to run Hartford. I wasn't aware that it's actually the Bishops who run the place."

"You do us a great disservice young man by insulting our efforts on behalf of the City of Hartford," Hanson said, beginning to lose his cool.

"Perhaps," Logan responded. "What exactly do you need my support for?"

"A plan that my colleagues and I are developing that would make a major contribution to the economic development of Hartford, in a peaceful fashion. The riots were a great embarrassment to the city this summer and they must be avoided in the future."

"I see," Logan said, nodding as if he were intrigued. He knew enough about these guys — roughly a half-dozen CEO's who ran the largest insurance companies in the country, all based in Hartford — to know that anything they did had only one objective and that involved putting money in their own pockets.

"Can you give me some details?" the reporter asked.

"Not at this time. We are working diligently to finish our plan and present it to the city by sometime next fall. You see it involves the suburbs as well."

An alarm bell sounded in Logan's brain. The suburbs. The suburbs were where all the white people who had moved out of Hartford had fled. He had no idea why, other than his dislike for the man in front of him and his general distrust for the business leadership of the city, but his stomach churned anxiously.

"So it's a secret?"

"For now. Yes," Hanson replied.

"Well, I'll ask you again. What do you want from me?"

"Just your talent with words and a promise of your support when we're ready to expose our plans," Hanson said, a smile coming to his face for the first time since they had convened the discussion.

"I don't make promises like that. And don't even think about offering me money."

The pallor of Hanson's face flushed with anger.

"Why, of course not, and I am insulted by your insinuation that I would bribe a reporter of The Hartford Times," Hanson said testily. "Who the hell do you think you are, boy?"

"Ah, back to 'boy.' I've been waiting for that. Brings back fond memories of our first meeting at your...cottage."

"Listen, Danny," Charles finally interjected, "that was all a big mistake. Mr. Hanson was pretty shook up about all that happened that night."

"If I remember correctly, he called you 'boy,' too, Charles. But I see you've overcome the slight. And what exactly is your role in this secret plan to save Hartford?"

"Well... I'm sure you remember that I'm studying economics at the Sloan School..." he began but was cut off by Hanson.

"My daughter Elina seems to be very infatuated with Charles, whom I must admit I've taken a liking to as well. I see a lot of my younger self in him."

"I'll just bet you do," Logan said, not able to resist the opening.

"It would seem likely that they will marry after graduation and I want to ensure Charles has a solid career ahead of him," Hanson said, ignoring the jab. "This project is something he's going to be working on with me part time until then. He'll be working with officials in the suburbs that are part of our planning, raising the capital... but I've already said too much. Let's just say he will have an integral role in the process."

"Good for you, Charles. I wish you every success, you've obviously earned it," Logan said, looking his former best friend directly in the eye. His voice was dripping with sarcasm.

Danny pushed back from his chair and stood up, looking down at Hanson. This farce of a meeting was over.

"Like I said, I'm on deadline. Call me when the secret's out," he said to Hanson.

He walked out the door and headed back to his desk. But on the way he ducked into a staircase and climbed to the rooftop, a place he often went when he needed to escape the bedlam of the newsroom and find quiet. It helped him to think.

But on this early afternoon, it wasn't quiet that brought Danny Logan to the rooftop of The Hartford Times building.

It was the only place he could think of where he could cry without being seen.

Hanson and his young protégé had asked for his help, but in the process made him feel small and insignificant. Every time he came near the Hanson's he was reminded of his lot in life that seemed to dictate that he would be their lackey forever. He looked up into the sky. It was still light out. Good. He couldn't see the stars yet.

A rush of shame came over him. To think he once thought he could defy the stars and his fate.

The door to the roof swung opened on its squeaky hinges. It was Holcombe.

"Your best friend is calling, Danny. That Smith Corona needs to be fed, the Washington story is definitely going to lead the paper tonight. C'mon. You've got to learn to win the war one battle at a time."

Logan looked at the personnel manager, strange as he was. The man was a good friend, although words to that effect would never be spoken between them.

"Yah, I'm coming, sir. Just need to catch my breath," he answered.

"I suppose I should be doing a better job of screening your visitors," Holcombe said. "You ain't over the broad, kid, and I guess I need to remember that."

"You don't need to fight my battles, sir."

"No, you're more than capable of standing up for yourself, Danny, impressively so. But every man needs someone to watch his back occasionally."

The two men were silent for a moment, and then exchanged knowing glances.

"C'mon Danny, let's get back to the war."

Hours later, Greaves and Holcombe dropped by unannounced and dropped the "Bulldog" edition on his desk. The Bulldog, or suburban edition, was first off the presses each afternoon. Across the top of page one ran the banner headline under Logan's byline:

War Protesters March On White House; More Than 100,000 Demand Withdrawal

In a sidebar story, Logan's piece on the rumors of a major push by the Marines in Vietnam's Que Son Valley in the Quang Nam and Quang provinces also ran on page one.

"Not a bad days work, son," Greaves said. "This Vietnam thing has a bad odor to it. I suspect the White House is going crazy about now, trying to find a PR spin to put on this thing. Every paper in the country picked up the story. The body bags are piling up and suddenly this is not a popular war. Stay on it."

"Yes sir," Logan replied, trying to hide his satisfaction. Holcombe gave him a salute when Greaves turned his back.

"One war at a time," he whispered.

Two weeks later, Logan was plastered across page one, top of the fold again with news of a major engagement between U.S. forces and Viet Cong in the Battle of Dak To in the Central Highlands of South Vietnam, less than 300 miles north of Saigon near the Cambodian border. By the time the fighting had stopped late in November, the U. S. had won a narrow victory but at a cost of more than 360 men killed in action and nearly 1,500 wounded. There was little celebration in America, as the foreboding sense of being trapped in an unwinnable war was settling over the country like dark, threatening storm clouds.

Logan had turned in another standout performance and he was being widely read in Hartford and across the state of Connecticut. In the newsroom, he was accorded the same respect as reporters seasoned by many more years in the business.

But it was gradually dawning on Logan that it was going to take more than The Hartford Times to continue to stoke the fire that was building in his belly. He was hungry for success and notoriety but more than anything, the respect that came with it.

At night, in the few restless hours he slept, he dreamt of stars once again.

Eight

~~~ ဏ ~~~

New Year's Eve, 1967

The specter of the war in Vietnam and an eerie truce on the streets of America's embattled cities cast a graveyard pall over the Christmas and New Years holidays across the country. Closer to home, by the very nature of the business, the newsroom of The Hartford Times was always filled with excitement over one story or another. But now there was a troubling tension hanging over the cavernous hall where the paper was written, a sort of dread of things to come. Logan found himself holding his breath every time he went to check the wires for breaking news. He wasn't alone.

"It's that feeling I get," Greaves shared with Danny over a New Year's beer at the Traveler's Spa Restaurant around the corner from the Times, a frequent

139

hangout for its reporters. "Like shit is going to start raining down on us and it isn't going to stop. I am really worried about where this country is going and especially the next 12 months. It's gonna hit the fan. I know it. Just call it a hunch."

"Can't' argue, boss," Logan responded. "When I'm in the newsroom, I'm almost afraid to check the wires or the networks for news. I'm looking over my shoulder when I walk home. The television in my kitchen is always set to a game — any game — so I don't have to listen to what's going on in the world. Strange feeling."

Several hours later, the beer had helped to ease the anxiety and despite their shared premonitions, the two men exchanged good wishes for the New Year and headed for home. Danny staggered the few short blocks to his one-bedroom apartment on Park Street. As he walked, he took in the neighborhood, studying its character, looking for signs of the community he had known as a boy. Sure it had its problems back then, and the culture had already been changing. But now...it was gone. In just the few years he'd lived there, the area had gone completely to hell. Crime was everywhere; you had to have eyes in the back of your head just to walk down the street. Greaves was right. Something was going to bust. Vietnam was a no brainer, the only question was where the continuing escalation would lead. But he found the state of Hartford even more worrisome. Racial tensions were running high in Connecticut's capital city, as they were across the country. It wouldn't take much of a spark for rioting to begin anew. Hartford was like a match waiting to be struck, and Logan bet that it would happen when the sweltering summer drove young, jobless blacks and

140

Puerto Ricans from their rat-infested tenements into the streets.

He used his key to open the door to the stairway to his apartment, quickly closing it behind him, then checked his mailbox. There was usually nothing but bills. Not today. Inside was a letter addressed to him in a familiar hand writing.

"Elina..." he thought with a new sense of despair. "Give it up, please..."

He carried it unopened up the stairs to his third floor flat, let himself in and reached for another beer. Logan threw the letter on the kitchen table and forgot about it. Uncharacteristically he turned on his small black and white television just as Walter Cronkite was reporting on the day's news in Vietnam. In the background was film footage of U.S. and South Vietnamese troops fighting somewhere in the Mekong Delta, where Viet Cong casualties were reported in the hundreds. It seemed that the November pronouncement by U.S. commanding General William Westmoreland, that the war was turning in American favor had credibility.

"I am absolutely certain that whereas in 1965 the enemy was winning, today he is certainly losing," Westmoreland said. Yet just a week later, Defense Secretary Robert McNamara resigned in protest over LBJ's rejection of his proposal to stop the bombing of North Vietnam, turn over ground fighting to South Vietnamese forces and freeze U.S. troop levels. It didn't add up.

Logan finished his beer while staring at the television, not even hearing Cronkite sign off with his signature, "And that's the way it is..."

His thoughts turned to his buddy Eddie Graziano, a real friend who had bailed him out when he was a train wreck after being crushed by Elina and had dropped out of UCONN. He'd given him a couch to sleep on and even made the job at The Times happen. Eddie had bypassed college, even though he probably could have gotten a college scholarship to play football. He just didn't want anymore to do with school. But after several years of bouncing from one dishwashing job to another, he enlisted in the Marines and was shipped to Vietnam less than a year later. Logan hadn't heard from him in a while and worried. He made a note to write a letter to him.

A letter. The thought reminded him of Elina's note sitting unopened on the table. He got up to get another beer and stopped to stare at it.

"Shit. Happy New Year to you too, Elina. I guess what ever you have to say couldn't make me feel any worse than I do." He tore it open.

"Dear Danny,

"I'm sorry I didn't get to see you at Christmas. Charles and I went to Jamaica for the holidays. It was a present from my mother and father. It was nice to sit on the beach for a few days without a care in the world. We had fun but I always think about what it would be like if you could be part of us again.

"As you probably know, Charles is working with my father on his "secret" project, something to do with Hartford, I think. It's good to see them working together and there's no question my father can do wonders for his career. He could help you too, if you'd let him. I know you two had a rocky start, but I think he's become more liberal in his thinking now and is no longer the bigot you met. Anyway, I know how hard you work but my father says there's not much money to be made in journalism. If you ever want me to say something to him about you, I'd be happy too.

"Charles and I live in a delightful apartment in Cambridge, such a great part of Boston. We would love for you to come up and stay with us some weekend. We have plenty of room and I know the three of us would have a marvelous time in the city. There's always so much to do. Hope to hear from you. Happy New Year!
Love always,
Elina"

Logan's face turned red with anger as he finished reading. With one hand he crumbled the note into a small ball and with his other threw his beer across the room where it smashed against the bathroom door. He closed his eyes as he watched the sudsy liquid drip down the scarred door, hoping the feeling of hopeless rage would pass quickly. He wondered how he could ever have fallen in love with someone so shallow and insensitive. Jamaica. A weekend together in Cambridge. It was as if she was completely unaware of what she had done to him. And then she had the incredible nerve to trash his job.

"I'd rather sleep in the street before I ever step foot in Cambridge and shovel shit than work for your father, Elina. You hear me?" he screamed at shadows in his apartment.

He was still steaming with anger when he grabbed his coat and headed out to a bar a few blocks away on Park Street. Logan was still there at midnight to welcome in the New Year with his impoverished neighbors. The thought came to him as a few dozen strangers toasted the coming year that he was actually right where he belonged. In the ghetto with a job that was probably going nowhere.

"Hooray for Danny! Hey Elina?" he slurred at his reflection in the mirror behind the bar. A few minutes later a fight broke out between a couple of partiers who'd had several too many. The cops pulled up in a black and white and ordered everyone outside. It was just as well. It wouldn't have taken much for him to start throwing punches himself, given his mood.

As he lurched his way home, he wondered what Elina and her boyfriend were doing to celebrate the New Year. Were they at a fancy party with lots of friends? Or were they in bed, celebrating in a lover's embrace? The sudden thought churned his stomach and he had to stop and vomit at the curbside. He fell to one knee.

She could still do that to him.

Nine

~~~ ❧ ~~~

Winter, 1968

The arms length distance between the newsroom of The Hartford Times and reality disappeared with a heartbreaking finality on January 21 as the Viet Cong launched a major surprise attack on U.S. Marines stationed at Khe Sanh in northwestern Quảng Trị Province. Hordes of highly trained Viet Cong stormed the U.S. camp slightly after midnight and at first were repressed. But desperate following attacks by the enemy resulted in penetration of the base, close quarter firefights and even hand-to-hand combat.

Fighting was so severe that the Associated Press broke a wire story that Gen. Westmoreland was arguing the need for a limited nuclear strike on the 20,000 North Vietnamese forces that were pounding the Marines at

145

Khe Sanh Combat Base day and night with artillery, mortar and rocket assaults. Sanity prevailed at the White House and the recommendation was rejected. But ultimately, 275 Marines were killed and 2,500 wounded.

"I guess your instincts were right, Mr. Greaves," Logan commented the next morning as he was writing the story for the first edition. "It didn't take long for the shit to start raining..."

Greaves was pale and didn't respond.

"What's up, chief?" he asked, sensing trouble.

"Khe Sanh is where Holcombe's kid is stationed," he replied, shaking his head. "Charlie's just sitting at his desk, staring out the window. He's waiting for the phone to ring, for a call from his wife to tell him there are Marine representatives at the house with news."

"Shit," was the only word that would come to Danny's lips.

"They've been counting the hours. The kid only had another 40 days to go on his tour," Greaves said. But ever the newsman, even a potential horror in his own newsroom didn't prevent him from pursuing a story.

"When you're done with the Khe Sanh piece," he ordered Logan, "start digging into how many Hartford kids are in harms way right now over there, and do the same for the state. I think we're going to be shocked by the number."

"I'm on it. I'll have Khe Sanh ready for you to look at soon, Jim."

"Ok. And do a little background work on Charlie Holcombe's kid, just in case."

Logan nodded without responding. The phone rang. Greaves reached for it and shook his head.

"Ok, I'll be right there. I'm going to drive him home," he said, his voice shaking. He slowly put down the receiver and turned to Logan.

"That was my secretary." He stopped, digging down for the courage to say the rest. "There are two Marine officers waiting for Charlie at his house. I gotta go. If it's what I think it is, I want a sidebar on the Holcombe kid on page one with your Khe Sahn lead. I'll call you with confirmation." He hurried off to meet Holcombe.

Danny Logan stopped writing for a few moments, trying to digest the meaning of what had just happened. The war had suddenly gone from being a news story to something deeply personal. He would never again write anything about Vietnam that didn't have the rusty odor of blood on his copy.

Greaves called an hour later.

"Write the Holcombe sidebar," he said quietly into the phone without explanation. There really wasn't need for one. "Make sure we have a headshot of the kid in his dress uniform and double check if we have other Hartford area dead.

"We don't know more about the kid other than he was KIA defending the Khe Sanh garrison in 'close quarters' combat. The Marines are telling us he was a real hero. They can't be more specific, so just use 'was known to have fought with extreme gallantry.' Got it Dan? We can do a follow-up piece when we get more facts. Don't pull your punches on the main story. These guys are telling us it was a real blood bath for both sides." He sighed. The days were getting heavier for the managing editor.

"I can't leave here right now, so do your best. I'm gonna get drunk with Charlie." The phone went dead.

The story led the paper that night. Young Charles Holcombe, Jr.'s death sent shock waves through the newsroom. Without instructions, a maintenance crew wrapped several of the Time's massive marble pillars in black bunting.

The next morning, as he did every day, Charlie Holcombe, Sr. slowly walked up the steps of his beloved Hartford Times, but this time took a moment to drink in the magnitude of the expression of sorrow hanging from the building. A guard inside saw him and called out. One by one, employees walked out of the building and met him half way down the stairs with a word of condolence, an embrace or just a silent handshake. They'd lost a member of the family to a cause they were deeply questioning. Holcombe was silent, already numb from grief but now overwhelmed by the compassion of his colleagues.

Danny Logan was one of the last to approach the personnel manager, who seemingly overnight had aged beyond his years. Logan was frightened by his appearance, worried for his wellbeing. Wordlessly, he stepped up and wrapped his arms around the older man and hugged him. Holcombe was taken aback at first, but slowly took his friend into his arms. Logan could hear him sob.

"Help me to my office, Dan, please. I have work to do," he said.

"Go home Mr. Holcombe, your family needs you, Danny replied, whispering the words in his ear.

"No. They'll be all right. We must stop this insanity. The Times can help. This is my family, too, and I need their help." He looked into Logan's eyes, pleading. "I need your help."

Logan stepped back and the intensity of Holcombe's stare touched his soul. The man was

148

shattered, but as usual, he was on a mission. The reporter wrapped an arm around him, helped him walk up the rest of the steps and took him to his office.

Holcombe immediately began shuffling through his paperwork. The funeral wouldn't be for another two weeks. Charlie Holcombe didn't miss a day or even an hour of work while waiting for his son's flag draped casket to arrive in Hartford.

At Holcombe's insistence, Logan kept him abreast of new events in Vietnam as the war suddenly escalated, shocking Westmoreland and the Pentagon staff who had felt as if the tide had been turning. Only once did he see the shattered man break down. It happened one night when the two of them were watching the CBS Evening News and Walter Cronkite announced how many young GI's had been killed that day.

Charlie Holcombe's jaw dropped. "Hundred's more," he said, almost whispering the words for fear that repeating them aloud would make it true.

"Mr. Holcombe..." Logan said, getting up to turn off the television.

"No, leave it," he demanded. "Look at the blood, Danny. All the blood... they're just boys. My God, Charlie was just a boy..." Logan and Greaves drove him home that night where they sat in his living room and drank scotch until after midnight.

On January 30, Tết, the Vietnamese holiday marking the New Year, the Viet Cong launched a series of surprise attacks across all of South Vietnam. In the next 24 hours more than 80,000 enemy troops struck nearly 100 towns and cities including most of the capitals. The U.S. Embassy in Saigon was brazenly attacked the next day.

U.S.-led forces repulsed most of the attacks and the bulk of the Tết battles were mopped up by the second week of February. But the damage was done to American confidence in winning a war they had less and less stomach for as body bags stacked up at a sickening pace. Reporters from all over the country, including Danny Logan of The Hartford Times were quick to point out that more than 1,500 young American boys had been killed and another 7,700 wounded in a "victory" that amounted to a PR nightmare for LBJ's presidency. Westmoreland, the commanding general who before Christmas had arrogantly boasted to a *Time Magazine* reporter that, "I hope they try something, because we are looking for a fight," was stunned by the speed and coordination of the attacks. Westmoreland's credibility was destroyed and he was replaced by June.

Logan had gotten a letter from his Marine buddy Eddie Graziano who had been in the thick of the Tết Offensive in the Battle of Huế, where intense fighting had virtually destroyed one of the major southernmost Vietnamese cities. Graziano had obviously tried to unload on his friend on the question of what the U.S. objective was in Vietnam, but the censors had blocked out almost everything of controversy making his words almost illegible. But one point came through clear.

"I'm scared, Danny, and I want to come home. Pray for me, pal," he wrote.

Logan began to feel the weight of guilt as he wrote day after day about the thousands of young American men who were being slaughtered for a reason the Johnson administration had yet been able to effectively communicate. Despite Holcombe's urgings to the contrary, he felt useless in the struggle. His words weren't making the difference he needed to feel.

"I'm going to enlist, Mr. Greaves," he announced after getting the letter from Eddie. "I can't watch this happen everyday and just write the words against this insanity... it's not enough."

Greaves wasn't shocked by his star reporter's abrupt decision. He remembered his own struggle during the Korean conflict, which he had ultimately succumbed to and left The Times for nearly two years. He had regretted the decision soon after he got to Korea.

"Yah, I don't blame you, Danny," the veteran newsman played along. "Better you get over there and start shooting real bullets at an enemy that is willing to die to hold on to his freedoms, primitive as they may be. You're not contributing much by just writing the truth — which, if you haven't noticed, Americans are clamoring for — in an effort to stop an administration with its head so far up its ass it actually thinks there's a point to this slaughter. I mean, who can argue with you, kid?"

Logan didn't catch on at first being so wound up about joining the fight.

"Yah, guys my age are..." he began to respond.

"Dying for nothing, Danny!" Greaves interrupted him. "This isn't like a frigging bar fight where your buddies are getting picked on so you jump on some guys back, damn it. This is about an enemy who sure as shit doesn't care about democracy and is hell bent to erase any memory of you from this planet. With a bullet, a knife or his own freaking bare hands!" He stopped. His blood pressure was so high his voice was echoing in his ears.

"Get the point, kid?"

Logan was incensed. He needed to lash out and Greaves knew it.

"Hit me if you have to hit something, Logan," Greaves said. "Then get your ass back to that typewriter

151

and fight the war — in your way. Your words can make a difference."

For a moment, Greaves was afraid the reporter was going to tell him to go to hell and quit. Just then Charlie Holcombe walked in, trailing a stream of wire copy behind him.

"Well, March 16th is turning out to be a very good day after all," Holcombe said, acting dumb to the loud conversation that had been taking place. "Thought you might like to know that Bobby Kennedy just threw his hat into the ring for the Democratic nomination," Holcombe said. "He's pretty clear about his platform — get out of Vietnam and civil rights. So, I thought..."

Logan was out the door running towards the newsroom before Holcombe could finish his thought.

Greaves laughed.

"You were saying, Charlie?"

"Actually, I didn't know what else I was going to say," Holcombe said, laughing. It was the first time Greaves had seen Charlie Holcombe so much as break a smile in two months.

"You know, it might be a good idea to get him closer to the action once in a while," Holcombe said. "Perhaps get him into a press pool for a couple of weeks."

"You mean get him on the ground in Vietnam?" Greaves replied.

Holcombe paled, realizing what he had suggested. "God, no. But hell, CBS plunked Cronkite right down on the front lines last month after the Tét Offensive and their ratings went through the roof. More importantly, what he reported pretty much destroyed any hope Johnson had of rebuilding support for the war."

"Not going to argue that. But Logan's too young, he'll go right for the action, risk be damned. Besides, we need him here. By the way, how's he doing in school?" Greaves asked, still pondering the suggestion.

"The Dean tells me he's not first in his class but he's showing up. He'll keep that II-S deferment until graduation. We'll have to re-strategize after that.

"The truth is Jim, we're not going to be able to hang on to him much longer. I've already had calls about him from the New York Times. Logan's building a reputation as a reporter that's going to give him opportunities bigger than The Hartford Times can offer. I say we give him every shot at learning while he's with us. Let's at least get him out in the street more."

That night, alone in his small apartment watching the evening news with Cronkite, Logan mulled over the conversation he'd had with Greaves and Holcombe. He still wasn't convinced that he shouldn't enlist and the television anchor's focus on reporting the war and the candidacy of Robert Kennedy didn't help. He should be doing more and wondered if people thought of him as a coward. He was despondent and more than a little confused. So much so that he finally broke down and reached out to the only person on earth he still felt the need to impress.

He wrote to Elina.

"Dear Elina:

I'm sure you are more than a little surprised to receive this. I can only say that I am perhaps as surprised that I am writing. But for the first time in a very long time, I feel so confused, so unsure of what I am doing. And I will admit that I still miss you terribly. I hope you will accept my apology for carrying on with such anger for so long and that you will believe I have never stopped being, 'This Boy.'

153

But I'm not writing in the hope of things changing between us, other than perhaps that we can be friends again. Truthfully, I hope you are happy with Charles and will enjoy together the fairy tale life that lies ahead.

The fact is, I'm writing just because I need a friend to talk to. I'm so lonely and uncertain, maybe more than I've ever been in my life.

I know you've seen some of my work covering the racial unrest here in Hartford and the Vietnam conflict. Those are the things that I think about day and night, the horrible truths that have created such an icy grip of contention and confrontation in our country. These are the issues that have caused fathers and sons to turn their backs on each other, to cause some to raise the flag while others burn it, for mothers to weep, for hatred and sadness to sweep our nation.

Listen to me. I sound like a politician. But I'm not. I'm just a lowly news reporter, a writer who presents the facts as he knows them in black and white. I'm not even so much as allowed to suggest my own opinion, and I think, very much, that is what is driving me somewhat crazy.

I've written about so much blood I almost need to get some of it on me. Sometimes I feel like I'm hiding here in the newsroom, while guys my age are getting killed because they've no one to run cover for them. I'm proud of what I do, but yet feel like I should be doing more. I would so much like to be with Eddie, watching his back, helping him to get home.

I want you to know that I've been giving thought to dropping out of school, quitting my job and enlisting. My boss, a great guy whom I deeply respect is dead set against it and argues that I can do more to end racial unrest and to stop the war as a reporter – bringing the facts to light – than I can carrying an M-16 through the jungles of Vietnam. Honestly, he flatters me, but I think deep down inside he's more worried that I'll end up as one of those numbers that Cronkite reports each night.

154

I've never been a coward in my life, but I feel like one. And right now I need someone to help me make a decision, not just because they're afraid of what might happen to me, but because they know and understand what I am feeling.

Not so many years ago, I thought there was no place in the stars for me, that maybe there wasn't one with my name on it. My brief taste of the life you lead (you won't believe this but sometimes, out of nowhere, I'll catch the smell of the ocean at Fenwick and my heart skips a beat at the memory) instilled in me an ambition I never thought I had. And to have the courage to say, 'I defy you, stars.' I still feel that courage, Elina, but it is my destiny that leaves me so puzzled. Is it as a Marine… or as a lowly newsman?

I hope you get a chance to write. How and what you think means more to me than you probably will ever know.

Danny"

Logan folded the letter without reading it and shoved it into an envelope. Despite the cold, he walked without a coat a block down Park Street and dropped the letter into a postal box. He knew if he so much as thought about what he had written, he never would have mailed it.

There was no sleep for Logan that night, and he didn't try to fight it. He walked back to The Times Building and worked the rest of the night helping out the rewrite guys who were pulling stories together from stringers who were calling in news from around the state. Near eight o'clock in the morning, he poured himself a fresh cup of coffee and hit the wires, poring over the teletype news stories that continued to rain upon the news room, day and night.

It was what a newsman did.

Ten

~~~ ॐ ~~~

April, 1968

Logan's instinct that the hiatus in racial violence in America's cities would be short-lived was spot on. But the spark that rekindled the blaze was an event that shook even the most hardened of segregationists.

The country had not yet recovered from Lyndon Johnson's shocking announcement on March 31 that he would not seek reelection in 1968 when less than a week later, shots rang out in Memphis, Tennessee. Martin Luther King, Jr., the man who had stoked the energy of civil rights protestors with his "I Have A Dream" of equality, fell dead on a motel balcony, victim of another lone assassin.

Danny Logan was at his desk when the news flash came in over the United Press International wire at

156

6:11 p.m., a scant ten minutes after King had been shot. Immediately, Managing Editor Jim Greaves was at his lead writer's desk trailing reams of teletype behind him and yelling assignments even as he read the details.

"It doesn't matter who shot him, the cities will be burning within hours," an ashen face Greaves said to Logan who looked up at him in confusion.

"Shot who? Who got shot?" Logan asked. He was oblivious to the assassination, deep in thought on a story he was writing.

"Martin Luther King," Greaves responded, "minutes ago in Memphis. Appears he was hit by rifle fire on the balcony of a motel." He paused, shocked by the sound of his own words. "Another good man. My God, what's happening to this country?"

Logan slumped in his chair in stunned silence.

"What are you doing, Dan?" Greaves said to him tersely.

The young man looked up at his boss.

"Just digesting… this is unbelieva…"

"Why aren't you writing the lead for the special edition we're going to hit the streets with ASAP?" he barked. "There's no time for 'digesting,' Logan, write the story and do your thinking afterwards."

"Yes, sir," the shaken reporter replied, inserting a clean sheet of paper into his well worn typewriter even as he said it. "Is he dead?"

"Wires say he's been rushed to St. Joseph's Hospital. Nothing further," a runner announced, handing Greaves an update to the breaking story, "other than eye witnesses say he was 'gravely wounded to the head.'"

"He will be," Greaves shook his head, battling his own emotions. "But it makes no difference to the story I

157

want you to write, Danny. I want you to put yourself in the shoes of a black man. Tell me what that man is thinking right this minute."

Logan looked at him, dazed.

"Are you hearing me, Logan? You've got 20 minutes to give me four takes. Get going."

But the reporter was already thinking even as Greaves barked his final instructions.

"*A black man. How does a black man feel at this moment?*" Logan silently repeated to himself. Words came to him. Rage. Frustration. Hopelessness. Sadness. Sorrow for King's wife and children. All of which he had to capture in less than 1,500 words without igniting even more hatred.

His fingers began flying over the keyboard as his thoughts and emotions came together, stopping only for seconds at a time to check from personal notes.

"When Rosa Louise McCauley Parks boarded a public bus in Montgomery, Alabama in December, 1955, perhaps the last thing on her mind was being arrested for refusing to give up her seat in the 'whites only' section. Certainly she had no intention of becoming an emotional icon of resistance to racial integration. This evening, when Martin Luther King stepped onto a Memphis motel balcony, surely he gave no thought to becoming a martyr for his inexhaustible efforts to right centuries of wrong, including giving Rosa Parks the ability to avail herself of any seat on any bus without fear of retribution.

"I have a dream," Martin Luther King said and millions of Americans came to share it. But like Camelot less than five years before, tonight the dream lies shattered in a pool of blood.

Insane vengeance and hatred has robbed our nation of another great man.

But to what end?

As unfathomable as this act of violence is the equally absurd notion that the nightmare perpetrated by King's murder will end the dreams of a great man and will stop his never ending freedom ride. The horrific irony is that this senseless crime will only spur on his vision.

Following John F. Kennedy's assassination, King heroically intensified his relentless push to force a begrudgingly slow shift in the country's attitude towards desegregation, culminating in the passage of the Civil Rights Act of 1964. At long last, this sweeping legislation made it a federal crime to discriminate based on race, color, religion, national origin or sex. It equalized voter registration requirements and prohibited racial segregation in schools, in the workplace and in facilities serving the general public.

When will the madmen understand that their selfish, cowardly acts of self-glorification only ensure the failure of their senseless bigotry?"

Logan worked another ten minutes then began editing his copy as he walked to Greaves' desk. He handed the managing editor his work.

"He died at 7:05 p.m.," Greaves said without looking up. He read Logan's copy and didn't notice the writer walk away, the need for a breath of fresh air overwhelming him.

He made his way to the rooftop and looked towards the city's North End. Already black smoke was curling up into the sky. The rioting, burning and looting had begun in Hartford as it ultimately did in more than 100 U.S. cities that night and in the days to follow. There were no words to calm the rage that filled the streets of America.

As he watched his city burn, Logan was overcome by the absurd contradiction of the violence that had broken out to protest the murder of a man who had only sought peace and equality. His story ran on the front page, opposite the cold, bloody facts. Unfortunately, it wasn't enough to quell the violence that night, nor did Logan for a minute think it would be. But for the next 72 hours, he went out into the streets to talk to angry people and politicians alike, trying desperately to find common ground that could be the basis of rebuilding at least Hartford's sense of community. Sadly, all he could muster from leaders of both sides was rhetoric, bluster and finger pointing. While his copy was applauded by the newsroom and in all corners of the city, he knew his words weren't enough to heal the wounds that had been festering for decades. The riots gradually came to a halt, but he knew the smoldering hatred felt by so many could spark again into flames in seconds.

After a week of living on coffee and sleeping at his desk, Logan was completely exhausted. Greaves sent him home for a couple of days of badly needed rest. He walked to his Park Street apartment with one eye over his shoulder. Tension still filled the air even after King had been buried.

A week's worth of mail was spilling from his box when he entered the lobby. He spent several minutes collecting it, but one envelope jumped at him from the pile. He recognized the handwriting immediately. It was Elina's. He'd been so preoccupied with the King tragedy and its aftermath, he had forgotten he had written to her. There was also a letter from Eddie.

He hurried to his apartment, threw the stack of mail on the kitchen table and grabbed a beer out of the fridge before opening either. He had an urge to read Eddie's first out of respect for his friend, but couldn't resist and tore open Elina's.

160

"Dear Danny,

I have not slept an hour since receiving your letter, and frankly Charles has been pestering me wanting to know why I'm constantly crying. I can't help it. The thought of you enlisting and going off to Vietnam terrifies me. My hands shake at the notion of it. I'll admit that it's the first time the whole mess has become real to me, not just a story that won't go away.

I know there are boys dying every day, Danny, and the more I read and watch what's happening, I am convinced it's all a terrible, grotesque waste. Despite Charles and my father telling me it's a righteous war, I also know their lives are not at stake. My father is too old to be drafted and Charles... well Charles is the kind of person who will always have a way out after he graduates next year. I know that's not very kind of me to say, but I'm beginning to recognize traits in him that are so much like my father's. But my God... these are just boys who are being slaughtered every day. How has it come to this? And I'm so embarrassed to admit how oblivious I have been.

I'm not blind anymore, Danny. You've opened my eyes. You can't go, do you hear me? It will only be more of a waste, not only of your talent, but perhaps even of your life. There's something else, too. I know in my heart that even if you live through it, you will not come home the same person. You will never again be... This Boy.

You owe me nothing... and a part of me thinks that maybe you would do this to punish me. Please, Danny, forgive me. Despite the fact that we are not together, I couldn't live another day if I lost you. You are in my heart in so many ways that it confuses me. I was so happy with you... I can't really explain what happened. But I know this. With or without me, you must continue what you are doing. Your boss is so right. What you do, your words, do make a difference. Trading that power to kill faceless people in the jungle for no reason that I can understand would be such a waste. To die for whatever confused sense of right that we're fighting for is beyond my comprehension.

Please, Danny, don't do this. I love you still and always will in some way. If you feel anything for me, you'll stay home and fight this war and its battles with your sense of right, your compassion and your typewriter.

All my love,
Elina"

Logan was stunned by her response, never dreaming Elina had such feelings left for him. He reread her words again, more slowly, savoring the emotions he felt from them. He was elated that she acknowledged his ability to write. It was a far cry from her offer to speak to "Daddy" about an opportunity for him.

As if fate had intervened to support her plea, Eddie Graziano's letter lay on the table, begging to be read. Logan tenuously reached for it, worried for his friend and the emotions his words might carry at this moment.

"Dear Danny,
It's about 3 a.m. here. We're on patrol taking a break about four clicks due east of Khe Sanh. Been doin' some weed with the guys, trying to stay mellow, you know? It's easier to pull the trigger when you don't care. But man I've been wanting to talk with you. Guess this is the only chance I'll have for a while.

Can you imagine me whining about missing Hartford, frigging Connecticut? I mean, all our lives, growing up in that shithole we called home, all we thought about was getting out, going somewhere to make something of ourselves. I remember that night in Fenwick thinking, man, this is where I belong. You know what? I was wrong, bro. No matter how hard I had it, Hartford was where I belonged.

I know that now, after spending six months in a real shithole... I mean a real one, man. This isn't just the jungle, it's like a scene out of a movie on an alien planet. And all around me are people that want to kill me in the worst fucking way. I mean it doesn't make any difference how many of these crazy bastards you kill as they come at you, they just keep coming, and coming. Sometimes my rifle barrel is so hot from shooting, the heat carries down into the stock and burns my hands.

I've killed so many people who want me dead. They want me gone from their country, gone from existence. They don't know why I'm here... and you know what? Neither do I. I don't belong here, Danny. I think of Hartford now and it tastes sweet, like ice-cold water on a steaming hot day. God, let me come home... if I could make it, I think I'd spend the rest of my life trying to rebuild it. Make it the city it could be for all of us, no matter what color we are or what neighborhood we come from. Remember when we could ride our bikes together anywhere we wanted to without being afraid? I want my kids to see Hartford like that again. I could do it. Hell, we could do it together, Dan. And Brother King would smile down upon us...

But I don't think I'm gonna get the chance, bud. I know I asked you to pray for me Danny, and I'm sure you have, but I don't think it's going to help. They're gonna get me some night on patrol, I know it, some nameless, faceless Gook who lives just to kill me and all the rest of the invaders of his country. I just hope they can bag me, man... I don't want to spend all of eternity sprayed out all over this jungle, rotting in the heat. I want to be buried in Hartford, so you and all the guys can come see me and we can talk like the old days. I can taste that sweet water again.

You catch the new 'Doors' album, Dan? Called 'Waiting In The Sun.' You gotta listen to Jim Morrison, he's so whacked out man on peyote or weed or something but he knows the truth about what's happening here. Just listen to

163

the song 'Five To One' and you understand he knows what the VC are thinking:

> *And it may take longer*
> *They got the guns*
> *But we got the numbers*
> *Gonna win, yeah"*

That's all you hear the guys humming when we're out on patrol. It's terrifying. We all know we're gonna get ours, it's just a matter of time. Morrison knows the truth man, he sees it. Why won't LBJ and his gang listen to him and get us out of here? Morrison tells the truth, Danny, he sings it right there for everyone to hear:

> *'No one here get's out alive!'*

Do whatever you have to Danny but don't let them ship your sorry ass here. Just keep on doing what you're doing, write some sense into the sorry motherfuckers who are keeping us here.

Don't think I'll be seeing you again, Danny, but know that I love ya, man. Sorry if I sound fucked up, guess I am a little baked. It's the only way to get through another day of this hell.

You can have any of my shit you want. Except my football jersey. If they can't bag me, bury that, ok? Just something that says I was here for some other reason than this shit.

Eddie

P.S. I know those SOB's have been censoring everything I've written to you so I asked a friend that just finished his tour to mail this for me once he got stateside. Somebody got to know the truth... tell them for me, Danny.

Tears flowed freely from Logan's eyes as he finished the letter from Graziano. His heart pounded from the anger and sadness that had built up inside him as he read Eddie's words. Stoned or not, his message was clear. And more horrifying than anything Logan could imagine.

But there was work to be done at home and with the help of God, he and Eddie might just do it together.

Three days later, as he was writing a story on Lyndon Johnson's signing of the landmark Civil Rights Bill of 1968, the phone rang in Logan's office. It was Holcombe.

"I've got a Juan Graziano on the phone for you. Sounds drunk. Came through the switchboard. You want it?" Holcombe said innocently.

A chill shot up Logan's spine as he waited for the voice of Eddie's father to come on the line.

He listened and said a few words that he couldn't remember later, and hung up the phone. For almost 30 minutes he sat motionless, staring into space. Someone noticed his catatonic state and summoned Holcombe.

"What is it Danny? What's the matter?" Holcombe asked after rushing to Logan's office.

The reporter waived him off. "Please, sir, just leave me be."

Holcombe persisted.

"What is it?" he demanded.

"Eddie."

Holcombe sucked in his breath, knowing.

"His father said there were no remains. He stepped on a land mine at Khe San. Three days ago."

"Dear God... when will this end," Holcombe responded. He put a hand on Logan's shoulder. "Go

165

home, Danny, take the day," he said, knowing there was nothing he could say or do that would matter.

"No."

"It's alright to grieve, Danny, I understand..."

"No, I have to write. Something about Eddie, something about the city he loved." Greaves suddenly appeared. He had been listening.

"Tell makeup to hold space for two takes on page one, top of the fold," he told Holcombe, his voice shaking just slightly. "And to leave room for a photo."

The managing editor turned to Logan.

"Write your story, Danny. Make the connection. You know what I mean, "Greaves told him.

Logan nodded, his emotions freezing his fingers on the keyboard.

"I don't know what..."

"Yes you do, Danny. Write it," Greaves prodded him.

Logan's hands began to move across the typewriter and as the keys hit the paper they printed letters that formed words. He fought to keep control of his emotions as he wrote. Great tears sat in the corner of his eyes, but he willed then from falling. There would be time for crying. Now was the time for writing.

"Today, the parents of U.S. Marine Eddie Graziano of Hartford were notified that their only son had been killed in action three days ago in Vietnam, near Khe Sanh. They grieve tonight for a boy not yet old enough to vote.

Eddie Graziano was my friend.

We grew up together in the South End. We played high school football on the same team. We washed dishes at Carducci's Ristorante.

But that's where the story ends.

166

For Eddie Graziano went to war, and I became a newspaper reporter and part-time college student.

Eddie enlisted because he knew he was going to be drafted otherwise. He couldn't afford to go to college and being a young, black male, he couldn't find a job in Hartford worth keeping — though I watched him try in vain day after day — so his opportunities for a draft deferment were extremely limited. And Eddie wasn't the type of guy to lie about anything, particularly himself. I on the other hand, born to bona fide South End Irish, got the break of a lifetime with a job at The Hartford Times and the chance to go to college and get a student deferment.

Eddie got an all expenses paid trip to war; I stayed home, safe and cozy.

There was much drama but little celebration when President Lyndon Johnson signed the landmark Civil Rights Act of 1968 on April 11, exactly a week after the assassination of Dr. Martin Luther King. In the ultimate irony, although the legislation significantly expanded federal laws aimed at creating true equality for all Americans, many U.S. cities were still smoldering in rage over King's murder even as the Bill became law. And three days later, half a world away, the irony continued in the death of a single U.S. Marine from Hartford in the jungles of Vietnam.

We may have laws that say we're all equal, but at least this writer wonders if they're worth the paper they're printed on.

Eddie went to war because he was poor and black. I got a job and went to college because I am the son of a white man.

As to his patriotism and his courage, color didn't mean a damn to my friend. But what he found in Vietnam left him disillusioned and very afraid. He wanted to come home, desperately, even to a city that had turned his back on him. Because he knew he belonged here and maybe could even make a difference in building the community he dreamed Hartford

167

could be. A community where peace, harmony and equality weren't just political buzzwords, but real life.

Just three days ago, on the very day he stepped on a land mine and his body was reduced to a bloody spray, the mailman delivered his last letter to me. It was different than his others because the military censors never had a chance to rob his words of the truth he tried for nearly a year to share with me. This one was carried into the U.S. by a friend of his whose tour was up, and mailed stateside.

I owe it to Eddie to share it with you, for as his final words say, 'Somebody got to know the truth...'

Forgive me, old buddy, for editing out a word or two here and there that some folks might find offensive. But here's your chance to talk to Hartford, the nation, to Lyndon Johnson and the Pentagon, and to every voter in the country who can put an end to this insanity.

So let it rip.

And when you're done, rest. You did your duty, even if it wasn't very clear what the mission was. Thanks for being my friend and you can be sure I'll be voting with you in my heart come November.

Semper Fi, Eddie Graziano. The stage is yours.

"Dear Danny,

It's about 3 a.m. here. We're on patrol taking a break about four clicks..."

Logan handed his copy to Greaves who read it silently. His red pencil never touched the paper. The managing editor handed it to a runner with instructions to file the story with United Press International as a special from The Times.

Logan made his way to the rooftop where he watched the sun set over Hartford, remembering good times with his friend. He never did shed the tears he

168

had managed to hold back. But he vowed to keep fighting America's wars from his typewriter.

An hour later, the tribute to Eddie Graziano was on the desk of every senior editor in the country under Logan's byline. It ran in every major newspaper in America over the course of the next two days.

Logan worked until midnight, afraid to be alone with his own thoughts. He tried not to think about the fear Eddie had expressed of his remains being scattered in the jungle. His worst nightmare had come true. Somehow he would summon the courage to honor his last request. He wondered how his parents would feel knowing their son's high school football jersey was the only thing in his coffin. But, as Eddie said, it would give them, and everyone who loved him, a chance to visit.

Finally, exhaustion overcame him and he began the slow walk home to Park Street. With every flicker and shadow cast by streetlights and passing cars, he swore he saw Eddie waiting for him on the other side of the street. Finally the tears came, and he sat down on a bench at a bus stop on Park Street, buried his face in his hands, and wept. Once the dam was opened, it was nearly an hour before he could compose himself again. Only the overwhelming urge to go home and fall into bed made him get up and walk again.

The stairs to his apartment were endless and he was almost out on his feet when he put his key in the lock. But it was opened. He pushed against the door with his fingertips and it swung free. Logan was so tired he didn't feel any sense of panic. He just walked in, unafraid of what he might find.

The television was on but there was no signal, only static. It was nearly 2 a.m. As he looked around, he knew the smart thing to do was walk out. But calling the

169

Hartford PD at this time of night in this neighborhood was hopeless. They wouldn't respond until morning.

Logan flipped on a light and walked through the kitchen and then into the dark living room. His heart beat faster from what he saw and stopped him dead in his tracks. Part of him wanted to run. Another part desperately wanted to be held.

There on his lumpy couch someone stirred under a blanket. He took another step closer.

The blonde hair poking out of the top of the blanket told him he wasn't dreaming.

It was Elina, sleeping.

Eleven

Charles Anderson's week had gone from bad to worse.

His future father-in-law, Don Hanson was pissed at him because he was behind in writing the plan they had secretly labeled "Greater Hartford Process." Anderson had concluded that the guy was so used to getting his own way on anything and everything that he didn't understand the complexities of dealing with the suburban shit-kickers who would make or break his deal.

On top of that, he was falling behind in his studies at Sloan and without a miracle would not achieve his objective of graduating at the top of his class in a year's time. For the first time in his academic career he was going to fall short of a perfect 4.0 for the semester. And, it appeared he was going to have to take summer classes to make up for some incomplete work.

That meant driving to Boston two or three times a week while he was working for Hanson. He didn't look forward to explaining that to his boss, who would definitely see it as a distraction to working on his project.

And finally, Elina had not come home last night. He had no idea where she was. If she'd gone home to Fenwick he would have heard from the old man. But he was fairly certain he knew why she hadn't come home. Charles Anderson had finally faced up to the fact that he had a drinking problem. A serious drinking problem. Not that acknowledging it changed anything. It was only ten o'clock in the morning and he had been sitting in a bar on the South Boston waterfront already for more than two hours. Breakfast had been three double vodkas, no fruit, no ice.

Anderson had spent most of the night sitting in a chair in their apartment in Cambridge staring out of a window that overlooked the Charles River pondering why everything was suddenly going to hell. About dawn he left, driving into South Boston. He needed to get away from the picture perfect life Elina had created for them in Cambridge and go somewhere that smelled like home. Someplace where the neighborhoods were rough and tumble, where the kids who walked the streets owned them. The kind of place he had come from. Just for a while, only to remind him of how good life was now. Or had been.

He wasn't sure when the drinking began. Maybe it was when Hanson pulled him onboard his project with all its inherent pressures and opportunities. Or it might have been when he had finally admitted that he knew Elina was still in love with Danny Logan. A guy he grew up with, who was once his best friend. The same guy whose girl he had stolen. Or at least that was the way it had appeared.

And now they were mortal enemies. Danny Logan wouldn't amount to any more than a news hack no matter how hard he tried. He would be insignificant all his life. So how could he be such a problem?

Charles, on the other hand, was already making serious money and useful contacts as an advisor to Hanson and he hadn't even completed undergraduate school. He was certain his life was blessed. In a couple of years, he was going to marry a stunningly beautiful woman who came with more money than even he dreamed was possible, was going to get his doctorate in economics, become a Wall Street whiz kid, make millions of his own, live in an oceanfront mansion... he could go on and on. He even occasionally allowed the Presidency to enter his thoughts.

Yes, he was blessed. Or would be if he played his cards right and didn't let Logan spoil his plans.

But spending most of everyday drunk and coming in at all hours of the night wasn't a sure way to convince Elina of his commitment to her. In fact, it wasn't just the booze that was a problem. He had been unfaithful to her countless times, even on their Jamaica vacation last year. And she knew. He couldn't put his finger on why he would risk everything for a drink and sex, but there it was, staring him in the face. The truth.

Now what was he going to do about it, he asked himself.

"Get your shit together, Charles," he thought, downing the last of his fourth double of the morning. "Find Elina before she can make any noise at home and upset her old man, and then tell her anything to get her back. Do what you must to make Danny Logan look like the chump he is. It shouldn't be too hard. For Christ's sake the guy's a reporter. A chimp could do the job."

He laughed out loud, attracting the attention of the bartender who shook his head. A sure sign for, "That's all for you, pal. Hit the bricks."

Well, he didn't mind as he threw a $50 bill on the bar and staggered out, shielding his eyes as he gingerly opened the door and stepped into the morning sun. "Someday I'll buy this joint and burn it down, just for the fun of it," he thought, thoroughly plastered. Money and power. That was all that mattered.

He looked up and down the street, unsure of his next move.

"Where the hell did I leave my car?" he slurred, then spotted it where he had parked it hours before, across the street.

It was hard to miss. The new 1968 Porsche 911S was a birthday gift from Elina and her parents. Tangerine on black with the silver and black Fuch's alloy wheels that made the car look like it was breaking the speed limit when it was parked. It was the most hot shit car he had ever seen, let alone owned. He almost couldn't wait until his five-year high school class reunion. He fantasized about pulling up in front of his friends and having Elina step out with him.

"Is that Chickie Anderson?" they'd asked. "No wonder he goes by Charles, now," he fantasized.

He fumbled in his pocket for the keys and staggered across the street, almost being hit twice by oncoming traffic. He was oblivious to it.

Anderson opened the car and started it. Just for a moment he rested on the high backed leather bucket seat and listened to the engine as he revved it. The vibrations and exhaust note coming from the rear of the sports car were soothing. Why couldn't everything in his life run as smoothly, he wondered?

He put the car in gear and pulled away from the curb, accelerating hard without bothering to check for traffic. A city bus swerved to miss him and nearly hit a car in the next lane head on.

As luck would have it, a South Boston beat cop witnessed the near catastrophe and used his hand held radio to reach dispatch. Only three blocks ahead, a city patrol car heard the call about the screaming Porsche, swung a U-turn and began looking for Anderson. A moment later, he passed the patrol car at nearly 80 miles per hour in the opposite direction, swerving through traffic like it was a racetrack. He had decided to go to Fenwick.

"That's where she'll be and I can explain everything," he convinced himself in his drunken state. "Her old man will understand. We can fix this."

He downshifted and swung in front of a small delivery van, causing the truck driver to slam on his breaks to avoid him. But Anderson had seen a sign for an entrance ramp on to I-90 West, the Mass Pike, that would start him on his journey to Saybrook, Connecticut and the safety of Fenwick.

He downshifted again and swerved the car on to the entrance ramp, then rapidly slammed the gearbox through third and into fourth gear. He was doing nearly 90 miles per hour by the time he merged with the heavy Mass Pike traffic.

Trouble was, there was no place to merge.

Anderson realized his mistake only when he recognized that the wall of cars he was fast approaching was crawling in a traffic jam. With nowhere to go and no way to stop in time, he swerved to the right into a concrete barrier that absorbed some of his speed. But not enough. The car's right front tire caught the retaining wall and climbed up the barrier, flipping the

175

car upside down and airborne. A moment later Anderson's Porsche hit the rear end of a Lincoln sedan at better that 60 miles per hour, shearing the rear end off the car. It came to rest buried in a Ford station wagon in the next lane carrying a family of five. There were three kids in the back seat.

The Lincoln burst into flames as did Anderson's Porsche. The driver of the sedan managed to free himself from the wreckage of his car and stepped out onto the highway shaken but otherwise unhurt. He quickly realized that the station wagon next to him was full of people and about to be engulfed by fire. He threw himself at the rear door, trying to wrench it open to free the trapped kids. The door wouldn't budge. The driver of the Ford, their father, also was unhurt and had better luck on his side pulling his children out of the car that was burning already. The driver of the Lincoln pulled the hysterical mother out of the front passenger seat of the station wagon and dragged her away from the burning wreckage despite her screaming resistance.

If the two Boston cops hadn't been right on Anderson's tail, he would have burned to death in the upended Porsche, it's roof nearly completely crushed. The flames hadn't yet reached the sports car, but with seconds to spare the two cops managed to yank Anderson's unconscious body from the pile of torn metal. It's tangerine orange color made the fire that much brighter when it finally began to consume the car.

The sound of ambulances screaming towards the scene filled the air while the Boston cops worked to stabilize Anderson, who had been badly injured. Visibly he had a gaping wound to his forehead and one of his legs was twisted crazily out of shape. He was in shock and had lost a lot of blood and there was no telling what kind of internal injuries he had suffered. The first medics on the scene immediately saw signs of ragged breathing and worked feverishly where he lay on the highway to insert a catheter into his trachea, suspecting that multiple broken ribs were restricting his ability to breath.

They loaded his badly injured body into the ambulance, which backed up the highway entrance ramp with the help of a half a dozen more police who had responded. With sirens blaring and lights flashing, the ambulance sped toward the financial district, its driver snaking his way through heavy morning traffic en route to Mass General Hospital on Cambridge Street.

Behind him, two medics worked frantically trying to keep Anderson alive until they could get him into an operating room.

"I don't know how many lives this guy's got left, but he just used up more than a couple," one of them remarked to his partner. "Keep on that bag, he's not breathing on his own," he yelled, referring to the reservoir bag placed over Anderson's mouth that allowed the medic to squeeze air into his patient's lungs.

"Got it, Sam. But his blood pressure is dropping. Don't know if we're going to make the hospital. For sure we have significant internal bleeding."

"Yah, but let's keep trying," he mumbled as he inserted an intravenous line into Anderson's wrist and began administering a sodium chloride solution to help offset the shock symptoms Anderson was displaying and maintain his blood pressure.

"Poor bastard is lucky he's out of it," Sam said. "With the shit he's got going on he'd be screaming with the pain. But I can't give him morphine or anything. You can smell the booze on him a mile away."

"Kind of early to be hitting the bottle, huh?" his partner said more out of curiosity.

"The clock has nothing to do with drinking, Frank. I have a feeling this guy was in a world of hurt before we met up with him. That fancy car don't mean shit."

They were silent again as they worked. The speeding ambulance was a difficult environment to concentrate in as the two medics were constantly fighting to maintain balance.

"Did you pull his wallet or one of the cops?" Sam asked his partner.

"Cop took down his information for the police report but gave me the wallet. I'll give it to the head nurse. His ID says he's a student at Sloan but comes from Hartford. They'll have to make a call to his kin."

"What's his name?"

"Charles Anderson." Sam shook his head and shrugged his shoulders. "Don't know the name."

"Me neither. But if he's a student at the Sloan School, there's a good chance we might hear it again someday."

"You're right. That's some school. But right now his future notoriety is in someone else's hands."

"What do you mean?"

"I mean I hope he believes in God. Charlie here is going to need his help to get through this."

Twelve

~~~ ❧ ~~~

The alarm clock jarred Logan out of a deep sleep. It was the best rest he'd had in weeks, even if it was only a few hours. He was officially off the clock at The Times for a few days, but he'd set the alarm for noon so he could call in and make sure he wasn't needed for anything. The paper was like an incurable virus. There was no getting it out of his blood.

He yawned and stretched in bed for a moment, trying to clear the cobwebs when his hand brushed a shape lying next to him. It was only then that he remembered. Good lord, he thought, it was Elina, still sound asleep. How could he have forgotten?

His mind raced as he tried to piece back what had happened last night.

"Elina," he had called loudly upon seeing her on the couch, intentionally waking her. "Why are you here? What's happened?"

179

She roused and stared at him for a moment, slightly confused.

"Danny..." she hesitated, not quite sure how to explain her presence.

"How the hell did you get in here?" forgetting his exhaustion for the moment. He was confused, not sure if he was angry or glad to see her.

"Well..." she hesitated, "I didn't want to surprise you at the paper again, I know you don't like that... so I found the building superintendent and asked him to open the door for me. He didn't mind..."

"Manny let you in? Did he hit on you..."

"No... geez, what do you think I am, Danny?" she said. He didn't answer.

"Danny!"

"Well, it would be just like him to ask for a... 'favor' in return, trust me. You don't know this neighborhood, Elina."

She got up and walked over to him.

"You still haven't told me why you're here, Elina. I didn't exactly expect to find you sleeping on my couch."

Wordlessly, she leaned forward and wrapped her arms around him, pulling him close to her. Logan didn't know how to respond, but he could feel the anger leaving his body as she held him.

"My father called me," she whispered. "He told me about Eddie and the incredible story you wrote about him. I had to come..."

"Your father?"

"Yes," she said looking up at him. "He said it was one of the most moving tributes he'd ever read. He said it actually had him thinking about the Vietnam War."

Logan could feel the tears welling in his eyes again.

"He died for nothing, Elina. There aren't even any remains. Nothing to bury."

"I didn't know him very well, Danny, but I'm aware he was one of the boys who saved me the night of my birthday. And I do know that he was your friend... a loyal one..." she said, hanging her head in embarrassment.

"Where's Charles?" Danny asked, harshly. "We all grew up together. Loyalty... I guess your boyfriend doesn't understand the meaning of the word..."

"I don't know if he's even aware, Danny," she said. "I just left. I... I was going to leave any way."

"What do you mean, 'leave?' As in 'leave him?'"

"Yes," she said without hesitation.

"You mean the golden boy has disappointed you somehow?" Logan responded sarcastically.

She let go of him and walked back to the couch, sat down and put her head in her hands.

"I need you to forgive me, Danny..." she said.

Logan was wary.

"If you recall, I've already been down that road. I've already said I forgive you... I'm sorry I didn't send flowers and chocolates, Elina. What do you expect from me?"

"No... I mean I really need you to forgive me. I've made a horrible mistake."

"Mistake?" he said. "Mistake? I really don't understand," Logan responded, truly confused.

"I let you go... the one person in my life who really loved me. I'm so sorry, Danny..."

He shook his head.

"Let it go, Elina. It's in the past and it is what it is. I'm tired of being angry and I really do want you to be happy."

"But you don't understand."

"Understand what? Why are you playing this frigging game? Just spit it out. What's the problem?" Logan said, loosing his cool.

She sighed, still crying.

"Charles has turned into a drunk, Danny. He hits me. And he cheats on me. All the time..." she said and Logan thought he could hear the sound of her heart breaking. He was familiar with it.

He felt the blood rushing to his head and clenched his fists even as his mind began to process what she was saying.

"He what...? Charles?"

"I don't know what's happened to him," Elina sobbed. "He's just such a different person now. So angry, violent. And drunk. Always drunk."

"Does your father know?"

"I don't think so. He seems to pull himself together enough to get through their meetings. But I know Daddy is not happy with his work and he's falling behind in school..."

"That brilliant asshole is having trouble in school? Now that I find hard to believe. All the rest of it... maybe it's just the real Charles Anderson coming out from hiding."

"He was so charming, Danny. I mean... that's what happened. I was so homesick and missed you so much and he was just there, always, to hold my hand. He was so sweet."

Logan turned away.

"Christ, stop it, Elina. I think I'm going to gag. Forgiveness only goes so far."

He couldn't help himself. His own rage bubbled over.

"Jesus. Do you know how naïve you sound?" he went on. "How could you ever have respected a man who screwed his best friend to the wall? Who threw away our friendship — just so he could get into your pants?"

She gasped.

"No... it wasn't like that at all," she cried.

"Yah, it was, Elina, only you were too immature and naïve to see through it. It's not you he wants, other than as a knockout broad hanging on his sleeve. What he wants is your father's money. That house. Power. That's what Charles Anderson is all about. He can change his name to Donald Duck for all I give a shit. It doesn't matter. He'll always be 'Chickie,' the ultimate con man. "

He took a deep breath before delivering the knock out.

"And he conned you out of the only real thing you've ever had in your whole, very blessed, life."

"What?" she asked, her eyes wide.

"My love."

She jumped from the chair and ran to him, throwing her arms around his neck.

"No Danny, please don't say that. Please don't tell me you feel that way. It's not to late..." she begged.

He pushed her back.

"God dammit, Elina. I'll say it again. What do you expect from me? You hurt me so bad I'll never get over it... and with the best friend I ever had as an accomplice."

Tears filled his eyes. This was too much.

"Do you know what that feels like? To have your heart broken into a million pieces? Do you?" he demanded.

She hung her head in shame, sobbing, a little girl who had everything in life, now beaten and humiliated.

It took a moment for her to respond. She took a deep breath and looked out the window.

"Yes," she said. "I do now." She sagged to her knees and buried her face in her hands again.

He couldn't bear it. No matter how much she had hurt him, he knew that he would never stop loving the little girl or the woman she had become. Hurting her only caused him more pain.

Logan walked over and put his hands on her head. She was weeping uncontrollably. He helped Elina to her feet and slowly pulled her close to him, his arms enveloping the girl in a blanket of caring.

"Elina," he whispered in her ear, his hands caressing her back and long blond hair. "I love you. I always will. I'm sorry Charles has hurt you so much."

He gently pushed her away from him and stared into her eyes.

"What to you want me to do? How can I help?"

She opened her eyes, stunning him once again with their beauty. It was like looking into liquid pools of green ocean, he thought. Suddenly, Elina reached up with her hands, held his face and stared into his own sad eyes. The urge to kiss him was overwhelming, but she was so unsure.

Logan took the decision away from her.

He abruptly pressed his lips to hers, hard, the months of unfulfilled passion taking over his emotions and preventing his better judgment from interceding. The kiss was long and deep, driven by both their need for comfort but also long held desire. Without breaking their embrace, Logan slowly began moving her towards the couch. Elina understood and wordlessly began unbuttoning his shirt.

Harsh shadows from the streetlights pouring through the unclosed drapes and the static drone of the off air television provided an awkward substitute for the soft candles and music Logan would have preferred. It was hardly the romantic backdrop that he had fantasized for years when he dared to dream of the possibility of this moment.

But it would do. And now nothing could stop them from satisfying their lust, born virtually the moment they had set eyes on each other as teenagers in another time, at another place.

Logan poured himself into their love making, holding back his own powerful urges to ensure that Elina was fulfilled. The two were locked together for what seemed like hours, he finding it impossible to be satiated or able to quench the smoldering embers of passion within her. And when finally they were spent, they held each other in as tight an embrace as they had on their final night together on the beach in Saybrook, years before, neither knowing it was to be their last until now.

Before dawn, they moved to his bed and Logan fell asleep in Elina's arms, falling into the delicious comfort of the first moments of peace he had known in years. He dreamt of the stars and of his place among them.

When the alarm clock broke the precious calm the next morning and welcomed in a day of joy he could not have imagined possible, Elina kissed him with renewed passion. Logan never did call the office, or for that matter give a thought to the paper. Nor did he turn on the television. The only world he cared about at that moment was lying next to him in his bed.

In a hospital operating room less than 100 miles away, surgeons were still working feverishly to try to save what remained of Charles Anderson's broken body.

And even as he lounged in blissful ignorance with the love of his life, for reasons he would never know or understand, Danny Logan's star began falling from the sky once again.

Thirteen

~~~ ℘ ~~~

By mid afternoon, Charles Anderson had been
moved into an intensive care unit at Mass General
Hospital after somehow surviving more than six hours
of surgery. His injuries were multiple and severe. But
most worrisome was the trauma his brain had suffered
as a result of the dramatic deceleration of the Porsche as
it rammed the huge Lincoln sedan. The sudden impact
threw Anderson into the steering wheel, which stopped
his body from being thrown through the windshield but
the inertia forced his internal organs, particularly his
brain and aorta to continue violently forward. In
essence, his brain bounced off the "brick wall" of his
cranial cavity. In his chest, broken ribs and a collapsed
lung were minor impact injuries compared to the
ruptured aorta he suffered when the horrific deceleration
tore it from his heart in the pericardial cavity.

He also had a severe gash in his forehead and had experienced a compound fracture of his left leg that was going to require additional surgeries before he would walk again. But the very fact that he was alive was a miracle. Twice surgeons rescued him from death as they worked feverishly to relieve the pressure on his brain and sew together his lacerated aorta.

His medical team had elected to place him in a drug induced coma, the theory being that the resulting reduced cerebral blood flow would reduce some of the swelling and pressure in his cranial cavity. His breathing was controlled by a mechanical ventilator the sound of which filled the air with the unsettling knowledge that this patient was not capable of breathing without life support.

Charles Anderson's day had begun badly. Now his life hung by a thread. And despite the dozens of hospital staff that milled about the Intensive Care Unit constantly monitoring his condition, the truth was, he was alone.

Had he been cognizant of his condition and the slight grasp he had on living another day, he would have been afraid. But to know that he was alone would have been even more terrifying.

Hospital administrators had been unable to reach his parents or any relative. The Sloan School informed them of his address and that they were aware he lived with someone, but could not give them a name or contact. They promised to track down his classmates and provide any information they could surface as soon as possible.

But for the time being, Charles Anderson, the man who had been immensely self-assured of his bright future and life of wealth and comfort, was locked in the unconscious grip of a coma. It was a world that some survivors of similar situations had described as a living nightmare. They recalled being able to hear voices, to sense touch and to feel fear. Worst of all was the incredible desperation they felt at not being able to communicate.

In fact, had Anderson been able to speak or even to scribble a message, he would have communicated a single word. A word that none but those few who appreciated his incredible ego and thirst for power would correctly decipher.

It was "No."

Not as in, "No, I cannot lose Elina." Or, "No, I did not mean to hurt anyone."

Inside Charles Anderson's tormented brain, the word "No" screamed over and over, mercilessly.

As in: "No, this can't be happening to me."

Fourteen

~~~ ℘ ~~~

"First of all, I'm going to buy you the best pizza in the South End. You haven't lived until you've tasted the pepperoni at Casa Loma on Wethersfield Avenue. I'm telling you, Elina, there are treasures like this all over Hartford," he told her after they finally got out of bed.

"Then I'm going to take you to Pope Park, where the flowers, the crocuses and lilies will just be starting to bloom. They're magnificent. And then after I've walked all that pizza off that skinny body of yours I'm taking you to dinner at the Hearthstone Restaurant on Maple Avenue for Prime Rib. It's two inches thick. If the mayor is there, I'll introduce you. Ok? So, hurry up and get ready!"

If Danny Logan had looked in a mirror at that moment, he wouldn't have recognized himself. His smile was as big and as real as it had ever been in his life and his heart was skipping with joy at Elina's unexpected return. He could not remember a single day in his life he when he'd been happier.

"Danny, are you sure? My father is always telling me how dangerous Hartford is..." Elina responded nervously.

"Your father? How the fuck would he know?" Logan responded angrily, his happiness suddenly interrupted by the mere mention of a man for whom he held no respect. A "Bishop." My ass, he thought.

"Your old man gets chauffeured around the city with a body guard. He wouldn't know the South End from the North End. Ignore him, please."

She was startled by his reaction.

"Danny, I know you don't..."

"No, you don't know how I feel about him, Elina. And please let's not allow your father to ruin a wonderful day. Or what little is left of it. Now c'mon...hurry up!"

He regretted snapping at her but inside was raging at the nerve of a guy who thought he had a finger on the pulse of the city. He didn't know squat. It was men like him who were preventing the things that desperately needed to happen in Hartford from even being considered. He had his own agenda, whatever that was. But Logan didn't want to think about that today.

Elina had disappeared into his bedroom. He found her combing her hair in front of his dresser mirror. Logan stood in the doorway for a moment, watching. He was still awed by how beautiful she was.

He came up behind her and wrapped his arms around her small waist.

"I'm sorry, I didn't mean to snap at you," he apologized.

She smiled into the mirror.

"It's alright, Danny," she said softly, turning in his arms and facing him. "I've given you good reason to be angry about a lot of things. But if we're going to have any chance at this, you'll need to remember your promise to me."

"Anything," he said, meaning it. "But what promise are we referring to? I mean a new Rolls Royce Corniche is sort of out of my league... at least until I get my next promotion," he teased.

"That's not what I mean and certainly not what I want from you," she said, an unusually serious tone in her voice.

She looked deeply into his dark brown eyes. They had such a sparkle today. And then she whispered two words to him, slowly.

"This boy."

Logan smiled.

"You have a good memory."

"Yes," she said. "Of a wonderful time in my life... that I made a complete mess of. But you promised to forgive me, no matter what, if I came back to you."

" I did," Logan said, gently kissing her forehead.

She stared up at him, waiting.

"And I do."

She leaned up and kissed him full on the mouth. It didn't take much of a spark to light their passion for each other.

He broke off the kiss.

"As much as I'd like to continue this..." he smiled at her confused look. "I need to eat, woman! C'mon, please?" he begged. "The best pizza this side of New York awaits us."

She laughed.

"Ok, cave man, let's go forage for food."

"That's the spirit," he said. "Shall we walk or cab it?"

"You have something against my Healy?" she asked in mock surprise.

"You still have that beauty?" Logan gasped.

"Pretty as the day I got her."

He stared at her in horror.

"Don't tell me you parked her on the street... please don't."

She looked at him oddly.

"Why, of course. It was too heavy to carry up to your apartment and I don't think it would have fit through..."

"Oh, Jesus... c'mon. Now, quickly. And say your prayers."

He ran down the stairs two at a time and burst through the hallway door to the sidewalk.

"Which way?" he called to Elina, a whole flight of stairs behind.

"Right."

Logan looked up the street and began running. He took a deep breath and sighed. It was still there. Tires and everything.

She finally caught up to him.

"What was that all about?" she asked, somewhat alarmed.

"You can't park something that valuable on the street around here. I'm amazed someone didn't jack it overnight. Guess no one around here knows what it's worth. Now if it was a Chevelle..."

She threw him the keys.

"Here, you drive. You look like you could use a little excitement in your life."

He laughed out loud.

"Elina, you've given me more excitement in the last day than I've had in five years."

He jumped into the drivers seat, turned the key in the ignition and the Austin Healy 3000 fired right up. The throaty roar from its exhaust was just as he remembered it.

"How sweet." He released the convertible top latches and with one hand pushed the canvas back to open up the roadster.

"Danny, it's only April!"

"Yah, isn't it great? We've got spring, summer and fall to cruise together," he laughed. "Wow, you do light up my world, girl."

She grinned.

"I think that's the nicest thing anyone's ever said to me," she laughed. "Say, whatever happened to the Chevy?"

"I left it at my father's when I went to UCONN. Haven't been back since. I'm sure he probably sold it for booze money."

"Amazing."

"What's amazing?"

From the sound of it, your father is as big a drunk as my mother. But she's never had to steal to support her habit. My father's done that... strangely because he loves her."

He began to drive and was quiet.

"We do come from different worlds, Elina."

She looked over at him.

"I know. So what?"

"No second thoughts?" he asked.

"Never again, Danny. And I've never been so sure about anything before. What my parents have is not what I want. What I want... who I want... is you."

194

A simple pizza became a meal to remember as Logan regaled Elina with endless stories of nights spent with his high school buddies at the Casa Loma Restaurant, feasting on Italian cuisine at the South End landmark. It didn't hurt that the wait staff greeted him by his first name and the chef and the owner both came to their table to see him and wink at his beautiful companion. This was his world and he was proud to share it with her.

The afternoon flew by as he told her his story of growing up in the South End with his friends Eddie Graziano, Chickie and the rest of the guys she met who worked at her birthday party.

"Thank you for taking me away from mourning over Eddie, Elina... I wish you had gotten to know him better. Ends up he was my real best friend," he said as the memories cooled their laughter for a few moments. "And I know he would have loved you. I wish I had been there when he died. Maybe I couldn't have saved him. But he would have known that I had his back."

Tears came flooding back to Logan's eyes, but he fought them.

"It's all right to be sad, Danny," she said. "Eddie would have been proud to know someone cared so much for him. But I think he would have been the first person to tell you not to waste your life fighting for a worthless cause."

"In fact, he told me just that," Logan said, hanging his head. "I just can't shake the guilt of not being with him."

"Just because you weren't with him doesn't mean you weren't fighting for him. In the way that you do best," she reminded him.

"I'll try to remember that, Elina. I love you for saying it."

195

Logan raised his beer and offered a toast.

"To Eddie, my friend," he said. "I hope you'll find peace now."

"To Eddie," Elina repeated and they drank together.

"That reminds me," Logan said, wiping the tears off his cheeks. "I've got to stop at the paper and make some phone calls. I need to talk to his mom and dad and a couple of the guys. I don't have a phone in the apartment. It will only take a few minutes before we go to Pope Park."

He pulled the Healy up to the curb in front of The Times building and opened the door for her.

"Come inside, please? Mr. Holcombe will get a kick out of seeing us together. He thought you were pretty hot..."

"Danny!"

"It might give him a reason to smile, Elina. He lost his only son a few months ago at Khe Sanh. Guy's been like a father to me."

She closed her eyes and shook her head, sadly.

"Will this ever end?" she asked.

"I hope so. And it was Holcombe who convinced me that in my own small way, with my typewriter, I might help stop the war. I think he's exaggerating, but I trust him. So, for the time being, this is how I'm going to fight for guys like Eddie."

He took her hand and they bounded up the stairs two at a time. This too was Danny Logan's world and he was proud to bring her here now, even to show her off.

"I'll bring you down to the newsroom and show you where I sit. But let's visit with Holcombe first," he said.

Charlie Holcombe was at his desk, deep in his work, head down and poring over some documents. He looked up in surprise when Danny and Elina approached. Logan suddenly noticed that he had that nervous look in his eye you could see when something was wrong.

"Hey, Mr. Holcombe, you remember Elina, don't you?" Danny said, hoping he was misreading the personnel manager.

"Why yes... of course.... of course I remember, how are you, dear?" he said, extending his hand. Then he was silent. The moment was as awkward as any he had ever shared with Holcombe, and there had been quite a few.

"Uh... Danny... uh, can I talk to you for a minute in private? I'm sorry to be so rude, Elina, but..."

Logan respected his friend enough not to question his request. "Elina, give us a minute, will you? I'll be right there."

She smiled. "Of course, but hurry up, we've got a walk in the park to take, remember? Crocuses, lilies?"

"I'll be right there, promise."

He turned back to Holcombe. His face was full of anxiety.

"What's wrong, Mr. Holcombe? I was supposed to be off today, remember..."

"It's not you Danny. It's Don Hanson. He's called here three times looking for you wondering if you knew where Elina was. It's something about Charles Anderson. An accident. A bad one. You don't have a phone, I was actually about to walk over to your place."

Logan stared back at Holcombe, not wanting to believe what he had said.

"Danny? I don't know what's going on with you two, but you must tell her. She needs to call her old man," Holcombe said. "Sounds pretty serious."

He shook his head, too stunned for words.

197

"You tell her. Please. I'll be at my desk." Logan turned and walked out of Holcombe's office.

"Are you sure?" he asked, but Danny continued walking. He hurried by Elina without a word.

"Elina, Elina," Holcombe called out into the hallway, "please come in here."

"Where did Danny go? Why did he just walk by me? What's happened?" she asked, the color draining from her face.

"You need to call your father, Elina, it's about Charles. Here, use my phone."

"Charles? What about Charles?" she asked as Holcombe dialed the number and handed her the telephone.

"Daddy? What's wrong?"

Holcombe watched as she listened. Her eyes went wide and then clenched shut. She raised a hand and covered her mouth as tears came to her eyes.

"Mass General?"

She listened in silence as Hanson answered her and then obviously began asking her questions.

"What? Now is not the time, daddy. And don't judge me. I'm leaving now." She handed the receiver back to Holcombe without another word to her father.

"Can you show me to Danny's desk, Mr. Holcombe?" she asked, tears streaming down her face. He reached into his pocket and offered her a handkerchief.

"Of course. It's just downstairs."

Logan was holding a string of wire service copy, but had been staring at the same page for minutes. He looked up when Holcombe led her to his desk. All around him, people had stopped whatever they were doing as they caught sight of the stunning blond.

"Hey, so here it is! Where I make my contribution to everything that ails society," he joked, waiving his arm around the tiny space, trying to avoid what he knew was coming.

"Oh, Danny... how..." she said.

"Shh...," he interrupted her, holding a finger to his mouth. "How bad is it?"

"Bad."

He reached for her and wrapped his arms around her slender frame. She buried her face in his chest and cried softly.

"You have to go." It was a statement, not a question.

"Yes," she whispered.

He held her tighter.

"Remember," he said.

She pushed back, looking up at his face. He looked so sad. She wondered if it was for her or for himself.

"This Boy."

She kissed him softly on the lips and turned and walked away. Holcombe followed her.

Danny Logan watched until she was out of sight, then dropped the wire copy he was still clutching in his hand. He walked slowly to the staircase and climbed the stairs to the roof.

Looking out over the skyline, he hadn't realized it was so late. The sun was low, it was almost five o'clock. They would have had just enough time to see the flowers in Pope Park. Elina would have liked that, he thought. Even this early in spring the scent of the crocuses and lilies filled the air in the beautifully landscaped city park. He would have explained to her it's fascinating history, and how he marveled that it's

199

lush grounds had somehow escaped the ravage that the rest of Hartford had suffered.

But it was too late for that, now. Perhaps it was a visit they would never make together.

He looked up into the sky. It was still too early to find the stars, and for that he was grateful.

He laughed to himself, holding back tears. In less than a single day he had gone from a state of exhaustion and utter despair to indescribable joy and boundless energy. He had experienced a few hours of a dream fulfilled, his heart nearly ready to burst from rekindled love.

Just like that, it was gone. The star with his name on it had been extinguished again in a split second.

He shook his head in wonder... and defeat.

Danny Logan walked to Pope Park alone that night and picked a few flowers to give to Eddie's mother. He drank too much with his devastated father. Then he went home and slept at the kitchen table.

He couldn't bear the thought of lying in his bed, the scent of Elina's perfume on his sheets a constant reminder of what he wanted so badly but could never have.

Fifteen

~~~ ℘ ~~~

June, 1968

Danny Logan stayed in the newsroom late into the early hours of June 5th to watch the television coverage of Robert F. Kennedy winning the 1968 California Democratic Presidential Primary. It was nearly 3 a.m. on the east coast when Kennedy, the hope of young Americans of all races and fervent Vietnam War critics, took the podium to claim victory in the hugely important primary, a vital step towards the Presidential nomination. The win had him trailing only incumbent Vice President Hubert Humphrey in the race.

The crowd of supporters at the Ambassador Hotel in Los Angeles numbered in the hundreds as they waited for Kennedy despite the lateness of the hour. They were euphoric. Even Logan, who had become a hardened cynic of government in general, felt the stirrings of excitement that Kennedy infused into the hyper tense social environment that was infecting the country. Violent protests involving race or Vietnam were a daily occurrence and Walter Cronkite continued to inform the American public at the end of every nightly newscast how many young men had been killed in the fighting that day.

The mood across America was dark, confused and divided. Minutes after Kennedy finished his remarks before a cheering audience, the word despondent would come to the minds of most people attempting to describe their feelings about America.

Logan watched Kennedy speak and felt a glow of hope stirring in his heart. The man was so inspiring, he thought, just the answer to the cloud of hatred, desperation and confrontation that seemed to be enveloping America. He was tired now, and had to be back in the office before 9 a.m., so he hurried back to his desk to grab his satchel filled with notes of stories he was working on and began walking out of the newsroom. Greaves booming voice stopped him in his tracks.

The managing editor was walking towards Logan's desk carrying a UPI wire bulletin. Someone turned up the volume on the television sets.

"God dammit, can you believe this…" Greaves shouted in anger, his emotions unusually visible to all. "When will this stop?"

He handed Logan the wire copy and the writer turned pale as he read.

"Los Angeles Radio Station WCCO reports that Senator Kennedy has been shot in the hip as he left the hotel."

"This says he's been shot in the hip... that can't be too..."

A runner approached with an updated bulletin.

"It was an error, he was shot in the head. It says he's still alive, but lying on the floor of the hotel kitchen, bleeding from the head and apparently unseeing. His wife is..."

Someone in the crowd shouted, "Oh, my God," and all heads turned to the television sets. The black and white still photograph was of a young Mexican boy cradling the Senator's head in his arms." Kennedy's face was withdrawn and emotionless. His eyes stared blankly upwards, as if he was unaware of the crowd that surrounded his motionless body on the kitchen floor.

A cold, eerie silence gripped the newsroom with only the television reporter's voice echoing through the chamber. TV camera's had not yet gotten to the scene, and the macabre photograph filled the screen for long, agonizing minutes.

Greaves finally broke the silence.

"Ok, everyone. Back to work. Let's keep a close eye on the wires for updates from the police and hospital. They're already announcing they have the shooter in custody, let's dig into that as well. We've got quite a bit of time before the Bulldog deadline so let's stay on this and be as current as possible right up until the press rolls. Get some people in the street comments during the morning rush hour. Feed everything you've got on the main story to Logan. He'll write the lead piece. Photo, I want to see everything that's coming in over the wires and I'll personally select our lead picture. It's possible the Courant won't be able to carry this even in their last edition because of the timing, so we may lead Hartford with the story." The Courant was Hartford's morning newspaper, a fierce competitor.

"Let's be proud of our work, as sickening as it is. Go to it."

The staff dispersed immediately and the hum of conversation began again. The television volume returned to normal. The newsroom had survived another shock and was back in business.

Through the rest of that bleak night and throughout the next day, Americans searched for news of the Senator's condition and his assassin's identity in their newspapers and in radio and television broadcasts. It was an excruciating wait that worsened with every passing hour.

Just after midnight on June 6th, Greaves spoke with the managing editor of the Los Angeles Times who was a close personal friend. He described Kennedy's situation as "grave" and told Greaves "we don't expect him to make it more than a few more hours." The managing editor called Logan in to his office.

"You did a good job on today's paper. Your lead was as good as any I've seen. It's hard to write a death watch," Greaves told him.

"Is it that bad?" Logan responded.

"Yes. Start mapping out a special edition. If he dies tonight, I want it on the street by noon tomorrow."

Four hours later, the newsroom went silent again, as Walter Cronkite interrupted regular programming with a Bulletin. Not a man or woman in the room didn't know what was coming, but they clenched their fists or buried their face in their hands as Kennedy's press spokesman, Frank Mankiewicz stepped up to a bank of news microphones. He took a moment before speaking, attempting to compose himself, then said the unthinkable.

"Ladies and gentlemen, I have, uh, a short... I have a short announcement to read, which I will read, uh... at this time," Mankiewicz began haltingly.

"Senator Robert Francis Kennedy died at 1:44 a.m. today, June 6, 1968. With Senator Kennedy at the time of his death were his wife Ethel, his sisters Mrs. Stephen Smith and Mrs. Patricia Lawford, his brother-in-law Mr. Stephen Smith, and his sister-in-law Mrs. John F. Kennedy. He was 42 years old. Thank you."

"Oh, dear God, what is to become of us?" someone in the newsroom said in shock. "How can this be?"

Greaves gave new instructions to Logan.

"Show me the three best photo's you have and we'll run it full page with just a headline. Ok?"

Logan nodded, his mind already pulling the words together that would make his story.

"It's not enough, Mr. Greaves," Logan responded. "We have to do more than just report the facts. I want to write a story about the impact of Kennedy's murder on one individual, one young American."

Greaves stared at his lead writer and nodded his head. "The man stood for a lot of good. We owe it to him to go the extra mile...or ten. Go get the story."

Logan had seen the wire service photographs of the young Mexican hotel busboy at the hotel and wondered what his role had been. For the next several hours he worked the phones, tracking down 17-year-old Juan Romero in the middle of the LA night. He finally reached him at the hotel where he had reported for work right on time.

"Juan Romero?" Logan asked.

"Yes, sir," the young boy responded.

"Juan, my name is Danny Logan and I'm a reporter with The Hartford Times. I'd just like to talk with you for a moment if you can…

"I must get back to work, Mr. Logan, but I can talk for a few minutes," the boy responded.

"Thank you, Juan, I know you have been through a difficult couple of days," Logan said. "Am I correct that the young man kneeling next to Senator Kennedy in the photograph taken right after the shooting was you?"

"Yes, sir, that was me," Romero said. "I just wanted to congratulate Senator Kennedy on winning the primary. I had delivered room service to him the night before and we talked for a few minutes. He told me to call him 'Bobby.' I felt so bad for the poor man. He was shot right in front of me."

"Who shot him, Juan?"

"The man they've identified. The guy with the two same names."

"Sirhan Sirhan," Logan probed.

"Yes."

"I'm not really calling to ask about him, Juan. What I really wanted to know is what you said to the Senator or what he said to you. Can you help me?"

"Of course."

"Tell me about it, tell me what you remember, Juan," Logan asked the boy.

"I watched him fall to the floor after the shots and saw the blood. I wanted to protect his head from the cold concrete. When I met him the day before, he had made me feel like a regular citizen, he made me feel like a human being. He didn't look at my color, he didn't look at my position. I felt so bad for him. I tried to hold his head."

Logan had a lump in his throat as he listened to the boy tell his story.

206

"Did he say anything, Juan?"

"Yes. First he asked, 'Is everybody ok?' and I told him, 'Yes, everybody's ok.' And then he turned away from me and said, 'Everything's going to be ok.'"

Romero paused. "I still feel so bad. Why did they kill him? I gave him my rosary beads to hold. One of his eyes was blinking real fast and his leg was twitching. I don't know if he knew I gave him my rosary. I hope so."

"I'm sure the Senator knew you were being so kind to him, Juan," Logan said.

"I hope so," Romero replied, almost in a whisper. "I mean, he shook my hand when I brought him room service, I didn't ask him to. He just put out his hand. Such a nice man."

"Are you OK, Juan?"

Logan thought he heard him sob.

"I don't know, man. I haven't slept in two days. I come to work because it keeps my mind busy. This made me realize that no matter how much hope you have, it can be taken away in a second."

Logan flinched at the words. The thought of Elina was never more than a syllable away.

"I think many people feel that way this morning, Juan. Thank you for your help. And thank you for helping a good man. I think he would have done great things for our country."

"Me to, Mr. Logan.

"God bless, Juan."

It took Danny Logan another 15 minutes to gather his thoughts after the conversation. Romero had asked the question on the minds of millions, especially the young.

Why was it that the most compassionate, inspiring and peace loving leaders in America had all been assassinated, Logan asked himself. What did that say for a country founded on such unassailable principles? He thought of the first words of the Declaration of Independence: "We hold these truths to be self-evident, that all men are created equal, that they are endowed by their Creator with certain unalienable Rights, that among these are Life, Liberty and the pursuit of Happiness."

John F. Kennedy. Martin Luther King. Robert F. Kennedy. All martyred for their pursuit of the rights of oppressed people. As a country, did we still share the beliefs of our founding fathers? He could no longer answer the question with any certainty.

Logan's head spun with the magnitude of the tragedy. And his heart hurt. He, like millions of other Americans had lost another hero.

He wrote the story of how one young Mexican-American immigrant had lost his own hero on the cold concrete floor of a Los Angeles hotel to an assassin's bullets. He wrote Juan Romero's story, the tale of the nameless boy in the photograph that had made page one of every paper in the country. He wrote how the young man had given Senator Kennedy his rosary as he lay dying, the only thing he could do for the man who had shaken his hand and made him feel like an equal, like a true American. And he while he lay dying, his words were still full of hope: "Everything's going to be ok."

Greaves read it once and set his red pencil down without ever touching the copy. Logan watched as his boss' eyes filled with tears. He looked up at his lead writer and shook his head.

"I can't do this anymore, Danny," he said. "I just can't. I can't handle the hate, the blood, I can't stand watching our country come apart."

He lapsed into silence, took a deep breath and blew it out slowly. For the first time, Danny Logan noticed how old his boss had suddenly become. The man had aged ten years in the last 12 months.

"Put the paper to bed, Danny. She's yours today. I need to put my head on a pillow for awhile."

"Mr. Greaves, we're all exhausted. Get some rest. You'll feel better. Let me get Mr. Holcombe to give you a ride home."

Greaves stood up and grabbed his baggy suit jacket. He ignored his briefcase.

"No, Danny. I need to walk," he said. "I'll see you in the morning."

At noon that day, The Times released a special edition dedicated to the murder and legacy of Robert F. Kennedy. The lead story by Danny Logan ran superimposed over the photograph of Juan Romero holding the head of the gravely wounded Senator Robert F. Kennedy, under the headline, "Kennedy: Everything's Going To Be Ok." It was a tribute to the slain candidate's bottomless well of hope and belief in America.

Logan left for home at 9 p.m. that night, having been at his desk for more than 50 hours. He passed by Holcombe's office on the way out.

"Glad you stopped by, Danny," Charlie Holcombe said to him. "Great job today. But I wanted to tell you that Elina called earlier. Forgive me for not telling you before, I just thought you needed to concentrate."

"No problem, Mr. Holcombe. There are few people in the world whose judgment I would never challenge. You're one of them. What did she want?"

"She wanted me to let you know that Charles Anderson came out of the coma today and is off the ventilator."

"Really?" Logan said, not sure if he was interested or not.

"Yes. And she asked if you could come to the hospital. Said she needs to talk with you about Charles."

Sixteen

~~~ ❧ ~~~

Logan was not prepared for the sight of Charles Anderson in the Intensive Care Unit at Mass General.

It wasn't the overall state of urgency that permeated the air in the specialized wing that made him anxious. Or even the array of monitors, ventilators, intravenous bags and other medical equipment that surrounded every patient in every room. It wasn't even the smell that permeated the entire unit: a combination of sickness, torn flesh, blood, medicines, urine… and even death.

No. What shocked Logan was seeing how little of Charles Anderson wasn't broken. No description could have prepared him for actually seeing how severely injured he was.

What little of his body that wasn't bandaged and visible was bruised or scraped. Even his once handsome face, half dressed because of the massive head wound he

211

had suffered, was one sickly yellow purplish bruise, evidence of the horrendous forces his body had endured as a result of the deceleration injury. Where there wasn't a bruise, there was chalky white skin that one would expect to find on a cadaver. His right leg was encased in a hard plaster cast from hip to toes and strung up in a frightening contraption that held it in traction high off the surface of his bed.

Elina met him in the lobby of the huge hospital the day after she had called asking him to come. Logan had rented a car and drove to Boston after work, unable to refuse her but also desperate to know what she had to say.

She was grateful to him, knowing that she probably couldn't guess at the emotions involved for Danny. She was prepared for any kind of reaction from him, particularly anger. But to her surprise, he gently hugged her and gave her a soft kiss on the cheek when they met.

"Are you alright?" he asked her.

"Yes. Tired. But I'm alright," she answered quietly.

"Let's sit for awhile," he asked.

"My father is in the ICU with Charles and his parents," she said. The mention of Hanson's name made his stomach churn.

"Thank you for coming, Danny, I know this was a lot to ask."

"Just tell me what his situation is, please," as he took a seat and pulled her down next to him.

She sighed. It was hard to tell him. Because Charles Anderson's condition defined the path her life must take. She wasn't sure if Danny understood or was still hoping she would come back to him.

What she described was at once terrifying but hopeful.

"He will physically heal," Elina began. "I mean... he will walk again, with a limp, but he will walk. He will live with a horrible scar on his forehead, but his ego will have to accept that. The tear to his Aorta is healing, miraculously, and it does not appear that he will have any long-term physical complications. It is beyond comprehension how he lived through that. He should have bled to death right there on the highway. The surgeons here..."

"What about his brain injury?" Logan asked, knowing Anderson's future depended on his recovery from his most grievous trauma.

Elina did not respond immediately. She wrung her hands, then clasped them beneath her chin.

"We don't know, Danny," she finally responded. "He has not spoken yet, although he appears to understand questions and what's going on around him. I've asked him several times if he remembers what happened, but he doesn't respond in any way. His doctors say that the x-rays and tests they've done show no blood clots or other life threatening conditions. But it's what they don't know that worries them."

"What does that mean?" Logan asked.

"It means they don't know yet if he has suffered any long-term cognitive intelligence impairment, or if there will be emotional or social consequences. It's possible he will behave without emotion or the exact opposite could happen. He could emerge from this in a constant state of rage."

"Jesus Christ. Has anyone given you a hard answer on anything? It's all what ifs..."

"Exactly, Danny. We don't know who exactly Charles Anderson will be or what he will become as he heals."

Logan ran his hands through his hair in frustration.

"Sloan? The investment world? All his plans of fame and fortune? Will he be able to pick up where he left off?" he asked.

"They don't know. Certainly not for some time — if ever. Chances are he will not be able to return to the Sloan School. He would never be able to keep up with his studies. At least not for the foreseeable future…"

"So what happens to him?"

"When he's ready to be released from here, he'll go to a rehab facility of some sort for both physical and mental therapy. Then…" She hesitated for a moment.

He watched as she took a deep breath, searching for the courage she needed to go on.

"Then he'll come live with me at the house in Fenwick. I'm dropping out of school to care for him and… well, we'll see where it goes from there."

"Meaning, you'll get married."

She dropped her head and stared at the floor.

"Just say it Elina, get it out," Logan demanded.

"Yes," she blurted out. "Are you happy? Yes. Charles will never be able to live on his own, alone, again. What would you have me do, Danny? Abandon him?"

"You were ready to do that just a few weeks ago, if I remember. I can still smell your perfume in my apartment."

A tear escaped, running down her cheek. She looked up at him.

214

"That was then, Danny. It was what I wanted. I didn't anticipate…"

"Save it," Logan said abruptly.

"Danny, please…?

"No, I mean it," Logan went on. "You don't have to explain. I've given up trying to understand how I lost you to begin with. But this… this… I understand."

She leaned forward and hugged him.

"He was once my friend. My best friend. That's over, but I still care for his wellbeing. Do what you must to take care of him."

She sobbed.

"Why are you crying?" Logan asked.

"Because I so want to be selfish."

He looked at her quizzically.

"Selfish?"

"This is not what I wanted, Danny. I know what my heart wants, and I want to give in to what it's telling me to do. But I can't. I can't just walk away from him when he needs me so much. It's no different than if my father were to abandon my mother because she's a hopeless drunk. Charles will be as helpless as she is."

He stood up, shaking his head. This conversation was over.

"Elina, if I gave in to what my heart is telling me, I would go home tonight and pray that Charles dies and that you can finally be   Guess you could say that would be a bit selfish, too."

He grit his teeth at the thought of what he was about to say.

"But I learned to give you up once before, and I'll learn again. We each need to get on with our lives. You've made your choices, I've made mine.

"Let's live with them."

He reached down to her with his hand.

215

"C'mon, I should at least say hello to Charles while I'm here." She took his hand and they went to the ICU.

Elina was right about his level of awareness. Charles immediately recognized his old friend but did not acknowledge him.

Danny stared down at the corpse-like figure on the bed and didn't speak. Instead he looked directly into Charles' eyes for several long minutes. He didn't have to speak the words for Anderson to understand what he was thinking.

You poor, dumb bastard.

You fucked up, buddy, and now you're paying the price. But despite your incredible disloyalty and amazing arrogance, you won the ultimate prize.

Don't ever forget it. Because I won't let you.

He turned and walked away without saying anything. Logan nodded to Hanson who was sitting in a chair in the corner of the room and wondered what he thought of his prized "student" now. The Hartford "Bishop" nodded back, a reflection of his cunning, not his manners. He needs me for something, Danny thought as he walked out.

Elina followed.

"What happened to the police issues, as if I don't know?" he asked her.

"Daddy took care of everything, somehow. There wasn't even a traffic ticket written," she said. "Thank God no one else was hurt."

Logan looked up at the sky and shook his head. Then his gaze turned to Elina.

Again, he didn't need to say the words.

She understood perfectly.

It was only when he got back in his car for the long drive home that he permitted himself to say anything.

"No one else was hurt, Elina?"

Seventeen

~~~ ❧ ~~~

Reeling from the mindless assassination of yet another disciple of peace, it would seem America might have taken a collective deep breath and rethought things.

Nothing could have been further from reality.

Bobbie Kennedy's body had barely been laid to rest beside his murdered brother John at Arlington National Cemetery when racial tensions exploded once again across the nation.

On July 16, rival gang confrontations in Wooster, Ohio escalated when police intervened and riots ensued, spreading into downtown Akron. One week later, a four hours long shootout between police and a Black Panther splinter group in Glenville, Ohio led to five days of riots. Seven people, including three police were killed in the unrest sparked by substandard living conditions in overcrowded, deteriorating minority neighborhoods, high unemployment among the city's youth and poorly managed segregation attempts by the city government.

And then, in August came the event that shocked not only Americans — but the world.

It was widely recognized that the United States continued to struggle with deeply ingrained racial prejudices that had exploded into a seemingly endless cycle of hate propagated violence and destruction in its cities. But as the world watched, the country that had so willingly paid such an enormous sacrifice for the cause of world peace less than 25 years before exposed just how ferociously divisive the Vietnam War had become.

As the Democratic National Convention convened in Chicago with the pain of Robert Kennedy's assassination and strong anti-war sentiment dampening any hope for enthusiasm on the floor of the International Amphitheater, outside more than 10,000 demonstrators gathered to protest America's continued involvement in Vietnam. Chicago Mayor Richard Daley's response was to confront the mostly college-age demonstrators with a 23,000 man armada of heavily armed city police and National Guardsmen.

On August 28, the demonstrators gathered in Grant Park with the intention of staging a peaceful demonstration. About 3:30 p.m. a demonstrator lowered the American Flag flying over the park. That was the spark that enflamed Chicago's blue-helmeted police who rushed in with flying nightsticks. Leaders of the Students For A Democratic Society movement who had organized the demonstration moved the crowd towards the convention being held at the Conrad Hilton Hotel to ensure that if the police or Guard used tear gas, it would envelope the city.

Predictably, Chicago police indiscriminately fired tear gas into the crowd as they marched into Chicago and continued to do so as the demonstrators massed in front of the Hilton. Police also used Mace at close range, mindlessly spraying the gas at demonstrators, spectators and even delegates making their way in and out of the convention hall.

News of the riots and the residue of tear gas spread inside to the convention floor even as nomination speeches were being given for Vice President Hubert Humphrey and Senators Eugene McCarthy and George McGovern.

"Do you believe this?" Greaves said to Logan as they watched the televised news coverage from the newsroom.

"No... frankly, I don't. I can't fathom what Daley is doing... he's single handedly turned this into a war zone. These are just kids...

"Oh, my God," he said suddenly, as a television camera zoomed in on a Chicago cop raining blows upon a young woman with his wooden nightstick. The relentless rage with which the cop went about his savage work was impossible to hide from the television lens.

The assault on the demonstrators was broadcast live by NBC for a full 17 minutes, Logan later learned. During the entirety of the coverage, the demonstrators chanted, "The whole world is watching." Indeed, the whole world was watching.

Logan was sickened by the violence and wondered how he could write an objective story on the riot and the Chicago police behavior. He turned to Greaves, who was watching another network's coverage of Sen. Abraham Ribicoff of Connecticut, who was nominating Sen. George McGovern for President as the violence was occurring.

"With George McGovern as President of the United States, we wouldn't have to have Gestapo tactics in the streets of Chicago!" Ribicoff said on live TV, looking up from the podium at an angry, mortified Daley. There was spontaneous applause from many of the delegates who were appalled by the violence outside. But millions of viewers all over the world watched in horror as the Chicago Mayor responded, "Fuck you, you Jew son of a bitch."

"There's my lead," Logan said, turning again to Greaves.

But the managing editor had dropped his head. Logan thought it was the shock of Daley's words. Several minutes passed before Greaves spoke. It was more than Daley's words.

"I was just a kid, an 18-year old Marine when I landed at Iwo Jima and Okinawa, " he said aloud, his normally strong, gravelly voice no more than a whisper. "I can still see all the boys laying dead or dying on the beach, the water red with their blood. Jesus Christ, it was awful..."

His eyes were full of tears but he wouldn't give in to them.

"They died proud because they were fighting for the greatest country on earth. I never questioned it, never asked why, we just believed. You know I still got shrapnel in my back?" he asked looking around at the dozens of faces who had turned away from the television to hear a man they all admired.

"My younger brother... he died at Normandy. Yet no one in my family, not one of us, questioned the sacrifice, the pain we suffered. Because we fought for freedom, we fought for what was right... God dammit, wasn't that what America was all about?" he continued, his voice rising with emotion.

"We were the greatest country... so proud... but now..."

221

He paused. Logan was alarmed by how pale he was.

"Now, for the first time in my life, I am ashamed of my country. I am embarrassed to be an American."

He wiped his eyes.

"I'm sorry, boys," he said to the anxious faces around him. "This is more than these old eyes can bear to watch."

He turned and began walking to his office.

"I'm hanging it up for the night, Danny. Need some sleep. It's your paper tomorrow. Make the calls."

"Yes, sir," Logan responded, somewhat shaken. It was the second time in as many months that Greaves had abandoned the newsroom in the middle of a tough story.

"By the way," Greaves said without turning around. You're right. Ribicoff is your lead. Make him the hero he was tonight."

He suddenly stopped and turned back to face Logan.

"You know, it just struck me."

"What," Logan asked.

"Our government."

Danny shook his head, confused.

"You can count the hero's on one hand." He shook his head. "The leaders, the men with vision and courage... my God..."

It was if he didn't want to say it.

"They're all gone."

Eighteen

~~~ ❧ ~~~

November, 1968

The Vietnam War dragged on through the tense summer months. The Pentagon launched new offensive operations in the Mekong Delta with little effect and the conflict remained mired in stalemate. With each passing day, America's support for the war effort weakened.

On October 31st, President Johnson, desperate to end the conflict before the upcoming elections, announced the commencement of Peace Talks in Paris in early November. Further, he ordered the cessation of all air, naval and artillery bombardment against North Vietnam. The news was promising but hardly enough to raise the country's barometer of hope as Walter Cronkite continued to announce the daily casualty counts on the evening news. The endless stream of flag draped coffins still poured into Travis Air Force Base in California.

Republican Richard Nixon was elected the 37th President of the United States on November 5th, narrowly defeating incumbent Vice President Hubert Humphrey. Nixon had campaigned on a platform of "Peace with Honor" in Vietnam and successfully created an illusion of having a "secret" plan to end the war.

Americans welcomed the end of 1968, a year of tragedy and violence and there were few reasons to celebrate. It was a country painfully divided on every front.

Perhaps the only uplifting news of the tumultuous year was the continuing success of NASA's Apollo program. The Apollo manned space program was an aggressive response to President Kennedy's 1962 challenge that the U.S. land a man on the moon before the end of the decade, "because we choose to do so." It was a direct attack on the post war malaise that he felt was an impediment to American progress and prestige around the world.

The most powerful nation on earth was desperate for an achievement to rally around. NASA's bold men, with brains equal to their enormous courage provided at least a taste of the inspiration that America hungered for at the end of the decade,

In mid November, the space agency announced a change in mission for the last Apollo flight scheduled for 1968. The new plan for Apollo 8, only the second manned flight of the program, shocked the country with its audacious undertaking. Leapfrogging its cautious testing schedule of multiple missions leading to a lunar landing, NASA management threw the rulebook away. It announced that the crew of Apollo 8 would, for the first time in history, leave the relative safety of Earth's orbit and travel to the moon. There, the crew would enter into a lunar orbit and circle the celestial orb that had been the dream of dreamers since Jules Verne had penned the science fiction novel, *From The Earth To The Moon* in 1865.

"NASA's taking a hell of a risk here, but the PR strategy is brilliant," Greaves said at a meeting of the writers he had assigned to cover the story. It was late. The last edition was already on the street.

"If this thing goes off as planned, those three guys will orbit the moon on Christmas Eve and head for home on Christmas day." He smiled, something he rarely did of late. "Brilliant. They'll have two days of page one, top of the fold headlines in every paper in the country and probably 50 million television viewers. For free."

Greaves singled out writers for technical features, close ups of the three astronauts and their families and the actual event. He saved the best for Logan.

"Danny, I want you to lead with whatever it is these guys say when they emerge from that first pass from behind the back side of the moon," he said. "In those words we'll find our headline, barring disaster."

Logan nodded.

"On it, sir," Logan responded. "I'll get in touch with NASA public affairs today, although I doubt they'll tip their hand," Logan responded.

"Right, but give it a shot," Greaves said, ending the meeting. "Ok, let's get back at it and hope we can make it through to the end of the year covering the Nixon transition stuff, boring as it is. This editor has had enough blood and tragedy for one year," he added sadly.

Abruptly, Charlie Holcombe came into the room just as the meeting was ending.

"Danny, hang back for a moment will you?" Charlie and I need to talk with you," Greaves said quietly.

Logan nodded and sat back down in his seat. His face gave away his concern. Unscheduled meetings with the managing editor and the head of personnel weren't to be taken lightly. What was this all about?

"Relax, Dan," Holcombe said, reading his apprehension. "The Apocalypse has been postponed. At least until tomorrow." He smiled, trying to ease the tension.

"Listen," Greaves said running this fingers through his thinning hair. "If you haven't noticed, I'm not getting any younger. And frankly, I'm not sure I can take another 12 months like these last. Emotionally or physically."

Logan nodded in silence, but didn't have a clue where the conversation was going.

"I'll bet you remember the day we hired you," he continued, leaning back in his chair, "and what Charlie here described to you about the qualities that make a newsman."

Logan nodded again.

"He told you, 'You wanna be a newspaper man, you gotta have a nose for news, ink in your blood and like the taste of newsprint for breakfast.' Am I right?"

Logan laughed. "Yes sir. I believe that's an exact quote."

It was Greaves' turn to laugh.

"I know it's an exact quote because that's what I told Charlie the day I hired him. And he's been using the line on every new hire ever since."

Holcombe just smiled, glad to be a witness to what was about to happen. He'd always had a good feeling about this kid.

"The problem is, those aren't just words. This game does get in your blood. In fact, it'll kill you if you let it. You see, the one thing we forgot to tell you is, 'Don't ever let it get personal.'"

Holcombe nodded in agreement.

"Unfortunately, I've broken my own rule, Danny," Greaves continued. "Everyday, every story, every take, every word... it's all become very personal now. I've forgotten how to leave my emotions checked at the door."

Logan had to say something. "Mr. Greaves, the reason everyone here respects you so..."

Greaves waved him off.

"I can't have them respecting me for showing my emotions and walking out when the big bell goes off, Dan. Just take my word for it."

"Yes, sir."

"And I need to do something about it."

"Sir..." Logan leaned forward in his chair. "You can't..."

"I'm not going to quit, Dan. Because you still have a lot to learn and I have more work to do. I'm about to become your full time teacher. Because effective January 1, you're the new Assistant Managing Editor. If it works out..."

"And it will," Holcombe interjected.

"You'll replace me as managing editor in a bunch of years when I retire," Greaves concluded.

Logan blinked rapidly a few times, then fell back into his chair, not sure he had heard his boss correctly. His face was void of any expression.

Greaves laughed at Logan's reaction.

"That's one of the things I like about you so much, Danny. You always take everything for granted," he said facetiously. Logan was so confused he took

Greaves literally until the managing editor allowed himself a broad grin.

"Earth to Logan, this is good news," Holcombe said, realizing that his prodigy was dumbfounded by what was happening.

"You've worked hard, kid. I couldn't be prouder of you," Greaves said.

"That makes two of us," Holcombe added.

Logan finally found his voice.

"You're not just kidding me here?" he asked, his voice cracking with emotion.

Greaves and Holcombe both shook their heads.

"Have you ever heard me joke about my newspaper in any way?" the Greaves asked.

"You of course heard him say 'My newspaper,' Danny," Holcombe said. "That's what's so profound about this conversation. I thought we'd have to wheel him out of here. But no... the man who has guided The Hartford Times for more than two decades has found someone capable to succeed him. And did I mention competent?"

Logan swallowed hard.

"I don't know what to say..."

"You don't have to say anything, Dan. Just watch and listen closely," Greaves said. "Even more closely than you have over these last few years. You'll learn fast, but frankly I already have enough faith in you to hand you the paper from time to time."

"Maybe you have too much confidence in me, sir. I haven't taken those opportunities lightly," Logan confessed.

"I know you haven't. Actually, I knew you were scared to death. If you hadn't been, if you hadn't shown me humility and respect for the awesome responsibility of reporting the news in a timely and accurate fashion I wouldn't have turned out the lights in my office. The truth is, a couple of the best papers we put out last year happened on days when I couldn't hack it and gave you the keys to the press room."

Greaves slowly pushed his lanky frame out of the chair and stood up, extending his hand to Danny Logan, the new Assistant Managing Editor of The Hartford Times.

"Thank you, Mr. Greaves, " he said shaking his hand vigorously. Then he turned to Charlie Holcombe.

"I remember being so green that I had to ask you what a 'take' was, Mr. Holcombe. I didn't deserve the opportunity you gave me."

"I'd say you've proven the contradiction of that to me a thousand times, Danny. I'm proud to tell people I hired you. Hell, you give me credibility," he said, laughing.

"Let's give it hell, Dan," Greaves said. "We both know 1969 is going to be no picnic for the country — or Hartford for that matter. I'm predicting it's going to be another long, dramatic 12 months that will leave us all a little breathless."

"I'm with you on that, sir. This country, and this city, are slow ticking time bombs. Let's hope Nixon can lead us out of this mess."

"I wish I had confidence in that, Dan. But I don't — any more than I have confidence in the Hartford municipal government stepping up to what ails this once great city," Greaves responded. "It's very important that you keep your ears to the ground, Dan. Let's hope this newspaper can be an instrument for change in Hartford. And on that note, I'm going home. Goodnight, fellas."

Logan took a deep breath and headed for his perch on the roof of The Times building. It was nearly 10 o'clock. The air was cold and winter was almost upon the small metropolis at which he gazed as the conversation with Greaves kept playing over and over in his mind.

Atypically, it came to him that he should celebrate somehow. It was the kind of news to share with a mom and dad, a best friend, a lover. The thought made him feel empty. A drink perhaps? No. For the moment, he wanted to feel something special — like he, Danny Logan was special, that he belonged to the stars.

A lover.

The urge came from his heart before traveling to his head.

What better way to celebrate than a phone call to the woman he loved?

"Don't even think about it, Dan," he whispered into the cold night air. But it lingered, taunting him.

Did he dare?

He suddenly remembered Romeo's response to fear.

"I defy you stars."

"You're going to regret this in the morning," he thought to himself as his heart won the battle.

Logan walked home slowly, wanting the time to think. He was nervous about the change in his career, but he knew he could handle it. What was unnerving him was thinking about what he was going to tell Elina.

Holcombe had insisted he install a telephone in his apartment in the event the paper had to reach him. Reluctantly he had obliged. Now he was happy to have it in the privacy of his own space. He telephoned Elina's Cambridge apartment but there was no answer. In his wallet he carried the number of the rehab facility that Charles had been admitted to and considered calling it. But he worried about how his news would be received given the challenge his old friend now faced.

Hell, he thought. I'm not looking to talk to Charles. He dialed the number.

He was connected to the receptionist at the hospital who surprised him with news that Anderson had been released the week before.

"Did he leave a forwarding address?" he asked the receptionist.

"I'm sorry. Did you say you were family?" she asked.

"No, just a friend," he responded, and suddenly recognized he was actually neither.

"I'm afraid I can't release that information," she replied politely. Before he even hung up the phone he knew where Elina was.

With Charles at the mansion in Fenwick. It was all going according to her plan.

He hung up the telephone and stared at it for the next half hour. It was nearly midnight when he finally summoned the courage to call her in Connecticut.

Despite the lateness of the hour, the phone rang only twice before being picked up by one of the household staff Don Hanson employed. Logan apologized for calling so late but inquired if Elina was still awake.

"Why yes she is, Mr. Logan, I believe she's tending to Mr. Anderson. Let me see if she is available to take your call."

The line went silent for only a few minutes. He heard Elina say, "I'll take it in here."

He braced himself for her voice, immediately regretting having made the call.

"Danny? Danny? What's wrong? Why are you calling so late?" she asked. He thought he heard a tremble in her voice.

231

"Elina… I'm so sorry. I shouldn't have called. Nothing's wrong. I just wanted to tell you…" He paused, losing his nerve. It wasn't such a big deal after all, he thought.

"What? What, Danny? Tell me what?"

He didn't answer.

"Danny, whatever it is, I'm all ears. It's so lovely to hear your voice. Tell me, please…" she begged him, sounding so sincere that he had to answer.

"It's so late, Elina, I don't know what I was thinking. And I haven't even asked about Charles…"

"Charles is fine," she said, not allowing him to change the subject. "Why did you call, Danny? I've missed you so much."

He felt the familiar flutter in his chest at her words. If only he could believe them.

"I, uh… well, you see…"

"Just spit it out for Christ's sake, Danny!" Elina responded, exasperated.

"Well… I was promoted to Assistant Managing Editor of The Hartford Times today," he said hurriedly, then paused. He thought he heard her suck in her breath "It's the first step to being named Managing Editor in a couple of years when Mr. Greaves retires."

Then there was no doubt that he heard the catch in her throat as she began to cry.

"Why, Danny Logan… that's just incredible. Incredible? It's remarkable! You're going to be one of the youngest managing editors in newspaper history, I'll bet. I've got to tell my father, he'll be…"

"No, Elina, don't tell your father, please," Logan said quickly.

"Danny, let it go…"

"No, I have my reasons."

232

"Oh, bother. But to hell with my father for now," she said. "I am so proud of you Danny. What an amazing achievement! We have to celebrate. I have to see you to give you a giant hug! What fantastic news!"

"Elina…" He felt the first pull at his heart strings. It was always the same.

"I don't think that's a good idea."

"When have we ever been a good idea…" she asked. He couldn't answer.

"Did you get your car back?"

"No."

"Don't you think… oh, hell, can you get one?" she pursued.

"Well…maybe. Why?" he asked.

"I'll meet you at Cornfield Point," she said, "at our beach, in two hours. You know where I mean." The line went dead.

Logan looked at the phone wondering what had just happened. He shook his head. Just as fast he dialed Charlie Holcombe's number.

"Hello?" a voice, groggy from interrupted sleep answered the call.

"Can I borrow your car?" Danny asked.

"What? Danny? Is that… what the hell. Why?"

"Don't ask."

Holcombe sighed. "Ok."

"Can you pick me up? I'll drop you back at your house."

Logan heard another sigh.

"It's the broad, isn't it?" Holcombe guessed. Logan didn't answer.

"Yah, sure. After all, you're going to be my boss." Holcombe hung up. He was outside Logan's apartment in 15 minutes.

"You owe me," he said to the reporter.

233

"I know. In many ways."

"No, just for this. It's against my better judgment." They rode in silence back to Holcombe's house in West Hartford.

"Thank you Mr. Holcombe," Logan said.

Charlie Holcombe closed his eyes and leaned his head back. Danny Logan was like the son he had lost.

"Don't let her break your heart again, Dan. Good night. Drive carefully." He got out of the car and walked into his house without looking back.

Logan made his way to Route 9 through Middletown and was in Old Saybrook in 40 minutes. He was 20 minutes early as he pulled Holcombe's Cadillac into Cornfield Point and parked in a dark spot near the beach.

Their beach.

He got out of the car and walked down to the water's edge, sucking in the fresh, ocean air. There was a full moon and the tide was out. It was also freezing cold and a wind was blowing harder by the minute.

"Hey handsome," a voice called out from the shadows. "Remember this place?"

Logan's heart stopped.

"How could I ever forget it?"

Elina stepped away from a wooden jetty ten yards away and he saw her in the moonlight.

He thought it possible that his heart might not restart.

"Congratulations," she said, running to him and wrapping her arms around his shoulders. She stared up into his eyes for a long, silent moment then leaned forward and kissed him with the same passion she'd had on their first date.

Logan's head was spinning, knowing that everything about this scene was wrong. But he couldn't break off the kiss. He held on to her as if she was hanging over the edge of an abyss.

"What are you driving?" she asked, pushing back from him.

"Holcombe's car..."

"What make is it, silly?

"A Cadillac."

"Bigger than the Healy, let's go," she answered and took his hand. "Lead the way."

"Elina..."

"I said we need to celebrate. There's no better way I can think of, Danny Logan."

"What are you doing to me, Elina? I'm not a toy..."

"What am I doing? Only what I've been dreaming about for the last eight months," she said, seductively. "Let's not think about it now, Danny. Later. Let's celebrate."

He led her to the Cadillac, fortuitously parked away from the streetlights and opened the door for her.

"It's not the Ritz... not even your apartment. But at this moment, it's our piece of heaven," she said, kissing him again before stepping into the car. He joined her, started the engine and turned up the heat.

"I don't know how long we'll need the heater," she laughed, pulling him down on top of her and reaching for his belt buckle.

He moaned in frustration.

"What about Charles?"

"He's sleeping."

Logan lifted his head and stared down at the woman he could not let out of his life.

"Later, Danny. Later."

His resistance was gone. He leaned back down and kissed her with the hunger of months of loneliness and need. Logan slipped his hands inside her blouse, cupping her full breasts. Elina felt him harden and wrapped her legs around his waist, urgently guiding him into her. She groaned with his thrust, unconsciously digging her fingers into his shoulders, holding on for the precious few minutes of mindless lust she had been fantasizing for months. Her desire for him had only grown in the years since the night they met at Fenwick, despite the distance and the impediments. She knew it would never be satisfied.

They coupled fast and hard, each craving every second together, the scent of their sex, the touching.

It was over too soon. They held their embrace on the front seat of the Cadillac, each afraid to let go. The reality of the inevitable was just too painful.

He spoke first.

"Charles…"

"Must we?" Elina whispered as she kissed his face over and over. "There's not much to talk about."

Logan closed his eyes. There was so much to talk about. But she had just given him the one answer he needed to hear.

"He's healing?"

"In some ways. But he will never be the same. And he needs me now, desperately, and what my father's money can give him."

He laughed. Or was it a whimper at the unfairness of it all?

"A life of ease, of gratification, entitlement. Is that what you mean?" Logan asked.

"No," Elina responded. "Therapy to learn how to walk again. To help him think again. Even to help him learn to talk again. That's what my father's money gave him."

He winced and spontaneously held her tighter.

"It's that bad?"

"He's making progress every day. Eventually he'll be able to live a semblance of a normal life, probably even hold down a job. But his Wall Street dreams are over." She paused, running her fingers through Logan's hair. "Charles Anderson is a man with a great future behind him. Not at all like you." Her eyes glistened with tears.

His heart hurt.

"Why did you leave me? Enough about being lonely..."

She sighed.

"I don't know. I was impetuous. And arrogant. Maybe I liked his big dreams. And the fact that he had no qualms about moving back to Fenwick." She stopped, sensing that she wasn't satisfying his question.

"I know that saying I'm sorry isn't enough."

He laid his head back on her shoulder.

"You'll marry?"

"Probably in a year." She said it without hesitation, almost mechanically. "It will be a marriage of convenience. His, not mine. But it must happen."

She hesitated. There was more.

"But I haven't been totally honest with you. There is another reason. So selfish, but so real. You see, I will lose everything if I walk away from Charles. My drunken mother adores him, my father somehow feels responsible for what happened. I honestly don't know why. But they've made it clear."

He pushed himself upright to better see her face.

"What is there to lose?" he asked. "A loveless marriage? A relationship with your mother — who drinks because she's so jealous of how your father feels about you? What are you saying? Face it, Elina, you are

237

living in the middle of an ongoing tragedy. A real-life farce."

"Don't be hurtful, Danny, this is hard enough."

"I'm not being hurtful, Elina," Logan reacted. "I'm trying to wake you up. You're throwing your life away. I don't understand why."

"Because there are only two things that mean anything to me, Danny. But right now, I can't have both. I can only hope that someday that dream will come true."

"What in God's name are you talking about?"

"All I want in my life is you… and Fenwick. I will love you always, Danny, you fill my heart. But Fenwick? It is the only place that brings me peace."

"I still don't understand what we're talking about here," Logan snapped. "You sound like Scartlett O'Hara describing 'Tara.'"

She tried to make light of it.

"You'll never understand, 'Rhett Butler,' but Fenwick, that house, it is my 'Tara.' It's not just what you see, it's not just wood and shingles and rooms and walls and windows. Fenwick is the fragrance of the ocean, the salt in the breeze, echoes of the pipers and gulls, the moonlight over the Sound at night. I've been gazing at the stars above Fenwick since I was a little girl and fell in love with every one I can see. It is my Tara, Danny, and I can never leave it."

"So, why would you? Why are you telling me this?" Logan asked, completely confused.

"Because my parents have made it clear to me that if I don't stay with Charles I will not inherit Fenwick. Now do you understand? They will take away a part of my dream."

She stared at him, begging him to understand with her eyes.

"I can't let that happen," she said.

He swallowed hard, knowing that he had never felt the same way about anything in life, with one exception. And he was holding her this very minute.

"Don't try to understand, Danny, please?" she implored him. "But will you do one thing for me? Even if I don't deserve it?"

"Like I could say no..."

"Would you try to believe that someday you might share my dream — that you might belong here with me?"

He laughed.

"Belong here with you? Aren't you going to have a husband?"

She let out a long sigh.

"I said he will recover enough to carry on the semblance of a normal life. If I know Charles, it's only a matter of time before he picks up his bad habits again. And my loyalty does have boundaries." She looked into his eyes again.

"Danny... our time will come."

He shook his head at the lunacy of their situation.

"For now, I am an unmarried woman who desperately wants another memory before I climb back into my car. Think "This Boy" could help me out?"

Danny Logan didn't hesitate to reach for her again.

Nineteen

~~~ ဢ ~~~

Christmas Eve, 1968

On December 24th, for a few hours at least, Americans enjoyed a brief respite from the racial strife, civil violence and war in Vietnam that had brought their country to the brink of despair. Ironically, the catalyst for the short-lived taste of goodwill was a drama played out more than 250,000 miles from planet Earth.

On that winter morning, nearly three days after lifting off from Cape Kennedy atop a Saturn rocket generating 7.5 million pounds of thrust to break free of Earth's gravity, the crew of Apollo 8 ducked their spacecraft behind the moon and out of radio communications with the Earth. The world prayed for Astronauts Bill Anders, Jim Lovell and Frank Borman. It would be 45 minutes of silence from the black void before NASA would know if the crew were safe and had entered into orbit around the moon.

The tension built as the minutes ticked by and millions of people around the globe held their breath. Finally, at exactly the moment it was scheduled to occur, NASA Mission Control in Houston, Texas reported they had picked up Apollo 8's signal: "We've got it! Apollo 8 is in lunar orbit!" Command Module Pilot Jim Lovell calmly responded, "Good to hear your voice, Houston." At Cape Kennedy, Houston, and at NASA tracking facilities around the world, celebration was mixed with a huge sense of relief. For the next 20 hours, Apollo 8 would orbit the moon only 70 miles from its surface before heading for home.

The Hartford Times led its first edition that afternoon with the joyful news that the Apollo 8 crew was safe and their mission thus far was a success. Danny Logan's piece focused on the intensity with which the entire world waited for the capsule to emerge from the dark side of the moon.

Apollo 8 Unites Earth In Prayer
By Dan Logan

"The world was united for a few minutes today, perhaps like it has never been united before. Millions of people, of every nationality, country, gender and religion held their breath and prayed as the three brave NASA astronauts who left the bonds of Earth disappeared into the foreboding black void of space behind the moon and out of radio contact with mankind. For three quarters of an hour, hope and goodwill encircled our world. And the heaven's shook with celebration from all points of the globe when at last it was heard: "Good to hear your voice, Houston."

At 9:30 p.m. Eastern Standard Time on Christmas Eve, in the most watched television broadcast in history, Anders, Lovell and Borman provided Logan the rest of his story for the special edition The Times put out that night. As the Apollo 8 spacecraft passed in front of the moon on its ninth orbit, they each read from the Biblical story of life from the Book of Genesis, verses one through ten. But it was Commander Frank Borman who said the words that gave 1968 the peaceful ending it hardly deserved:

"And from the crew of Apollo 8, we close with good night, good luck, a Merry Christmas – and God bless all of you, all of you on the good Earth."

The Times printed a full-page photograph of the Earth taken by Bill Anders as the crew flew through the lunar sunrise. It was the first photograph of the entire planet ever taken by a human. Borman's words made up the headline:

Apollo 8: "...and God bless all of you, all of you on the good Earth."

Greaves called the newsroom together, every man and woman having worked tirelessly for two days. He had champagne wheeled in from the kitchen for a toast. It was not the kind of thing that happened often at a newspaper — any newspaper. Ad revenues and circulation were down at every newspaper in the country because of the growing influence of television news. But extraordinary work demanded an extraordinary act by the beloved managing editor. Even Lou White, the paper's rarely seen publisher who focused nearly solely on the business of keeping the newspaper financially sound, came down to join in the celebration.

"Great work, all of you," Greaves said. "It certainly feels like Christmas for the first time in a long time, eh?" There was nervous laughter in the room. There had been weeks of speculation that the managing editor would step down at the end of the year.

"I don't have to tell you that this has been a long, hard year. For America, for Hartford... yes, even for The Times. But we never gave up the fight to bring the news, and bring it right, to our readers. And as a newsman, I'm very proud of that and proud of all of you. Someday, we may look at this night as The Hartford Times in its finest hour."

Applause broke out spontaneously. "There wouldn't be a Times without you, Jim," someone yelled from the crowd. The cheering grew louder.

"Thank you, but you exaggerate," he responded. "To some our newspaper is just that. Ink on newsprint. But we know the truth," he said. "The ink on that newspaper is the blood, sweat and tears we put into it every day."

He paused.

"1969 is right around the corner gang, guaranteed to be as chock full of shock and dismay as the last year. But that only means we've got to work that much harder to ensure that The Times remains the best newspaper in Hartford... hell, in the country." The cheering rose to the high ceiling of the newsroom and probably could be heard up and down Broad Street.

He raised his glass.

"To the men and women of The Hartford Times, Merry Christmas, Happy Hanukah and may God bless us all."

They downed their champagne and cheered again.

"Now, before we leave this church of ours to the poor bastards who've got the night desk, there's something I want to share with you."

There was a collective groan.

Greaves laughed, knowing their expectation.

"Now that's not a very proper way to congratulate our new Assistant Managing Editor, is it?" he yelled.

The room went silent.

"Let's hear it for Dan Logan."

There was a whoop and a loud roar of approval. Logan was mobbed by his colleagues, who, despite his young age shared great respect for the prodigy of Greaves and Holcombe.

"Dan starts his new job January 1," he added. "It's not all good news for him. He's going to be moving into the office next to mine."

Laughter filled the building.

"Anything to say, Dan?" Logan asked.

Danny Logan shuffled forward awkwardly, uncomfortable with the attention.

"No, sir... except, I'm proud to be here, I'm proud to work with all of you. This is the only place in the world where I've ever felt like I truly belonged. " He paused for a moment, realizing how true that was.

"A very Merry Christmas and Happy Hanukah, everyone," he concluded, raising his glass to his colleagues. All but those covering the night desk and the team assigned to covering the news of Apollo 8's three-day journey back to Earth headed for home and a day off for the Christmas holiday.

Greaves wrapped his arm around Logan and shook his hand.

"Well done, Dan. The Apollo 8 coverage was spectacular. We'll sell out the special edition, guaranteed. Get some rest. Got any special plans for tomorrow?"

"Uh, just family, Mr. Greaves," he lied.

"Well, that ought to be fun," he replied. "My place will be jammed tomorrow with my kids and grandkids. Lots of laughter for the kids and cheap scotch for the adults. Why don't you come by later for the latter?"

"Thank you sir, but I'm sure my mom will be guarding the door to keep me there. I don't see them much."

"Yah, you sure are a busy guy with work and school. You gonna be able to handle it?"

"Try and stop me," Logan laughed.

As he left the building that night, Logan considered paying a visit to the rooftop in the hope he might catch sight of a shooting star. But the combination of fatigue, adrenalin and the growing despair of another Christmas alone pushed him out the door for the long walk home. It was bitterly cold and a mixture of snow and freezing rain was falling, making the walk that much more miserable.

His apartment was dark and empty when he arrived, as it always was. He usually didn't notice, but tonight was different somehow. He had no Christmas tree or even a candle or trinket to suggest it was a special time. Why would he? He couldn't remember ever celebrating the holiday, even as a kid. His father would be at a bar all day and his mother usually passed out drunk on the couch. All he remembered of Christmas was standing on Main Street, watching the animated Christmas Village display atop the portico of G. Fox & Co. with hundreds of other spectators. He would stand

245

there for hours, wanting so much to be part of the holiday excitement. But that was as close as Christmas ever got for him.

Merry friggin' Christmas, he thought. He tried to think about his work instead. Tomorrow would be a good chance to go in and move his office so he could hit the road running after the holiday. He had schoolwork to catch up on as well. He convinced himself that he could keep busy until the distraction of the holiday passed.

As he contemplated the great relief of getting some rest, the shrill ringing of the telephone that jarred the silence of his lonely night startled him. He let it ring. But whoever it was persisted. It rang and rang.

"What the…" Logan finally got up to answer it. It had to be the paper, he thought. Maybe there was a problem with Apollo 8. Who else would be calling so late?

"Hello?" he said gruffly into the receiver.

"Danny? It's Elina… I knew you were there," the voice said.

He was too surprised to say anything.

"Danny?" the voice called again. He winced at the sound of his name coming off her lips.

"Elina… to what do I owe the pleasure?" he finally said, embarrassingly tongue-tied.

"I just wanted to share with you how impressed my father has been by your writing the past couple of days," she said. "Why, all this evening he's been telling our guests that he knows you personally. I know his opinion…"

It was Christmas. A time to be charitable, Logan thought.

"That's very nice of him," Danny interrupted. "It was a great team effort, but a real pleasure to write something positive for a change."

"I can imagine. You were brilliant, Danny. I'm still so proud of you," she said.

He let it go.

"How's Charles?"

"Improving every day. He's able to walk without assistance, just using a cane. His speech is almost normal and he's actually shown a sense of humor lately. That's a major brain function improvement."

Logan rolled his eyes. Yah, Charles always was the life of the party, he thought. It was on the tip of his tongue, but he let it pass.

"I'm glad." He was already out of small talk.

Long seconds of awkward silence followed. Then she abruptly blurted out the real reason for her call.

"My father would like to invite you to Christmas dinner, Danny," she said quickly, then, "Don't say no, please…"

"What? He what?" Logan was completely taken aback.

"He wants you to join my family for Christmas dinner," she repeated.

"I thought that's what you said. Now tell me, Elina, why would your old man want me at your Christmas dinner table? You sure he didn't mean that I should come and join the help? Sorry, my TV dinner is already thawing."

She ignored his sarcasm.

"He really has grown to respect you a great deal, Danny… if you can believe that," she explained.

"Your father told me exactly how much he respected me the first time I met him, Elina. Some things are hard to change. Certainly, some things are also hard to forget, " Logan snapped back.

"Danny…"

"Elina…" He was about to take her head off at the lunacy of the call, but stopped himself.

"Look… I'm sorry. Forgive me, I don't mean to say hurtful things. But this is a bad idea."

"You said that the last time we got together," she pleaded.

"And I was right. Our little soiree has only made living without you that much harder." He regretted the words the instant they came off his lips. "I'm sorry. I shouldn't have said that."

She wouldn't back down.

"Come for me then, please?" she pleaded. "We can bundle up on the porch with a bottle of brandy after Charles is tucked in."

"And what will Charles think of all this?" he wondered aloud. "I find it hard to believe that he intends to share your affections…"

"Oh, Danny, that's just mean," she responded, brushing his sarcasm aside.

"Actually, I know Charles would really enjoy the opportunity to talk with you," she responded. "Or, more honestly, to try and win back your friendship. You will find that he has been humbled in many ways."

"Humbled? Charles? Elina, please don't make me laugh. I'm having a hard time feeling sorry for him. You make your own bed…"

She was silent.

"Jesus, you can't expect me to…"

"Danny, I pray that you never have to ask for a second chance. Because then you would know some of what Charles is going through."

"I'm afraid you think I'm a bigger man than I am, Elina. I'm fresh out of empathy."

"No. You're wrong. I know exactly what kind of man you are," she fired back. "You are full of compassion and care for others. That's what makes you such a great reporter and writer. But you're just plain angry with Charles."

You don't know the half of it sweetheart, he mumbled.

"What was that?" she asked.

"Nothing."

There was silence again.

"Interesting," she continued. "You found it possible to forgive me, but you can't forgive a man who was your best friend. A man who made a mistake."

"There's a big difference, Elina."

"And that would be?"

"I love you," he said impulsively. It just came out.

"Ouch…"

He sighed. "Sorry… the truth hurts, doesn't it?"

"Yes," she said. But it's also true that the relationship you two shared growing up isn't just going to disappear like it never happened. You were much too close for that to happen. The truth is you're both hurting."

Logan's anger was simmering just below the surface of the next words that would come out of his mouth. He had to force himself to be silent.

"Look," Elina said. "We could do this this for hours. It won't change anything. But maybe I still believe that Santa Clause will bring me what I want for Christmas. If you can find it in your heart to be with me tomorrow, despite how you feel about my family… and Charles… you would be giving me the best present ever.

Dinner is at five o'clock. I'll make sure there's a place set for you."

Silence.

"I love you, Danny. Merry Christmas," she said and hung up.

Logan held the phone to his ear for several minutes, trying to resist the temptation to call her back and tell her just how angry he was. Instead, he followed Paul Carducci's advice one more time in his life and counted to ten.

He hung up the phone and stared out the window.

It was still sleeting outside. Park Street was deserted and the road and sidewalks were covered in a slippery white slush. The neon lights of bars and bodegas cast a wild array of fluorescent colors up and down the street. A wreath hung in the window of one of the bars. The words "Feliz Navidad" circled it in flashing Christmas lights.

This was his world now, he thought silently. Not Fenwick.

What was she thinking?

"Fenwick," he said aloud, mocking the name.

He closed his eyes and imagined the house on the ocean. He hadn't seen it in years.

Suddenly, a vision of Elina's world came to him. The mansion that meant so much to her.

There would be a huge wreath of real spruce boughs decorated with a carefully tied, red velvet ribbon hung on the massive solid oak front door. A polished brass knocker of a bust of Father Christmas would be set in the middle. Inside, the grand foyer would be awash in a sea of potted Poinsettias that led directly to the great dining room. There a superbly cooked goose would be the centerpiece of a long exquisite dining table dripping with silver platters and utensils, fine china and Venetian crystal. The magnificent house would be decorated with Christmas trees in every room and there would a roaring fireplace. The scent of pine hung in the air. In the background was the ever-present crash of the ocean surf.

Fenwick.

Was that where he belonged?

No. Not by a long shot. But wouldn't it be nice to see what it felt like...

Just once.

He picked up the phone again.

"Mr. Holcombe?"

He heard a sigh at the other end.

"When?" Holcombe asked, instinctively knowing why he had called.

"Tomorrow. Until late."

There was silence.

"No. Let's do it now. I need to be here in the morning for my wife," he said. His voice cracked. "She's... she's having a pretty hard time."

He grimaced. How could he have forgotten about Charlie Jr.? They must be in agony.

"Oh, shit, I'm sorry, I shouldn't have called," Logan said, kicking himself for being so insensitive. Elina and Fenwick faded away.

"On the contrary, it's like a tomb here, Danny," Holcombe sighed. "Sometimes it feels like we have a contagious disease. People don't know what to say, so they don't say anything. That's hard enough. But you really don't understand reality until the holidays roll around and the empty chair at the table screams out at you.

"Charlie Jr. isn't coming home again..." Holcombe said the final words with a fatalism that was frightening to hear. But he was a newspaperman. And

251

that's how the world worked for men and women who dealt with tragedy and horror all the time, even when it touched them personally.

"Mr. Holcombe..." Logan was reaching deep for something to say. A writer should be able to do that, he thought. He blurted out the first thing that came to mind.

"Could I invite myself over for a drink? Things are pretty lonely here, too," he said, suddenly wanting to be near the man who had done so much for him as he grieved.

Holcombe perked right up.

"Why, Danny, that's a lovely idea. Arlene will be delighted. When can you come?" he said, an obvious tone of relief tingeing his words.

"Well..."

Holcombe laughed out loud.

"I forgot. I guess that would be just as soon as I can pick you up. See you in 20 minutes. And for Christ's sake, wear something festive. We've seen enough black around here to last forever."

"Festive? I'm not exactly..."

"Fake it." He hung up the phone.

Fenwick? Festive? His head was spinning. Then the craziest idea hit him between the eyes.

He threw on his coat and hurried down the stairs and ran up a block to the bar with the wreath with the flashing lights. He knew the owner. They spoke about Hartford a lot.

Hector Julian looked up from wiping down the bar top when he saw Logan walk in the door.

"Danny, my friend. Feliz Navidad!" Julian greeted him cheerfully. "That was some piece you wrote today, mi amigo. Go look, I have it taped on the wall over the urinal in el baño," he said, pointing to the only bathroom in the place.

"Now that's the big leagues, Hector, but thank you for the compliment. Big day for America, hey?"

"You're right, my brother. America could use a few more big days. But let's not talk about that while Santa Clause is in the air. What can I get you, the usual? On the house."

"No thanks, Hector. Actually, I was hoping to do a little Christmas shopping..." Logan answered.

"Logan? You been drinking already? Sage Allen is right up the street, maybe still open," he laughed.

"I don't think they have what I need, amigo," Logan answered.

Ten minutes later and $50 lighter, Logan walked out of the bar with his presents, shopping completed courtesy of his friendly bar tender. He walked back to his apartment and waited outside for Holcombe.

No more than five minutes later, the light blue Cadillac Seville pulled to the curb and Holcombe beeped the horn. Logan climbed inside with his treasures.

"What have we here?" Holcombe asked.

"Christmas presents. Something festive. Like you asked."

Hell, I would have been happy if you had worn a red sweater," Holcombe laughed.

When they pulled into the West Hartford driveway, his wife Arlene was waiting at the door. You could tell that she'd had a rough day by her red-rimmed eyes. She was wringing her hands.

"Hello, Danny, Merry Christmas," she said sweetly, hugging him.

"Merry Christmas, Mrs. Holcombe. I brought you something. He reached into his bag and pulled out a small Poinsettia plant that Hector had sort of wrapped in red foil paper.

"Oh, Danny, how thoughtful of you," she said, hugging him again. He felt her tears on his neck as she wrapped her arms around him. Charles Holcombe Jr. had been one lucky guy until his luck ran out.

He turned to his mentor and reached back in to the bag.

"And this is for you, Mr. Holcombe... or maybe the three of us can share it," he laughed. It was a quart of Johnny Walker Black, the most expensive bottle of scotch Hector had in his bar.

"Hell, that thing will sit there unopened for another 20 years, amigo," Hector had complained, then laughed. "I bought it on impulse. Not a big calling for expensive scotch in Puerto Rico."

Holcombe shook his head appreciatively. "You have good taste, son. At least in scotch," he laughed.

"Don't start on the poor boy, Charlie," Arlene admonished him. "You have a say over his paycheck... not his heart."

"Yes dear," he laughed and kissed her on the cheek. "I'll go crack this open."

"Wait, I have one more thing for you... for both of you. Something 'festive,'" Logan said, winking at Holcombe.

He pulled the blinking wreath out of the bag.

"What the hell?" Holcombe said, laughing.

Logan placed it in the center of the picture window in their living room and plugged it in. "C'mon outside. Close your eyes."

He led the couple out to the front walk. "Stop. Now open your eyes," he said. The words "Feliz Navidad," circling the bar room wreath, were blinking on and off every few seconds lighting up the front yard with a bright red glow.

"Mr. Holcombe, I guarantee you there's not another one like it in your neighborhood!" Logan said, grinning.

"I love it!" Arlene laughed aloud, slapping her hands together and giggling. Charlie Holcombe beamed at the sight of his wife laughing, her broken heart distracted by the ridiculous present. He turned spontaneously and threw his arms around Logan.

"Thank you, my friend," he whispered into Danny's ear. "You made her smile. I didn't think it was possible."

The three stood for a few minutes in the falling sleet, enjoying the only Puerto Rican Christmas wreath hanging in the well-to-do West Hartford neighborhood.

Finally Charlie Holcombe dragged them back inside and poured each a drink of the aged scotch.

Holcombe pulled his wife close to him.

"A toast" he said, "to the man who's going to steal my car again in pursuit of the wealthy heiress…"

"Charles," Arlene said, pinching him.

"Ow, I'm just kidding," he laughed.

"To Danny Logan," he continued, "best damned hire I ever made. Best friend, as well. Merry Christmas." They drank.

Holcombe's faced tightened.

"And to my son, Charles Holcombe Jr.," he continued, pausing to pull his wife closer still as she sobbed, "whom we miss this Christmas Eve and every day. May you rest in peace, son and know that you will always be in our hearts and our every thought." They drank again.

"And finally Charlie Jr., know that your friend Danny Logan is going to sharpen his quill even more

255

this coming year to help convince the world that this bloody war has to stop. He may not carry a gun, but he's just as lethal.

"'Scribe,' do me proud in your new job," Holcombe concluded. Danny was so touched he could do no more than nod, acknowledging a promise made.

They drained their glasses and several more after that as they sat in the living room and sang together while Arlene played Christmas Carols on the piano.

At 2 a.m. he bid them adieu and drove Charlie Holcombe's car home to Park Street. Hector let him hide the expensive car in his gated and locked rear lot for safekeeping. Then he climbed the stairs to his apartment once more and let himself into the darkness.

Bone tired, he sat at the kitchen table and mulled over the thought of calling Elina to let her know he was coming for dinner. He decided it was too late and put it off until the morning. He hoped his courage would still be intact and shook his head in confusion. Perhaps he should just show up.

He forced himself to stop thinking about it, instead recalling the impromptu celebration he had just come from. And he smiled at the thought of his first real taste of Christmas.

Logan wandered back to Holcombe's plea that he carry on with fervor the literary anti-war battle that was so personal to the grieving father. And then he remembered the words he sang while Arlene had played, *I Heard The Bells On Christmas Day*, the lyrics actually part of a poem written by Henry Wadsworth Longfellow, entitled *Christmas Bells.*

"...Peace on earth, good will to men..."

How brilliant and courageous he thought, as he recalled from his college studies of Longfellow's poetry the background behind the poem.

Longfellow had finished the seven stanzas on Christmas Day, 1864, despite grieving over the tragic accidental death of his wife in a fire and the paralysis his son had suffered after being wounded in the battle of New Hope Church in Virginia during the Civil War. Longfellow's heart was broken, yet he had somehow summoned the strength to continue to write and even to pen his hope for peace and good will amongst his countrymen.

Logan marveled at the writer's courage to continue on with his life and work despite the unimaginable emotional burdens he carried.

How did he go on?

His own sorrows paled by comparison to Longfellow's, yet he couldn't help but relate to the despair he must have suffered. Longfellow was already a celebrated poet by the time he wrote *Christmas Bells* and his personal tragedies were widely known. By comparison, Danny Logan was a virtual unknown outside of Hartford, and he hid his personal life and emotions carefully.

As a journalist, he was slowly finding his place in the stars, but so long as he was alone, his universe would be a dark place. There was only one person in the world that could ever lead him into the light, and she was the fiancé of another man. She was also the heiress to a fortune built by her father, who undoubtedly considered him a lesser man. He knew that Elina would never be his and with agonizing remorse that their relationship would never amount to anything more than painful verbal sparring that ended in desperate passion to satisfy their physical longings.

Danny Logan struggled with his all or nothing conclusion, but it was the truth and he had to face it.

At what cost, he wondered?

Somehow he had always been able to carry on while hiding his personal sorrow. Now, deep within him were the growing doubts that a life lived in lonely despair was not a life worth living at all.

Tomorrow he expected to witness a day of joy and family celebration unlike anything he had ever experienced. It would tell him a lot about himself — perhaps how much pain he could endure as an outsider looking in.

Logan put his head down on the kitchen table and closed his eyes for the first time in more than two days. Two days filled with elation, celebration, compassion, uncertainty and despair. It was a roller coaster of emotions that was wearing him down.

He had one final thought before falling asleep from exhaustion.

Could he find the strength to live without Elina?

Or, was he too weak to stop the descent into perpetual loneliness and depression that he knew had already begun.

Twenty

~~~ ❧ ~~~

Christmas Day, 1968

Christmas morning dawned much too early for Danny Logan, who needed at least another 12 hours to catch up on his sleep. The Apollo 8 coverage had sucked his energy reserves dry and the quart of Johnny Walker that he had helped the Holcombe's demolish resulted in him sleeping awkwardly bent over the kitchen table. What little rest he got was hardly refreshing.

The sun was streaming through the blinds of the living room window as he pried his eyes open and tried to get his bearings. His head was pounding and he was stiff from sleeping in such an awkward position. The muscles of his face were wrinkled and lopsided from resting on the hard table.

And then it hit him. Not that it was Christmas morning, not that he had a day off from work, but that he had decided to accept Elina's invitation to dinner at Fenwick.

Immediately, he was filled with anxiety. The thought of seeing Elina should have mitigated the discomfort of having to be in the company of Charles and the Hanson's. But Logan's deep rooted feelings of unworthiness, confirmed the very first time he met Don Hanson and his drunken wife, as well as Anderson's despicable disloyalty would not allow him to focus on enjoying the time with Elina. Instead, he unconsciously began stoking his fires for a confrontation.

All morning he fussed over what to wear, when to arrive and whether he should even call Elina and tell her he was coming. He kept telling himself that it was just a common courtesy, but the side of him filled with hatred for the bigots awaiting him at Fenwick overruled him from doing the right thing. It was only when it dawned on him that it might make Elina's Christmas more enjoyable if he called and politely accepted her invitation that he relented.

At noon, he called her. He was surprised when she answered the telephone.

"Danny! I was so hoping it was you," she said at the sound of his voice. He sensed her genuine delight and he relaxed ever so slightly.

"I just wanted to wish you a Merry Christmas and to accept your invitation for dinner... that is if it's still..." he stumbled.

"Of course!" she said. "I'm so happy. When will you come? Please come early?"

"Well, if I can ever decide what to wear, I could be there by three," he said.

260

"Any jacket and tie will be fine, Danny," she laughed. "No one is going to judge you by how you dress."

"Are you sure about that, Elina?"

"Danny..."

"I'll see you about three." He ended the conversation quickly. His sharp mouth would only hurt her.

He scurried around the apartment looking for a gift for the Hanson's, kicking himself for not thinking of it the night before. Then an idea came to him, but he'd have to stop by the paper. He put on his least wrinkled shirt and slacks, grabbed the tie he wore to interviews at City Hall and his one and only sports jacket then hurried out of the apartment.

Holcombe's car had survived the night at Hector's and he headed to The Times building. He went immediately to the printing press room where he knew he could find the press proofs from the Apollo 8 special edition. If Don Hanson was as big a fan of his story as Elina said he was, it would make a fine gift. It took him only a few minutes to find it and he looked it over with satisfaction. He remembered that same feeling when he had given the front page of the special edition a final look before authorizing it to be printed. He carefully wrapped it in sheets of fresh newsprint, then pilfered a red Christmas bow off one of the wreaths hanging in the building. It was perfect. On the way out, he stopped by his office in search of one more thing.

Logan opened his top desk drawer and there it was, the precious little piece of torn cardboard lying nearly forgotten in the bottom corner. It was his ticket stub from the night that he and Elina had gone to Shea Stadium to see the Beatles in August 1965. Their first date. She had often told him how much she cherished

261

the stub she kept because it reminded her of their illicit trip into Queens with him, right under daddy's nose. He began to reminisce over the wonderful time they'd had that night, the start of something he thought might last forever. The memory began to sour Logan's mood again so he forced himself to shake it off. He shoved the ticket into an envelope and put it in his jacket pocket. Now she'd have the pair.

Driving to the shore, he found himself excited to be seeing Elina without having to hide in the shadows. It was the first time he would ever be with her without having to sneak around. Then he remembered her idea of them "snuggling with a bottle of brandy" on the porch after Charles retired. Back to square one.

At exactly ten minutes to three, he pulled up to the mansion and parked the car in the street. He thought it would be presumptuous to pull into the driveway. Not that the Cadillac didn't fit into the environment. Hanson's new Rolls Royce Corniche was parked in front of the five-car garage, but there was also a Lincoln, two Caddies and Elina's Austin Healy. Logan figured the cars alone were worth more than ten years of his salary. He laughed when he thought of what a sight he must have been to Hanson when he pulled into the driveway with his primer black '57 Chevy hot rod the night of his daughter's birthday party.

For a moment he actually gave Hanson the benefit of the doubt. He wondered how he would have felt as a father watching someone like him ogling his daughter when she appeared by the pool in that skimpy white bikini. He could remember the scene like it was yesterday.

But just as quickly, he remembered how Hanson had treated him. Like so much trash. Logan didn't think he could ever make such a snap judgment like that about anyone. But then again, he wasn't a bigot.

"Oh, hell… here we go," he whispered aloud as he grabbed the package he had for Hanson and made his way to the front door of the mansion. It was on the ocean side of the house and the view, even in the biting cold of winter, made him pause and stare out over Long Island sound. The smell of the salt air, the waves breaking against the beach, the sky full of nothing but blue for as far as you could see. There wasn't a rooftop or a bridge or a telephone poll or anything to interrupt the incredible panorama.

He began to understand how Elina felt about Fenwick. A person could do some very serious thinking sitting on the porch staring out over that masterpiece. It reeked of a calmness he had never experienced before. A seagull suddenly flew across the horizon, and at first he thought of the bird as intruding on the horizon that had him mesmerized. An intruder? No, he quickly concluded. The gull belonged here. And therein was the problem.

Danny Logan didn't.

"Screw you, bird. But Merry Christmas," he said and laughed at the absurdity of it all as he walked up the steps to the porch. He stopped at the top of the stairs and took a deep breath. The huge wreath was on the door, just as he expected. The doorbell was 20 feet away. His heart was racing so fast it was like he was facing the last few yards to the summit of Mt. Everest.

He grabbed hold of the stair railing and clutched, seconds from turning and running back to the safety of his borrowed car. The only thing that saved him was Elina.

"Danny, you're here! Merry Christmas!" she squealed, flinging the front door open to greet him. Caught. His chance to run was gone.

Behind Elina were her parents, all smiles at the arrival of their guest. Logan swore he saw Don Hanson flinch as Elina ran to him on the porch and gave him a huge hug and a kiss on the lips.

She wrapped her arm through his and escorted him to the door. He felt like he was wearing lead boots.

"Mom, Dad, you remember Danny," she said excitedly.

"Of course," Don Hanson said, warmly extending his hand to Logan. "Merry Christmas, Danny, helluva story you wrote on that crazy Apollo 8 adventure. Brought tears to my eyes."

Logan shook his hand.

"Thank you Mr. Hanson, but as you might imagine, there were a lot of people involved in putting out the Apollo 8 special. I..."

"Nonsense. There always has to be a leader, son, and I can smell one from a hundred yards away. You're going to run that paper some day," Hanson said.

Logan looked at Elina, wondering if she had mentioned his promotion. She shook her head. "I wanted you to tell them, Danny," she whispered.

"Tell us what, Elina?" Hanson inquired.

"I really don't remember you," Betty Hanson abruptly interrupted the conversation. She slurred her words.

"What did you say your name was?" she asked Logan.

Danny smiled and looked at Elina. Her eyes were closed with embarrassment.

"Mother, please..."

"Betty," Hanson said, taking his wife by the arm, "this is Danny Logan, a friend of Elina's we met many years ago. He's going to join us for Christmas dinner."

"Oh, how delightful," she said letting her husband lead her back into the house. "We must have a drink before dinner, David."

"Danny, it's Danny, Betty," Hanson said. They disappeared inside leaving Logan alone with Elina.

"I'm sorry. She's drunk already. She's always drunk," Elina apologized.

"It's ok," Logan responded. "You'll remember that both of my parents are alcoholics. I know the drill."

"I keep pressing my father to get her some help but he can't bear the thought of her going to one of those dry out places."

"It's called rehab, Elina. That's too bad. She has so much to live for and your father obviously loves her. If she got help she could find a new life." He tried to be supportive, but Elina wasn't buying it.

"She's a bitch, Danny, a spoiled bitch. She's ruining his life, embarrasses him constantly. He's had to stop bringing her to company functions. The worst part is she won't admit to having a problem."

"Well, don't worry about me. I'm hard to embarrass. If she wants to call me 'David,' that's ok, too," he laughed.

"Oh, god... now I need that drink," Elina said, exasperated. "C'mon, let's go hit the bar before dinner and have a drink with Charles."

"Charles... oh yes, Charles."

"Danny, be ok with this, please? I meant what I said. He sorely misses your friendship."

Logan turned and looked out over the horizon again. The endless blue sky calmed him. The sun was setting already.

"Yah, let's go say hello to Charles."

"Please?"

"Elina…" he took a deep breath. "Let's just see where this goes."

She looked into his eyes, pleading, then led him into the house. He hadn't been inside the house in years, and even then only for a few minutes. But he immediately remembered the darkness of the interior. Such a beautiful house should be full of light… and life, he thought.

They walked through the long foyer, which was decorated with a virtual field of Poinsettias just as he had predicted, and into the living room. The fireplace was roaring and the smell of pine was everywhere.

Charles was sitting in a high-backed chair covered in dark brown velour. He sat unnaturally upright with his legs together and his hands resting on his knees. His hair had thinned out and was combed straight back. As Danny came around to face him, he was shocked by his old friends appearance.

The accident had scarred his forehead noticeably, but it was the look in his eyes that alarmed Logan most of all. They were distant, as if focused on something outside the room. He look awkwardly uncomfortable and out of it.

The sudden appearance of Danny Logan seemed to bring him back. A smile came to his lips and he slowly and gingerly stood up to greet him.

"Danny," he said in a subdued voice that Logan didn't recognize, "it seems like a million years. How are you?"

"I'm well, Charles," Logan said, shaking his hand. "More importantly, you seem well on your way to recovery."

266

"Well, I think we can rule out hockey or football as next career moves, but I'm coming along. A few aches and pains that are annoying, but they will leave me in due time. I read quite a bit... economics still fascinates me but it's real estate that has my eye at the moment."

He sat back down and resumed the awkward posture.

"Really..." Logan was caught off guard. There was so much the two needed to talk about, but Anderson had skipped right by the past.

"Yes, there's this bridge project being speculated, fascinating..." Anderson replied.

"Bridge?" Logan sat down across from him.

"Yes. A ten-mile span from Long Island to Old Saybrook. Crossing the Sound. It would have a major impact on real estate here. Perhaps on the economy of the State."

"Charles, you know that's just someone's pipedream... and besides, you and Danny have so much to talk about," Elina interrupted.

One of the house staff appeared before the conversation could continue. "May I get you a drink, sir?" she asked.

"Oh, thank you," Logan responded, glad for the disruption. "Elina, why don't you do the honors?"

"I'll have a scotch, neat, please," Doris. "Danny, with ice?"

"Yes, please."

"And the same for Charles," Elina said.

"I'm studying for my real estate license, Danny. Did you know that?" Charles was eager to pick up the conversation.

"Why no, Charles, the last conversation we had on the subject of your career was the kingdom you were going to build on Wall Street," Logan said, somewhat sarcastically but meant in jest.

"Wall Street no longer holds my interest, Danny, the real money to be made is in real estate and locally at that. Frankly, I was tired of Sloan..."

"Ah, I can understand the study of economics must be a real challenge, even for someone with a brain like yours..." Logan knew he had misspoken before the words were off his lips.

"The brain, yes, the brain. It seems mine does not function quite the way it used to," Anderson said without hesitation. "But I am comfortable that other capabilities will overcome what I've lost."

"Charles, forgive me, that was rather insensitive of me," Logan apologized.

"I'm sorry, why? No hurt feelings here, Danny. That may be one of the ways that my brain has changed, in fact. I am no longer as emotional as I used to be. That's a good thing, wouldn't you say?" Anderson responded.

Logan didn't answer immediately. He felt like he was talking with a robot.

"I'm not certain how to answer that, Charles. In my line of work, emotions are a liability that must be kept in check. But they certainly have a major influence on forming opinion."

Anderson turned and looked at Elina.

"To that end, what is your opinion of me now, old friend?" Anderson asked out of the blue.

"Charles..." Elina was as startled as Logan by his question and the almost arrogant tone in which he had asked it. It seemed to smack of, "I really don't care."

She turned to Danny, hoping he wouldn't lose his cool. But her guest wasn't about to be baited.

"Charles, I know you've been through a terrible ordeal. Our relationship before or after your accident shouldn't get in the way of your recovery. Let's leave it at that. Frankly, I don't dwell on the past," he lied.

"Of course you do, Danny. We were best friends. And I did the most despicable thing to you. I was disloyal and I stole your girlfriend."

Anderson didn't even blink as he said it, but turned back to Logan.

"Yes, you did, Charles. That's history. Over and forgotten," he lied again for Elina's sake.

"Is it? Or did you come here today to torment me, to punish me?" Anderson asked, stone faced.

Logan let out a sigh. He was beginning to think he'd made a big mistake. Not more than five minutes had passed since he'd arrived and already he was being challenged.

"Look…" Logan said, desperately trying to keep his cool, but he was loosing the battle.

"What do you want from me, Charles? To react in someway? Do you want me to come over there and kick your ass and make a fool of myself? Are you really dumb enough to want to piss me off?" His voice was rising with every word. Elina gasped.

"Oh, Charles… please, just shut your mouth. He came here to be your friend."

Anderson laughed.

"It wouldn't take much to 'kick my ass' these days, Danny, but I guess you already know that."

"What I know is that it's a waste of ammunition to shoot at a falling target, Charles," Logan responded. "But if you insist on continuing this ridiculous conversation, I'll be on my way." He stood up to leave.

Anderson laughed again.

"I'm just screwing with you, Danny."

269

Logan walked over to Charles, his fists balled, and stared into the listless eyes of his former friend.

"Don't," he said, his voice dripping with long unresolved anger.

Charles dropped his head, genuinely frightened by the rage he saw on Logan's face.

"Do I need to repeat it, Charles? Don't fuck with me," he said, pronouncing each word slowly for emphasis.

Charles looked up again, his eyes watering.

"I need you to be my friend again, Dan. But I don't know how it can happen after what I did." His tone had abruptly changed.

He paused.

"And I know you still love her."

Behind him, Logan heard a groan.

"Well... old buddy," he said sarcastically. "That's my problem."

Doris entered the room at that moment with their drinks.

"Thank you, Doris," Logan said and downed his scotch in a single swallow. "I would appreciate another, if you wouldn't mind. I'll take it on the porch please. I feel the need for some fresh air before dinner." He turned and began walking out of the room.

"Danny..." Charles called.

"Save it... for when your brains make their way back. You seem to be sitting on them at the moment." Logan went out to the porch to cool off. Elina walked by Charles without a word and followed him.

It was cold outside and the sun had set. The sound of the ocean was just beneath him but the darkness nearly hid the Sound completely. Only the phosphorescent tips of the shallow water surf made the shoreline visible. He looked to the moon, rising in the east. It was in the last day of its waxing crescent phase so only slightly more than a third of the lunar surface was visible. But it was enough on the clear night to take its place among the stars. He laughed to himself. This was not the time or place to look for his own elusive star. He needed to calm down. There were many reasons for him to leave Fenwick on this night, but he refused to be chased away by Charles Anderson's insane behavior.

He felt a touch on his sleeve.

"Forget it, Elina," Logan said without looking at her. "He doesn't know what he's saying."

"I don't know where that came from, Danny. All he's talked about all day is how good it was going to be to see you."

"I said forget it. He obviously needs more time to recover."

Elina took his arm and held it. He wanted to push her away, but resisted. It was obvious that she was living in a very stressful environment and he was not about to make it any worse. In fact, he was glad he had come now, if for no other reason than to show her kindness at Christmas. His experience with the Holcombe's the previous evening had taught him something. They were real people suffering from enormous grief. Yet an act of kindness had helped them to weather the nearly unbearable time. He considered sharing the story with his hosts, but wondered if they would understand.

Doris brought them their drinks. Silently, Elina took her glass and touched Danny's.

"To the stars," Logan toasted. She smiled and they drank.

"Thank you, Danny. Most men would have run from this crazy place. But you're not most men."

271

He didn't respond. The sweeter she was to him, the more it hurt.

Instead, he asked the question.

"So when are you getting married?"

She drained her glass.

"Ah... that," she said softly. The crashing waves nearly drowned out her response.

"Yes, that."

"I'm trying not to think about it, Danny," she finally said.

"Sort of a strange response, Elina." He turned to look in her eyes.

"Helping someone to recover is one thing, Danny. Signing up to babysit an angry lunatic is another. I'd rather we not talk about it. At least not tonight."

"I understand," Logan said. Although he didn't at all.

He changed the subject.

"What's this bridge thing all about?"

"Oh, it's some craziness some Long Island developers are trying to push. It will never go anywhere. But he's fixated on it, thinks he can make a fortune by getting involved. My father just ignores him every time he brings it up," Elina responded.

"Speaking of your father..."

"I'm sure he's upstairs with my mother trying to sober her up so she doesn't fall into her soup at dinner. I'm sorry you had to see that."

"Like I said, no problem.

She gazed out over the horizon. "I've tried to count them, you know."

"What?"

"The stars. There are just too many," she said.

"All you need is one," Logan answered.

272

"My father could give my mother the moon and the stars, in fact, they're probably the only thing he hasn't given her. And all he wants in return is for her to love him and stand beside him. No matter how much he accomplishes in life he will die with a broken heart. Isn't that sad?"

In the dim light of the moon, he saw a tear roll down her face.

"Yes, Logan agreed. He reached over and put a finger to her chin, turning her face towards him.

"But I understand completely."

She reached for his hand on her face.

"Dinner is served," Doris called from the door.

Elina turned away, dabbing at her eyes.

"I've suddenly lost my appetite," she said.

Logan rose to the occasion and extended his arm for her to hold.

"Oh no you don't. You're not going to get away with dragging me all the way out to this nut house without feeding me," he said.

She threw her head back and laughed out loud, immediately extinguishing her tears.

"Ah, you've finally caught on to us. We have invited you to Fenwick to fatten you up, get you drunk and make you one of us. We have a cell all ready for you tonight."

He leaned over and kissed her cheek.

"This is the best Christmas I've ever had, you know," Logan admitted.

"Actually, the only one. It's amazing..."

"I agree," Elina said. "That is really sad."

"No, you misunderstand me. What's amazing is that the first Christmas present I've ever received is to share dinner with the most beautiful woman in the world... whom I happen to absolutely adore."

He felt her shudder on his arm.

"Come, let's see if Charles has regained his sanity, your mother her sobriety, and your father his respect for a poor boy from the South End of Hartford."

She laughed again.

"You taking bets?"

"Do I look like a fool?" Logan answered.

They marched inside. Danny had a fleeting thought that he was about to experience what author Lewis Carroll had envisioned when he wrote, "A Mad Tea Party" in *Alice in Wonderland*.

Half way through a feast the likes of which Logan had never partaken, he wondered if he had the wrong novel in mind. It was if Scrooge had visited the Fenwick mansion while he and Elina were on the porch and spread his newfound spirit and humanity on the Hanson household.

Charles and Betty Hanson gave no evidence of their challenges and Elina's father could not have been a more gracious or welcoming host. It was if the first two hours of his visit had never happened. The conversation was light, with Hanson talking endlessly about the Apollo program.

At dinner's end, following an exquisite raspberry creme brulee dessert and a 1961 Cálem Colheita tawny port that Hanson explained he had shipped from Portugal just for the evening, the host offered a toast.

"First, allow me to express my gratitude that these two fine young men have graced our Christmas table this year," he began, lifting his glass to Charles and Danny. "I have come to respect you both a great deal, and if I had been fortunate enough to have been blessed by the son I always wanted, both of you would be outstanding role models for him. Charles, I wish you continued and speedy recovery, and Danny, continued success in the news business. There is no doubt in my mind that you will someday run The Hartford Times. So to Charles and Danny, may peace, happiness and good fortune fill your lives."

Then he turned to the women in his life.

"To my lovely wife, Betty, Merry Christmas my one and true love. I promise to keep you warm through yet another winter here in Fenwick and hope that we will share many more together." He paused. His profound love for the woman was obvious. Deep inside Don Hanson, Logan concluded, was the soul of a man with compassion lost in venality. He was capable of crushing the masses for an extra dollar of profit, but would carry his drunken wife to bed and lovingly tuck her in without judgment.

"And finally, to my darling daughter, Elina, the sunshine of my life. My hope is that you will find true happiness in life, and that you will always find it here in Fenwick. And to that end, I have just yesterday given my attorney instructions to redraft my Will, leaving this house and all its furnishings to you upon my passing."

Elina gasped, her perfectly manicured hands rising quickly to cover her gaping mouth. Betty Hanson showed no emotion, a well-practiced behavior, Logan guessed.

Hanson laughed at his daughter's surprise.

"I do this, Elina because I know how much this house means to you and that you will always care for and respect it. And also, of course, because I love you. Merry Christmas, sweetheart."

Elina burst into tears as Charles and Logan applauded. Betty sat quietly and said nothing.

"Daddy," she said, rushing to hug him, "I don't know what to say. There is nothing in this world that is

275

more dear to me than Fenwick — with the single exception of your love."

Logan squirmed in his chair. Where had he heard that before?

Hanson was elated as he held his daughter. Gratifying her was possibly the only joy the man had left, Logan decided.

"Danny, Charles and I are going to enjoy a cigar and brandy by the fire. Care to join us?" Hanson asked.

There was nothing in the world he wouldn't rather do, Logan thought to himself.

"Why thank you, Mr. Hanson. But I actually must be in the newsroom early tomorrow morning with the Apollo 8 team close to home. It's time for me to say goodnight and thank you for a lovely Christmas."

"Ah, a shame, but I understand. As I said earlier you're work on that marvelous adventure was nothing short of stellar. Very proud of you, Danny."

Logan knew he meant well, but somehow felt like one of the servants getting a pat on the back.

"Thank you sir," Logan said, feigning sincerity. "By the way, I've left a small token of my appreciation for you under the tree in the living room."

"Well, I must go and take a peek. Thank you, Danny and Merry Christmas."

Elina took his arm as her father left with Charles. Doris helped Betty upstairs to her changing room. They were alone.

"I know you were serious about leaving, but I was also serious about that brandy and the porch I mentioned last night. Especially the 'snuggling' part," she said to Logan.

"Elina, you are incorrigible," he responded, but did not resist being led to the porch. There he found a small wicker love seat, a blanket and a silver tray with two chilled snifters of brandy awaiting them.

They sat on the couch and Danny threw the blanket around them.

"I'm not kidding, I've got to hit the road pretty soon."

"I know," she whispered.

"But before I do, congratulations," Logan began, passing her a brandy. "I know how much this house means to you."

"I had no idea he was going to do that," Elina said. "I thought he would wait until after…"

He changed the subject, grateful that she hadn't finished the sentence.

"I have another question, but first I have a Christmas present for you."

She sat bolt upright on the couch and squealed with happiness. "Really? For me?"

"It's not much… but it's something that meant a lot to me… and I hope to you," he said, painfully aware of how romantically challenged he was. He reached inside his jacket pocket and pulled out the envelope."

She grabbed for it. He pulled it back. It was a game lovers played, wasn't it? He handed it to her. The sparkle in her ocean green eyes was dazzling.

"Merry Christmas."

Elina tore open the envelope, closed her eyes and reached inside. She felt the torn cardboard stubb and pulled it out, biting her lip as she realized what it was.

"The Beatles. Shea Stadium. The best night of my life. The best date of my life. With you." She held the tiny piece of paper to her chest.

"Now I have the pair, I keep mine with my other secret things in my bedroom. Things that mean the most to me."

Elina put her lips to the ticket.

"I have nothing for you."

"I've already told... you gave me the best Christmas present ever. The first one. It will always be the best."

She wiped her eyes.

"Now what was the other thing you wanted to ask me?" she said, still clutching the ticket.

"Yah. Can you tell me what the hell just happened in there? Did the Good Fairy sneak in and sprinkle 'Pixie Dust' over the dining room table while we weren't looking? I mean... everyone was so sane..." He smiled but he was genuinely puzzled.

"Welcome to my world, Danny. That's why I was so surprised by Charles' reaction earlier. Let us just agree my family is exceedingly dysfunctional and prone to brief fits of lucidity. But I emphasize 'brief.'"

She sipped from her snifter.

"It's getting very cold out here, Ms. Hanson," Logan commented.

"It's ok. One of the great joys I get from living here is being so in touch with the ocean. And with that comes the heat and the cold. Another joy is being completely removed from the world, if and when I choose," she answered.

Danny looked up at the stars and shook his head.

"The latter has little to do with Fenwick, my lady. Rather, it has to do with one's net worth."

"Why is it always about money with you?" Elina asked, annoyed. "There is more to life than money."

"I couldn't agree more," Logan laughed. "But money allows one to ignore reality and even to create your own. You would find that a person is much more focused on the value of money when it means the difference between eating or not. I speak from experience."

She snapped at him in irritation. "Are you always going to hate my wealth? It's not like I did something wrong!"

"No, you didn't do anything wrong. It's your destiny to be wealthy. And no, I don't hate you for your money. But the reality is money is the great divider between us. You are a have, I am a have not. From a relationship perspective, it's hardly a formula for success.

"To put it bluntly, Elina," Logan continued, "I don't belong here, I am a square peg in a round hole in the village of Fenwick. Your father was very flattering tonight. But do you think he would ever accept me as an equal — or as a son-in-law? I think not."

"My father... that was a long time ago under very difficult circumstances..." she said, trying to defend the indefensible.

"Yah, I dared to admire how pretty you were. Look, it's ok, it is what it is. It will be a cold day in hell before I am accepted into your social circle," Logan responded.

"I don't believe that. Charles... before his injury... was well accepted by our friends, by this community. And he certainly has no wealth of his own."

"That's because Charles is a chameleon, Elina, once smart and savvy enough to be able to change his stripes at the mere immersion into an environment that attracted him. He dreamed of money and power even when we were growing up. He had the rich kid act down pat before he even met you." Logan paused.

"I sound harsh?" he asked.

"Yes," she said.

"Maybe. But from the sound of our earlier conversation, you don't seem quite as convinced about him as before."

She turned away and began to cry.

"Shit. The whole point in coming today was to put a smile on your face. I'm sorry," he apologized.

Elina swung around on the couch and pulled him close.

"Kiss me. Now. Hard."

And he did. Long and lovingly. It went on for several minutes. They were seconds away from taking it to the next step.

Not this time.

Danny broke it off and stood. He drained the last of his brandy and turned to her.

"Merry Christmas, Elina, Lady of Fenwick. Thank you for having me. It was my first Christmas. An enlightening experience." He walked to the staircase that would bring him back to his car.

He stopped and turned back to her.

"And did I mention very enjoyable?"

"No," she pouted at his leaving.

"Or how beautiful you looked tonight?"

"Well, perhaps once… or twice…"

"Or that I love you?" He winced as the words came off his lips. That wasn't what he wanted to say. It only made the hurt that much worse. He really did lose control when he was with her. It was time to move on with his life.

"Not nearly enough," she said.

He smiled. But it was a sad smile.

"And that, Elina is probably a good thing."

He hurried down the staircase without another word and went straight to the car. Every ounce of him wanted to climb back up to the porch and take her in his arms. To tell her that he would fight Charles, her father or any other obstacle in the way of his having her.

Forever.

Instead, he pulled out of the driveway, stopped at the street corner and paused to look back at the mansion. He knew that she was waiting for him to come back, and hesitated for a moment. But sanity prevailed.

"No. You're just fooling yourself, pal," he said aloud.

"You will never belong here."

He gunned the big car and raced to the highway.

It was time to go home.

Twenty-One

~~~ ❧ ~~~

1969

New Year's came and went with American anxiety reaching new heights. Even before his inauguration to succeed Lyndon Johnson as President, Richard Nixon took aggressive steps to bolster the public's confidence that the war's end was in sight.

On January 1, a full 20 days before taking the reigns of government at one of the country's most critical junctures in history, Nixon appointed Henry Cabot Lodge, the former ambassador to South Vietnam, Republican Senator from Massachusetts and 1960 Republican vice presidential candidate to be the chief U.S. negotiator at the Paris Peace Talks.

In his inauguration speech, Nixon said "...the greatest honor history can bestow is the title of

282

peacemaker. This honor now beckons America..." The country prayed that this new man and his handpicked negotiator could end the bloodshed.

But Nixon, ever a calculating if not ruthless gamesman, was surreptitiously playing multiple hands as the Peace Talks began on January 25th in Paris.

In one hand, he was softening the rhetoric of war, boosting American hopes.

In the another, he simultaneously escalated the war, ordering the commencement of Operation Dewey Canyon, the last major American offensive of the conflict. Nixon's strategy was to stop the flow of North Vietnamese men and weapons into South Vietnam. Although the campaign was publicly declared a success, more than 300 U.S Marines died and over 700 were wounded in the exercise that ultimately led to the clandestine U.S. bombing of Laos, only ten kilometers from where Operation Dewey Canyon was fought.

And in still another slight of hand, Nixon had Secretary of State Henry Kissinger secretly performing back door negotiations at the apartment of a French intermediary with the North Vietnamese representative Xuan Thuy.

Americans would eventually learn that Nixon was not above exceeding his presidential powers or any other nuances of the law that might get in his way.

The U.S. media was paying close attention to the war in the first half of 1969, as racial tensions in the country seemed to waver during the winter months.

"It won't last," Mr. Greaves. "I'm telling you, the riots will start again. I know for a fact they will in Hartford because nothing is being done to fix the problems that led to the riots of the last three years."

"I hope you're wrong, Danny," Greaves said. "But I suspect not."

283

"This time, Hartford is going to light up like Detroit, I can feel it," Logan predicted.

For the moment, Hartford was quiet. But in the jungles of Vietnam, the war bled on as Nixon and North Vietnam President Ho Chi Minh played a gruesome chess match.

In late February, the Viet Cong launched more than 100 offensive operations throughout South Vietnam in response to the Dewey Canyon campaign. Saigon became a favorite target of the VC and dozens of civilians were slaughtered daily. On February 25, North Vietnamese Army regulars launched a surprise raid on U.S. Marine fire support bases near the de-militarized zone. Before dawn, 36 more Marines had died in the fierce fighting. Nixon retaliated by resuming the bombing of North Vietnam and ordering U.S. troops to go on the offensive in the DMZ for the first time in over a year. To many Americans, it appeared we were losing ground.

Nearly 545,000 American troops were now stuck in the quagmire and some 34,000 had been killed in action, a toll greater than the U.S. loss of life in the entire Korean War. Despite the American sacrifice, bloodshed and heartache, the billions of U.S. dollars being poured into the war machine and nearly five million tons of bombs dropped on the enemy — more than two and half times the explosive power used by the U.S. military on two fronts in all of WWII — the conflict was a stalemate.

In March, a frustrated Nixon dug in deeper and increased the B-52 bombings, covertly spreading the war into Laos and Cambodia in an attempt to shut down North Vietnamese supply lines along the borders. In less than a month, the *New York Times* broke the story triggering massive public and congressional protest.

In May, the Army's 101st Airborne began a murderous ten-day assault on Hill 937, the military designation for Dong Ap Bia Mountain in the A Shau Valley. Only 1.9 miles from the Laotian border, it was yet another futile attempt to cut off the supply pipeline the North Vietnamese had established along the border. Strategically, the mountain meant little to success or failure for the American military in the Vietnam conflict, but military brass were fixated on taking the hill. Among the troops fighting fierce resistance from the well-entrenched enemy, 937 was know as "Hamburger Hill" because of the way the troops fighting the battle "got chewed up like hamburger." It took ten days, but U.S. forces finally took the hill on May 20 at a steep price. In all, 72 U.S. troops were killed and 372 wounded

Inexplicably, on June 5th, the order was given to abandon Hill 937. Reaction at home was swift and sharp. Key members of the Senate were highly critical of the needless casualties and *Life Magazine* ran a special edition showing photographs of the 241 men killed in action in one week in Vietnam, including some from the Hamburger Hill Battle. The American public was aghast at the massacre and public opinion now solidly aligned behind the anti-war movement that was growing by the day. For Nixon and the Pentagon geniuses that had dug a bottomless pit into which America was pouring its young men, it was the lowest point of the entire war.

Managing Editor Jim Greaves and his assistant Danny Logan pushed the Hamburger Hill debacle for days across page one, never missing the opportunity to emphasize the illogic of U.S. military strategy and the horrific price being paid to win and unwinnable war. Logan interviewed Connecticut's high profile senior senators, Abe Ribicoff and Tom Dodd who leapt at the opportunity to lambast Nixon and the Pentagon for the waste of young American lives, calling it "senseless and irresponsible."

By July, Nixon was facing such vehement public and political outcry that he was forced to begin troop withdrawals. He announced that 800 troops from the 9th Infantry Division would be sent home. It was but a fraction of the U.S. Forces in country, but it was a start. And more importantly, Nixon pledged that withdrawals would continue in 14 phases between July 1969 and November 1972. It was the first time the President had hinted at a timetable for ending the war.

Holcombe couldn't hide his pleasure with his prodigy's work when he stopped by Logan's office after a meeting with Greaves.

"God dammit, Dan, it's the press that's going to end this war, I know it," he said. "Your fingers on a typewriter are as lethal as any M-16," he said.

Logan was still uncomfortable with such praise.

"Mr. Holcombe, I'm very grateful for your confidence in me, but the pressure on Washington to end this disaster is coming from many different directions. And it will only grow stronger. We can only hope that Nixon will find a way to expedite a magical formula for 'Peace with Honor' that will satisfy his ego. Personally, I don't think the average American would care if we just packed our bags in the night and were gone by morning with no explanation."

Holcombe shook his head sadly.

"I'm confused there, Dan..." he said, shaking his head.

"If that's how it ends, does it mean my son died for nothing at all? But at the same time, will it mean someone else's son doesn't have to die?"

Logan was silent. He didn't know how to respond.

"I tell you, I lose sleep over that question alone, Dan. I want something for Charlie's life. Some rationale. Some meaning. But I'm afraid, in the end, there won't be one. And I don't know if I can live with that..."

This was a conversation to have in a bar with a bottle and two shot glasses, Logan thought.

"Mr. Holcombe, I know it's not much, but I can only imagine that the parents of the thousands of boys who won't be coming home when this is all over are asking themselves the same question," Logan responded.

"I think the only way you'll ever find peace is to do what you're doing. Fight to stop the killing."

Holcombe buried his face in his hands.

"Charlie would be proud of you for that, sir."

Holcomb shook his head and left for his office. Logan wondered how the man got out of bed everyday with the burden he carried.

* * *

Even while Logan was sharing the emotional conversation with Holcombe, another more fateful drama was playing out not 50 miles away at the edge of Long Island Sound at the Hanson mansion in Fenwick.

Despite round the clock surveillance of Don Hanson's beloved wife by the house staff, at four o'clock that afternoon, Betty Hanson had somehow managed to slip out unnoticed and made her way down the treacherous seawall staircase to the beach.

She was inebriated and it was a miracle she hadn't fallen and killed herself on the weathered stairs. Only the hardening of years of drinking allowed her body to even function. Her resistance to alcohol had reached a point where she could still walk and talk after drinking enough to kill the normal person.

Wearing a signature Chanel jersey and slacks and an array of jewelry that simply dripped of wealth, Betty Hanson was as impeccably dressed as always and appeared ready to entertain a house full of guests. For a woman in her early 60's who had abused herself with alcohol for longer than she could remember, she was still a handsome, if not beautiful woman.

Friends as well as the envious would say she was blessed with a husband who adored her, a spectacular home with a view only God could create and the wealth to fulfill any fantasy.

But if anyone ever took the time to ask, Betty Hanson would tell you that she was cursed, a lonely, despondent women who's only identity was as a socialite married to a powerful business executive. There was no real Betty Hanson. The young Radcliffe graduate of many years before, full of inspiration and aspiration had simply disappeared, overwhelmed by a lifestyle that demanded of her a Stepford-like existence.

Now, lost in a cloud of alcohol that impaired her ability to reason, she had decided that today was the day she would find her new life.

By ending the hell that each day had become.

Staggering to the water's edge, she turned and looked up at the mansion she had once thought of as Cinderella's castle, so taken was she by its' magnificence. She sipped from the martini glass still in her hand, then tossed her head back and drained it. With all the anger she could muster, she threw the empty glass at the sea wall to smash it. It fell harmlessly to the sand yards short of its target.

Hanson nearly fell over in drunken, hysterical laughter. What a lady she had become, she thought. She couldn't even smash a martini glass in indignation. Not so long ago it had become her trademark for impetuous behavior, an excuse for her husband to rush her away from whatever god-awful social event to which he'd dragged her as his trophy bride.

She kicked off her Chanel sandals, each landing in the salt water and sighed. There was a time she wouldn't wear them in the rain for fear of them being ruined.

Reaching around, she unabashedly unzipped her cream-colored silk shorts and let them drop to the sand, then pulled her matching blouse over her head and threw it into the surf. She took several steps into the water and awkwardly removed her bra and panties, taking a moment to watch them float away. Betty Hanson was now stark naked and raised her hands over her head in joy at the sense of freedom that overcame her. In the house, a member of the kitchen staff watched her antics in confusion, not knowing what was about to happen. She ran to fetch Elina or Charles.

But Betty Hanson hadn't come this far to be denied. With more purpose than she had felt in decades, she began to walk out into the mild surf. It was high tide, and within only a few yards, her head was just above the water. Then she pushed forward into the ocean, launching into a slow crawl that took her another 50 yards or so from the safety of the beach. When she stopped, she realized she was exhausted and was desperate for a nap. With only a single last thought, she opened her mouth and let herself sink below the surface.

"Where did my life go?" she asked as the water that filled her lungs robbed her of the ability to answer her own question.

* * *

The telephone on Logan's desk rang and he reached for it. It was the receptionist. Odd, he thought.

"Yes?" he answered.

"Mr. Logan, I have a Ms. Hanson on the line for you. Shall I put it through?"

Danny sat upright in his chair. He hadn't heard from Elina since Christmas day. He glanced at his watch. It was near nine o'clock."

"Yes, please," he said, sounding more assured than he felt.

"This is Dan Logan," he said, feigning ignorance.

"Danny?" Elina said. She'd been crying.

"Elina... I'm so surprised to hear from you," Logan answered.

"My mother is dead. She's killed herself. Can you come?" she pleaded.

"What? She did what? Oh, my god, Elina..."

"I need you," she said.

He didn't hesitate.

"Yes. Give me an hour." He hung up the phone.

He sat at his desk for a moment, silently absorbing the few words Elina had just said. It didn't dawn on him until later that he had never told her that he was sorry for her loss. He poked his head in Greaves office and told him he had a family issue to tend to. He nodded, unquestioning.

As Logan walked to the parking lot, his head was spinning with questions and judgments. He wondered how it was that a woman who on the surface had so much could be so unhappy. And why did Elina call him? How could he possibly help? Where was Charles?

But then he spied his new girlfriend waiting for him just where he had left her that morning, and at least for a moment Fenwick faded away. It was the car he had bought after his last promotion, the only thing in the world that could drag him away from his darkest thoughts.

It wasn't much to look at, but his purchase was by design considering the neighborhood he lived in. It was a 1963 Triumph TR4, a British roadster very similar but far less powerful than Elina's Austin Healy. And it needed plenty of help, but that too was by design. Many a night after work he crawled under the old sports car, slowly rebuilding it in the safety of Hector's back lot. He worked with a single droplight but was good with tools and liked the feel of a wrench in his hands. Bringing the old car back to life was therapeutic, like massaging a lover's aches and pains away. The effort made you both feel better.

The car was black where it wasn't rust and had a red leather interior that needed some new hides and a lot of thread. But he didn't mind its' obvious shortcomings. She purred when he drove her because he had fixed all that ailed the car with his own brains and hands. In a way, the TR4 was like the mistress he didn't have and it occupied, a least partially, the hole in his life.

He felt his blood begin to roil as he pulled off the tarp that protected her insides while he was at work. A new top was not in the budget yet. It didn't matter. He reveled in driving the convertible hard and fast and the feel of the summer air buffeting against his face over the low windshield. And there was the sense of freedom that came with his hair (which had grown considerably longer over the last year) being wildly tousled by the wind rushing over the small, two-seat cockpit. He could only describe it as a kind of natural high: being at one with the road and the open air as he expertly shifted through the gearbox on winding country roads, listening to the roaring exhaust with a faint smell of gas and oil filtering into the cockpit. It wasn't quite a religious experience, he thought, but guessed it would be as exhilarating.

He thought of Elina whenever he drove the sleek sports car and in the time he spent at the wheel at least, his heart soared.

She started right up and he blipped the throttle a couple of times to warm up the four-cylinder engine with its dual Stromberg carburetors. He smiled. But then remembered why he was about to drive to Fenwick. The smile disappeared from his face.

Less than an hour later he pulled onto Pettipaug Avenue in Fenwick and stopped a short distance from the mansion. There were cars parked everywhere. Hanson had a lot of friends. He noticed at least two police cruisers.

It came to him as he studied the great house that for some reason it intimidated him. How was it he wondered that a structure of wood and stone could make him feel inferior, like less of a man? He couldn't answer the question, but he knew the feeling was genuine.

He parked some distance away and walked slowly to the house, pausing again as he had on Christmas day to take in the ocean. It was dark again, but the sound of the shallow water surf and the smell of the ocean was invigorating, almost like a shot of adrenalin. He'd need it for what was ahead.

Logan made his way up the stairs but was only half way up when Elina met him and threw herself into his arms. Charles stared down at them from the porch.

"Danny," she said, hugging him and kissing his neck. "Thank you for coming... I need someone to talk to so badly..."

"I'm so sorry," he finally told her. "What happened?" She just shook her head and hugged him again.

Logan took her hand and led her back down the staircase to the beach. They walked half way to the waters edge and sat on the sand, still warm from a day baking in the sun. The police had long since completed their investigation and were gone. Her clothes and the unbroken martini glass had been recovered as evidence. The only remembrance of Betty Hanson on the beach that day was footprints that one would have to search to find.

"Oh, Dan," Elina explained, sobbing. "She'd been drinking all day... like everyday... but came down to the beach about four o'clock for some reason. She had to have snuck out of the house because all the help were supposed to be watching her."

She paused, wiping tears from her cheeks.

"My father is a mess. He can't understand..."

"I'm sorry for him, too, Elina," Logan said sincerely.

"He hasn't really seen her in days. She'd still be sleeping when he left for work in the morning and was passed out drunk by the time he got home. He carried her to bed every night."

"How awful... for all of you..." Logan said.

She leaned over and put her head on his shoulder, tears rolling down her cheeks.

"You said she killed herself?" Logan asked, confused.

"Yes. The police said she drowned herself. One of the kitchen help saw her do it. She took off her clothes and went into the water then stopped to look back at the house. But then she dove in and kept swimming out into the ocean until she couldn't go any more... and disappeared."

"They haven't found her?"

"The police divers found her body about six o'clock, before the tide pulled her out into the sound," she said.

"There was no one with her?"

"No," Elina shook her head in remorse. "She wasn't easy to be with, Danny. I think she hated me."

She cried aloud while Logan stroked her disheveled, sun-streaked hair.

"Jesus Christ, she's dead," Elina said, as if understanding it for the first time. "Why would she do that to my father? He loved her so... gave her everything..."

Logan was silent, letting her talk.

"Why Danny, why would she do that? It's so cruel!"

He stared into her beautiful eyes for a moment before responding.

"I don't know, Elina, I don't. Perhaps we'll never know. She didn't leave a note, or a letter... some explanation?"

"No, not that we've found," Elina said, lying back on the sand.

"You know she's needed help for a long time," Logan continued. "She was hurting... I don't know why. But I know from experience that drinking numbs the pain. Maybe being drunk didn't work anymore. Maybe she couldn't stop the pain."

"Why would she be in pain? She had a husband who adored her, everything she could want..." Elina sobbed.

"She had everything, Elina, you're right. Perhaps everything but companionship and purpose," Logan blurted out. He regretted it at once.

"What do you mean, Danny? My father was always there to hold her hand."

"It seems she spent all her hours rambling around this house, under guard, Elina. What she needed was help."

A fury appeared in her eyes.

"Are you blaming me? My father? Do you think we wanted her to kill herself?" she answered, her voice raised.

"I said nothing of the kind, Elina, calm down. I came because you said you needed to talk to someone. Here I am. I'll just nod my head up and down if you prefer," Logan responded.

"I'm sorry if I was harsh, it wasn't intended. Far be it for me to second guess your life," he said.

She sat back up. "I could have gotten more sympathy from Charles, and he just stares out the window as if nothing has happened."

Logan let out a loud sigh.

"I am sorry, Elina, for your father, too. But I think it's important that you put this into perspective and face facts."

She turned to look at him, defiance on her face.

"You hated your mother. She was a psychological mess who needed serious help. Your father gave her everything but what she needed."

He paused when she didn't respond and looked out over the faint light on the horizon across the Sound.

"It's not going to help you by blaming her now, it simply isn't. And it won't help your father who I'm sure is dealing not only with grief right now, but guilt and regret as well.

295

"I'm sorry if I've hurt you. I would never do that intentionally. But eventually you have to stop living in fantasy land and this seems like a pretty good time to start."

She turned away.

"I think it's best that I leave now, Elina. Again, I'm deeply sorry for your loss." He got up to go and glanced up at the house. Charles was still looking down at them. Someone else who needs some serious help, he thought to himself.

He leaned over and kissed the top of her head and made his way back to his car. She didn't follow him.

At the corner of Pettipaug Avenue he stopped the car and looked back at the house again. Betty Hanson's absence was invisible.

It was still a house of misery.

Twenty-Two

~~~ ॐ ~~~

July, 1969

On July 21, at exactly 10:56 p.m. EST, the world came to a virtual standstill as a lone American astronaut sprang from the last rung of the lunar module *Eagle's* ladder and stepped onto the moon. For the 500 million people in 196 countries who watched in wonder as television broadcast Neil Armstrong's first step onto the dusty, grey lunar surface, a sigh of relief and a cry of celebration in more than 6,900 languages could be heard around the Earth. It was perhaps the most unifying event in the history of mankind, and for a moment, the world's ills took a back page.

In the newsroom of The Hartford Times, where reporters had gathered around televisions for ringside seats at man's most incredible adventure, Assistant

Managing Editor Dan Logan gave the go ahead to print the special edition commemorating the accomplishment.

"One Small Step for Man... One Giant Leap for Mankind"

It was the headline that graced the top of newspapers across the country as well as The Times. Editor's Greaves and Logan couldn't conceive of a more powerful or moving message than the first words Armstrong had spoken, as he became the first man to step on the moon.

The Apollo 11 mission, culminating with the first manned landing on the moon, was the capstone of President John F. Kennedy's challenge to the country on September 12, 1962 before 35,000 people at Rice University. Logan, only 16 years old when Kennedy delivered one of the most memorable speeches of his all to brief presidency, had been excited by the sheer audacity of Kennedy's call. Personally giving the "go" order to roll the presses for a newspaper expressly written to celebrate the martyred president's dream was a high water mark for the young editor. But the irony of the accomplishment by a country mired in war and violence at home and abroad was not lost on him.

"Why is it that a country that has the ability to build a machine comprised of billions of components that didn't even exist just a few short years ago, that is capable of carrying men 250,000 miles into space, landing on the moon and safely returning..." he paused, shaking his head in frustration. "If we can manage all that how is it that we can't find peace in our own cities and streets, treat men as equals and stop fighting wars with no purpose? Why can't we stop killing each other?"

Greaves drained his shot of "Wild Turkey" and placed his shot glass gently on the polished counter at *Franks Restaurant* on Asylum Street where they were enjoying a celebration. He beckoned to the bartender for another round.

"If I had the answer to that question, do you think I'd be sitting here with a mug like you?" Greaves kidded his assistant.

"Hell, the only kind of fighting I can stomach anymore is in a boxing ring. Dammit, I miss watching Ali... Hey, there's Willie Pep," Greaves smiled, spying the great Hartford Featherweight champion. Pep waved at them.

"Now there was a champ..." Greaves said in a low, almost melancholy voice.

Logan ignored the unusual tone and pressed on with his question.

"Really bugs me, Jim, I don't know how this country can hold itself together..."

His drinking partner suddenly held up his hand to silence him.

"Stop it, Dan," Greaves harshly interrupted him. "Don't you get it? I don't want to talk about it!"

He drained his glass again and ordered another.

"Look," he suddenly exploded. "I was a fucking Marine on Iwo and Okinawa. You know what I went through for this country? Can't we just celebrate something we did right for a fucking change? No one died, no one was the good guy or the bad guy. It was nothing but great stuff. A victory for the whole fucking world. Can't we just take a break from the horror? Can't we? Shit happens!"

He threw down another shot.

"No. I guess we can't. Because it will all be forgotten by tomorrow when we have to go back to work and follow up on that jackass Kennedy getting caught with his pants around his ankles in Chappaquiddick and the latest rumors about some kind of civilian massacre our guys did in some frigging Nam hootch. And did I mention that I have to take an extra dose of laxative tomorrow so I can get ready to stomach listening to our asshole president announce his personal "Nixon Doctrine" in a couple of days? Ok? You hear me? I don't want to talk about all the bullshit in the world. I just want to get drunk. We did something good today. The end. God dammit!"

Logan was stunned. He'd had no idea Greaves was on the brink.

"Stupid bastard Kennedy. Could have been the next president. Maybe we could have had one with a brain for a change. But no, the rich brat has to go thinking with his dick. I'd punch the son of a bitch out myself if I had the chance just for being stupid. And for making America look stupid again. My country. The one I fought for. The one my buddies died for. I'm sick of it. Just sick of it."

He drained another shot and called the bartender over. Logan waved him off, but that only enraged Greaves more. "Give me the fucking bottle, " he said. "I told you, tonight, we're getting drunk."

Logan didn't respond, letting his boss cool off. This was so unlike him.

"Ok, chief, let's get drunk and celebrate," he said.

"Shit, celebrate..." Greaves responded, and pounded down another shot.

He was quiet for a minute, staring into his glass. Then he just blurt it out.

"Mary has breast cancer."

Logan's heart sank. Mary Greaves was a saint, mother of three girls and grandmother to four boys and three girls. She was the only woman Jim Greaves had ever loved. He poured them both another round.

"How bad," Logan asked.

"Biopsy was positive. They're going to take a look day after tomorrow. She may end up having a double mastectomy. Then chemo and radiation. They'll make the decision during the surgery."

Logan swallowed hard at the nightmare scenario.

"Shouldn't you be home, boss?"

"No, she wanted to spend the night with her girls. They're having a sleepover at the house. I was told to stay away. We're going to spend tomorrow together and I'll bring her to the hospital the next morning. You may not be seeing me for a while, pal. You got the helm."

Logan nodded. "I'll take good care of her skipper. Where you sleeping tonight? Why don't you come to my place. I got a couch, you can have the bed."

"Beats the Salvation Army, pal. Thanks. Sorry I couldn't answer your question. I'm afraid I'm all out of reasons for why shit happens. It just does." A single tear rolled down his cheek."

"It's going to be all right, Chief, believe me," Logan offered.

"Yah. We both know that, Dan," Greaves responded not believing a word of it. He drained another shot.

Logan carried his boss to his car that night and up the long flight of stairs to his apartment. Greaves was dead on his feet as Danny deposited him on his bed and took off his shoes before covering him with a blanket. He looked down on the man, already snoring, wondering how long it had been since he'd had a peaceful night's sleep.

Logan sat at the kitchen table, exhausted and drunk. He heart ached for Jim Greaves. He was a good man. Mary was a sweetheart. They didn't deserve this, he pondered. In an alcohol fog, his thoughts wandered to his last conversation with Elina when she faced tragedy. Her behavior was so different. She could only blame everyone else. On the other hand, Greaves would have taken a bullet to protect his wife from what she was facing..

Elina came from everything, a world where there were no wants, where hubris was passed on generation to generation. Like Logan, Jim Greaves came from nothing, where everything you had, you earned. Two very different worlds. But if ever there was proof that money doesn't buy happiness... Unlike Elina, Greaves had earned a bit of joy in his life despite having to scratch for it.

Why did God crush a man who knew where he belonged and made no excuses for being who he was?

Logan was too drunk to pick up the phone, but impulsively he did anyway.

"Elina..." he said when she answered the phone. It was late.

"Danny," she replied, sleep in her voice. "What's wrong?"

"Did I wake you?" he asked although knowing he had.

"Just needed to hear your voice. Long day." His voice was empty.

"You sound terrible. I don't understand. The paper was fantastic. My father talked about it all night," she replied.

"Yah. We did good."

"So...

"Just needed to hear your voice," he repeated. "Lonely."

"Are you drunk?

"Yup. Big time."

"Alcohol makes people sad, Danny. I know. Get some sleep, you probably haven't seen a bed in a couple of days. Maybe we can get together tomorrow?"

He wanted to say yes so badly tears came to his eyes. But he didn't. Instead, the sudden jolt to his emotions made him angry.

"Oh, sure...behind Charles' back? Or will he wait in the car while we make a fool of him... and ourselves?"

"Danny... that's the booze talking."

"You're right, Elina. I'm sorry. I shouldn't have called. Good night." He hung up the phone quickly.

He put his head down on the table. What was he thinking?

The phone rang. He stared at it, confused and angry. It had been a mistake to call; it would be a bigger one to continue the conversation. It kept ringing. And tears he'd been holding back for so long started to fall.

Eventually, the ringing stopped.

But not his tears.

303

Twenty-Three

~~~ ℘ ~~~

"Have you even seen such a total contradiction in terms? It's almost obscene," Greaves commented to his editorial staff while holding up a press proof of the August 16 Hartford Times. The lead story on page one carried the headline "Throng of 500,000 Jamming Roads To Rock Festival."

"I don't understand, Jim," Logan replied, thinking he was on the hot seat for a story he had written. "I mean, these are all kids who are camping out in Woodstock, New York to listen to rock n' roll. It's all about the new hippie culture, you know, peace and love. It's a helluva lot more upbeat than the latest disaster in Vietnam or another one of Nixon's lies."

"No, you misunderstand me, Dan. In column one we're covering the horrific Tate and LaBianca murders out in Los Angeles, supposedly committed by some desert hippie cult. Peace and love... and cold-blooded murder? What the hell is this 'Flower Power' thing about anyway? I'm lost." The journalists, most in their late 20's and early 30's, laughed.

"The world is changing Chief, kids have stopped listening to Frank Sinatra and Frankie Lyman. Now they're into the Rolling Stones, Sly and the Family Stone..." the paper's arts and music editor commented.

"Sly and the family what?" Greaves said, bringing another laugh.

"I think what's of more pressing concern," Logan interrupted," is the unrest that began last Sunday night on the South Street Green."

"What do we know about it, Dan," Greaves asked, quickly turning to the seriousness of Hartford's simmering unrest.

"Well, you all know we ducked a big one in June when the Puerto Rican community rioted for a couple of days. Mayor Uccello's curfew worked and quieted things down pretty quickly, but there were shots fired and a lot of looting. The fuse has been lit.

"Last Sunday, the Puerto Rican leadership informed the Hartford Police that the Commanchero's, a local biker gang, had assaulted an elderly Puerto Rican gentleman on the Green. All hell broke loose when the cops didn't react and there have been 53 arrests in the week since. I'm afraid that another spark will ignite the North End. Tempers are very short in the Black Caucus and the cops are uptight. We could have expected Kinsella to make more promises. I don't know what to expect from our new Mayor. One can only hope that the Honorable Mrs. Uccello understands the gravity of the situation."

"Anyone want to take that bet?" Greaves asked in jest. There was silence in the room.

"Ok, that's it. Everybody keep your ears close to the ground and be careful. See ya tomorrow, boys," the managing editor said.

Ironically, the match that started the inferno came from The Hartford Times itself two weeks later, in an awkward attempt to educate Hartford residents about the Puerto Rican population, their history, traits and place in the community. The paper's strategy was to help open discussions between the Puerto Rican and White leadership in the City.

Unfortunately, the naïve reporter who wrote the piece, which ran on page one on August 31, unintentionally insulted the Puerto Rican population who were already angry about their living conditions, medical care for their children and what they claimed to be constant instances of police brutality.

It wasn't bad enough that the reporter was critical of the smells that emanated from their neighborhoods due to the unusual foods they prepared, but he also took issue with the brightly colored clothing they were prone to wearing and their habit of leaning out of apartment windows and loudly chatting with neighbors in a foreign language. But the worst was saved for last.

The reporter interviewed a fireman who didn't hesitate to identify his Puerto Rican neighbors as "...pigs. That's all, pigs... They dump garbage out of their windows. They live like pigs."

He ended his story with a quote from a South End resident that drove by the South Green near where Logan lived everyday commuting to work. "They throw stones at my car and at my wife's car. They insult women on the street. They should all go back to hell where they belong."

Greaves and Logan both missed the story in editing as it was written on the City side. It was published with verbatim quotes under the innocuous headline, "Puerto Rican Trek to Hartford Began in 1945 With Farm Jobs."

Logan read the paper from cover to cover that night as he always did before leaving.

"Holy shit," was the best he could muster when he stumbled over the article. He alerted Greaves immediately.

"We better batten down the hatches, skipper. We're gonna get killed for this and it will be a miracle if things don't explode on the streets."

He went back to his office, already strategizing how the paper could apologize to the Puerto Rican Community without doing further harm. There was no saving the hapless reporter.

Mayor Ann Uccello was on the phone to Greaves within the hour.

"Have you lost your mind, Mr. Greaves? What could you possibly have hoped to accomplish by calling a large percentage of Hartford's population — who are already angry — 'pigs.' Yes, you called them 'pigs.'"

Greaves was almost spitting into the phone in embarrassment, promising he would do whatever was possible with the editorial staff to make up for the harm done.

"I'm afraid that's going to be too little, too late," Mr. Greaves," she said. "For all the good The Hartford Times has done to represent the minority population of this City, you have just wiped it out." She slammed down the phone.

Greaves wasted no time, and called the news and editorial staffs together to explain the situation and strategize.

307

"First, anyone with a pencil get out on the street, now. Call me with what you see and hear. Second, you guys on the opinion page, I want you to put a spear through this paper for its stupidity. It's your dream assignment. Let me see it before it goes anywhere. I've got to deal with our publisher first. Lou White is not going to be happy. And the lawyers, of course." He paused, taking a deep breath.

"But at the same time, our job is to report the news. Understood? What happens, what we see, what we hear, we report. That's our job. The people who need to apologize will do the apologizing. You do your jobs. Any questions? Then go to work. And be fucking careful."

Logan returned to his office. The phone rang.

"Logan," he answered curtly,

"Dan, how are you," the voice said in a voice meant to be charming.

"Excuse me? Who is this?" Logan said tersely to the stranger. What timing to call with small talk, he thought.

"It's Charles, of course. I wonder if you have a few minutes to talk about the bridge," Charles Anderson said.

"Charles? Charles Anderson?" Logan asked in surprise.

"Yes, of course, Dan. How are you?"

"I'm well. Charles," Logan responded. "You want to talk to me about a bridge?"

"Yes, don't you recall our conversation before Christmas dinner? I told you all about it…"

Logan was already exasperated with the conversation. He didn't have time for this. Not now.

"Charles, I remember our conversation well... in fact, how could I forget it? But I vaguely remember you mentioning something about a bridge..."

"From Long Island to Old Saybrook, Dan, it's really a brilliant idea, can make us all a fortune," Anderson went on.

Logan wondered how much Anderson had recovered from his head injury.

"Charles, frankly, I'm in a bit of a spot here right now, I really can't talk about this now. Perhaps sometime later in the week."

"Please, Dan, I just need a minute of your time and for you to write an editorial supporting the project," Anderson pleaded.

"Charles... I don't write editorials... and I certainly wouldn't recommend one without knowing a lot more about this project, which frankly, I've never heard of before. Now if you'll excuse me, I have to get back to work. Goodbye, Charles."

"But Dan..." Anderson went on talking for several minutes before realizing Logan had hung up.

He had already forgotten about the conversation when Greaves came into his office. The man had virtually turned grey in the last month after his wife's surgery had shown her to be riddled with cancer. Even with the double mastectomy, chemotherapy and radiation, doctors had given her less than a year to live. Greaves came in every day but arrived late and left early, handing much of the responsibility of running the paper to Logan and Holcombe. He was a very sad man.

"Hey Jim, how goes it," Logan asked as his boss sat down in front of his desk.

"I could have lived without this screw up Dan. My mind is somewhere else. I should have caught up

309

with what the City desk was up to. I need you to double up for me..."

"No problem, Jim, and by the way, it's every bit as much my fault. You can tell that to White if he wants someone to swing. More importantly, how's Mary?"

Greaves hung his head and clasped his hands.

He paused before responding.

"It's hard to lose someone you love, Dan. I've seen a lot of death in my lifetime. But it's just ugly, just so painful to watch her die. In agony. And there's nothing I can do to help her."

"Jim..."

"I swear... I could put a bullet through my head right now if I didn't know how much harder it would make everything for her and the kids."

"They need you to be strong for them, Chief. You know that..." Logan offered.

"Yah, I know. But I'm not feeling very strong, pal. All I feel is empty."

At nearly that same moment, a West Hartford patrolman was also sharing an empty feeling after a confrontation with a 16-year-old Black youth that had left the teenager dead on a Hartford Street.

At noon that day, Officer Keith Marshall of the West Hartford Police observed a stolen Cadillac being driven by a young Black man by the name of Dennis Jones. There were two others in the car with him. Marshall radioed the information to the West Hartford Police Headquarters who alerted Hartford Police that the car had crossed over the city limits and was now on Mark Twain Drive. As Marshall followed, suddenly, the Cadillac sped up to over 80 miles an hour and proceeded onto the Mark Twain extension, then abruptly skidded to a halt. The occupants, including Jones ran from the car.

Marshall jumped from his cruiser and climbed to the top of a nearby embankment where he spotted the three suspects running towards a wooded area. He called for them to halt but without letting off a warning shot, quickly aimed at one of the youths and fired. The officer's shot hit the fleeing Jones in the left buttock, but unfortunately also struck an artery. The teenager was dead from loss of blood before an ambulance could arrive. Hartford Police were on the scene moments later.

Less than 30 minutes later, while Greaves and Logan were still talking, the phone rang again.

Logan stabbed at it.

"Logan," he said gruffly, aggravated by the interruption. It was a reporter who had staked out the Hartford Police Station on Morgan Street looking for news

"We've got trouble, Dan," the reporter said. "A 16-year old Black kid was shot and killed just a few minutes ago by a West Hartford cop. I don't know the details, but word is crowds are massing in the North End and on the South Green."

Greaves took the news hard.

"This is going to explode," he said. "We've already got the Puerto Rican community up in arms. Whatever happened with this kid is sure to light up the Black neighborhoods. Say your prayers."

All Sunday night, Hartford simmered with building anger. High police visibility seemed to keep things calm. But on Monday morning, Labor Day, the fires began.

Rioting crowds took to the streets in the Clay and Arsenal areas of Hartford and began firebombing buildings, looting stores and ambushing police patrol cars with barrages of rocks and bottles.

311

Danny Logan, over Greaves' protests, grabbed a photographer and headed out into the worst of the rioting. He wanted to talk to people, to find out exactly why they were so angry.

He and the photographer made it as far as the shopping district on Main Street before being prevented by police from going any further. In the distance, shots could be heard. There had been reports of sniper fire in the area. Logan decided to walk in anyway. Ahead he could see smoke rising.

As they got closer, Logan realized what was burning was the Ropkins Branch Library. The reporter was stunned. He turned to the first person he could find and asked why someone had set fire to the library.

"Why would someone do that?" he said as firemen braved thrown bricks and bottles while they tried to contain the fire. "It's a library. Why burn books?"

"Man, why not?" an older black man responded. "Big deal it's a library. It don't do much for the community. The City closes the doors before it gets dark so a working man can't make use of it. My kids can't even do their homework there. Far as I'm concerned, they can burn the whole damned City. Ain't doing nothing for me and my family."

A shot rang out and a bullet ricocheted off a car Logan and his photographer were standing next too. They hightailed it back to the police roadblock.

"Scary down there, ain't it?" someone called out to Logan. He looked over at a middle-aged Puerto Rican man, one of hundreds just watching the violence.

"You ought to see it through my eyes," he said.

"What do you mean," Logan replied.

"I came here because I want to live better," the man said. "I always work hard every day. I am no pig... no pig. I was arrested last night by the police. The handcuffs were too tight...they cut my hands. They throw you onto a truck and boot you in the rear end. They don't treat white Americans like that."

"What's your name, sir," Logan asked. "I'd like to quote you."

"You don't need my name," he replied. "I got enough trouble with the cops. Let's just say I speak for thousands of... what do you call us? 'PR's?'" He turned and walked away without another word.

Before the end of the day Hartford's North End had suffered massive damage from the explosion of violence that swept over Hartford like a firestorm. More than 40 square blocks were ablaze. At least 100 businesses had been looted and torched and 50 people were under arrest. A Hartford policeman had been shot in an ambush on Albany Avenue and tear gas enveloped the streets as far as City Hall. Mobs fought in the streets with Connecticut State Police and City cops.

It was a war zone.

Logan ran the news desk for nearly three days before Greaves forced him to get some rest. Every edition of The Times was filled with man in the street interviews, reports from police and firefighters and the latest efforts of City Hall to bring the unrest to a halt.

To her credit, Mayor Ann Uccello had courageously walked into the crowds the very first night of rioting to try and calm the rioters. But clashes with the police continued unabated for more than 24 hours and looting and firebombing for more than two days. The Mayor held several press conferences, which Logan himself covered, but they did little to quell the rioting as she unwittingly stereotyped members of the Puerto Rican and Black communities and had little to offer in terms of what efforts had been made to placate their

313

concerns. Logan openly challenged the Mayor to discuss the progress she believed had been made in improving living conditions in the Black and Puerto Rican neighborhoods since the 1967 riots. She ducked the question.

"This activity was instigated by agitators and carried out by hoodlums who would steal no matter what the social conditions," the beleaguered Mayor responded. Shortly after she announced that a citywide curfew would be put into effect immediately and imposed a state of emergency. Nonetheless, the riots and fire bombings continued. By Friday, State and local police had made more than 500 arrests and the Hartford jail was overwhelmed. Prisoners were transported to available holding cells in Haddam, Connecticut.

Remarkably, the NAACP failed to take on City Hall during the riots, but instead issued a weak statement condemning the violence.

"The violence and lawlessness is due to the reprehensible behavior of a small number of Blacks and Puerto Ricans. The NAACP deplores and condemns these actions," a spokesman read, unwittingly pouring even more fuel on the fire by not taking the opportunity to recognize the deplorable social conditions   in Hartford.

The Black Caucus wasn't having it. "The power structure reacts to riots and violence. This is the black man's only power," said John Barber, the group's spokesman.

In City Councilman Collin Bennett, a strong proponent of revitalizing the North End and improving conditions for the growing Puerto Rican community, Logan finally found the response he needed for The Times to begin the process of helping to calm angry rioters.

"The riot is evidence of poor relationships and lack of communications between the city government and members of the Black and Spanish-speaking community," Bennett said. "This segment of our society feels that there is no one to represent their interests in City Hall, and this has been partly responsible for the increased tension."

The Hartford Times coverage was as fair and balanced as Greaves and Logan could ensure. But it was Logan, after Uccello finally lifted the curfew and state of emergency over Hartford on September 8 — a full week after the riots had started — who summarized the wreckage of the 1969 riots in a column on page one.

"The categorical failure of Hartford's leadership to recognize the social and demographic changes that have been brewing in our city for more than 30 years is an indictment of generations who have ruled with an iron fist and a blind eye from City Hall.

What was once a great metropolis is now a half-burnt out shell of ruin and decay divided by hatred and bigotry. The exodus of Hartford residents, some with family roots extending to 1637 continues at an alarming pace. And what was once America's richest city for decades after the Civil War is now one of the poorest in the nation. Poverty is as endemic as is the epidemic of intolerance that separates our neighborhoods into ghettos aligned by the pigmentation of skin.

Why is this happening now? Just a glimpse at the issues that are enraging intelligent people provides a partial, but nonetheless devastating condemnation of city government: almost no enforcement of housing codes, delayed school construction, blatant segregation, and the exorbitant prices paid by Blacks and Puerto Ricans for food and housing in their crumbling neighborhoods. And that's just the tip of the iceberg.

315

Is there time to mend the ways that have brought Hartford to this state? To lift the crushing burden of hatred that has brought Hartford nearly to its knees? Of course, given the full commitment of Hartford's leadership — government, business and social — to push past the racism that is eating at the very foundation of Hartford as we watch.

That will take intelligence, heart, compassion and determination to work together, openly and honestly in a manner that aims to recreate a thriving city that is proud of its heritage and broad demographics. Certainly, we need no more of the political rhetoric that has blazed from City Hall this past week and served only to heighten the flames that consumed Hartford's economy — and soul. Sadly, it would seem that Martin Luther King Jr.'s sage definition, "A riot is the language of the unheard," was indeed unheard and unconsidered by our Mayor.

So, friends, neighbors and citizens, it comes to this:
The time for Hartford is now. Or, it is never."

Jim Greaves spent most of the next day fielding the calls of politicians and neighborhood leaders screaming for Danny Logan's head.

The managing editor held his own, despite the weariness he was feeling from his own battle. The love of his life was slipping away, day by day. If not for the distraction of the newspaper, he would have gone mad. Despite his strength, having Dan Logan as his rock-solid understudy gave him the strength to weather the political storm that was stirring winds strong enough to topple The Times. And the sad truth was, as his most recent conversation with Publisher Lou White had confirmed his suspicions, The Times was on shaky grounds. Television and the evening news, the extraordinary change in demographics and the overwhelming poverty that sometimes ruled out even the purchase of a twenty-cent newspaper was eroding its circulation base at a frightening rate. Taking unpopular stands with those who bought and advertised in the paper was not the brightest strategic move to fight the economic challenge.

But it was the right thing to do.

"Lou, so long as you see fit to employ me as managing editor of this newspaper, not even a direct order will keep me from printing the truth," he told the publisher.

"Have I ever asked you to do differently?" White asked bluntly.

"No."

"Then don't expect it to start happening now. I may not be much at a typewriter, but I'm every bit as much a newspaperman as you are, Jim, and don't forget it."

Greaves nodded with pride in his own boss.

"How's Mary?" White asked. The look on Greaves face told him all he needed to know.

"Listen, Jim," he said despite Greaves silence. "You've done a first rate job in building a strong editorial team downstairs. Particularly this kid Logan. Put your faith in them. They won't let you down. Take the time you need with Mary. Every minute is important. I know." White had lost his own wife two years earlier.

"But there is one group that I'm going to need your help with. They aren't my favorite people, but they carry some considerable weight in this burgh and they have something to say. A proposal they want us to listen to, clearly looking for The Times' support," White said. "We at least need to listen, Jim."

Greaves cocked an eye, puzzled by the identity of the group.

317

"Who are they?"

White shook his head, not enjoying the squeeze he was putting on his managing editor. But it had to be done.

"They like to call themselves, 'The Bishops.'"

Twenty-Four

~~~ ⁓ ~~~

November, 1969

Then came perhaps the worst nightmare of all: My Lai.

While Americans continued to be rocked by violence at home and in the jungles of Vietnam, no horror screamed out at them as vividly as the murder indictment filed against Lt. William Calley in early September for the massacre of Vietnamese civilians in the tiny village of My Lai in March 1968. The story was barely covered by the news media because details were so sketchy. Logan, preoccupied with the Hartford riots almost missed the first wire service stories but put a reporter on it. His gut told him the details were going to be explosive.

319

Logan's instincts were correct. On November 12, New York Times reporter Seymour Hersh broke the story of the My Lai Massacre in which he reported the outright murder, rape and mutilation of unarmed Vietnamese civilians by U.S. soldiers under the command of Lt. Calley. As many as 500 innocent men, women and children were slaughtered in the insanity ordered by Calley, who by first hand accounts, machine-gunned dozens of civilians himself and ordered men under his command to do the same.

The American anti-war movement exploded in outrage and the response from around the world was outright condemnation. Calls for the immediate withdrawal of U.S. troops from Vietnam came from every corner.

For the President, the news was devastating. He had made some progress during the summer in earning the trust of Americans. Public reaction to his "Nixon Doctrine" proved favorable with nearly three-quarters of the American public approving. The plan promised no future involvement of U.S. troops in ground style wars while continuing to provide military and economic assistance to countries facing communist aggression. He also ordered the withdrawal of an additional 35,000 troops from Vietnam. Americans believed their new president was making progress on his campaign pledge to end the conflict "with honor." But the My Lai massacre erased any vestige of "honor" from the country's involvement in the war.

"Can you believe that son of a bitch is arguing that My Lai was an 'aberration' by the military?" Logan said loudly at the news budget meeting the following morning. The front page of the previous evening's edition had led with a horrific photograph of civilian Vietnamese bodies piled up in an irrigation ditch. Logan had approved the wire service shot but was sickened by it. "This is a symptom of how screwed up some of our guys are getting fighting a war no one wants — especially the poor bastards fighting it."

"The evidence is mounting that there are severe morale problems in the ranks," added Dick McGrath, a ten-year veteran of The Times who had been solely covering the war for the last two years. "The ranks are full of guys doing everything from smoking marijuana to shooting heroin to help them tolerate another day in that hell hole. We're also getting reports that there have been as many as 200 'fraggings' in just the last ten months."

"What in hell is a 'fragging?'" Greaves asked.

"It's a military term for attacks on officers by men under their command using fragmentation grenades or other explosives. Officers who are unpopular with their men are particularly at risk," McGrath said.

"My God, we're turning on ourselves," Greaves replied in astonishment. "We are surrounded by chaos. When even the military breaks down, order is lost. Next we'll find out the White House is corrupt."

"Anyone want to take odds on that?" someone yelled from the back of the room. There was laughter but Greaves shook his head in worry.

"I agree, Chief," Logan replied. "But I'm worried the dam is about to burst. The anti-war movement has grown exponentially in the last year. I think it's only a matter of time until the college campuses erupt in protests. Last month's 'Moratorium' peace demonstration attracted over 100,000 people in Boston alone, mostly students who heard George McGovern demand an end to the war. The media covered the story worldwide. In fact, North Vietnam Prime Minister Pham Van Dong sent a congratulations message to the organizers."

"Yah, and the White House handled that well," Greaves said sarcastically.

"I thought it was one of our esteemed Vice President's most shining moments," McGrath piped in. "I mean how many of us could claim authorship of such pearls of wisdom as, 'In the United States today, we have more than our share of the nattering nabobs of negativism.'"

There was more laughter in the room, but it was a nervous reaction. No one thought any of it was really funny. It was all too tragic to be humorous.

"But seriously, to write off hundreds of thousand of protestors as 'dupes' of the communists is outrageous. And it gets worse. This morning, Agnew was quoted as saying the students who protested are 'nothing more than an effete corps of impudent snobs who characterize themselves as intellectuals.' Ladies and gentlemen, that's the vice president of the United States speaking. Imagine. That man is literally a heartbeat away from being the president. God help us."

"We have anyone covering the next 'Moratorium' protest in Washington on November 15th?" Greaves asked. A couple of hands shot into the air.

"Good, let's make the most of the opportunity. I want the story to lead the paper."

That Saturday, some 500,000 anti-war protestors descended on Washington D.C. in the largest demonstration in American history. Nixon was stunned as he watched from the Oval Office as 40,000 protestors walked single file down Pennsylvania Avenue, each carrying a placard with the name of a U.S. soldier killed in action or a Vietnamese village destroyed in the conflict. The protest left no doubt in the President's mind that he had lost the support of the American people in his efforts to force Hanoi to agree to peace terms. Americans wanted peace now and all U.S. troops withdrawn immediately.

Despite his outward calm, Nixon was enraged. But to the public, he conveyed an air of indifference.

"Now, I understand that there has been, and continues to be, opposition to the war in Vietnam on the campuses and also in the nation," Nixon said at a press conference. "As far as this kind of activity is concerned, we expect it; however under no circumstances will I be affected whatever by it." The quote was carried by every newspaper and media outlet in America, including The Hartford Times, serving only to further incite the anti-war movement and leave Nixon's few war supporters shaking their heads.

Greaves and Logan shared a beer later that night at the Traveler's Spa bar after the last edition had been put to bed.

"I just don't get it. Nixon has to know that he's lost all support for the war. You would think he would turn this whole bloody mess over to the South Vietnamese who by this time sure as hell ought to be able to fight their own battles," Greaves said.

"He must know something we don't Jim. I haven't a doubt that this guy has another card to play before he folds his hand. And that makes me very nervous. Word has it that there's even been discussion of a 'nuclear' option," Logan replied.

"Can you imagine? I mean, even having that thought?" Greaves said, rolling his eyes.

"If that little ditty ever went public, I think American's would be treated to our own version of the storming of the Bastille. The White House would be ground zero for the anti-war movement. The reaction to any escalation of the war will be extraordinary."

"Well, we aren't going to win the war by drinking it away, although I wouldn't mind trying," Greaves said. "Hate to leave you buddy, but I have to go home to my Mrs."

"How's Mary feeling?" Logan asked but dreaded the response.

"The days are getting shorter, in every respect," he said. "I just wish I could take her pain away. But there is nothing I can do now but hold her."

He hung his head with the burden.

"Thanks for asking, Dan," Greaves said without looking up.

Logan watched him walk out of the dimly lit bar, his head down, shoulders stooped. Physically, he was a shadow of the man he was six months before. His wife's illness had taken a terrible toll on him as well.

"There goes a very sad man," he whispered to himself. The sight caused him to contemplate the price of love.

One moment love could fill your soul with joy, he thought. In the next, heartache. Elina had taught him that much, at least. But would he give back those few weeks they had spent together, even knowing the outcome? Would Jim Greaves have fallen in love with Mary if he knew the end would be so desperately sad?

A phrase suddenly came to him, words that he remembered reading in a college English poetry textbook but had never really considered. He repeated them slowly to himself.

"Tis better to have loved and lost, than never to have loved at all." The brilliant English poet, Alfred Lord Tennyson could have had Greaves in mind when he wrote the phrase, Logan reflected, but the author must have been referring to love that had been fulfilled. Jim and his wife had been married for more than 30 years.

On the contrary, there was no joy in his love for Elina because it never had or would be satisfied. He had tasted love, and it was bitter.

"Sorry Al," Logan talked into his beer glass. "I have to disagree. Sometimes its better to have never loved at all."

He drove the black Triumph home to Park Street trying to erase the image of My Lai and the sorrow Greaves was facing. The idea occurred to him that he might need a day off to regroup.

That wasn't about to happen anytime soon.

Logan no sooner unlocked the door to his apartment than he heard the telephone ring. He answered it without hesitation, worried that it might be his boss calling. Instead, he heard the voice of a man, vaguely familiar, asking for him by name.

"Is Mr. Logan available, please?" the voice asked.

"This is Dan Logan. Who's calling?"

"Dan, this is Don Hanson, Elina's father and..."

Logan didn't let him finish.

"Yes, Mr. Hanson, how are you? What an unexpected pleasure," he lied.

"Yes..." Hanson paused, caught off guard by Logan's cordial response.

"I'm doing well and Elina and Charles asked me to give you their... regards," Hanson replied.

Logan ignored the comment.

"I never had the chance to speak to you directly after Mrs. Hanson passed," Logan said. "I am terribly sorry for your loss."

"Thank you for that, Dan. I loved Betty dearly. But, as you know, she was fighting some demons that proved to be stronger than my love for her. I miss her. I spend much more time at the office now trying to keep busy."

"I hope time helps to heal your grief, Mr. Hanson. Now, what can I do for you? I've just come in from work myself."

"You do keep long hours, Dan. I'm quite impressed," Hanson complimented him.

"Don't be impressed. It's the nature of the beast."

There was an awkward pause.

"So..." Logan asked.

"I'm sorry, Dan," Hanson said, slightly befuddled. "Actually, I wanted to make this request of Jim Greaves, but I recently learned that his wife is quite ill and didn't want to intrude."

"That's kind of you, but it means you had to settle for second fiddle," Logan responded, making no attempt to hide his sarcasm.

"Quite the contrary, young man. Frankly, I thought you would be the harder sell."

"And what exactly are you trying to sell us, Mr. Hanson?" Logan responded. He couldn't help the edge in his voice. "The Hartford Times is not in the business of buying news. We find it and report it."

"Dan... I'm not trying to sell you anything. What I'm asking you to do is listen to a small group of Hartford businessmen who have a proposal to make," Hanson said calmly. He did not want to engage Logan in an argument. "We believe that what we have to propose can change the future of the City of Hartford and bring the violence to an end."

"Interesting," Logan said, genuinely intrigued. "And who are these businessmen, besides yourself I assume?"

"They are the CEO's of Hartford's largest employers. There are five of us. Lord knows I detest the name, but some call us the 'Bishops' of Hartford."

Hanson waited for a response. There was none.
"Dan…"

"I know your group, Mr. Hanson, you already told me about your friends, the 'Bishops.' A long time ago," Logan finally said.

"First, I'm not convinced that you are so uncomfortable with the name, 'Bishops' as it defines well your power over the city. Second, I will say that I have long wondered where you've all been hiding as it has to do with the critical revitalization of Hartford. Especially in the minority neighborhoods."

"Think what you will about the 'Bishops'; what people call us is unimportant," Hanson replied. "And as to hiding, trust me, what we have to show you will prove that we have been doing anything but."

"What I'd most like to hear are the facts as they are today, Mr. Hanson."

"Facts? What facts, Dan?" Hanson asked.

"Well, for one thing, I'd like to see some data on your minority hiring practices. From what I understand, the number of Blacks and Puerto Ricans employed by your own company can be counted on one hand. I suspect the numbers will be similar in the companies run by the other 'Bishops.'"

"Well you have to understand…"

"Second," Logan interrupted, in no mood for bullshit, "I would like to see how much your companies have invested in minority programs, low income housing, schools, etc."

"And why would you want all this information, Dan? The past is the past. We want to talk to you about the future of Hartford," Hanson replied in defense.

"Hartford's future wouldn't be nearly as bleak if the 'Bishops' had gotten involved in its past. Big business has done nearly nothing to create jobs, improve the neighborhood schools and spur the local economy. You look down on the ghettos and blight of Hartford with disgust and get driven to and from your mansions in the suburbs in fancy limousines. Don't think for a minute The Hartford Times is going to help you shout out to the world that you've suddenly found religion without first examining your past reluctance as well as the business reasons for your new motivation."

"I assume you speak for Jim Greaves as well."

"I believe you will find that you are correct in your assumption, Mr. Hanson. We'd both be delighted to hear your proposal and to support it if the Editorial Board of The Times is in agreement. But that is going to require that we invest in you, and your fellow 'Bishops,' as well."

"Invest in the 'Bishops? Whatever do you mean?" Hanson asked, shaken by Logan's acerbic response.

"It means you have to earn our trust, and the trust of the people of Hartford, Mr. Hanson."

Hanson did not respond immediately.

"Mr. Hanson, its late, perhaps we should consider this conversation at another time," Logan said.

"No. We are eager to unveil our ideas. Will you meet with us?" he asked.

"Only if you are willing to answer the hard questions The Times will have for you. If that is the case, you can call my secretary in the morning and arrange for an appointment."

"No, Dan, I would like to invite you and Jim to Fenwick to first broach our idea. Then, given your concurrence, we will be pleased to discuss our proposal with the Editorial Board of The Times... along with any other questions they may have."

"Mr. Hanson, this is quite unusual. The Times does not wish to be identified with secret meetings with the 'Bishops' in the suburbs."

"I'm asking you to come to my home and have a drink while we tell you about our ideas. That's all. There is nothing Machiavellian about my invitation," Hanson replied. "If anything, it will eliminate the possibility of stirring up false ideas or expectations if we are all seen gathering at The Times."

Logan paused, considering Hanson's point.

"Ok. Let me discuss this with Jim and I will call you tomorrow. When would you like to meet?"

"Saturday afternoon, if that is convenient for you."

"You'll hear from me tomorrow, Mr. Hanson. Good night." He hung up the telephone.

Every bone in Logan's body ached with suspicion of Hanson and his cronies. But he knew he couldn't just go with his instincts. His relationship with Hanson and the complication of his feelings for Elina made it impossible for him to be completely objective. Logan thought to call Greaves but decided to wait and talk to him in the morning.

Jim didn't arrive at The Times until mid-morning. He poked his head into Dan's office to greet him. He was ashen.

"Hey boss... you look tired," Logan said sympathetically."

"Yah... it was a long night, Dan. But that's ok. I know we won't have many more together."

"Jim...I don't know what to say," Logan responded. "Sit down for a minute. Let me get you some coffee."

The two sat in silence for a few minutes as Greaves pulled himself together.

329

"I held her all night, Dan... It's all I could do. The morphine isn't helping her anymore. She's really suffering." Tears rolled down his cheeks as he opened up to his friend. "I just want to run away from this, make believe it isn't happening."

He buried his face in his hands.

"Oh my God... what did I just say. She's all I've got."

Logan came around his desk and put a hand on Greaves' shoulder.

"It's ok, Jim. You're just letting off steam. Mary knows you'll always be there for her," he said.

"This is so frigging awful, Dan, I don't know how much more I can take." He shook his head in frustration. "Listen to me. She's the one who's suffering and I'm crying about how much I can take. Jesus Christ, what's wrong with me." He wept into his hands. Logan closed the door to his office and closed the blinds.

"Boss, when's the last time you had any sleep?" Logan asked.

"I dunno..."

"You gotta crash, buddy. C'mon, just lay down on my couch for a few minutes."

Hours later, Greaves awoke to Logan handing him another cup of coffee.

"I thought you'd like to see the press proof of the Bulldog edition," he said, trying to get him to focus on something else for a little while. "After all, you're in charge. We need you, Jim."

Greaves rubbed his eyes, struggling to clear his head.

"Thanks, Dan, I really needed to put my head down for awhile. I've been sleeping that long? Everything ok here?"

"Sure. Drink your coffee. Then there is something I need to talk to you about," Logan said.

"Oh, shit.

"Nah, nothing so important. Just need your advice."

"You got my attention. What is it," Greaves said.

"Got a call from Don Hanson last night."

"Don Hanson? CEO of Mutual Insurance? Didn't he just lose his wife?" Logan winced. He had to make sure his boss was focused on the real issue with Hanson.

"What did he want?" he asked, then remembered. "Oh, never mind, I already know. Lou White told me to expect a call from him. He and the 'Bishops' want to come in and talk, right?" Greaves said.

"Yah, something about a proposal that will change the future of Hartford and put an end to the violence. He wants to meet with you and me and bring his friends," Logan explained. "He said he called me because he didn't want to bother you at home right now."

"Nice of him. He's not known for his kindness. Well, we have to hear them out, at least. When's the meeting?"

"That's the thing. He doesn't want to meet at The Times. He's afraid all those Hartford big shots gathering at our place will bring undue attention to their proposal, too soon. He invited the two of us to his place at Fenwick, on the Old Saybrook shore for a casual meeting over a drink. Then, if you think his proposal is worth bringing to the Editorial Board, he'll drag his gaggle of Bishops in their fleet of limos to The Times for a hearing."

"Gaggle of Bishops? You don't much like this guy, do you, Dan?"

"Can't say that I do, boss. I don't like what he stands for, his lack of involvement when his company really could help, his dismal record of minority hiring, and..." he paused.

"And?

"It's a personal thing, Dan," Logan confessed. "He's the father of a girl I used to be involved with. He made it quite clear a long time ago that he thought I was nothing but trailer trash from the South End, hardly good enough for his princess."

"Oh," Greaves responded calmly. "So I guess that means it's going to be a struggle for you to be objective."

"I don't know. I'd like to think I'm enough of a professional to be able to separate two issues that have no connection," Logan admitted, "but I want to be absolutely sure. That's why I can't take this meeting alone, Jim. I know the timing is terrible for you, but I need you to take the lead in deciding if what these guys have to offer is either legit or a con job. Whatever your decision, I'll do the work to prove you're right..."

"Or wrong." Greaves finished the sentence for him.

"Listen, Dan. I understand your feelings and I appreciate your being man enough to admit that you have a bias going in. But here are the facts. These guys are important to us. They spend a lot of advertising dollars that we need badly and also buy several thousand newspapers from us everyday. Every executive of these companies gets a free subscription to The Times as a reward for... for... well, I guess for staying awake at their desks past 4:30 in the afternoon."

Logan looked at Greaves, wondering if he had just heard what he thought he had heard. The managing editor burst out laughing at the puzzled look on Logan's face.

"Hell, I don't know why they get free newspapers, but they do," he laughed. "And between the advertising spend and the subscription money, the so-called Bishops are helping to keep this paper afloat. I know I don't have to tell you that circulation is continuing to trend down. There's a whole bunch of reasons for that, as you know. Employment, literacy and of course, Walter Cronkite and his buddies at CBS, NBC and ABC who are eating us alive with news the family can watch rather than read."

"I know all that, Jim, but what are you telling me? We're just going to buy whatever they have to sell? Has it come to that?"

Logan watched warily as he saw color creep into his boss' cheeks. Greaves was pissed.

"Have you ever seen or heard me suggest we sell out to anyone when it comes to the validity of the news we report?" he snapped. "Have I ever given you reason to believe that I would even consider jeopardizing The Times' reputation? Have I?"

"I'm sorry, Jim..."

"The fuck you're sorry, junior. When the day comes that I give anyone fair reason to think I'm trading the veracity of this newspaper to sell a few more copies or book ad space, you won't have to lodge a protest. I'll fire my own ass. Understood?" He slammed the palm of his hand down on Logan's desk.

"Loud and clear," a chastised Logan responded.

"But you're absolutely right about one thing, Logan," Greaves added.

"Yes, sir?"

"You are sorry..."

Logan hung his head in embarrassment. Greaves grinned.

"Now that you understand the reason that we must at least take the meeting, set it up. But do so with the complete reassurance of your managing editor that if this proves to be a con job, The Times will prove that it is and say so. The opposite is also true. As I said, understood?"

"Yes, sir," Logan smiled, grateful that he had gotten away with only a tongue lashing after questioning Greaves' integrity.

"When?"

"Saturday afternoon. I'll work out the details."

"Let me know. And Dan..." Greaves' tone softened. He wrung his hands.

"Thanks for the shoulder. And for being such a good friend." He stood, raised his arms to stretch and walked toward the door of Logan's office.

"I gotta get home tonight. My help has to leave early and Mary can't be alone. Ok? Goodnight, Dan." He left the door open behind him. Logan had the helm again.

He worked for several more hours, seeing that the last edition was put to bed then headed for home, skipping his usual beer at the Travelers Spa. He had an important phone call to make.

He dialed Hanson from his kitchen.

"Hello?" a light voice sang into his ear. He felt his stomach tighten. He hadn't considered that Elina would answer.

"Elina," he said as coolly as he could, "it's Danny. I'm calling for your father. Is he available?"

"That's it?" she said in irritation. "Not even a 'how are you?'"

"Uh... yah, sorry. How are you, Elina?" he asked awkwardly.

"Just fine," she said curtly. "I'll get my father." He heard the telephone drop and Elina walking away. Several minutes passed. He was being punished, no doubt.

Hanson eventually picked up the telephone.

"Dan, my apologies. I just got the message you were holding," he said, a confused tone in his voice.

"No problem. Listen, I spoke with Jim, he agreed to meet at your place Saturday afternoon," Logan said.

"I'm delighted. I assure you it will be time well spent," Hanson said.

"Mr. Hanson, what I said last night still goes. We'll listen, but there is no guarantee of The Times' support for your project. And Jim is in total agreement that we should discuss the other issues I raised," Logan said directly.

"I understand," Hanson agreed. "Shall we say two o'clock? You know the address."

"Fine."

"And Dan, thanks for setting this up," Hanson said.

"We'll see," Logan responded, not about to give any suggestion that he or Jim were keen to support the Bishops.

"Right. Hold on a minute, will you, Dan? Elina would like to speak to you."

She was talking before he could respond.

"I want to apologize, I wasn't very polite. You took me by surprise," she said.

"My fault. I wasn't thinking. I hope you are well," Logan replied.

"We're doing all right. My father stays very busy. It's his way of processing grief."

335

"And you?"

"Well, Charles still takes a certain amount of handholding, although he has earned his real estate license and opened a small office in Old Saybrook. He's working on his bridge fantasy."

"Yah, he called me at a bad moment a while back, wanted to talk about it. I've never heard anything about the project."

She changed the subject.

"I understand you'll be visiting?"

"Yes, your father has a proposal he'd like to present to The Times. Jim Greaves will be with me," Logan said.

"Will you have time to talk?" she asked. "I miss 'This Boy.'"

"Elina." He didn't know how to respond.

"You said you'd always be there for me. No matter what," she said. "I just want to talk with you about something."

"I'll try. It's awkward. Jim's wife is gravely ill, I doubt that he'll want to hang around very long."

"Have him drive and I'll bring you home," she said. "I'll let you drive the Healy..." she added, seductively.

"We'll see. Either way, I'll see you Saturday."

As he hung up the telephone, he felt the stirrings that always accompanied any contact with Elina. He could not get her out of his system. He wondered if she really needed to talk or if there was something more to it. It was on his mind when he went to bed and he tossed and turned all night.

On Saturday, Jim drove and Logan briefed him on the people they were meeting.

"You know Hanson," he said. "He runs the biggest company and largest employer in the state. He's been the Mutual CEO for nearly ten years but was virtually invisible during the troubles in Hartford. I would bet he had the ear of Kinsella and share the same inside track with Mayor Uccello. He clearly seems to be the leader of whatever it is the Bishops intend to propose.

"Mutual has done virtually nothing to improve employment opportunities in the city. There are no more than a handful of minorities employed by the company in anything more than janitorial, mailroom or maintenance jobs. The same can be said for his counterparts."

"And they are...?" Greaves asked. "I know most of these guys, but refresh my memory."

"Well, along with Hanson there's Walter Stinson, Chairman and CEO of Standard Corp.; Michael Wright, Chairman and CEO of Anderson & Roberts, Inc.; Stephen Malloy, Chairman and CEO of Liberty Freedom Assurance Corp.; and Arthur Lettrell of American Insurers Corp. Not one of these guys brought home less than a half million dollars in salary, bonus and stock options last year. Hanson personally earned a salary of $750,000. His total package was worth nearly $2 million."

"And why are they known as the 'Bishops?'"

"For the last decade or so, these guys have all sat on the city's important charity boards and there's no question they are their financial and political patrons. Not much has happened in Hartford without their blessing, and consequently, from what I've seen, not much has happened. But there's no doubt that at least our last two mayors have been beholden to the Bishops. I think what's finally made them crawl out from under their... excuse me... made them come forward now is the most recent violence. They were personally embarrassed by it and are afraid it's going to hurt their businesses."

"And your feelings on that?" Greaves asked.

"They damned well ought to be embarrassed to be the business leaders of a city that has earned a national reputation for bigotry, had 40 square blocks burned down by its people in protest of their treatment and living conditions and it sure as hell ought to hurt their businesses. That's what I think," Logan answered angrily."

"We may have to sit you on ice for awhile before you join the conversation, Dan," Greaves laughed. Logan smiled, but wondered why Greaves was taking this so lightly. He wrote it off as the man having more important things to worry about.

"Well, who knows? Perhaps they realize it's time for them to use their power and influence to get development moving and concentrate on some of the socio-economic issues that are overwhelming our city. But I wonder if they know what a loaf of bread or a quart of milk costs," Greaves answered in jest.

"Doubt it. Or what it takes to provide adequate medical care for a newborn."

"Touche. Boy, you really don't like these guys, Dan. You're going to have to hide it. Unless they give us fair reason to pick a fight."

"I know. I'll behave. But I told Hanson to be ready for some hard questions."

Greaves tried to lighten things up.

"I've always liked the Connecticut shore, especially around Old Saybrook. Mary and I used to rent a cottage at Cornfield Point when the kids were small. We're early. Let's take a ride past the beach, ok?"

338

The last time Danny Logan had been to Cornfield Point, he'd spent several hours in the front seat of Holcombe's Cadillac making love to the girl he still dreamed about nearly every night. He winced when they pulled up and Greaves stopped the car. They sat in silence for a few moments watching the tide surge in and out at the water's edge. Jim opened a window and said he loved the smell of the ocean. All Logan could think of was the fragrance of Elina's perfume.

"We better get going," Greaves said. "That reminds me. We have to talk about how we're going to play the 'Lottery' story." He was referring to the first draft lottery to be held in the U.S. since World War II. Congress had finally gotten around to realizing the existing conscription process was heavily weighed towards minorities and the poor, and anyone with a rich uncle or political pull could usually escape the draft. The new Draft Lottery randomly assigned numbers from one to 365. If you had a birthday in the low numbers, chances are you'd be drafted.

"Yah, we've got Thanksgiving next week and then it will be on top of us. December 1. Another great day in American history," Logan said sarcastically.

"By the way. How are you doing in school? I've been meaning to talk to Charlie," Greaves asked.

"Ok. Holding my own."

"Good. Hang on to that II-S deferment. This damned thing in Vietnam is going to drag on for a bit longer, I'm afraid," Greaves offered.

The Editor in Chief pulled the car into Hanson's driveway.

"Holy shit!" he said. "Will ya look at the cars. I probably ought to park this old Chevy in the back with the help." The Hanson driveway was full of Cadillacs and Lincoln stretches, and of course, the owners Rolls

Royce. Several drivers were sharing a smoke as they waited for their charges.

"Never thought I'd get an invitation to this castle," he said. "Mary always wanted to see the inside of one of these places. I'll have to spend some time with her tonight describing it. That is, if you don't set fire to it before I get a chance to look around, Dan," he said, a twinkle in his eye.

"I promised to behave."

"Do that."

They walked around to the front of the mansion and Greaves stopped to take in the ocean. "Look at that view," he said. "Imagine waking up to that every morning."

"It wasn't enough for Betty Hanson. That's exactly where she killed herself."

"No shit? Hard to believe. It seems like they had everything," Greaves said.

"Jim, take it from me. Don Hanson would probably give all of this away for just one day with a woman like Mary."

Greaves looked back at the ocean to compose himself, then wrapped an arm around his assistant.

"Thank you for reminding me, son..." he said, a catch in his throat.

Hanson met them at the door.

"Jim, Dan, thank you for coming," Hanson greeted them, extending his hand. I'm certain you'll find the trip was worth the effort." Logan was pleased that Greaves didn't respond but only nodded.

Hanson led them into his library, a place Logan had not seen before. As he swung opened the oversized double doors, four men rose from their seats to greet them. Logan stopped dead in his tracks.

Before him was a room unlike any other in the dark house, full of color and natural light that poured in from from a huge bay window directly behind Hanson's desk. The carpet was a bright blue wool pile so dense and thick that it absorbed a visitor's weight. It felt like walking on a sponge, he thought. Three sides of the rectangular room were lined ten-feet high with books that overlooked a sitting area of several high-backed chairs and facing couches. They were all upholstered in a mocha-dyed young cowhide that had richly aged from the sunlight. The room had the fragrance of leather, expensive cigars and brandy and reeked of wealth and power. The only art exhibited on the walls were stunning three-quarter length portraits of his late wife and Elina, and to Logan's surprise, the press proof of the Apollo 8 front page that he had given Hanson as a Christmas gift.

Greaves saw the look on Logan's face and laughed. His mouth was hanging open.

The distinctive decorating that separated this room from the rest of the mansion's rather depressing interior only confirmed for Logan that its owner was a man of many personas. On one hand, he was a ruthless corporate autocrat whose every whim was considered a directive. On the other, he was an affectionate and devoted husband and father. Still another Don Hanson was a man supposedly committed to the future wellbeing of his birthplace and a willing benefactor to the City of Hartford. Logan wondered which man he would see today.

"Gentlemen, I know you all have met the Managing Editor of The Hartford Times, Jim Greaves but you may not have made the acquaintance of the new Assistant Managing Editor, Mr. Dan Logan. Dan, why don't you introduce yourself while I get us a tall brandy."

Logan had recovered enough to walk forward and shake the hand of each of Hartford's business elite who were, to a man, endearing in their introductions. He held a confident smile on his face, but inside he was in turmoil. A voice in his head kept saying, 'You don't belong here.'

Suddenly, the doors to the library swung open again and in strode Elina.

"Elina..." Hanson greeted her with pride, delighted that she had honored his request to greet his guests. He beamed with pride at his daughter. Again, his guests rose to meet the newcomer, but the look in their eyes was one of admiration for the beauty that had joined them.

At once she unleashed her incredibly disarming smile that radiated throughout the room, a skill that made every man present feel as if he had been chosen for her singular attention. Her gaze swung around the room to each man, stopping only a moment longer to catch Logan's eye. He realized that he was holding his breath.

Elina Hanson was more beautiful than he had ever seen her, now a young woman who had lost the adolescent devilishness that had seduced a hundred boys. Dressed in dark Armani silk slacks that made her legs go on forever and a loose fitting cream colored blouse casually unbuttoned to a hint of her décolletage, the blonde with eyes as green as the ocean was the Lady of the Fenwick manor. If her mother had taught her anything, it was how to take instant command of a room full of men. Even the slight scent of her perfume seemed to overwhelm the aroma of brandy and cigars that was literally imbedded in the mahogany clad walls.

Danny Logan allowed himself to think that at least for a little while, this stunningly beautiful woman had been his. His heart ached at the thought.

"Gentlemen, my daughter, Elina," Hanson said. Each of them had met her at business or social engagement of one sort or another, but shared the appreciation that one never tired of studying her beauty.

"Gentlemen, good afternoon and welcome to Fenwick," Elina said. "I believe I know you all with the exception of this charming man..." She walked to Jim Greaves and extended her hand.

"Elina, this is Jim Greaves, the esteemed Editor in Chief of The Hartford Times," Hanson said, introducing him.

"Ah, Mr. Greaves, I have heard so much about you and I do so admire your newspaper's stance on many issues," she said with sincerity, bringing an immediate smile to the Editor's face.

"Thank you, Ms. Hanson. We try," he said, pointing his brandy glass towards Logan in acknowledgement of his partner's contribution.

"Yes," she said. "I am very familiar with Dan's byline. He's come a long way in a very short time, wouldn't you agree, Mr. Greaves?"

"That he has," Jim answered with a genuine smile.

"It's so nice to see you all and to meet you Mr. Greaves. I hope your discussion is fruitful and you enjoy your stay."

With that, she turned and walked out, leaving a sudden void that caused each of Hanson's guests to take a long pull from their brandy snifters.

"Gentlemen, let us begin," Hanson said immediately. "I know our guests have limited time this afternoon." He nodded to Greaves, offering his respect for the man's grief without addressing it.

"All of us want to thank you, Jim and Dan for accepting our invitation today. We hope to share with you a proposal that will not only excite you as it has to do with the future success of the City of Hartford, but also cause you to engage the support of The Hartford Times in supporting it," Hanson began.

"Walter," he said, raising his glass to Walter Stinson, chairman and CEO of Standard Insurance Corporation, Hartford's second largest employer, "why don't you begin by sharing your thoughts on why we began our efforts."

Stinson smiled and nodded.

"Of course, Don," Stinson responded. "I've been looking forward to this."

Logan had an odd sensation that he had met the rotund Stinson somewhere he couldn't place. Then it hit him. The man was almost a twin for William Howard Taft, the 27th president of the Unites States. He sported a huge handlebar moustache, a look that was at once dated for a man of his age, but ironically one returning in favor with the longhaired hippie culture. He guessed him to weigh well more than 300 pounds. His presence was almost clownish, but he was renowned for being no one's fool and a man who ruled his company with an iron fist. His voice was deep and commanding.

"I'm sure you will agree with me gentlemen that the Hartford business community has been greatly embarrassed by the violence and rioting that has plagued our city over these last three years," Stinson began. "My colleagues and I have been particularly offended by the lawlessness displayed by a few that grew into riots of national recognition. I say this because each of us represents companies that have been generous

344

benefactors to the city, particularly in the arts and the parks of the West End. Indeed, we have each personally made generous contributions to the continued beauty and sophistication of Hartford..."

Logan could feel the hair on the back of his neck stand on end as Stinson went on in his pontificating style. He glanced over at Greaves who was squinting his eyes as he concentrated on listening to the man. It was impossible to tell how Jim was taking what he was hearing.

"And so," Stinson went on, "this small group, or 'The Bishops' as we are known, determined to do something about this abhorrent situation as it appears our municipal government is incapable of responding in any way." He paused, looking around the room for indications of agreement.

Logan watched as Don Hanson shifted uneasily in his chair, certain that Stinson was not connecting with his audience. In fact, he was moved to interrupt his colleague and redirect the discussion before disaster set in. It was already too late.

Hanson read the situation correctly because if had known Jim Greaves better he would have recognized the redness creeping up the Editor's neck as anger about to explode. Logan had just caught the changing expression on his boss' face.

"Uh, Walter, if I may interrupt you... I believe it's important for Jim and Dan to know this is...I mean to say, our efforts..." Hanson was already shaken.

Greaves spoke up to Logan's surprise.

"Walter, I think what Don is trying to say is that although we appreciate your personal ... excuse me, it's hard for me to believe it but you did say 'embarrassment'... at the recent demonstrations, The Hartford Times couldn't give a rat's ass about your

345

business or personal contributions to the arts and parks of the city."

Stinson's eyes went wide.

"In the event you have not understood the cause of the riots, I suggest you invite members of the Black and Puerto Rican communities to your office where they can tell you why their people burned 40 square blocks of ghetto in protest."

"And what exactly would they would tell us, Mr. Greaves?" The question was asked by Michael Wright, chairman & CEO of Anderson & Roberts, Inc., the nation's largest reinsurance firm and a major Hartford employer. He was a tall, thin but imposing man with black eyes who tended to smirk in such a way as to suggest, 'you, my friend, are a dumb shit.'

Greaves had seen the look before but had never been its target. The redness had crept into his cheeks.

"What they would tell you, Michael is that they are enraged over the indecent, reprehensible housing conditions in their neighborhoods that neither the city or your cash rich companies have done anything to correct despite repeated promises. And they would tell you they are angry because they can't buy a job at any one of your corporations, are price gouged at every turn and have been continually promised new schools for their children for the last 20 years. And they would also share with you their frustration and despair with not being able to get proper medical care for their children when they become ill. Why? Because they are too poor." He sighed.

"Is that enough? Have I given you enough reasons why the minority residents of our city rose up in violence? Because, if you wish, I could go on for at least another hour citing other equally egregious indictments of our municipal government... and each of you."

Greaves stared down each man in the room. He wasn't the least bit intimidated by men who could buy and sell him. They disgusted him.

"That's why they burned 40 square blocks, Michael, fought with police and would have torn City Hall down brick by brick with their bare hands if given the opportunity. Trust me, they were in no mood to thank you for donating the latest Renoir to the Wadsworth collection. The fact is, they can't afford to buy a ticket to enter that illustrious museum that was built when the City of Hartford was the richest in the nation, not one of the poorest."

He looked around the room and then to Logan.

"Have I left anything out, Dan? If I recall, that's what angry people told you to your face when you went out in the street during the riots and asked them why they were burning the city." He waved his hand around the room. "That took some courage, wouldn't you all agree?" There was silence. "I didn't think so. You never would have thought to go out in the street and ask a man why he was burning down his own home. Because you're all cowards."

Greaves paused and drained his brandy.

"Now... unless you gentlemen have something to tell me that is somewhat less obscenely self serving than what I've heard and really has to do with the enhancement of the future of the City of Hartford, Dan and I will be making our way to the door." He stood.

Don Hanson did as well.

"Jim, I apologize. That is not how any of us, including Walter intended to set the stage for our proposal. I think Walter was just conveying some frustration."

Greaves turned to Stinson.

"Well, Walter, you sounded like an idiot. And an asshole," Greaves said, his own anger at the boiling point.

Stinson appeared stunned.

"Please, Jim, have a seat and let me tell you why we asked you here," Hanson pleaded.

"I'm all ears, Don. But I think I'll need another brandy to continue this conversation."

They all waited in silence as Hanson brought Greaves another drink.

Hanson began anew.

"Actually, Jim, you have well summarized the focus of our proposal. The issues you spoke of are real, and we know it. Perhaps our companies have not done enough to help. But we'd like to change that.

"What we believe is required to avoid continued violence and to improve the living conditions of our minority brothers is an extensive effort to revitalize the city. That means new housing, new schools, new jobs... a new community, if you will," Hanson said.

"I take it you're planning on rebuilding the North End... or what's left of it, I should say," Greaves responded.

"In a way."

"What do you mean, in a way?"

"I will explain. Very discreetly, we have created a new non-profit organization called 'The Greater Hartford Process." Its members are all Hartford employers and its intent is to revitalize the city by expanding the business district into the area that once was the North End. We intend to create a whole new community in the suburbs that will house those displaced by the riots and those whom are dissatisfied with their current living environment."

"You mean, those who are tired of living in the ghetto," Logan interjected.

"However you want to say it, Dan," Hanson replied curtly.

"Wait a minute, I'm confused," Greaves said. "You're going to build a whole new community in the suburbs? For who? Tell me again?"

"Like I said, for those displaced by the riots or who are unhappy with their current housing situation," Hanson said.

Greaves shook his head.

"If I understand correctly, your plan is to move the minority population of Hartford into some new development outside of the city. You're going to move the poor out of Hartford."

"Yes, but you say it with such a negative tone, Jim."

"You're just taking out the trash, Don. That's all your plan amounts to. You've created a secret organization that has buckets of corporate money to build a camp for Hartford's minority poor and you're going to call it a solution," Greaves said, shaking his head incredulously.

"That's not our intention at all. It's to provide a fresh start to..."

"That will allow you to turn Hartford into an oasis for wealthy white people."

Greaves leaned forward in his chair and stared at the carpet, shaking his head in amazement.

"And who is the lucky suburb that is going to agree to this wholesale transition of our Black and Puerto Rican citizens?" he asked without looking at any of the Bishops. "Or have you decided that yet?"

"Actually we're in negotiations to purchase 1,600 acres of property in Coventry, but that has not gone public yet in Hartford or Coventry."

"Coventry? A town of, what, 8,000, maybe 8,500 white residents? And you're going to move how many of Hartford's minority citizens there?" The tone of Greaves' voice was becoming increasingly angry.

"We believe the number is somewhere in the vicinity of 20,000 people," Hanson answered.

Greaves drained his second brandy.

"Is that it? Is that all there is, Don? That's the proposal you want my newspaper to support?"

"Jim, there are many more details to share with you that will involve education, social services, job training and even economic development. You're not giving us a fair hearing," Hanson responded sharply. He was not used to being dressed down — by anyone.

"Does anyone at City Hall know about this?" Greaves asked.

"There are a few insiders."

"Insiders. That's a good way to describe them, Don. White people who haven't got a clue what's happening outside their offices."

"Listen, Greaves." It was the voice of Arthur Lettrell, chairman and CEO of American Insurers Corporation.

"We have a tremendous amount of time and money invested in this plan and we deserve to be heard. There's too much at stake. Our businesses can't bear another embarrassment like the Labor Day riots.

"The truth is there simply isn't room in Hartford for people not qualified to work in the insurance or banking industry, that's just a fact. The people who aren't employable are either going to have to stay in the ghetto or go back to where they came from. Take the

Puerto Ricans for example. Do you think they belong here? They have no skills and we shouldn't be encouraging them to come here. Hartford has become an unloading dock for people who want nothing more than a handout from City Hall. You probably think I'm a racist, but the truth is this issue has nothing to do with race, it's all about economics.

"Now we have a plan that will give these people a fresh start with new housing, jobs and schools. And it needs to be heard. Will you help us or not?"

Greaves was silent. Then he nodded.

"Yes, Arthur, I'll give you a hearing," he said.

"Thank you," Lettrell responded, clearly proud that he's brought the man to his senses. "I'm glad you see it from our perspective."

"I'll give you a hearing because this is wrong on so many levels I don't even know where to start," Greaves continued. "You can bet The Hartford Times will print your plan in all its' details to ensure that people who can see beyond the color of someone's skin can scream and holler about how the white rich guys of Hartford plan to fix their social issues: by getting rid of them and leaving the problem for someone else to wrestle with. And you can bet The Hartford Times will print every word they say, as well."

"Jim..." Hanson began to plead.

Greaves wouldn't have it.

"Hell, Don. You should be ashamed. All of you. You say you abhor the riots, but what you're doing is going to give the Blacks and Puerto Ricans in our city a reason to go back to the streets. Didn't you hear what Martin Luther King said? For that matter, didn't any of you read what he said in The Times?

'A riot is the language of the unheard.'"

351

He stopped to let the profound words sink in. "But one more time, no one stopped to listen to the people asking for help.

"Let me put this in terms I know you can all understand," Greaves continued.

"What the fuck were you guys thinking?"

He hung his head, embarrassed to be in the same room with the most powerful people in the city of Hartford.

"Don, I've heard all I need. I'll be in touch next week to set up a meeting with The Times' Editorial Board. In the meantime, Dan and his staff will begin digging into the 'secrets' of The Greater Hartford Process to ensure that we have a balanced story. Thanks for the brandy."

He stood up and walked to the doors. "Dan, you still planning on finding your own way home?"

Logan nodded.

"See you on Monday then." He left the room and Logan followed him out. The Bishops sat in stunned silence.

Greaves stopped on the porch, looking out over the sound. The sun was already low in the sky.

"Guess I should have listened to you, Dan. That was quite incredible," he said.

"Yes. But I'm proud of you, Chief. A lot of men would have rolled over and played dead confronting that much power," Logan responded.

"You're going to meet all kinds of people in this job, Dan. Some are worth listening to, some not. Some are just out to scam or intimidate you. What they were suggesting amounts to nothing more than a Potemkin village."

Logan's brow furrowed. He'd never heard the reference.

"It's Russian. It refers to something built for the sole purpose of fooling people into believing that a situation is better than it really is.

"But I learned a long time ago, there's only one kind of respect that means anything in this world. Self-respect. If I had agreed to support those guys, I would have sold out Hartford and my own self-respect. And that, I would never do. After Mary, it's all I have." He patted his friend on the back.

"See ya back at the ranch, dude." He began to walk toward his car, then stopped and turned around.

"Hey Dan, don't mean to pry. But do you know what you're doing with his daughter?"

Logan was surprised by the question. He also wasn't sure how to answer it.

"Yah, I think so," he replied.

"Be careful, son. You're in for a world of hurt if you get fooled."

Logan laughed.

"A 'Potemkin' type situation?" he asked.

Greaves smiled.

"You're a smart kid."

Logan watched as his boss drove away, waving as he turned the corner. Then he walked back to the house and up the stairs to the porch. He looked back at the Sound again, remembering Greaves' observation.

"Imagine waking up to that every morning?"

He let himself back into the house, looking for the living room. He could smell the smoke from a roaring fire and heard voices.

"Can I help you, sir?" a voice asked from behind him.

He turned to find one of the several housekeepers who worked in the Hanson household. He didn't recognize her.

353

"Yes, thank you. Dan Logan here to see Elina. She's expecting me. "

"Yes, of course, Mr. Logan. I believe she's in the living room with Mr. Anderson. Please let me show you the way," she said politely.

He laughed. "I've been here several times, but still can't find my way around. This house is so big..." They passed the doors to Hanson's library. They were still closed. He heard loud voices inside.

The housekeeper led him down a long hall and they abruptly entered the living room.

Logan froze, seeing but not believing the scene playing in front of the fireplace. The maid, embarrassed, said, "Oh, excuse me," and turned back. But he was paralyzed. His mind screamed, 'look away!' but his eyes — the gateway to his soul — were locked on the betrayal he had stumbled upon.

Elina and Charles were embracing, joined in a passionate kiss. She had one hand on the back of his head, her fingers running through Anderson's hair. His hands were low on her waist, caressing.

Charles saw him first. He was startled and broke off the kiss at once. "Dan," he greeted him as if a long lost friend had come to visit. Elina looked, then closed her eyes and turned away. It was not how she wanted to break her news to Logan.

"Elina," he managed to whisper, completely ignoring Charles. Inside he could feel his heart being ripped into tiny pieces. His chest ached. He waited for her to say, "It's only a dream, Danny." But she was silent.

Charles persisted. "Dan, it's so good of you to come. I've been wanting to talk with you about the bridge project, but now is certainly not the time. Not with such good news to share."

Logan swallowed hard and tried to calm his racing heartbeat. He looked to Charles.

"Good news?" he asked, his voice breaking.

Anderson looked surprised. He reached for Elina's hand. "Elina? You told me Dan was coming to visit. You haven't shared with him..."

He didn't hear the rest of what Charles said as he babbled on. Logan only wanted to beg Elina for an answer.

"Why?"

"...the marriage won't be until spring, of course. We'll wait until May or June so we can be married on the beach. I was hoping you would be my best man, Danny. I mean, I know we've had our... "

Anderson carried on, unaware his voice was just a hollow echo in Logan's ears. He was still fixated on his question.

"Why, Elina? Why did you do this to me?" He stared at her, speaking the words through his eyes, unable to say them.

"Danny, forgive me" she finally spoke, crossing the room quickly to take his hands. "I wanted to tell you... I didn't mean for you to...you see, Charles has made such great progress in his recovery and has helped me through my mother's death. We've become so close..."

Logan could not speak. He looked deeply into her eyes and poured his heartache into her. Her complexion turned white as Logan let go of her hands and walked out of the room. He panicked when he couldn't immediately find the front door, like a rat trapped in a maze. Don Hanson stepped out of the library as he passed and grabbed his arm. "Dan, can we talk for a moment? This has all gotten terribly confused..."

Logan brushed by him without answering and found his way to the porch where he paused to take a deep breath of the cold ocean air. Tears were streaming down his face as he stumbled down the stairs then walked past the limousine drivers and kept on going to the end of the driveway. He turned around and stared at the great mansion. Elina was on the porch calling him to come back. To tell him more lies.

There was no going back, he thought. Not ever.

But sitting alone in the back of a nearly empty Shoreline bus hours later making his way back to Hartford, it happened again as it always did when he thought of Elina. He forgave her. His love was too strong to hate her.

Out of nowhere, the song, their song, came to his mind and for mile after mile in the solitude of the bus the desperate lyrics of John and Paul played on and on in his mind. He didn't care about the music, it was the words that he hung on to.

That boy took my love away
Oh, he'll regret it someday
But this boy wants you back again.

That boy isn't good for you
Though he may want you too
This boy wants you back again

Oh, and this boy would be happy
Just to love you, but oh my
That boy won't be happy
Till he's seen you cry

This boy wouldn't mind the pain
Would always feel the same
If this boy gets you back again

356

Somewhere along the long drive home he fell asleep, still humming the words to their song, lost in the fragile hope that they gave him. Logan awoke with a start at Union Station when the bus pulled into Hartford. He thought of calling a cab to take him to Park Street but decided to walk, strolling beneath the dim yellow light of the streetlamps. He was tempted more than once to stop into a bar, but he knew where that would lead and his heart would still ache in the morning. Better to keep walking and remembering.

It wasn't until he was alone inside his apartment, sitting on his couch and staring at its blank screen that he finally decided what to do. He picked up the phone.

Charles answered.

"Let me speak to Elina," Logan said.

"Now Dan, let's talk…"

"Chickie, I don't want to hear your bullshit. Put Elina on the phone.

"Dan, I really need to talk to you about the bridge," Anderson replied.

Logan lost it.

"Fuck you and your fucking bridge. Put her on the phone, Chickie. Now!" he screamed into the phone.

He heard Anderson inhale sharply, then drop the phone. Elina picked it up almost immediately.

"Danny… I'm so glad you called. You left…with so much unsaid." He could tell that she'd been weeping.

"Elina, there's no more to say. I only called to make sure you understand how I feel."

"What do you mean?" she asked.

"What I mean is I think you're making the right decision. Marry Charles and get on with your life. Live. Find happiness with him at Fenwick. End of story," Logan said firmly.

"But what about us?"

His face felt hot.

"What do you mean, what about us? There is no us!" he said in anguish.

"My God, Elina... don't you see what you're doing to me? Why can't you see any of this through my eyes?"

He heard her crying on the other end of the phone.

"There is no story, Elina. Not one about us."

He listened to her sobbing for a moment, but was undeterred.

"Please tell Charles for me that I won't be his best man for reasons he well understands. And I won't be at the wedding, Elina, so please don't invite me. It ends here. Now."

"Danny," she pleaded, desperation in her voice. "Please, talk to me some more."

"No. No more talking. No more lies. No more waiting. Don't you see? I can't. I just can't go on like this." He stopped, summoning up the courage to do what he had to.

"Elina... listen to me closely.' His voice cracked but he forced himself to go on.

"I love you more than life. When I think of you, I feel like a teenager in the summer. You go to my head like the fourth of July. It's all colors and fireworks and my heart hurts. No, Elina. I can't wait anymore. I don't belong with you. Believe that."

"Danny... my heart is breaking," she cried. He wondered if Charles was listening.

"Mine too, Elina. But for something that never was. I have to go now. Just remember how much I love you. And I'll always be 'This Boy.'"

"No!" he heard her cry as he hung up the phone.

358

It was done.

He put his face in his hands and sobbed until the morning sun broke through his window.

Twenty-Five

~~~ ❦ ~~~

The year ended very much like it had begun: the country was divided over an endless war that was being waged seemingly without purpose, and the streets of American cities were filled with racial tensions. The only good news was that the 60's — a decade that began with new hope and visions of Camelot but ended in a nightmare of blood, despair and division — came to an abrupt, unresolved close.

In mid-December, desperate for any sign of an end to the relentless conflict in Vietnam and the interminable stream of body bags arriving at Travis Air Force Base, American's cheered at Nixon's decision to reduce U.S. forces by another 50,000 men. By year's end, a total of nearly 115,000 troops had been sent home during the course of 1969.

But heavy on the minds of every citizen was the inescapable fact that 40,024 mostly young American boys had died in the steaming jungle war. And very few could define the reason why.

The President's public stance was that U.S. forces were turning the tide and "victory with honor" was in sight. He continued to express confidence in the Peace Talks being held in Paris. But his closest confidantes and advisors, those who had supported the war most vigorously for so long, were losing faith.

On December 20th, the beaten, frustrated chief U.S. negotiator of the Paris talks, Henry Cabot Lodge, resigned along with his senior deputy, Lawrence Walsh. An anonymous American source reported to the press: "We are at rock bottom now in these talks, so it really doesn't make any difference who sits around that table."

The Times led with the story, continuing to push its anti-war editorial stance.

"On one hand, my guts tell me it's good news that Nixon is rebuffed at every turn from pushing his own agenda. This 'peace with honor' bullshit is going nowhere. You'd think he'd get the message and find a back door out fast before he's embarrassed anymore.

"But on the other hand, Nixon the 'cornered rat' scares the shit out of me. I worry that he's going to do something crazy," Greaves remarked at the morning news budget session.

There was general agreement from his staff.

"He's got two choices from where I sit," Logan contributed. "Pull out or escalate. We're seeing signs that he's reducing the 'force majeure' that the Pentagon has been bragging about for years through troop reductions. But I think he's intentionally misleading the American people and his real intent is to escalate. That doesn't have to mean greater troop strength. He could go nuclear or expand into neighboring countries that are

361

known to be aiding the communists. I don't know. I just have a hunch that 'Tricky Dick' is up to his old games."

The veteran reporter Dick McGrath piped in with his own thoughts.

"But even Nixon has to understand that the anti-war movement will explode beyond anything we've seen to date if there is even the hint of escalation," McGrath said. "If he goes off half cocked and starts B-52 runs over Cambodia or Laos it'll be 'Katy bar the door.' Hell, Abbie Hoffman and Tom Hayden will overrun the White House with a million college kids. I guarantee it."

Greaves leaned back in his chair and rubbed his eyes. He was exhausted from caring for his wife and trying to manage the newspaper. The anti-Nixon sentiment was so strong among his writers, he worried they might overstep the facts with speculation.

"Well," he said, "let's stay close to everything coming out of the Pentagon and our friends inside. Just because we're a small city newspaper doesn't scare me away from breaking a story — if we have one."

"Speaking of breaking a story, do you have a schedule for when Don Hanson and the Bishops will be visiting us," Logan asked.

"Sounds like a bad Vegas act," someone mumbled to laughter.

Greaves didn't join in. He was not looking forward to discussions with the Greater Hartford Process founders.

"Yes," Greaves responded. "I spoke to Hanson a couple of days ago. He asked for the rest of the month to better prepare their presentation. I told him I thought that would be time well spent. We'll meet right after New Year's. I'll inform those of you who will need to attend the meeting."

"How about summarizing your meeting with the Bishop's for us, Jim," Charlie Holcombe asked.

Greaves didn't respond immediately, thinking back to the contentious meeting.

"No, I don't think I want to do that, Charlie. I don't want to preempt or prejudice what the Bishops have to say. I have some strong feelings about their proposal, but I think it's in the best interest of The Times that all of you decide the merits of it yourselves.

"In the meantime," he said, looking at Logan, "I want you to put a few guys on this story immediately. We need background on the Greater Hartford Process, its members and financial supporters, etc. I'd also like to get a handle on who at City Hall is in the know and if there has been any input from... no, make that contact with the Black Caucus members and other community leaders. Let's get ready to spell out the whole story. We can't depend on getting all the details and an unbiased presentation from the Bishops. I want balanced coverage across the board. The Times will take a position at the right time, but only after this thing has been completely vetted. Is everyone clear on that?"

"I think we got your drift, Chief," Logan answered for the group.

"Ok, that's a wrap. Let me see the front page as soon as you have the press proof, Dan. I need to get home early tonight."

Logan nodded as the room cleared. Only he and Holcombe hung behind.

"How's she doing, Jim?" Holcombe asked. He remembered having to work through the grief of losing his son. Greaves was a wonder to him. His juggling act of continuing to manage his responsibilities at the paper while caring for his wife called for iron man endurance.

Greaves folded his hands beneath his chin and leaned forward onto the conference room table.

"If God has an ounce of compassion, he will take her tonight, Charlie," Greaves answered, his voice shaking. "Lord forgive me, but she is suffering so terribly."

Logan put a hand on his boss' shoulder. There were no words that could possibly comfort him.

"Jim, why don't you head home and I'll bring the proof to you as soon as I have it, ok?" he said. "Go and be with Mary."

Greaves turned and looked at his junior assistant, his eyes empty of emotion. He slowly nodded then got up and left without speaking again.

"Nice thought, Dan, he's completely exhausted," Holcombe said as he watched Greaves leave. "We cannot fathom what that man is going through right now." He hesitated. "I lost my son, but I was spared from watching him die. Sometimes you just have to wonder what the big guy is thinking..."

Logan sighed.

"I don't know, Charlie," he responded, a hint of anger in his voice. "I lost my faith so long ago. Eddie died for nothing and now Elina is getting married. I don't know what to think anymore other than that God is a callous, vengeful son of a bitch who does horrible things to good people."

Holcombe sucked in a deep breath and exhaled loudly. Logan was afraid he had offended him.

"You know, Dan..." he began and then stopped. Logan saw his eyes were wet.

"When Charlie Jr. died, I wanted to die too. And for a long while I actually thought I would. I had so much rage inside. I'd lie awake at night next to Arlene and listen to the sound of the blood in my veins racing through my heart so fast I was sure it would explode. And all the while I would silently curse God and dare him to take me too."

He wiped at his eyes.

"And then something happened," he continued. "Somehow, watching Arlene in her inconsolable grief made me forget my own rage. She was out of her mind with sorrow. I knew I had to help her or I would lose her, too. But I wasn't strong enough to do it on my own. I had barely enough courage left to get down on my knees and ask God to forgive my craziness and bless me with his help. It was all I knew to do…"

He reached for his handkerchief, tears now streaming down his face.

"He heard me, and I was able to hold Arlene together. We pray together a lot now, for Charlie and for each other. And we've come to accept that it wasn't God who took him. It was evil… in the form of those idiots in the Pentagon, lying, deceitful politicians, the military industrial lobbyists… everyone who has contributed to waging an unjust and unnecessary war. That's who killed my son.

"And you know what, Dan? It isn't God who is taking Mary Greaves from the man who loves her unconditionally. It's cancer," Holcombe continued. "Jim doesn't blame God. But he's angry that she is suffering so horribly and that so little has been done to find a cure or some way to ease her pain. We've poured billions into Southeast Asia fighting for no reason. That's money that could have been used to fund research to help people like Mary. Instead, we've only begun, investing pennies on the dollar for cancer research in comparison to the staggering sums being poured into buying bullets and building bombs. Trust me, that's what my dear friend Jim is angry about."

He paused, leaned back in his chair and stared at the ceiling.

"Just imagine how ludicrous the world is to people like Jim and I..." He dabbed at his eyes again.

They were silent for several moments as Logan digested what Holcombe had said.

"I'm sorry, Charlie, I didn't mean..." Logan began.

"No, Dan, don't be sorry. I'm not angry with you or at how you feel. I know that your own heart is broken. You lost Eddie and now Elina. They were precious to you. But don't blame God for it."

Holcombe got up to go back to his office.

"I don't expect you to understand all of what I said now, Dan. The wounds are too fresh. Perhaps someday you will find some peace with what's happened in your life."

"Thank you, Charlie," Logan answered. "I'd never doubt anything you believe. It's just..."

"It's just that we all need to blame someone for things we can't understand. It makes it easier to rage if you have a target. Well, take it from this old man that life gets easier when you finally understand who or what the right target is." He got up to leave.

"What say we get a beer tonight, hey? I'm parched as hell from all this preaching," he smiled and left.

Later that afternoon, Logan drove to the Greaves' home in Hartford's West End with the press proof for that afternoon's edition. The paper led with the resignation of Lodge as the chief peace negotiator in Paris. The couple lived in a large brick English Cottage on Scarborough Drive, a lovely neighborhood where they had raised four daughters. He noticed many of the homes were gaily decorated for Christmas. There were no signs of the holiday at the Greaves residence.

He parked the TR in the circular driveway and noticed Charlie Holcombe's Cadillac by the front door. He rang the doorbell and Jim's oldest daughter, the spitting image of her mother, answered and showed him in. It was quite obvious that she had been crying. He waited nervously in the foyer for his boss.

A few minutes later he emerged from a hallway with Holcombe by his side. Jim's eyes were red and he was a bit unsteady as he walked. Charlie Holcombe was holding on to his arm to steady him.

"Dan, thank you from bringing this," Greaves said quietly. "If I had waited…"

Holcombe helped him. "Mary just passed a few minutes ago, Dan," he said. "Her entire family was with her."

"Yes. Isn't it wonderful, Dan?" Greaves said, bravely trying to keep his composure. "She isn't suffering anymore. Thank God. Yes, thank you God."

Logan, having no idea what he had walked into, was stunned and speechless. He could only think to put his arms around the man he admired so much and hugged him.

"I'm sorry, Jim," he whispered into Greaves ear. "I'm sure she knew how great your love was for her."

"Perhaps, Dan. I've learned that no man can truly express the depth of his love for another human being, even for your wife or child. Not even a writer can do it."

"I'm sure she knew, Jim," Logan insisted, knowing no other way to console him.

"You brought the proof, I see," Greaves said, taking it from under Logan's arm. He opened the oversize file jacket and scanned the page. Long minutes passed while he assessed the content and makeup of the page.

"It's good, Dan, as usual. But do me one favor, please. Bump up the point size on the Lodge headline. I want our readers to understand that a great man has thrown up his hands in utter frustration with an impossible task. Let's send Nixon another pointed message. He won't know it, but this one's for my Mary."

"Of course, sir, I'll rework the head myself," Logan responded. Holcombe's words from their conversation that afternoon came flying back to him.

"Thank you. I won't be in for a couple of days, Dan. Take the helm, pal."

"God bless you sir. If I can help…"

"You already have, Dan. Get back to work," he smiled, patting him on the shoulder.

Holcombe walked him out to the car.

"I'm sorry, Dan, I never had a chance to call you," he apologized. "I feel terrible that you had to walk into that."

"No need for apologies, Charlie," Logan answered. "In fact, I think it has helped me understand a bit more clearly what we spoke about this morning. I'm grateful that I could bring him something that helped him to focus on the right target."

Holcombe smiled.

"Are you the same kid that once asked me what a 'take' was?" he asked in admiration.

"Yes sir. And I'm grateful that you gave me the answer instead of showing me the door."

Logan drove back to The Times where he called the staff together and gave them the news. The response was sobering. Then he immediately reworked the lead headline for the afternoon's edition.

Lodge Quits Paris Talks
In Protest Of Stalemate

"We Are At Rock Bottom"

Logan grabbed the first copy off the press and handed it to a runner.

"Hey kid, you got a car?" he asked the 17-year-old kid.

"No sir," he answered, embarrassed.

"It's only a matter of time, pal, keep working hard. Here," he said, tossing him his own car keys. "Take this out to Jim Greaves' house on Scarborough Street. Make sure you hand it directly to him. Tell him it's from all of us."

"Yes sir," the teen beamed. "What kind of car?"

"Black TR4. Wire wheels. You can drive a four speed?" Logan asked.

"Born with a stick in my hand, boss."

"Good. Bring it back in one piece… or don't come back," he smiled as the kid ran off.

Logan managed the paper for the final 11 days of the decade with boundless energy in the absence of the managing editor. Simultaneously, he pushed his staff to prepare for the upcoming visit of the Hartford Bishops and to cover the debacle in Vietnam with even greater scrutiny.

Taking Holcombe's lesson to heart, he pushed Elina to the back of his mind, and focused himself and the newspaper he was steering — albeit on a temporary basis —toward the right targets.

In his wildest dreams, Logan could not anticipate the crisis' that would further rock America's confidence within the very first months of the new decade.

Or the divisiveness that would take an even uglier hold of his city.

Twenty-Six

~~~ ℘ ~~~

January 3, 1970

Logan looked around the room at the staff reporters, editors and opinion writers who were listening intently to the presentation being made by Don Hanson of Mutual Life Insurance. He studied the faces of the people who, for the last three years, had covered the riots in Hartford and braved the violence in the streets to hear the protests of demonstrators first hand. He noticed the intensity in which they were listening, but also the distrust and even scowls that lined their faces. Jim Greaves and Charlie Holcombe were listening too, saying nothing, letting the Bishops put it all on the table. The air was thick with cigarette smoke and the familiar aroma of black coffee.

371

F . MARK GRANATO

What Logan heard Hanson describe as "the sure plan to save Hartford from itself" sounded even worse the second time he listened to it, this time as the CEO went into details. He wondered if Hanson knew that his argument was transparently racist and that he was forever labeling himself as a bigot. The words he spoke came from the perspective of an intolerant, wealthy white male who had studied the city crisis with one explicit intent: take back Hartford and purge it of the unwelcomed minorities that had descended upon it like a swarm of opportunistic locusts.

Hanson missed entirely the dark cloud of suspicion that permeated the Bishop's plan simply because they had developed it in secrecy. That one fact just about doomed any hope of them gaining the support of The Times.

He also missed the fact that once made public, the Greater Hartford Process plan would do more to further the division of the city's inhabitants than even the riots.

Greaves, who had buried his wife less than two weeks before, sat stone-faced as Hanson rambled. But Logan knew that inside, his boss was struggling to hold back the fury he felt. Privately, he had confided in Logan, Holcombe and The Hartford Times' publisher, Lou White that he would resign before supporting any part of the Bishop's plan.

"All these bastards are doing is working to rid Hartford of the poor so they can build themselves a corporate version of Disneyland in the North End," Greaves said, making it clear there was no room for debate over his opinion. "Our city will forever be tarred as an island for white power. And ironically, although Hanson and his cronies are too blind to see it, Hartford will become the target of every racial equality movement

372

in the country. This will be the single largest socio-economic blunder in American history."

Logan was having a hard time listening and glanced out the conference room window. It was the first Saturday of the New Year and although it was only slightly after noon, the skies were dark with snow-filled clouds. There'd be at least a foot of it on the ground before the weather cleared, he thought, already anxious about the drive home. The TR was always an adventure in the snow. It was a cold, miserable day in every respect, and the discussion in the conference room wasn't making it any warmer.

Finally, Hanson concluded his remarks.

"And with that, gentlemen, I'm sure it is clear why we have come today seeking the editorial support of The Hartford Times and your personal confirmation."

Hanson smiled and Logan thought he was expecting applause. Instead, what he heard was dead silence from the dozen members of The Times staff in attendance.

Finally, out of sheer desperation, Hanson asked for questions.

"Surely, you must have some thoughts on our proposal or need further clarification? We will be pleased to answer any questions," he said, slowly scanning the room.

It was Charlie Holcombe who broke the ice.

"Mr. Hanson, being the personnel guy for The Times, I have a keen interest in jobs. I wonder... your proposal goes to great lengths to promote the creation of jobs in Coventry designed for the black and Puerto Rican communities. Well, instead of resettling these minority neighborhoods outside of Hartford and rebuilding an entire section of the city, which I must say strikes me as a place that would very much carry your own image and likeness, have you given any thought to creating jobs for these people in your own companies?"

Hanson visibly paled.

"The truth is, these people don't have the necessary skills and perhaps the intellectual…" the CEO began.

He was abruptly interrupted before he could finish. There was angst in the room, as Logan had guessed, and it was about to let loose.

"Let me get this right," Art Planeta, the paper's senior editorial writer interrupted. "You're going to build a $200 million community in Coventry and move 20,000 Hartford minorities into it — how that will all happen is still a mystery to me — but supposing it does happen, where will these new jobs come from for people you claim have no skills? And did I hear you begin to say, no brains?" Tom Lynch wasn't just irritated. He was angry.

"No, of course not, that is not what I meant to imply," Hanson replied quickly.

"You don't imply it, you said it."

Hanson was smart enough not to argue.

"What I meant to say is that we will work to encourage new business development in the Coventry community we envision that will support the skills of the people we move… I mean… who choose to move there. Clearly you can envision the possibility of this plan actually helping the town of Coventry to grow its economy and for industry to begin to develop around the University of Connecticut, which is located not far away in Storrs."

"Boy, that's one hell of a leap," someone mumbled.

Holcombe jumped back in.

"It still seems like an awful lot of trouble to go through, not to mention a massive investment in a community that has no connection to Hartford, when we have not yet explored the possibility of training the available workforce in the minority neighborhoods and putting them to work in Hartford. That is, in your businesses. And, by the way, wouldn't that bring new investment into the city by other business owners who might envision rebuilding the North End in a manner appropriate and attractive to the cultures of people of color? "

"And get rid of what's left of the city's slums and ghetto's — properties which are mostly owned and have been historically neglected by your businesses," Dick McGrath added.

Another anxious voice joined in.

"Who knows about this in City Hall? And has the town of Coventry even been approached? Why all the secrecy?" The questions came from Tom Lynch, the State Editor responsible for news outside Hartford.

Hanson squirmed in his chair. Before he could respond, Michael Wright, chairman & CEO of Anderson & Roberts spoke up. He was clearly aggravated by the tone of the questioning.

"No, we haven't approached anyone in Coventry yet. Any man with business sense would know that we have to have the support of the City of Hartford before we could take that step. Who knows about this in City Hall? Only the Mayor has been briefed but I assume he has shared it with some of his closest advisors. As to secrecy..." The tall, thin man glowered at Lynch. "Again, if you knew anything about business you'd know this kind of a deal has to be announced at the right time, by the right people. Can you understand that?"

Lynch, a tough, 20-year vet of the paper who had worked his way up from a job on the loading docks stood up from his chair and stared across the table at Wright. The South End boy wasn't about to take shit from anyone.

"Listen, you motherfucker," he said in a voice that left no question about his mood. "You're not fooling anyone with this crap. This is a scam from the get go and I can tell you that the town of Coventry is going to go nuts when they hear about your grand plan. I'll let the City-side guys worry about how the Black Caucus and the Puerto Rican leadership are going to react. But I'll tell you this. You'd best have your 'rent a cop' security guards in your front yards the day you announce this frigging disaster because you five assholes are going to jumpstart the riots of 1970 all by yourselves."

He began walking out of the room, but turned back, not quite finished. "And God damn it, I hope the hell they burn your houses down this time because you're the reason why Hartford is such a shithole now. You greedy pigs have destroyed this city with your arrogance and total lack of compassion. You're not trying to save Hartford, you're trying to save your own fat, spoiled asses."

He turned to Greaves and apologized.

"Sorry, boss, but I can't listen to any more of this bullshit. And if there's a vote put to the group, you know which column I'm in." He leaned down and got in Hanson's face.

"Hell no."

Lynch left the room, slamming the door behind him.

Greaves laughed out loud. Every head in the room turned in his direction.

376

"Michael, I want to thank you. You are a master of diplomacy and subtlety," Greaves began.

"What...?" Wright was confused.

"If you hadn't been such a wiseass with that man — who by the way has the respect of every Time's staffer in this room because he earned it — we might have danced around the obvious for the rest of the afternoon. But no. You saved us from wasting our time. Because you were so obnoxious, you got Tom to say what we, I suspect, are all dying to tell you."

"And that is?" Wright said sarcastically.

"You don't have a snowball's chance in hell of getting the editorial support of this newspaper for your self-serving, goofball of a plan."

It was Wright's turn to laugh.

"And you think this piss ant little newspaper is going to stop us?" he shot back.

"Christ, Michael, shut up. Haven't you done enough damage?" Hanson said to his colleague.

"That's alright, Don, let me answer him," Greaves said. "I don't know, Wright. Maybe this 'piss ant little paper' can't stop you. But we're sure as hell not going to help you."

Hanson leaned forward to say something, but Greaves waved him off.

"No more, Don. We're not buying. And I'll tell you how this is going to work. You go ahead and make any announcement you want, do any deal you wish, The Hartford Times sure as hell can't stop you. But the day you make your announcement, The Times will be ready to support the facts and the factions who will undoubtedly oppose your plan. And we will be relentless in our efforts to discredit your intentions so long as it takes to derail this con job."

Hanson and the other Bishops appeared to be in shock.

"Am I clear about that, gentlemen?"

Hanson's eyes narrowed.

"Do you know how much you're going to cost this newspaper in advertising and circulation, Mr. Greaves?" he threatened.

"Down to the penny, Mr. Chairman. And I've already discussed that possibility with Lou White."

Hanson smirked. "And his response?"

"Let me quote him: 'So be it,'" Greaves responded slowly, emphasizing each word. "You are forgetting the difference between my world and yours, Hanson."

The Mutual Insurance CEO waited.

"A newspaper is built on integrity and honesty. Without either, we can't survive. Consequently, we can't be bought."

Greaves looked around the room at his staff.

"Anyone like to add something? Did I miss anything?" he asked. His face was red with rage.

Dan Logan stood up next to his boss.

"I think I speak for all of us, sir," Logan answered. He turned to the Bishops.

"Good day gentleman. Tell your limo drivers to be careful, the roads look slippery."

McGrath walked over and opened the door for Hanson and his colleagues who left quietly.

No one else moved, waiting for Greaves to say something.

"Well…that's that. I guess I have to go to confession tonight," he said. "But will somebody help me here, I'm a little confused."

He put a hand to his chin, pulling at it as if he were deep in thought.

"Is mugging a Bishop a mortal or venial sin?"

The room erupted in laughter that grew into a standing ovation for the managing editor.

Several weeks later, the Bishops scheduled a press conference and announced their plan to "revitalize and rebuild" the North End and to build a new community in Coventry to house the 20,000 Hartford minority citizens who would be displaced by the Greater Hartford Process Plan.

As predicted, most city officials, the Black Caucus Puerto Rican neighborhood leaders and the entire town of Coventry was blindsided by the plan. Also predictable was the outrage of all affected constituencies. No matter how hard he tried or how eloquently he spoke of the merits of the plan, Don Hanson was met with the mistrust of community leaders that had been building for decades. The fact that the effort had been conducted in a shroud of secrecy only inflamed the aura of deceit that enveloped the project. In the town of Coventry, when dumbfounded town officials recognized that Greater Hartford Process had already secretly moved to acquire a 1,600 acre tract to build the proposed new community, they threatened legal action to block the development.

The Hartford Times carried the story on page one, but not under a banner headline. The story, written by Dan Logan, presented only the facts as described by Hanson and the Bishops, but also quoted the exceedingly negative reaction of civic leaders extensively. For the next three days, every faction of Hartford that felt offended and deceived by the secret effort besieged City Hall. The mayor and councilman were quick to disown Greater Hartford Process as the "pipe dream of the Hartford corporate community." They left Hanson and his fellow Bishops hanging out to dry with the rest of Hartford's dirty laundry.

True to their word, the Bishops pulled millions of dollars in advertising and circulation from The Times, inflicting a financial wound on the paper that would never heal. Nevertheless, The Times' presses continued to roll each afternoon, even if the news hole was a bit smaller and a few thousand less copies were printed.

"We'll get through this, Jim, I know we will," Logan assured his boss who had just sat through a dismal meeting with the publisher.

"I don't know, Dan," Greaves said. "Our friends the Bishops have no idea how much damage they've done to the city. This was not the answer, but their proposal has spawned a whole new cycle of racial distrust. I simply don't know how Hartford can survive on its present course. Clearly, leadership will change. In fact, I guarantee we'll see black or Puerto Rican leadership elected at City Hall within the next two elections. That will help, but only if the remaining white population and the corporate fathers support them."

"Corporate 'fathers'?" Logan said, surprised by the term.

"I think our friends the Bishops have pretty much seen their day as powerbrokers. My bet is they will disappear from view and retreat to the sanctity of their palatial CEO offices to lick their wounds. Frankly, that's a good thing in my mind.

"Because ultimately, all they've succeeded in accomplishing is further dividing our city."

"Sad isn't it?" Logan said."

"In so many ways," Greaves responded. "But I suspect you have a specific point."

"In a little more than a hundred years, Hartford has gone from being the wealthiest city in the country to a city with a great future in its past."

"Extraordinary," Greaves answered.

"But maybe we shouldn't be so pessimistic. Perhaps something will cause a profound change in Hartford's future. I haven't a clue what that could be," Logan said.

"Well..." Greaves paused, thinking.

"You know there are those guys talking about a bridge..."

Twenty-Seven

~~~ → ~~~

May, 1970

Greaves and the entire newsroom staff were mesmerized by the image of their President on television rationalizing his intention to invade Cambodia.

Nixon had gone on the air on April 30 at 9:00 p.m. EST to announce to a shocked nation that he had ordered the escalation of the Vietnam War into neighboring Cambodia.

"The madman did it," Greaves said. "He's just upped the ante despite all his assurances to the contrary."

"It is not our power but our will and character that is being tested tonight," Nixon told anxious Americans. "The time has come for action."

Logan was equally stunned. Just ten days before, the President had ordered a further reduction of 150,000 troops within the next year. It appeared to most Americans that Nixon was focused on pulling out of the Vietnam quagmire. It was a cruel blow to a war-weary nation. Nixon, us usual, spun his message to rationalize his contradictory decision.

"Ten days ago in my report to the nation on Vietnam I announced the decision to withdraw an additional 150,000 Americans from Vietnam over the next year," Nixon said. "And at that time I warned that if I concluded that increased enemy activity in any of these areas endangered the lives of Americans remaining in Vietnam, I would not hesitate to take strong and effective measures to deal with that situation. Despite that warning, North Vietnam has increased its military aggression in all these areas, and particularly in Cambodia.

"Tonight, American and South Vietnamese units will attack the headquarters for the entire Communist military operation in South Vietnam. The key control center has been occupied by the North Vietnamese and Viet Cong for five years in blatant violation of Cambodia's neutrality.

"I realize in this war there are honest deep differences in this country about whether we should have become involved, that there are differences to how the war should have been conducted.

"But the decision I announce tonight transcends those differences, for the lives of American men are involved. The opportunity for 150,000 Americans to come home in the next 12 months is involved. The future of 18 million people in South Vietnam and seven million people in Cambodia is involved, the possibility of winning a just peace in Vietnam and in the Pacific is at stake."

Americans didn't buy it.

"Just when the bastard has you convinced, he shows you his real hand," Logan replied.

"This is going to ignite the anti-war movement," Greaves observed. "Let's get Dick McGrath in here."

At dawn on May 1, 36 B-52s dropped nearly 800 tons of bombs on the southern border of Cambodia in the first stage of *Operation Rockcrusher*, a mission to eliminate 40,000 Viet Cong troops and vast quantities of weapons stored in the neighboring country. At 08:00 hours, a massive artillery barrage began followed by another hour of aerial strikes by U.S. tactical fighter-bombers. Then, some 10,000 American troops supported by an additional 5,000 South Vietnamese soldiers crossed the border into Cambodia. Even the Cambodian government was shocked by the surprise invasion.

The U.S. media swung into high gear demanding answers from the White House and the Pentagon. A tsunami of protest and outrage surged toward Nixon from all corners of America and around the globe. It was clear that the President's pronounced Vietnam strategy was a ruse.

Protests against the war now came from nearly all segments of the American population including congress and business leaders who demanded that Nixon end the illegitimate invasion of Cambodia at once and pull out of the Vietnam War.

And then came reports of Nixon's address to employees of the Pentagon hours before the invasion began that not only further inflamed the huge student-based anti-war movement, it showed signs of the President beginning to unravel emotionally.

"You know, you see these bums, you know, blowing up the campuses," he said. "Listen, the boys on the college campuses today are the luckiest people in the world — going to the greatest universities — and here they are burning up the books.

"I mean," Nixon continued, "storming around about this issue, I mean you name it get rid of the war, there'll be another one."

Greaves was appalled.

"Lead with the invasion and the latest updates we can get on military losses," Greaves told Logan. "Dick, get to Dodd and Ribicoff and get a statement. Then I want a sub-head and a sidebar on Nixon's view of the student anti-war movement and quote the incoherent son of a bitch exactly as he said it."

The Times front page that afternoon echoed the country's disenchantment with their president, who had once again misled them.

President Orders Invasion of Cambodia
Congress Demands Review of Decision

Nixon Labels Student Radicals "Bums"

At a meeting of the news staff that night, McGrath briefed Greaves, Logan and key reporters on the mood on college campuses across the country.

"We may be on the verge of a complete meltdown. I'm talking about a nation-wide campus strike," McGrath said. "The student response to the Cambodian escalation has shocked the White House. And of course Nixon calling all these kids "bums" hasn't helped.

"But already, Princeton, Yale, Rutgers, Ohio State, and the University of Pennsylvania are out and more are planning to strike beginning tomorrow. The National Guard is already on campus at the University of Maryland and there are 5,000 kids right this minute protesting at Stanford despite heavy police presence and indiscriminant use of tear gas. Fire bombings of ROTC buildings have been reported on numerous campuses."

McGrath just shook his head, looking over his notes.

"Trust me gentlemen, this is going to get a lot worse before it gets better."

"Any word on local activity? University of Hartford, UCONN, etc?" Greaves asked.

"Both schools are planning demonstrations tomorrow morning. I suspect there will be a sizeable crowd. I still can't get over the fact that we had 10,000 people in Bushnell Park last week at the Moratorium. I'm planning on driving to Storrs in the morning to cover the UCONN protest," McGrath replied.

"Logan, you should stay clear of the University of Hartford, being a student there. But have somebody cover it," Greaves ordered.

By noon the next day, more than 100 colleges and universities had shut down, their students on strike in protest of the war and Nixon's treachery. More would follow.

Dan McGrath called in from the afternoon UCONN protest the next day.

"Dan, you'd have to be here to believe the anger these kids are feeling. I've been watching them burn draft cards for the last hour. That may not seem like much, but it's a felony and they couldn't care less. At least eight students have been arrested; there will be more before this is over. I suspect more of the same is happening at schools across the country."

As The Hartford Times first edition was being circulated later that afternoon, violent student protests were erupting all over the nation. But at Kent State University in Kent, Ohio, there was an ominous feel to the campus demonstrations fed by the intolerance of State and local government.

By the time Ohio National Guardsman arrived on the Kent State campus later that night at the order of Governor Jim Rhodes, the University's Reserve Officers Training Corps building was in flames. Tear gas was deployed to disperse the students and numerous arrests were made. ROTC buildings were a favorite target of the anti-war movement. The Kent State facility was just one of many to end up in ashes.

But emotions continued to rise on the Ohio campus and demonstrations persisted on May 3rd. Rhodes, speaking at a press conference at a Kent firehouse fanned the flames even more.

"We are going to eradicate the problem. We're not going to treat the symptoms. And these people just move from one campus to the other and terrorize the community. They're worse than the brown shirts and the communist element and also the night riders and the vigilantes", Rhodes said. "They're the worst type of people that we harbor in America. Now I want to say this. They are not going to take over the campus."

Instead of calling for calm, the Governor's foolhardy rhetoric made it clear he had blood in his eye. The stage was set for tragedy.

At 8 p.m., hundreds of students gathered for another demonstration on the campus Commons, but within 45 minutes, Ohio Guardsmen were using tear gas to break up the rally and several students were bayoneted. Kent Mayor LeRoy Satrom ordered an 11 p.m. curfew.

Another demonstration was planned for the next afternoon on May 4th at noon. Despite the university's efforts to ban the protest, more than 2,000 students gathered on the Commons. The National Guardsman almost immediately used tear gas to disperse the crowd, but high winds made it ineffective. Many fled the scene, alarmed by the aggressiveness of the Ohio Guard which seemed determined to clear the Commons of all protestors. Nearly 80 Guardsman began advancing on hundreds of students who held their ground with fixed bayonets on their M1 rifles

Then suddenly, at 12:24 p.m., with the smell of tear gas heavy in the air and shouts of "Pigs off campus" echoing across the Kent State University Commons, 28 Guardsman opened fire without warning on the unarmed students. Some 67 rounds were fired into the crowd in 13 seconds of insanity.

Deathly silence descended over the Commons but was quickly replaced by the screams and cries of the survivors who stood over the bodies of four dead or dying students and yelled for ambulances for nine others who were seriously wounded. A girl could be heard screaming in shock and disbelief, "They didn't have blanks, they didn't have blanks. No, they didn't." Most students had believed the Guardsman's rifles were loaded with blank rounds. They were tragically mistaken.

In the newsroom of The Hartford Times and in other newspapers across the country, the steady hum of reporters and editors conversing and the machine gun like chatter of typewriters all came to a screeching halt as the word "Bulletin" began to appear across television screens and the wires service teletypes streamed "Breaking News: Four Dead in Ohio."

"No. That's impossible," Logan whispered as he watched the recorded images on the television and was handed the wire service copy.

"They shot kids. Oh my God, they shot kids," Greaves said standing next to him.

The managing editor watched and listened for a few moments then hollered to Logan, "Tell makeup to stand by for a new page one and get McGrath and come into my office."

He quickly handed out assignments.

"Dan, you work the lead story, make sure you get identities on those kids who were killed or wounded, they deserve at least that. Find out what led to the Guard being there at all and who ordered the shooting. Your story will lead.

"Dick, get whatever the Ohio Governor is saying and find out what role he's had in this, if any. Also, get what you can from the White House, I can't believe Nixon won't issue a statement, although it will probably be passed our deadline by the time those assholes finish spinning this."

He turned to Logan again.

"Dan, get someone to do a round up of what's happened already and what is happening at colleges and universities. You can bet there won't be many administrations willing to risk staying in session after this debacle. If this happened once, it can happen again. We also need to hear from the National Guard. I don't even know who the hell the senior honcho is, but get somebody on it."

Logan called his news staff together and handed out assignments as Greaves had directed, adding a few more of his own.

"Kent State owns page one this afternoon guys, but lets get as broad a sweep of the rest of the academic world as we can. Get calls into Dodd's and Ribicoff's offices and don't take no for an answer. Get a statement from those guys or tell them we're going to go with "refused to comment."

He paused.

"Can you believe this?" he allowed himself just a moment to allow the reality to set in before returning to the crisis.

"Go get it, guys, and get it right," he ordered his staff of reporters. "We meet back here in an hour to share what we know."

They scrambled out the door of Logan's office.

"And let me see available art for the lead, ASAP," he hollered to a photographer that was in the dispersing group. Inside, his stomach churned at the pictures he knew would be available. Logan leaned back in his chair and closed his eyes. Strangely, it was times like this when he missed Elina the most. He often dreamt of just talking with her, sharing his feelings about so many things that filled his days. And he imagined how comforting it would be to hold her after a particularly emotional day, like this one.

An hour passed and details of the tragedy on the Ohio campus were sketchy. Logan's office filled with reporters ready to report whatever news they had. Greaves stood in the doorway, listening.

Dick McGrath was first.

"Well, surprisingly, the White House didn't waste much time getting Nixon in front of the press corps, but considering what he said, they might have been better off dragging their heels. I quote our 'beloved' president, " he said sarcastically.

"This should remind us all once again that when dissent turns to violence it invites tragedy. It is my hope that this tragic and unfortunate incident will strengthen the determination of all the nation's campuses, administrators, faculty and students alike to stand firmly for the rights which exist in this country of peaceful dissent and just as strongly against the resort to violence as a means of such expression."

"You're joking," said Tom Lynch, the State editor. He could hardly be heard over the chorus of cursing that erupted in the room.

"Nothing spiritual, no apology... he didn't say anything to humanize the situation?" Logan asked in disbelief.

"That's what he said, and the AP and UPI reporters were only too happy to let him hang himself. What I read you is a verbatim of the wire service stories.

"Who the hell is counseling this madman?"

"One wonders how he can survive this," added Bill Planeta, the senior editorial writer. "But 'tricky Dick' always finds a way."

"What did we get from the Ohio Guard?" Logan continued.

"I got this from the National Guard PA officer in Columbus," McGrath said. "The Guard is reporting that they responded to 'sniper' fire.'"

He paused, trying to compose himself. McGrath's anger was obvious.

"I quote," he continued. 'Sylvester Del Corso, Adjutant General of the Ohio National Guard said in a statement that the Guardsman had been forced to shoot after a sniper opened fire against the troops from a nearby rooftop and the crowd began to move to encircle the Guardsman.' End quote."

"The PA also told me that the Guardsmen were under standing orders to take cover and return any fire. That's supposedly what they did. However, the press that was at the scene and numerous students who were involved in the demonstration or just watching heatedly denied that there had been any sniper fire. The students admitted to throwing rocks, but swear there was no 'sniper' fire from any rooftop."

"Sounds like a weak cover your ass ploy to me," Lynch said. There was loud agreement amongst his colleagues.

Greaves spoke up.

"Until somebody debunks the sniper story, we will report the allegation as 'unconfirmed and challenged by eyewitnesses.' Clear? We're not in a position to deny. But let's try to get a reporter who was there to make a statement."

Logan nodded. "Dick, get on the phone. Jim's right." McGrath hurried from the room.

As he was leaving, a young reporter, a black kid hired only a few months before right out of Columbia University's journalism school came into the room with breaking news off the wires.

"Dan," Stephen Dunn interrupted, "this is important.

"What is it, Steve?" Logan liked this guy. He had the same fire in the eye that he had when he first got a chance as a reporter.

"This just came over AP," Dunn said. "Apparently at least 37 major college and university presidents have released a letter to Nixon urging him to move for immediate termination of the war. They warn him of a complete alienation of academia from supporting the government and that they believe further escalation may result in massive and violent student protests. There's also a list of schools that have already shut down on strike and many administrations are taking the action without waiting for students to demand it. It's over 200 now, including all the Ivy League schools."

"Steve, give me three takes on their letter and combine it with an update on the campus situation. I want to run a sidebar on page one," Logan ordered. Dunn grinned and hurried off.

Greaves liked what he heard, but the picture wasn't complete.

"Dan, we need an update on what's happening on the Cambodian border. How far U.S. forces have penetrated, how many killed, if we're calling the invasion a success or not. And also, let's find out what the Cambodian government is saying. They were as blindsided by this as anyone."

"Yes, sir, good call. Dick has the best Pentagon sources." He scanned the room for the photographer he'd asked to get page one art for him. He wandered in just as Logan was about to ask.

"Smitty," Logan yelled. "Where you been? I asked for those photo's an hour ago."

"Sorry, Dan, I didn't like the early stuff, it was mostly self serving crap the National Guard had released. This is what I was waiting for." He handed him an 8x10 inch photo that had just come off the AP wire. Logan took it from him and flinched, closing his eyes after a glance.

It was a photo of a young girl, screaming as she knelt over the dead body of a young student who had been caught in the Ohio National Guard barrage of fire. Logan thought he was going to be sick. He passed the photo around the room.

"Do we have identities on these kids, at least the ones who were killed?" he asked, struggling to regain his composure.

Len Smith, the photographer, answered.

"AP is identifying the victim in this picture as Jeffrey Miller, 19 of Plainview, New York and the girl is Mary Ann Vecchio. No details available yet on her. The other victims were Allison Krause, 19 of Cleveland; Sandra Scheuer, 20 of Youngstown; and William Schroeder, 19 of Cincinnati. There were nine others wounded, identities have not been released as of yet." He paused to scan some additional wire copy.

"Oh my God," he whispered.

"What is it, Smitty" Logan pressed.

"UPI is saying that Miller and Scheuer died instantly, Krause and Schroeder within an hour. A reporter says that none of their bodies were less than a football field away from where the Guard fired, hardly posing a threat, and that two of the four, Scheuer and Schroeder weren't even involved in the protest. They were just walking between classes."

He dropped his hands and looked up at the ceiling, incredulous.

"Jesus Christ, they were frigging murdered." His voice broke as he struggled to finish the last sentence.

The room went silent at his words. The truth was almost unbearable.

"Good work, Smitty, we'll go with the Miller photo," Logan said, trying to keep everyone focused. "Get that copy to Dunn, please, tell him to write a side-bar with as much information as he can get in the next hour on the victims."

"Yes, sir," Smitty answered in a low voice, sickened by what he had just learned.

Lou White suddenly spoke up. No one had noticed the publisher wander into the briefing.

"I'm sorry, I was in a meeting with circulation when all this went down. I just heard. It's real, isn't it... I mean, it really happened?" he asked in disbelief.

"Yes, Lou, it happened," Greaves responded.

"My daughter is a sophomore at Ohio State..." White said shakily.

Greaves understood with a parent's instinct what he was searching for.

"There's been reports of violence at Ohio State over the last 48 hours, Lou," he said to the shaken publisher. "But I believe the demonstrations are over and the University has been shut down. Go call your daughter. If you can't reach her let me know. I'll put some guys on it... we'll find her.

"She's ok, Lou," Greaves said. "I know it."

"Thank you, Jim," the publisher said, his eyes wet.

The managing editor waited until White was out of ear shot before speaking.

"I don't have to tell you that what you just saw is very much the same reaction every parent in this country will have when they hear what's happened," he began. "It's a parent's nightmare. An absolute, ultimate horror. Remember that when you write your copy. It will make you choose your words more carefully and to be sure what you're reporting is accurate.

"I don't mean to lecture you, you're all professionals whom I have the greatest respect for. Guess I've written too many stories about dead kids and seen too many weeping parents at their funerals. Keep at it guys, good work." He walked back to his office.

Logan looked around.

"There's not a damn thing I can say that tops that, guys," he said. "Let's put this paper to bed and get it out. It's one we'll never forget."

Feverishly, The Times editors and reporters worked for the next two hours to make their stories as current as possible and still make the Bulldog edition deadline. Greaves and Logan poured over the press proofs before they had even dried.

"Despite how we feel, there's still an awful lot of people out there unconvinced that Nixon is leading us down the wrong path," Greaves commented as they read. "One would think this would be the final straw. I have my doubts that our president will back down. If anything, he'll be irritated by this. His statement makes that pretty clear."

"You watch... the White House PR machine will be cranking out one tidbit after another over the next months, every one designed to convince the American people he's winding down the war, while behind the scenes he'll be doing the exact opposite," Logan responded.

"You know what this is really about, Dan?" Greaves asked. "Nixon's ego won't allow him to be the first president to admit to losing a war. It's all about him. Not the body bags."

The two signed off on the proof and the edition went to press. Logan rolled it up and brought it back to his office. Later that night, exhausted, he stared in awe at the words on the page. It was all so unbelievable. He had been chasing Vietnam-related news for half a decade and should no longer be surprised by anything, he thought. But even 12 hours after watching the Bulletin break on television, he was still in a sort of shock.

Four Ohio Students Killed At Kent State; Troops Fired On Unarmed Protestors

Sniper Reports Unproven; College Chiefs Tell Nixon To End War Immediately

The irony had hit him after the paper was on the street. The Ohio National Guardsmen who fired on the unarmed students were, for the most part, the same age as the kids they had killed. Most had joined the Guard to escape the draft into the regular Army and a certain one-year ticket to the Vietnam War.

The nausea came over him so suddenly he had to run for the bathroom. Logan retched over and over, the image of kids killing kids burned into his brain. Finally, his stomach emptied, he slumped down next to the toilet, resting against it.

He had a sudden urge to call Elina, just to talk to someone. But he knew it was a bad idea and nothing good would come of it for either of them.

It was at that moment that the thought came to him.

"This Boy" was a one-way street.

Twenty-Eight

~~~ ઝ ~~~

May 16, 1970

It was a brilliant spring morning, the kind that one celebrated after a long, cold winter. Warm sunrays cut through the cloudless, crisp blue sky bringing promise of an early summer. Logan sped down Old Boston Post Road towards the Connecticut shoreline in his low-slung sports car, the top folded back. The wind coming over the low raked windshield buffeted against his face but the fresh air was supremely refreshing after months of long days and nights confined to the smoky newsroom or his dark, lonely apartment. He could almost feel the blood rushing through his veins again, like a changing of the tide.

But despite the invigorating break from his daily tedium, his thoughts continually turned back to the

398

events of the past weeks as he drove, and he was powerless to leave them behind. There was a bright side to his preoccupation however. He could avoid thinking about the real reason for his trip on this Saturday morning and the inevitable outcome.

Only half way through the month, he was certain that May 1970 had been the most tumultuous and remarkable time in his life. He would never experience another spring without his thoughts wandering back to these days, which were so filled with shock, sorrow and confusion.

It seemed every day had brought some new blow crashing down upon the nation. The Cambodian invasion and Nixon's callous treachery, the sudden recognition by congress that America was being led down a primrose path towards an inescapable defeat. The astonishing response of the anti-war movement, which had seized the moment to escalate its own agenda. The campus riots and demonstrations that ultimately shut down over 450 colleges and universities and caused more than four million students to strike in protest of the futile war and the deceit of their president. The murder of four Ohio students, cut down by the overreaction of their own peers who were dressed like soldiers and armed like warriors only to avoid the very conflict that their victims were protesting. A president, whose cold-hearted response was nearly as devastating as the crime he had undeniably precipitated.

All that had happened in just four days, yet America would never be the same.

And then, on May 8th came the mass demonstration of 100,000 war protestors in Washington and 150,000 more in San Francisco. The mood of the demonstrators was so angry and violent that it caused Nixon's closest advisors to worry about the possibility of a national insurrection. The president was evacuated to Camp David for his own safety for two days and troops from the Army's 82nd Airborne Division were called up to occupy the Executive Office Building of the White House to protect the administration. In a bizarre twist, upon returning to Washington on May 9th, Nixon impulsively snuck out of the White House and met spontaneously with a group of 30 to 50 protestors on the steps of the Lincoln Memorial. There he awkwardly attempted to open a dialogue about his efforts to end the war. Witnesses said the president was rambling and condescending in his remarks, leading most to question his emotional state.

Logan could feel the air turn slightly cooler as he approached the shoreline but reveled in its feel. He powered the sleek Triumph TR that he had brought back to life through the twists and turns of the old two-lane blacktop, exulting in each crisp throw of the shifter. He needed to do more of this, he decided. But his thoughts almost immediately returned to the momentous times.

Just yesterday, he had worked closely with Jim Greaves to put out another memorable edition of The Times, leading with the story of two more student anti-war protestors who were dead at the hands of overzealous cops at Jackson State College in Jackson, Mississippi. More than 75 local and Mississippi State Police responded to the demonstration by a hostile crowd, but again opened fire on the unarmed students without warning. When the 30-second barrage was over more than 460 bullets had struck the dormitory directly behind the demonstrators, blowing out every window in the front of the building. And 21-year-old Phillip Gibbs, a student and father of an 18-month-old son, and 17-year-old James Earl Green, a high school student who was walking home and stopped to watch, lay dead in the street. For hours after, the streets of Jackson were filled with the sound of ambulance sirens racing to save the lives of 12 more wounded.

In the same edition, The Times ran a Pentagon press release announcing the overwhelming success of *Operation Rockcrusher*, the campaign to invade Cambodia. From a logistical standpoint the mission was already a huge success, according to the new military commander of U.S. forces in Vietnam, General Creighton W. Abrams. He claimed 11,000 enemy soldiers had been killed and another 2,500 captured with the loss of 338 U.S. troops killed and 1525 wounded. The Pentagon report also claimed seizure of a massive quantity of weapons and stores.

Yes, from a military perspective, Logan thought, *Operation Rockcrusher* was an undeniable success.

But at what cost? The victory would hardly be satisfying to the parents of six murdered students, 21 others who had been shot, and hundreds who had been beaten or gassed by police and the National Guard.

He was still mulling over the question when he came upon the last stretch of road before his intended destination. It was the narrow, two-lane Bridge Street causeway that passed over an ocean inlet and led to the village of Fenwick. He pulled the car over to the side of the road before proceeding to think things over. It was nearly 1 p.m. A time on a day that he knew he would never forget. That's why he was here. To watch what was about to happen, so there could be no doubt, ever.

It was Elina's wedding day.

He sucked in a deep breath, tasting the salt air on his tongue and pulled his car on to the causeway. He drove its length slower than he ever had before, with each roll of the tires bringing him closer to witness something he really didn't want to, but had to.

Logan made the left hand turn into Fenwick, then drove the mile or so to within a couple hundred yards of the Hanson mansion. He pulled the black Triumph off to the side of the road, a long way from the hundreds of guest cars parked on the street and Hanson's back lawn.

He got out of the car and pulled the collar up on the light windbreaker he was wearing. With dark sun glasses and his hair now considerably longer than the last time he had seen Charles, Elina or Don Hanson, he doubted that he would be recognized from a distance.

From the back pocket of his blue jeans, he pulled the folded and tattered invitation to Elina's wedding and reread the words printed on it for perhaps the hundredth time.

Mr. Donald Hanson
Requests the honor of your presence
At the marriage of his daughter
Elina Marie Hanson
to
Charles Edward Anderson
On the 16th of May, 1970
1 p.m.
The Hanson Cottage
18 Pettipaug Avenue
The Village of Fenwick
Old Saybrook, Connecticut
Reception to follow

He had never responded to it, in fact had only opened the envelope last night. Logan knew what was inside the perfumed envelope when it arrived in his mailbox weeks before, but couldn't bring himself to open it. The announcement in the social pages of The Times had shocked him. He had been able to push aside the envelope, but his own newspaper forced him to look.

The photograph of the bride in The Times column displayed Elina in all her glory. She would be a stunning bride, he knew. And that was when he decided that he had to see it happen with his own eyes. But only from a distance, where she could not see him or know that he was watching. He told himself that he didn't want her to be aware that he still cared and that was why he had to hide.

Last night, he had finally admitted that was a lie. The truth was that he couldn't come close to her because she would see the heartbreak in his eyes.

Logan hurried across the street and walked behind a tall hedge that hid him from the mansion. He figured that Hanson's neighbors would all be at the wedding so he could find his way to the beach without being noticed and settle in to a hiding place from which to watch.

His plan worked. He watched in a daze as she came down the weathered staircase on the arm of her father and walked across a bed of roses spread out on the sand to a waiting Charles Anderson. Logan was several hundred yards away but could still hear the soft music of a harp and violin playing in the background. The ocean lapping at the water's edge supplied a gentle rhythm for the musicians. There were hundreds of people in formal dress watching.

Logan looked on as Hanson stopped and lifted her veil then softly kissed his daughter's cheek. And then he gave her hand to Charles.

It was at that moment that Danny Logan knew he couldn't watch anymore. He broke from his hiding place and sprinted back to his car where he sat behind the wheel for several minutes, his hands trembling. Finally, he started the car and drove away from Fenwick.

But this time, he didn't look back.

Twenty-Nine

~~~ ❧ ~~~

June, 1973

Dan Logan thought there had never been a more sullen celebration in the history of the Traveler's Spa Restaurant.

The place was like a second home to most of the editors and reporters who frequented its bar almost every night after work, and it was usually filled with cheery banter. But tonight the long faces around the room gave away their emotions as they had gathered to send off their brilliant managing editor into the sunset of retirement.

Jim Greaves, who had lived and breathed The Hartford Times for 33 years, more than two decades of them as managing editor, was living up to his promise to relinquish the reigns when his self-imposed mission of working to end the Vietnam War had been fulfilled.

"Lighten up, you bums," he said after taking the microphone from Lou White who had given an emotional introduction.

"There's beer to be drunk tonight, and a paper to put out tomorrow," Greaves said, determined that this night wasn't going to be his wake. "Nothing changes, really, only the names and faces of those who do the drinking and the writing." He was successful in getting a laugh out of the packed house.

"You know, I'm a pretty lucky guy. Why? Well, first of all because I get to sleep in tomorrow morning. It's been a long time since I've done that." Half-hearted laughter was all the crowd could muster. They all knew Greaves would be up at the crack of dawn.

"But seriously, I do consider myself a lucky man. Because after all these years, I really only have two regrets in my life. The first is that my Mary, the absolute love of my life, isn't here to celebrate with me and that we didn't have a few years to eat dinner together at a normal hour." There was more laughter, but the poignancy of his words was lost on no one.

"The second is that I wish I could have retired a bit earlier, in fact a lot earlier. That, of course would have meant that the Vietnam War had ended a long time ago, as it should have. Sometimes, usually when I've had a beer or two too many, I think that maybe if all of us, if all newsmen had worked just a little harder to bring the truth to the American people, perhaps there wouldn't have been so many body bags, so many grieving parents... so many lost boys." He looked over at Charlie Holcombe, his dear friend and confidante. Holcombe's head was bowed.

"Yah, that's one of my regrets."

405

He paused, fighting to keep his composure.

"But then, when I sober up," he continued to welcomed laughter, "I remember what a remarkable thing we all did, what newsmen and college kids and priests, teachers and parents and every American who was ready to take a stand... what we all did to force the end of that futile disaster. And it makes me proud. Proud of you, proud to be an American, proud to have been a part of it. In the 33 years I worked at the Hartford Times, I believe our effort was the most important contribution ever made in the history of this great paper, and I'm damned proud of that."

The editors, writers and pressmen all rose together to applaud him, but he wasn't finished. He held up his hands to let then know there was more.

"So, I'm done here, can't do any more damage," Greaves said, smiling. "You'll have to live with the demands and whims of young Dan Logan here. But don't let the fact that he's not old enough to have to shave everyday fool you. Underneath that baby face is the heart of one tough newsman, who has the instincts — and the balls — of an editor three times his age. He will lead you well." The applause for Logan was genuine.

"But I can't leave without a toast. No editor can retire without saying something quotable," he smiled and raised his glass.

"And so, to The Hartford Times, the greatest afternoon newspaper in the country and to the men and women who make it so. And to that date in history that will forever be etched into my brain — January 27, 1973 — the date the Peace Accord was signed in Paris. May those who died in vain and those who lost a loved one know that they will never be forgotten." Greaves raised his glass in tribute.

"Salute."

"Salute," the crowd responded and drank up.

"And one last thing," Greaves continued. "Newsmen know if they work a story hard enough the truth will always rise to a headline. It's sort of like cream, it always rise to the top. Well, there's a certain truth that needs to be exposed in the coming months, and again it has to do with our government at the highest level."

He looked around the room, into the eyes of the people who had served him so faithfully in his career. "You all know what I'm talking about. Our president won his job back, that's a fact. How he did it is something that's being analyzed by a lot of people, including reporters of The Hartford Times.

"I well remember talking with some of you that June morning in 1972, just about a year ago, when the AP broke the story on the Watergate break in. We all laughed that only Nixon would be paranoid enough to authorize a burglary of the Democratic National Party Headquarters when he already had an insurmountable lead in the polls. Not so funny today, is it?

"The only thing we know for sure is that the whole story has not yet been heard. That's because the truth has not yet been found. Once again, it is your job, as newsmen, to bring the truth to the American people." He paused, on the brink again.

"The Times has never backed down from the truth, no matter how big or powerful or scary it was. Don't start now. We all know that hell hath no fury like a president scorned..." Greaves improvised to nervous laughter. "But no president can continually scorn the law, either. Justice must prevail." He paused and scanned the crowd again, invigorating them like he had so many times in the past.

"So. I leave you tonight with one final assignment. Find the truth. Write it. Print it. That's your job."

The restaurant went silent.

"And with that, thank you for sharing with me the best years of my life, thank you for your loyalty and dedication and know that you will all be in my heart for the rest of my days."

The roar inside the small restaurant was loud enough to shake the stately columns of The Times building, blocks away.

Later that night, sitting at his kitchen table, Logan reflected on the tumultuous years he had spent at the right hand of a man who had taught him so much. He only hoped that he could be half the managing editor that Greaves had been.

He remembered that night in April, when he and Greaves had watched the president tell a broken nation that he was about to expand the war into Cambodia. His boss had turned to him as the words came out of Nixon's mouth.

"Dan, what you are witnessing is an unmitigated disaster. But it's also the beginning of the end of the Vietnam War... and Richard Nixon. It's just going to take some time."

How right he had been.

That single decision not only energized and focused the massive anti-war movement, it erased any sense of confidence Americans had in Nixon's promise to end U.S. involvement in Vietnam. But worst of all, trust in their new president was replaced by bitterness and hostility.

The invasion of Cambodia also ended any sense that Nixon had a bona fide plan for ending the war. To many American's, including members of the government, his own administration and high-ranking Pentagon brass, he also lacked the emotional maturity necessary to affect a strategy of disengagement. His "Peace with Honor" slogan rang hollow from the moment he announced his decision to escalate the war, and his callousness in responding to the Kent State murders came to define his personality.

Despite the "success" of the invasion in terms of the number of enemy killed and seized weapons and materials, the incursion failed to convince North Vietnam that it could not support the high cost of waging the war. Instead, the enemy became even more aggressive in its military operations and took full advantage of the domestic and political turmoil in the U.S. Ultimately, the invasion jumpstarted congress into taking actions to curb the presidents' reckless disregard for the limits of his powers and his dependence on secret campaigns such as the bombing of Cambodia that had begun months before.

It was the U.S. media that discovered the deceptions and reported them resulting in a backlash that stunned the White House.

Within two years, congress passed the Cooper-Church amendment outlawing the presence of U.S. troops in Cambodia and Laos, and the War Powers Resolution effectively ending Nixon's ability to wage war without the approval of congress. In the end, Nixon's abuse of power had weakened the U.S. position at the Paris Peace talks rather than strengthened it. By January of 1973, it was over. Nixon had lost much of his ability to wage war, and because of the growing Watergate scandal that was slowly eating away at his presidency and his ability to focus on anything but saving his own skin, the Peace Accord was finally signed on January 27, 1973. It was hardly "Peace with Honor," Logan thought.

The final tally: 58,315 American troops died in the conflict and more than 153,000 were wounded. The pain and suffering of the survivors was incalculable.

Yet, somehow, Nixon had won re-election. Logan was still shocked that the Democratic candidate, Sen. George McGovern had been completely overwhelmed in the 1972 campaign. The Nixon campaign machine had successfully positioned the Democratic nominee as the "abortion, amnesty and acid" candidate through skillfully planted leaks that defined his platform as pro-abortion, pro-amnesty for Vietnam draft dodgers and supportive of the legalization of marijuana. None of it was true. Coupled with complete disarray in the McGovern camp, the nearly complete withdrawal of U.S. troops from Vietnam that took away the urgency of peace and Secretary of State Henry Kissinger's carefully timed pronouncement that "Peace is at hand" days before the election, and McGovern never had a chance. A healthy helping of dirty tricks from the Nixon campaign was the coup de grâce that befuddled and derailed the Democratic ticket.

But now "Tricky Dick" was in a tight spot. The bungled Watergate break in had set off a media hunt that already had led to a consistent pattern of criminal activity aimed at keeping a Republican in the White House. And now, America was beginning to believe that the path led right to the Oval Office.

In his first year as managing editor, Logan knew he would have to manage a team of reporters that was increasingly obsessed with the Watergate investigation and the Select Committee on Presidential Campaign Activities. Despite his own bias, he swore he would be strong enough to maintain objectivity.

The phone rang. He glanced at his watch. It was nearly 2 a.m. Now what...

"This is Dan Logan, " he answered.

"Dan, It's Dick McGrath. Sorry to disturb you so late. Sounds like you weren't sleeping," he said. Logan picked up a familiar background. McGrath was calling from the newsroom.

"Dick, what's wrong? Why are you at work?" Logan asked.

"I got a call from a PR guy at Mutual Insurance Corp. about midnight. He said it was important, asked if we could meet at The Times. I came in."

"So what's up?" Logan asked.

"The guy handed me a press release. Said he wanted The Times to break the news."

"What news?"

"Don Hanson, Mutual's chairman and CEO died about 10:30 tonight. Appears to have been a stroke. He was being driven home to Old Saybrook..."

"Fenwick, you mean."

"Uh, yah," McGrath said, surprised by the correction. "Driver didn't know what to do, pulled into a fire house in Middletown. The firemen called an ambulance and did CPR but he was DOA at the hospital."

"The PR guy... he say why he wanted The Times to break the story?" Logan probed.

"I asked the same thing. What he said was only Dan Logan knew the real Don Hanson. The CEO apparently left specific instructions with his PR department as to what they were to do in the event of his death. The guy said he was just following instructions."

"The 'real' Don Hanson," Logan repeated. "Let me tell you, Dick, I did know him outside the office. He was a complicated man. I think I understand. Let me

411

sleep on this. There's nothing we can do until tomorrow anyway." He was silent for a moment, thinking.

"Did this guy mention if the family is aware?"

"I asked. He told me his daughter was called to the hospital. Apparently his wife passed away…"

"Yah, I'm familiar with the family situation. Think I'll give the daughter a call just to be sure this is what she wants," Logan said.

"Think that's a good idea, Dan. Usually this would already be on a wire by now. He was a well-known businessman and I think Mutual is still the city's largest employer. And after the Greater Hartford Process dust up a few years back, it's a front page piece, agree?"

"Yes, agreed. Ok, talk to you in the morning unless something changes. Get some rest, Dick," Logan said. "You sound tired."

"Jesus…" McGrath said, surprise in his voice.

"What?" Logan asked.

"You already sound like Greaves… good night… 'boss.'" He hung up.

Logan recalled something Jim Greaves once told him was a key element to his success as a manager.

"Care, Dan. Care about your people and their lives. Don't interfere, but let them know you do care about more than how well they spell."

"Amazing how some lessons just stick," he thought to himself. Care. Just a couple of weeks ago, Greaves and Charlie Holcombe had shown they meant it when Danny Logan, their protégé, walked across a stage wearing a cap and gown and proudly accepted his college diploma at the University of Hartford. Greaves and Holcombe rose to their feet and shouted his name in celebration.

After the ceremony, Logan sought them out in the crowd.

"Thank you, Charlie and Jim. This never would have happened without you pushing so hard," Logan said.

"Get over here, kid," Holcombe laughed, reaching out and wrapping his arms around him. "Best hire I ever made," he whispered into his ear.

Greaves did the same. Logan had become the son he never had.

"Don't let all the attention go to your head, Logan. We just didn't want the Army stealing our best typist," Greaves laughed. Then they bought him dinner. The two men were the closest resemblance he had to a family.

The memories made him think again about that word: care. Greaves taught him to care. He should be big enough to pick up the phone and call someone who probably needed to hear that someone cared on this night.

He dialed a number he knew by heart despite having called it so few times. To his surprise, Elina answered the phone.

"Hello," she said wearily, her voice tinged with sadness.

"Elina, it's Danny," he said.

"Danny? Danny Logan..." He heard her sob. "How long has it been?"

"Three and a half years," Logan responded more quickly than he wished. "I know this is awkward, but I just wanted to tell you how sorry I am about your father's passing," he said as genuinely as he could. "I know you loved him very much."

"He was a very special man, Danny, and treated me like a princess. But you know all that... it's just as

413

well. He had a massive stroke and if he had lived, he would have been a shadow of himself. He was so active... it would have tortured him."

"I'm glad you've come to grips with that, Elina, but I'm sure you are heartbroken," Logan responded.

"He lived a good life, was so successful. The only pain in his life came from the woman he loved so much. He never really recovered from losing her, despite how much she had hurt him. I hope he's found peace at last."

There was a moment of silence.

"Elina, I know this is difficult, but I need to discuss something with you," Logan said, exceedingly aware of the inelegance of his timing.

"I understand, Danny. What is it?"

"A PR representative of your father's company met with one of my reporters tonight and asked that The Times break the story tomorrow," Logan told her. "Frankly, I was quite surprised. Are you aware that this was your father's request?"

"Yes. I am," she said without hesitation.

"I'm not sure I understand," Logan replied.

"Danny, you know my father was a very complicated man," Elina responded. "I'm not stupid. I know that he had a reputation as a tyrant at work and that he was very difficult to do business with. On the other hand, he lived for his family. Danny, he never once complained or raised his voice to my mother, despite the alcoholic bitch she was. And he would do anything for me. He had a lot of respect for you, what you made of yourself and he thought you might be the only newsman who would understand there was more than one side to him."

"Yes, I did see him in different lights," Logan answered, "but I'm not sure what he expected of me..."

414

"All he wanted was some indication that he was more than a businessman... that he loved his family," Elina said, sobbing again.

"Ah..." Logan did not want to continue the conversation. "I think I understand, Elina. I will personally write the story announcing his death and will indeed mention his dedication to his family. But I cannot go farther...to make him a hero or something bigger than he was... I just don't want your expectations to..."

"Danny... don't fret. I know what my father was. I know all about the plan he and his friends had for the City of Hartford. I wasn't a fan... I only hope that people will appreciate that there was a human quality to the man. That besides being a ruthless businessman, Don Hanson was a loving husband and father. No more."

Logan was silent.

"Danny?"

"I'll do my best," he answered.

"Thank you. "

"Good night, Elina," Logan replied, desperately wanting to end the conversation before he blurted out "Are you happy with Charles? Do you remember 'This Boy?'"

He never got the chance.

"Good night, Danny, and thank you for calling," Elina said and hung up.

The next morning, he called Dick McGrath into his office and handed him two takes, his story on Don Hanson's death. McGrath read it and raised his eyes in surprise.

"Interesting. This guy was a son of a bitch to work with. He seemed to hate the press . This bit about him being a devoted husband and father comes as a real surprise. He was the kind of guy you figured only had one thing of consequence on his mind: making money. This will come as a surprise to a lot of folks. Play it on page one?" McGrath said.

"Yes. Below the fold, but run his photo. He was Chairman and CEO of the state's largest employer. That should justify it."

The story ran that afternoon and was picked up verbatim by the news wires.

There was no comment from Fenwick.

Thirty

~~~ ✌ ~~~

August, 1974

"Well, that's that..." managing editor Danny Logan said with little emotion as he watched the televised coverage of Richard Nixon, the 37th president of the United States, board a helicopter with his family to begin his trip to San Clemente, California.

The irony was not lost on the room full of newsmen who also watched the man who had just been forced to resign the most powerful job on Earth as he turned to the crowd and flashed his famous "V" for victory sign. It was August 9th, 1974, a little more than a year and half after Nixon had won a second term in the biggest blowout in presidential election history, losing only the State of Massachusetts and the District of Columbia.

417

The embattled president had finally succumbed to resignation rather than face the certainty of impeachment for his role in the Watergate break in and other crimes during his administration. Nixon's long effort to connive his way out of the scandal ended with the release of the "Smoking Gun Tape" on August 5th that gave evidence that he had knowledge of the burglary and participated in a cover up of the crime. He was already facing the House Judiciary Committee's three articles of impeachment that had been adopted at the end of July: obstruction of justice, abuse of presidential powers, and hindrance of the impeachment process. Still, he had enough votes in the House to possibly avoid punishment as he had throughout his career. But with this new evidence and all support gone in the House and Senate, the president faced certain impeachment and removal from office. On August 8, he resigned the presidency, effective the following day when Vice President Gerald R. Ford would be sworn in as the 38th President of the United States.

There was a smattering of applause in the newsroom as they watched the Marine helicopter lift off from the south lawn of the White House. But Logan shook his head. It was a good day for democracy and justice served, but it was a bad day in the history of America. He saw only two good things in the tragedy he had just witnessed: one, the American nightmare of a presidency under investigation for criminal activities was over. And two, the process had proven that in the United States, no one — not even the president — was bigger than the law.

Even as the disgraced president was being spirited from Washington, on a small spit of sandy shoreline at the end of a secluded road in the hamlet of

East Marion, New York near the tip of Long Island, another form of conspiracy was about to be born.

Though not destined to make the international headlines of the consequence of the Watergate scandal, the secret meeting that was about to take place would eventually generate its own controversy and a plan to outfox the will of the people.

"There are millions to be made here, Charlie," said the man sitting with Charles Anderson in the backseat of a black Cadillac limousine with New York license plates parked near the waters edge. "All we have to do is convince the right people to do the right thing. Capisci, my friend?" the man in the dark grey, sharkskin suit asked Anderson.

He was Stephano Vaccaro, a man who was neither a fan of the seashore or the wealthy playgrounds of Long Island — the Hamptons and Shelter Island. He never quite felt comfortable around old money, clambakes, and white shorts and topsiders; preferring instead the bars, steak houses and thousand dollar business suits of Manhattan, a little more than an hour away. He was born and raised in Queens, but today called Manhattan home. He liked looking out the floor to ceiling windows of his 10,000 square foot, 40th floor apartment on Fifth Avenue, one of the world's most elite addresses. From his perch high above the city bustle, Vaccaro, better know as "Big Steve" looked down on an unobstructed view of Central Park and midtown.

"Yes, I understand, Steve," Anderson replied. "But I've told you before, I prefer 'Charles,'" he corrected his host.

The Sicilian-born Vaccaro laughed softly at the thought of the skinny, pathetic real estate salesman who had married into money admonishing him for something so insignificant. How could this idiot have

419

the "coglioni" to…" He couldn't be bothered to even finish the thought. If "Charles" had any idea of who he was getting involved with, Vaccaro thought, he never would have gotten in the car.

"Of course, 'Charles,' my mistake," he said.

"No problem," Anderson replied with confidence that he'd stood his ground. He knew he was dealing with a powerful New York City real estate developer with huge resources and it was important that Vaccaro understand that just because he was from Fenwick, he couldn't be pushed around.

What Anderson didn't know was what "powerful" actually meant. Vaccaro was actually the head of a discreet, organized crime family that focused on the Manhattan real estate market and its many lucrative opportunities to act as a "fixer" for legitimate building and project developers. Sometimes all that was needed with an uncooperative zoning commissioner, contractor, building inspector or any number of the myriad nuisances that crept up in the high roller real estate game was a little "nudge" to change their viewpoint. The Vaccaro family was powerful enough to be a member of the New York based Mafia "Commission" — a sort of council that helped the family bosses maintain organization and delineation of territory.

The average person wouldn't recognize the name Vaccaro like they would Gambino, Bonanno or Lucchese. "Big Steve" avoided the bright lights of publicity like the flu. He was convinced that running silent and deep within the bowels of City Hall and the businesses they influenced was the family's ticket to stability and fortune.

But for some reason that he couldn't quite put his finger on, this particular project intrigued him, even though it had all the makings of a media circus. What was it about a bridge that had gotten under his skin? It was against his nature to look at a project outside his sphere of influence. This was out of the city and it wasn't a building. A bridge?

Maybe it was the money he saw hidden under the millions of rivets, hundred of thousands of iron girders and miles of steel plating that would eventually take the shape of a 10-mile long span over the width of Long Island Sound between East Marion on Long Island and Old Saybrook in Connecticut in a little beach town called Cornfield Point. Cornfield Point? At first he thought he was losing his edge. It was like connecting two hick towns. What was the point?

Cash. Tax free cash, and lots of it.

Or perhaps it was just the thought of the Vaccaro family being part of such a massive... no, mind-bending project that turned him on. He wanted to be part of this action, so much so that he could taste it. So much that he would be patient and deal with a wormy little rodent like Charles Anderson if he had to. Vaccaro knew he had his end of the "The Bridge" well in hand. But it was the other end that worried him. Not the necessary "fixes" that he knew would be awaiting him on a project of this magnitude. A lot of money would change hands to get things done. What bothered him is what he didn't know about the little burgh in Connecticut. It was like an itch he couldn't scratch. Something about this Cornfield Point was itching at him, but he didn't know what it was.

And that's why he needed Anderson.

For a man who only needed to nod to have an uncooperative project participant chained to a cinder block and dumped in the East River, Vaccaro was not physically intimidating. In fact, he was quite the

421

opposite. With his receding, slicked back grey hair and horn rimmed glasses and only standing five and a half feet tall, he could easily pass for an accountant. One had to study his face to know there was more mystery behind those glasses.

His olive complexion, prominent nose and black eyes told you that he was of Mediterranean descent. But it was his lips that caught your attention. So thin and bloodless, his mouth was just a straight line across the space between his nose and chin. He never smiled or frowned, and his lips barely seemed to move when he spoke. It was when you noticed that everyone stopped talking when Vaccaro said something through that slit in his face that you realized this was a man who could make you or quite literally break you with a word or a simple gesture.

Charles Anderson was oblivious to the power of Stephano Vaccaro and the reputation of the family he ruled with an iron will. He only knew that he finally had a willing partner — a well connected one, at that — to help him achieve the dream that had intrigued him from the moment he'd read about it in the back pages of the Sunday New York Times. It was a three-inch story about an engineering study involving a proposed bridge between Long Island and Connecticut that involved a large amount of real estate that he was quite familiar with. And it had occupied his every waking moment since.

What no one knew, including his lovely bride of just more than a year, was how deeply he resented his inability to get anyone, including Elina and his late father-in-law to share his obsessive interest in the project. Nearly everyone he approached wrote off his infatuation with it as a symptom of his injury. Some, like Elina, listened intently to assuage his passion but only to

422

be polite. He had nearly begged the recently deceased Don Hanson to engage with him on the benefits that the Sound crossing proponents were touting, and even attempted to interest him in investing in the effort. Hanson, grieving over the death of his wife wanted nothing to do with it and bluntly told him so.

Finally, Anderson had also reached out to Danny Logan, still considering him an old friend and oddly oblivious to the destruction of their relationship, and had been sharply rebuffed. Consequently, although Charles hid his disappointment well, in actuality he was harboring a growing anger over what he felt was contempt for a project that had become deeply rooted in his daily existence. He couldn't stop thinking about "The Bridge." It had become his life's work completely supplanting his long held plans for a career on Wall Street.

There were no medical tests to prove it, but Charles's head injury had substantially altered the frontal lobe functions of his brain, particularly as it related to problem solving. He was also suffering from left and right brain dysfunctions that had resulted in impaired judgment and an inability to envision the "big picture" of a complex situation.

But the most troubling result of his frontal lobe injury — and equally invisible — was the impairment of Anderson's ability to make good choices or to envision the consequence of his actions. And although he was completely unaware of any of these changes, Anderson's predilection to achieve had gone from an academic route to an impulsive one, where risk taking was the center of his thinking and the path to which he believed he would be rewarded.

In short, Charles Anderson had become a gambler who gave little thought to the consequences of failure. In sharp contrast, the man sitting next to him in the Lincoln gave much consideration to the possibility of failure. He had a simple rule. Failure was unacceptable. It was a law that defined the behavior of the Vaccaro family, who lived and died by it.

"The key here, Charles, is to convince the people of those little towns…" Vaccaro hesitated.

"Old Saybrook, Cornfield Point and Fenwick," Charles Anderson interjected.

"Right," Vaccaro, replied, nodding. "The key is to convince them that the bridge will make them rich. We offer them twice what their properties are worth. Who could turn down such an offer?"

"The people who own mansions in Fenwick might not be so enticed," Anderson quickly replied. "They're already wealthy, old money actually. It's going to take more than twice…"

"Than three times, I don't really care. Just buy those properties. The bridge can't happen unless the developer can acquire the land necessary for that huge interchange that will connect it with I-95, Route 9 and…

"Old Boston Post Road."

"Yah, that one too." Anderson winced at Vaccaro's cavalier reference to one of America's oldest highways, with roots back to the early 1700's. The man had no appreciation for New England history.

"Why wouldn't the State of Connecticut just seize the properties by 'Eminent Domain?'" Anderson asked.

"Because it would take years and result in a hell of a public fight. No governor, not even Tom Meskill would attempt it. He'd get murdered by the press."

"So we buy up the properties and offer the developer a deal he can't refuse, right?" Anderson asked, somewhat uneasy at how simply Vaccaro saw all of this happening.

"Look, Charles, you're a smart guy. This isn't rocket science. Get your friend at that newspaper to help you. You stand to clear $10 million if you pull this off. Is there any way I can make this any clearer to you?"

"No, I understand," Anderson said, bristling inside at how Vaccaro spoke to him.

"Get it done, Charles," Vaccaro said calmly.

"You wouldn't want to disappoint me."

Thirty-One
~~~ ❦ ~~~

January, 1975

"We're in real trouble, Dan," Lou White said without pulling his punch. "You know the paper has been in decline for a long time. In the last ten years, our circulation has dropped by nearly half. We're printing 75,000 papers a day." The publisher shook his head.

Logan knew this day would come, but still hoped it wouldn't.

"I'm sorry, Lou. I've given it my best shot...my guys give it their all..."

"Dan, there's nothing to be sorry about. It has nothing to do with you. It's life. Shit happens. Things change. Who would have dreamt the population of Hartford would drop by 50,000 people in a decade? Who could have foreseen the impact of television on

426

newspapers? Especially afternoon newspapers." He laughed aloud. "Thank you Walter Cronkite and Roger Mudd."

Logan laughed too at the irony. Cronkite and Mudd, just two of the greatest journalists to ever report a story had helped to begin the process of taking down an entire industry. It was the beginning of the end for newspapers.

"What do we do?" Logan asked, hoping White would have a miracle plan up his sleeve.

"We write on until we can't make payroll. Then we shut down the presses. I'm not going to lay off another employee of The Times. This is not their fault and we'll go down together," White responded.

"How long do you think we can continue?"

"If we can slow down the circulation decline... maybe a year, year and a half," the publisher said. He was struggling with his emotions.

"We'll work twice as hard, Lou... find new ways, come up with new ideas..." Logan fired back.

"No, Dan... let's not make the mistake of selling our pride with gimmicks and contests and the other bullshit tricks we've seen that don't work anyway. What I want you to do is continue exactly what you're doing. Report the news with integrity, with honesty, with principle. That's what Jim Greaves taught us both. I'm not about to change now. Our last paper will be as good and as principled as the first.

"End of discussion. Get back to work," he said, concluding their conversation with a smile and leaving Dan Logan intact with the thing that was most important to him. His pride.

He got up and walked out of Logan's office, only to do an about face and come back.

"I forgot. I got a call from the First Selectwoman of Old Saybrook this morning. It was about that Long Island Sound bridge thing you guys ran last week. She was complaining that we didn't mention the heavy pressure that residents of Fenwick and Cornfield Point are getting from some local real estate guy trying to buy their properties. Apparently the offers are huge and she smells a rat," White said. "I told her we'd look into it."

"We just did a review of the engineering studies that Nelson Rockefeller initiated as Governor of New York before becoming VP under Gerry Ford," Logan responded. "It wasn't much of a piece, certainly we didn't express any opinion. It was just background. It's a pipedream, Lou," Logan responded.

"Not according to Barbara Manning, the first selectwoman. "She says the town is pretty hot and bothered by the whole thing. Got them worried."

"Who's the real estate agent, did she say?" Logan asked.

"Yah… um..." White closed his eyes trying to recall the name. "Anderson, that's it, a guy by the name of Charles Anderson."

Logan visibly paled.

"You ok, Dan?" White asked.

"Yah. Anderson. Ok, I'll talk to Tom Lynch and have him look at it."

"Thanks, Dan," White said. Logan was on his phone before the publisher was out of sight.

"Tom, c'mon over, will ya? Need to talk," Logan said.

He pushed back in his chair and looked out the window into the parking lot at his forlorn TR. The little sports car had been plowed in for the last three days. He would so much rather go outside and dig out his pet than get into what he knew was going to be a Charles Anderson scheme.

"Tom," he said as Lynch walked in. The State editor had responsibility for The Time's coverage of the suburbs, including towns like Old Saybrook.

"Tell me what you know about 'The Bridge?'"

"The Bridge? You mean that cockamamie thing that Rockefeller was pushing before he got kicked upstairs to the empty office next to Ford?" he laughed.

"Yah, that bridge."

"Somebody got a problem with the blurb we ran last week?" Lynch asked.

"Well, it's got some folks in Old Saybrook a little rattled."

"Listen, Dan... that thing has been kicking around since 1957," Lynch said. "It was first proposed by some group that called themselves the Montauk Beach Company. Essentially they proposed to build a bridge or tunnel across the Sound to Connecticut citing all kinds of economic nirvana. They got no reaction from either New York or Connecticut, but when the Chesapeake Bay Bridge Tunnel that connects the Delmarva Peninsula with Virginia Beach was built in 1964, the idea got dredged up again. That particular structure cost over $200 million but today it's a very important north to south connector for the State of Virginia and a huge success. It's something like 17 miles long...

"Anyway, that got the Rockefeller gang in Albany all excited and they looked at a bunch of different crossing points, finally settling on a 10-mile stretch between a little hamlet called East Marion on Long Island and Cornfield Point in Old Saybrook. Rockefeller held a press conference and made a big deal about this thing sometime in 1966 and got the Long

Island people all in a twitter. Problem is, Rockefeller's people forgot to mention their plans to one Governor John Dempsey in Connecticut who didn't take very kindly to being blindsided. "

"Whoops," Logan interjected, fascinated by Lynch's dissertation.

"Whoops is right. Dempsey's response was, 'We'll form a study group,' which is politician–speak for 'we'll get back to you in about a century.'"

Logan laughed out loud.

"Actually, Senator Ribicoff and Congressman Stewart McKinney did a good job of killing funding for anymore feasibility studies for a good three years. In the meantime, both New York and Connecticut committees looked at this thing and came up with all sorts of pros and cons, most predictable, none completely convincing."

"Pros?" Logan asked

"The Islanders argued that it would increase tourism and provide an evacuation route if a hurricane the likes of 1938 ever walloped them again. That was a valid argument because there is no way to move several million people to the mainland quickly. The only transportation across the Sound now is a couple of ferries.

"And of course proponents in New York all argued that the bridge would open up new business markets for both states and create job opportunities without the need for relocation... the kind of stuff you'd expect to hear from any developer and none if it very specific. Somebody even had the nerve to suggest it would be a boon to Hartford. Of course, property values would rise and taxes would go down, said the local politicians. All pie in the sky. The only real, immediate benefit would be the jobs created by the construction itself, which a couple of years ago was said to be in the neighborhood of $640 million. I'd say we're talking a billion bucks by now. It would be a godsend to the construction trades, but of course that's temporary."

"That leaves the cons..." Logan said.

"Which are frankly more emotional than economical," Lynch said. "First off, Connecticut doesn't believe the tolls levied for such a drive would ever be enough to pay for construction let alone maintenance of the bridge. Second, they argued there would be huge environmental impact on the Connecticut shoreline — short for it would wipe out Old Saybrook and the little boroughs and village beaches like the North Cove, Fenwick, Cornfield Point, Saybrook Manor, Chalker Beach, Indian Town, Knollwood, etc. That section of coast at the mouth of the Connecticut River would have to be bulldozed to make way for a monster highway interchange connecting the bridge to I-95, Route 9 and Boston Post Road. But the loudest argument against it was that the span would have no real benefit to Connecticut. No one on this side bought the New York business arguments, especially Ribicoff. And I would have my doubts that our new Governor, Mrs. Grasso will have any interest in the project. She's got more than enough to keep her occupied.

"To tell you the truth, I thought the idea had pretty much died until recently when some commercial developers got into it."

"Who are they?" Logan asked.

"Don't know, Dan, I'd have to get into it more deeply."

"Do," Logan said. "And I want you to quietly do some digging on a real estate agent by the name of Charles Anderson. He's supposedly making some outlandish offers on properties in some of the places you mentioned. Fenwick and Cornfield Point."

"Ok, we'll get on it," Lynch said.

"And Tom, don't be surprised if my name floats to the surface somehow. It shouldn't, but I don't want you to be surprised. Anderson and I go way back and he married a girl I had a relationship with. Her father was Don Hanson..."

"The CEO of Mutual who died not long ago?"

"Yes. One of the Hartford 'Bishops.' And you'll recall Greaves and I were not fans of the Greater Hartford Process those guys were selling."

"Why are you telling me this, Dan?" Lynch asked, surprised by Logan's candor.

"Just telling you in the spirit of complete disclosure, Tom. I'm not involved with Anderson or the Hanson family in any way. But I was. And come to think of it, Anderson even called me a couple of times looking for the paper to support this bridge project. I had forgotten about it. At the time, I brushed him off."

"Ok, thanks for being so open. Your relationship is not going to get in the way of what we find or write, is it?" he asked the managing editor.

Logan just stared at him in response. The look on his bosses face was all he needed to know.

"That's what I figured, Dan. I'll get back to you soon as we dig into this," Lynch said.

Logan kicked back in his chair again and put his feet up the desk. He had to fight the urge to call Elina and find out what she knew, hell, if she knew about her husband's activities. He couldn't believe that she would be party to the destruction of Fenwick. That house meant everything to her.

In fact, at that very moment, Elina Hanson was meeting with a decorator discussing her plans to

432

renovate and redecorate the mansion that she had acquired upon the death of her father. She still mourned her father's loss, but the darkness of that old place made it even harder. Hanson had left his entire estate to her — worth more that $100 million — and she was determined to breathe new life into the mansion. She knew her father would have approved.

"I want this house to be full of light, for the sun to wash it every day," she told the decorator. "These hideous drapes…" she said, touching the brown window dressing in the living room that her mother had always kept closed, turning the space into a sort of tomb," I want them gone, first thing. Burn them, please."

"Elina," the decorator interrupted her client, "you do realize that your plans, although stunning, are going to cost a fortune. I just don't want you to be disappointed when I start bringing in materials and the bills begin to pour in."

"Deliah," Elina said, "this is something I've dreamed of since I was a little girl. I love this house. It is a part of me. But it is filled with sadness. I want you to fill it with life! I don't care what it costs."

"Elina, I've been doing this for a living for more than two decades and you're the first client I've ever had who's given me a blank check. I promise the end result will be everything you've wanted."

"Perfect!" Elina responded. "Come, I have a wonderful bottle of champagne and a light lunch for us to continue to work and celebrate."

Charles Anderson suddenly appeared in the doorway.

"Hello dear," he said to Elina. "And who is our guest," he asked cordially, walking across the room to meet Deliah.

433

"Why this is Deliah Stone, a decorator I've hired, Charles. We're beginning our work on renovating this old place. She has some wonderful ideas. I'm so excited," Elina said, beaming.

"Oh," Anderson said without trying to hide his surprise. "I wasn't aware. We must talk later," he said cheerfully and disappeared into her late father's study.

Charles had taken over the office after his death without discussing it with Elina. She still hated to see her husband enter the room. It held so many memories of her father. But she held her tongue, not wanting to hurt her husband's feelings and didn't want to argue with him about a sentiment she really couldn't articulate.

Anderson closed the doors to the great room into which he had rarely been invited when Hanson was alive. He sat at the desk where his father-in-law had ruled his company when not in the office and fumed. Here he was trying to convince their neighbors to sell their homes to him and Elina was redecorating. The incongruity would certainly be noticed and he was already fighting enough suspicion as it was. He would have to broach the subject with her soon.

He was not expecting a pleasant conversation, but in the world where Charles Anderson now lived, logic was sometimes illogical.

"She'll understand," he thought to himself with confidence.

"In Elina's eyes I'll be twice the man her father ever was."

Thirty-Two

~~~ ❧ ~~~

The roar could be heard the length of Trumbull Street.

With a sellout crowd of 10,507 watching, New England Whalers Center Gary Swain pulled up on the ice for a 15-foot slap shot and snuck the puck into the right corner of the net at 5 minutes 45 seconds of overtime to cap a comeback victory over the San Diego Mariners. The fans went wild.

The uproarious celebration by the standing room only crowd on January 11, 1975 said great things about the future of hockey in their city, as the Whalers won their first home game in the Hartford Civic Center. Or so the sportscasters said.

Logan and Dick McGrath had attended and for both it was their first taste of hockey. Until now, the sport had limited interest in Connecticut with the closest teams located in New York and Boston. It seemed like

435

an odd fit when owner Howard Baldwin and his partners decided to call Hartford home after playing second fiddle to the Bruins in Boston for several years, but the Greater Hartford area had a hunger for sports.

Unable to land an NBA or ABA basketball team, the city settled for a hockey team, a winning one at that, and at least for a while, it seemed they had bet right.

"I don't know, Dick," Logan said while walking out of the arena. "Is hockey going to cure Hartford's ills?"

"C'mon," McGrath said. "Did you look around at that crowd? I'll bet you one in 20 fans is a Hartford resident. And the entire audience looked like you and me. White guys. I think we need to remember this is entertainment, not a cure for Hartford's socio-economic issues. It might bring a few new restaurants to the city and maybe a couple dozen jobs, but not much more. We'll see."

With the decline of Hartford's Bishops, it was left to commercial developers to come up with a game plan for Hartford, and although there were a few fits and starts, the population of the city continued it's decline, restaurants came and went and store fronts along Main Street were boarded up. The riots may have been fading memories, but they had done immeasurable damage to Hartford. The glory days for the City of Hartford were over.

But developers of "The Bridge" were beginning to push the economic benefits of the span to Hartford, arguing that it would bring businesses and jobs from Long Island. There was a loud silence from the city that had gone hockey mad and from representatives of the towns involved who wanted no part of the plan.

Still, the New York Developers pressed on and Charles Anderson's instructions from Stephano Vaccaro

436

remained "Buy at any price." The New York money backing the project wanted the parcels of shoreline property required for the project in their back pockets before they launched an army of lobbyists to invade the capital and twist the arms of legislators.

"How are you coming with that story on "The Bridge," Logan asked as he and McGrath walked to the Travelers Spa for a beer after the game.

"Well, I'm going to talk with the First Selectwoman in Old Saybrook tomorrow. She's got some strong opinions. I'll fill you in after that and after I hear back from the guys looking into the developers. I'll tell you this: I think we have a story that's going to surprise a lot of people."

At that very moment, nowhere was there more surprise than in the living room of the mansion on Pettipaug Ave. in Fenwick.

"Charles," Elina said quietly, her voice shaking, "have you lost your mind?" She went to the bar in the dining room and poured herself three fingers of scotch. The glass shook in her hand. She felt terribly afraid.

"Elina, my love, this is the chance of a lifetime," he said. "We can sell this old place for three times what it's worth, maybe more. That's... say it's $6 million. You could never get that kind of money..."

"It's not about money, Charles! I have money. And don't say 'we' can sell Fenwick, because it is not 'we' who owns it. This house is in my name. I will never sell it, at any price."

"Be reasonable, Elina," Charles demanded. "This is my chance to make something of myself. All I need to do is convince the old codgers around you to sell these rundown mausoleums. For more money than they have ever dreamed of!"

"Charles," she said, walking to him, "don't you understand? They'll never sell, or at least the vast majority won't. These homes, cottages, whatever you want to call them, they've been passed down by families for generations. They are more than just 'properties,' as you refer to them, they are family homes, heirlooms! Your plan will never work. Perhaps some owners in Cornfield Point and up the coastline might sell, but I'll bet there won't be more than a handful." She was pleading with him to understand.

"Can't you appreciate what these homes are worth to their owners? They wake up each day and look out over the Sound. They live with the tides lapping at their front doors, with the cries of seagulls... its like music. With the smell of the ocean, the taste of salt in the air. Why... it's like living in a world you can only dream of. Can't you see it, taste it, smell it? Can you put a price on that? Can you?"

"I think you're insane, Elina," Charles said angrily. "All that matters is what they're worth on the market. This place is just bricks, mortar, shingles, plaster. You can replace it in a second. And yes, you have money. All the money one could ever want. But I don't. This is my one chance to make my fortune. I lost my only other opportunity with the accident — which never would have happened if you weren't sleeping with Danny Logan! You owe me this, Elina!" Anderson screamed at her, his rage nearly out of control. "And I will have it. Sign the purchase agreement now," he ordered her.

"I will not," she yelled back, "never." She was stunned that he blamed her for the accident. "I would die first. And whatever chance you lost in that accident was of your own doing. No one told you to get drunk and drive like a madman!"

"Well let me tell you, if I don't make this happen, there's a very good chance that I will die. The people who are developing the bridge aren't used to being refused."

She stared into his eyes, shocked by what he had just said.

"Charles... what have you done? What promise did you make and to whom?" she demanded."

"To some people in New York... people that are more ruthless than even your father was... can you believe that, Elina?"

"Oh my God..." she said and turned away from him, suddenly sick to her stomach.

She whirled around and threw her drink at him. The glass shattered on the wall behind him, off target.

"Get out, Charles, do you hear me? Get out! And don't ever come back!"

Anderson ran at her and punched her in the face several times, knocking her to the floor where she lay helpless. Then he kicked her in the ribs and laughed.

"I'll leave, bitch. And I won't be back. But that doesn't mean this is over," he screamed and walked out of the house. She heard the front door slam as he left. Minutes later she listened to the powerful roar of his Jaguar as he raced out of the driveway and turned down Pettipaug Avenue at an insane speed.

Elina lay on the floor, blood dripping from her nose and mouth. It hurt to breathe. Doris, her housekeeper ran into the room and gasped. "Oh, Elina, what happened? Let me get a cloth to stop the bleeding. Oh, my god..." She ran to the kitchen and hollered to the cook to call for an ambulance.

Elina raised herself up and looked out the window where she had just had the old brown curtains taken down. She could just see the ocean. And then everything went dark.

She came to in the back of an ambulance that was speeding down Route 9 to Middlesex Hospital in Middletown. Doris was holding her hand while a medic checked her vital signs.

"Elina," Doris said, "what happened? Did Charles do this?" she asked. The housekeeper had been with the Hanson family for decades. She was more of a mother to her than her own had been.

"Yes," she sobbed. " He's insane, lost control. He wants me to sell Fenwick."

"Sell...our home?" Doris asked again, shocked at the thought. It was as much her home as Elina's. "But why?"

"I don't know, but I'm very afraid, Doris. I think he's gotten himself in trouble," she said. Her mouth hurt and her breathing was ragged. She winced.

"Try not to talk, Mrs. Anderson," the medic said. "The doctors will want to see if you have any broken ribs. Just relax."

She squeezed Doris' hand.

"Just one thing, Doris, please..."

"Anything dear."

She closed her eyes.

"Call Danny for me... tell him I need him to keep his promise."

Thirty-Three

~~~ ~~~

He was at her bedside within the hour, so upset he could barely speak. Logan had done his best to forgive Charles Anderson, but now seeing her in the hospital bed it was all he could do to control his rage. Elina's face was bruised and bloodied, her nose was broken and doctors had inserted an intercostal cathether through her chest wall and into her right lung to drain blood that had accumulated when Anderson kicked her in the ribs. She was sleeping, the result of a sedative they had given her to calm down and an intravenous morphine drip.

It was best that she was unconscious, he thought. He didn't want her to see him so upset. Logan pulled Doris out into the hall.

"Do you know what precipitated this, Doris? Has Charles been acting strange lately?" he probed.
~~~

She smirked. "No stranger than usual, Mr. Logan. He's an odd one, if I do say so. But I'd never tell that to Elina. I frankly don't know how she feels about the man. They certainly don't act much like newlyweds."

"What do you mean?" he asked.

"They sleep in separate rooms, for one. Never spend time together. She's completely involved with redecorating the house. And when he's around, which isn't very often, he spends his time locked up in Mr. Hanson's study. He's out every night, not in until late. A real mystery man."

"Did you hear what they were arguing about?"

"No. I only know what Elina told me in the ambulance when she woke up. Charles was trying to make her agree to sell the Fenwick house. Can you imagine? There is no place on earth that is more precious to her."

He grit his teeth. "Anything else, Doris? Do you remember anything else?"

"Only something I overheard in the market last week when I was buying some groceries. A couple of friends of mine, housekeepers for some of our neighbors were telling me that Charles had been around to visit their employers with the same idea. He wanted to buy their properties. From what they overheard, the amount of money he was offering was quite staggering."

Assured by doctors that Elina would be all right and would continue sleeping comfortably, Logan got to a phone and called Tom Lynch. It was nearly two o'clock in the morning.

"Tom, I'm sorry to wake you so early in the morning," he apologized.

"It's ok, Dan, must be important," Lynch replied groggily.

442

"It is. I'm at Middlesex Hospital in Middletown with Elina Anderson, the daughter of the late Don Hanson and the wife of that Old Saybrook real estate agent we were talking about earlier, " Logan explained.

"Yah, I know about Anderson. I have some things to talk to you about. He's involved," Lynch replied.

"I need to know now, Tom. Anderson beat the shit out of his wife because she refused to sell her house at Fenwick. Apparently he's been pressing other owners."

"Jesus... Well, it fits what we have to tell you. Let me round up the guys I've had working on this with me and we'll meet you in the office. Give me a couple hours, ok?" Lynch replied.

"Thank you, Tom. Apologies to your family."

"Comes with the job, Dan, but thanks for saying that."

Logan checked on Elina again. Doris was still with her. He leaned over her bed and kissed her on the forehead.

"You still love her, Mr. Logan," Doris said. "I can tell. Elina made a very big mistake letting you go."

Logan smiled. "She did what she had to, Doris." He looked at the beautiful blond woman lying in the bed again, telling himself he had let his pride get in the way. He should have fought harder for her.

"I'll be back, Doris. Please call me at The Times if anything changes."

"I will."

Logan drove back to the office in a daze. What had come over Charles to make him react that way? Why was he pushing her to sell? The answers were in "The Bridge," he knew, certain that Lynch's team had it figured out.

443

He got to the paper and walked the newsroom for a few minutes, talking with the night desk guys. They were busy doing rewrites from stories being called in from all over the State by reporters who never quit reporting the news. He remembered his nights on the rewrite desk. They were exhausting but exciting.

Logan put on a pot of coffee and went to his office to wait. He sat and leaned his head back to close his eyes for a few minutes. He fell asleep almost immediately

Images of Elina on the night of her 17th birthday came flashing into his mind. She was so beautiful in the skimpy white bikini that drove her mother to distraction. It had driven him and Charles...

"Dan, are you sleeping?" someone said, shaking his arm. It was three a.m. on the button and Lynch and two reporters were there to brief him.

"Sorry, guys, been a long night. Guess I didn't give you much of one, either," he apologized.

"Stop fretting the small stuff, boss. These guys couldn't wait to share with you all the juicy news they found in New York. And my conversation with the First Selectwoman of Old Saybrook was equally eye opening."

Lynch turned to one of the State-side reporters, a young man with a scruffy beard who Dan didn't know very well.

"Dan, do you know Phil Stanning? He's been working State for about a year, "Lynch said.

"I'm embarrassed to say I don't know him as well as I should," Logan admitted. "I think that's about to change."

Lynch laughed. "And this is Bob Keane, joined us last summer. Both good men who have already made The Times a better newspaper." Logan shook hands with Keane, a tall lanky kid who couldn't have been more than 20 years old. But he could see the fire in his eyes.

"What did you guys find?" the managing editor said impatiently. "But I should back up. Tom, did you share with these guys the reason for our early morning meeting?"

"Yes, and like I told you on the phone, it fits. The pressure to sell, I mean. I can't speak to this asshole Anderson getting violent, but as you're going to learn there's no doubt he's under some personal pressure. The kind that would make you consider thumb screws if given an option," Lynch said. "He's probably scared to death."

Logan winced. Charles, what have you done, he thought.

Stanning began.

"As you know, Mr. Logan, it was Governor Rockefeller of New York that got the ball rolling on the bridge idea. But he ran out of gas when he joined the Ford ticket as vice president so the project languished for a while."

"Right," Logan said. "Call me Dan, Phil."

Stanning grinned. "Yes, sir Mr. Logan."

The managing editor just grinned and shook his head.

"Then suddenly about a year ago, a private developer started things up again, working the engineering scheme and literally swarming the New York legislature and Long Island pol's with lobbyists. They've been successful. Most Long Island residents are upbeat about the project and the legislature has been sold on the economic promise. They also like the evacuation route aspect the bridge presents."

"Who's the developer?" Logan asked.

"It's a group of private investors who call themselves 'Sound Crossings.' Catchy, huh?" Stanning laughed.

"Yah," Logan responded, finding no humor in anything he was learning.

"I dug into the investors, Mr. Logan," interjected Bob Keane. "They are a tight group, but I found a few cracks. And they lead to some interesting people. People who appear to represent various factions of the construction industry, many of whom have ties to the New York families."

"Families? You mean organized crime?" Logan said, nearly coming out of his chair.

"It's going to take a lot more work to dig out this story completely, but we've already got confirmation on at least one of the partners who is a member of the New York City Mafia Commission. Stephano Vaccaro, head of the Vaccaro family," Keane continued.

"Holy shit," Logan said, stunned. "Oh, Charles, you silly boy," he said aloud. A sudden thought occurred to him. "Guys, give me the room for a minute. I have to make a call."

Dan jumped on his phone the minute the office was cleared. He dialed the number and Doris picked up.

"Doris, thank God I got you," he said. "Is Elina ok? Any change?"

"No, she's still sleeping, don't worry," Doris said.

"Listen, I should have thought of this. If Anderson shows up…"

"I'll scratch his eyes out," she said without hesitation.

"No, don't do that, Doris," Logan said. "Charles is in trouble. I don't know what he's capable of. I'm going to make a call and get some security guys to join

446

you. Ok? You sit tight and I'll come back sometime this afternoon. Call me when the guards get there."

Logan dialed the number of Charlie Holcombe. The personnel manager picked up the phone after only two rings. It was only four in the morning.

"Charlie, it's Dan. Sorry..."

"What's wrong, Dan, what do you need?"

"You never fail me, Charlie..." Logan gave him a quick rundown and asked him to pull a few strings with the Chief of Police in Hartford who Holcombe knew personally.

"Yah, I know the Chief in Middletown, too, but better he hears it from one of his own. Bet you we have a cop outside the door within a half hour."

"Thank you, Charlie, as always."

"You know, Logan, you never did take my advice," Holcombe said, laughing.

"What was that, Charlie?" Logan asked.

"I told you to forget about that broad the day I hired you. Guess I'm glad you didn't take my advice."

"I'm not so sure, Charlie," Logan said, sighing. "Elina is like my Achilles Heal. But I can't let her down now. Make the call, Charlie, please."

"I'm on it." The line went dead. Logan called the reporters back in.

"Ok, sorry about that. So we know at least that there's bad money involved here," Logan summarized.

"Bad people is more like it, Dan," Lynch said. "We've got enough to bring Vaccaro's interest to light in a story, but more work will need to be done before we can start publicly identifying the other families involved," Tom Lynch said. "We could get killed in lawsuits if we're not careful."

"You're right. But we've got enough to write the first story indicating all is not well, agreed?" The three reporters all nodded.

"What did you find out about Anderson?" Logan asked.

"Now there's a piece of work," Lynch said.

"Tell me about it," Logan answered. They all stared at him. "Forget it, it's a long story. What did you learn?"

"First, he's been a busy guy, knocking on doors sending letters, making calls, all in an effort to get beachfront owners primarily in Fenwick and Cornfield Point to sell their properties to him."

"Directly to Charles Anderson? That makes no sense, the guy has no money of his own that I know of," Logan said.

"No, he's representing 'Sound Crossings.'" There was silence in the room.

"He's trying to scoop up the shoreline property they'll need for the highway system connecting the bridge," Logan guessed.

"Precisely," Lynch agreed. "And get this... he's making offers of two and three times the appraised property values. To be paid in cash."

Logan whistled.

"That would make instant millionaires out of the people who own places in Fenwick..." Logan surmised.

"But that's been Anderson's problem, Dan," Lynch fired back. "The owners are already millionaires, many times over. They aren't inclined to sell what to most of them is a priceless commodity. Land with the most outrageous views of the Sound... I mean, have you ever been to Fenwick and watched the sun set? And although there aren't any mansions in Cornfield Point, well, I'd give my left nut to retire in one of the beachfront cottages... just spectacular."

"So, Charles Anderson has been running up against a brick wall?" Logan asked.

"Granite is more like it. And the resistance from the people who live along the shoreline to the bridge itself is quite remarkable. It would take a gun to their heads to make them vote in favor of building the damned thing. Pardon me for the pun, but the bridge is dead in the water as far as I'm concerned.

"As Old Saybrook's first Selectwoman, Barbara Manning puts it: 'We don't intend to be the town at the end of the bridge.' Truthfully, I've seen the plans and Old Saybrook would turn into a giant, sprawling highway interchange connecting I-95, Route 9 and Boston Post Road. The town would cease to exist except for gas stations and fast food restaurants."

Lynch shrugged his shoulders.

"We got the start of what I think could be a big story. So what do we do, boss?" Lynch asked.

"We can only write what we know. Anderson is a time bomb and the Long Island people need to know how they're being set up. But you guys need to expect to be called by the Attorney General's office. This is too big a political bomb for him to ignore. Meskill will order it if he doesn't pick up on it himself. Write the story. We'll slug it for page one, but not the lead. Below the fold so we won't be accused of sensationalism. Do expect to hear from lawyers, so write the story with that in mind."

He scanned the faces of the three reporters looking for questions.

"Ok? Excellent work. This is the stuff Pulitzer's are made of," he grinned. Lynch and his guys were stunned at the statement.

"I mean it. This is solid investigative journalism. Never forget the power you have. So use it carefully and get it right the first time. Now go home and get a few more hours of sleep before you hit it. This needs to be ready for today's Bulldog edition."

Lynch grinned like a Cheshire cat. "Ok, boss, but if it's all the same to you, I think we'll grab some coffee and get at it. We've got notes to compare. See you at the budget meeting in a few hours. I'll have an update."

"Thanks, guys. Me, I'm heading back to Middlesex Hospital to check on Mrs. Anderson's condition. I'll be back."

The phone rang as the room cleared. It was Doris.

"Mr. Logan, Mr. Anderson came a few minutes ago and tried to see Elina," she said breathlessly. "I wouldn't open the door and he was very angry. The nurses tried to make him leave, but then the strangest thing happened."

"What, Doris."

"Three policeman showed up and took him away... in handcuffs! Mr. Anderson kept asking what the charges were but the police wouldn't answer him, they just took him away."

Thank you Charlie Holcombe, Logan thought to himself.

"Good job, Doris. Elina doesn't know how good a friend you are to her. I'm coming back now, but I have to make a stop first. See you soon. Is she still sleeping?"

"Yes, Mr. Logan, like a little girl."

"Listen, you must do me another favor?" Logan said.

"What's that? Of course..."

"Please call me Dan. All my friends do. See you in a little while."

450

Logan hurried out to the car and made his way to Route 9 even before the morning rush hour. But instead of going to the hospital, he drove to the Middletown Police Station where he figured Charles Anderson was being held.

He spoke to an officer at the front desk.

"Yes, Mr. Logan. My boss has been expecting you. Second floor, turn right. Got the name Chief on the door."

He took the steps two at a time. Chief Bill Sullivan was waiting for him on the landing.

"Hello, Dan," Sullivan said, extending his hand. "Desk Sergeant told me you were on your way up. Been expecting you."

"Hello, Chief. Wanted to thank you personally for having those uniforms at the hospital this morning."

"No problem. We have a distinct distaste for wife beaters in my house. Wonder what got into the rich, spoiled brat," he said, not even trying to hide his sentiments.

"I'll tell you what. Read this afternoon's Hartford Times and you'll begin to understand. That boy is in a heap of trouble. He doesn't have a clue."

"By that, I assume you don't mean slapping his wife around. She'll have to file charges and even then it will probably be just a misdemeanor," the Chief said.

"No, it's a bit bigger than that," Logan said. "I'd tell you more Chief, but we need to clear it all with the lawyers before I say anymore. Anyway, you'll read about it this afternoon."

"Good. The little peckerhead deserves it," he said with a grin.

"Can I see Anderson, Chief? I assume you've got him in lockup?" Logan asked.

451

"Dan, I'm sorry. We couldn't hold him without charges. If the Mrs. wants to file, I'll get in touch with the Chief in Old Saybrook and one of us will pick him up."

"You mean he's out there?" Logan asked, alarmed.

"Yah, 'fraid so. Though he won't be going near the hospital. Made sure of that."

Logan let out a sigh.

"You worried, son?" the policeman asked.

"Yah, I am. This guy is getting desperate. No telling what he's capable of."

"Well he can't get near her at the hospital. And if you can get Mrs. Anderson to file assault charges I'll have his ass in a cell in a heartbeat. But even that won't hold if a judge sets bail, which he probably will," Sullivan said.

"Ok, thanks Chief. I appreciate all your help. If I can ever…"

"We're even, Dan." Logan looked him in the eye, puzzled.

"I read The Hartford Times every night during that stupid Vietnam War. My son came home missing a leg… but he came home. You and your guys did a helluva job covering that mess. Without hiding your feelings. I'm grateful."

"That's quite a compliment, Chief. Thank you."

"Go find your boy," he grinned.

Logan drove to the hospital, hoping Elina had awakened. He wasn't disappointed.

"Danny, you came. I knew you would. He's trying to take Fenwick from me…" she sobbed. Her face was swollen and bruised. A broken rib and the catheter in her chest made breathing painful.

452

"I'll get the son of a bitch, I swear, Elina," he said, losing his temper.

"No Danny, please," she pleaded. "He's not himself... since the accident. His judgment is so poor, he's fixated on all the wrong things... and he's in trouble. I'm so afraid..."

"Don't be... but he should be afraid. He's gotten himself involved with the wrong people. The kind that don't tolerate failure," he said.

"You know...?"

He reached for her hand.

"Yes, we've been working on a story. I didn't know until recently that Charles was involved. He's up to his neck in this. You want to press charges?" he asked, already knowing the answer.

"No... I can't, it would be like kicking a hurt puppy."

"Christ, Elina... that's at least one of the reasons you married him. The guy's got to get his shit together somehow," Logan barked. He had no sympathy for Charles Anderson.

"You don't understand, Danny. His brain isn't firing on all cylinders. He'll never be right, he has to have a babysitter. This is partially my fault. I didn't pay attention, didn't pick up on his obsession." She buried her face in her hands again and wept.

"But you're right," she suddenly said with anger in her voice. "I married him because I felt sorry for him and because I was so selfish about Fenwick. It was a mistake. I gave up the only person I've ever loved for all the wrong reasons." She looked into Danny Logan's eyes.

"This Boy," she said, squeezing his hand.

He slowly pulled away.

"I don't know, Elina." She stared at him, surprised.

"I don't know if I can go through this again. You've broken my heart so many times," Logan whispered.

She closed her eyes but the tears came anyway.

"We'll talk about us later," she said. "But please, please Danny, help me to save Charles."

"He shook his head. I don't know that I can. The story that will come out this afternoon will discredit him and he'll probably lose his real estate license. But it will put him in a spotlight that might save him from men who would kill him otherwise. Do you understand?"

"Yes," she said.

"You know him better than I do now... will he be strong enough to weather the humiliation?" Logan asked.

"I don't know," Elina said, slowly shaking her head. "I just don't know."

"There's no choice, Elina. This is bigger than Charles. I can't tell you how the story ends," Logan explained.

"I know, Danny. We have to find him..."

"You're asking a lot," he said.

"Danny, please," he heard her call to him as he walked out.

"More than you know."

454

Thirty-Four

~~~ ℘ ~~~

February, 1975

The Times broke the story that afternoon and within hours, as Logan had predicted, the Attorney General of Connecticut held a press conference to announce a thorough investigation of the proposed Long Island Sound bridge project, and in particular, 'Sound Crossings.' The New York Attorney General made a similar announcement the next day. The bridge was dead and Old Saybrook rejoiced. But from the perspective of The Hartford Times, the story had just begun.

Elina was released from the hospital several days later, tired and sore, but her body would heal. Emotionally, she was confused and frightened. Charles had disappeared and neither Danny Logan nor the Old

455

Saybrook police could locate him. All feared the worst as weeks went by with no word on Anderson's whereabouts.

Logan remained in constant contact with Elina and tried to convince her to hire private security at Fenwick. She wouldn't hear of it.

"I know what he did to me, but Charles was out of control. I'm not afraid that he'll come back to hurt me. I'm afraid for him," she said.

Logan's responsibilities at The Times kept him there late into the night as he managed both the newsroom and the circulation crisis with Lou White. But on weekends he drove the TR to Fenwick and stayed with Elina.

Although they were comfortable together, Logan made sure he kept their relationship on a 'close friends' basis. The idea that her husband might reappear at any moment unnerved him. He wasn't afraid of Charles; he was afraid to open his heart again. But it was unavoidable that they would spend quiet time together, and at night, in the cold of winter, they would often cuddle under a blanket in front of a roaring fire in the newly redecorated living room.

"Maybe it's the drink, but this house seems to be brighter and more open every time I visit," he said. "You are doing an amazing job on this place. It is so warm now, so enticing... I can imagine this is how you always saw it," Logan commented one Saturday night as they were enjoying a brandy after dinner, sitting together on the couch by the fireplace. As usual, Doris had prepared a spectacular meal for them and retired to her bedroom immediately after. She didn't attempt to hide her affection for Logan.

Before Elina could comment, Logan had abruptly jumped off the couch and walked to a window that looked out over the driveway. His face was drawn with concern.

"What's wrong, Dan? Something got you spooked?" Elina asked.

"I thought I saw headlights, or maybe a flashlight," he said. "I'm going to take a look outside."

"No, don't Danny. It's freezing out and I'm sure it's nothing," she said.

"I'll just be a minute," he said, grabbing a flashlight and wrapping a scarf around his neck.

Elina got up and walked to him.

"Please be careful," she said, and unexpectedly reached up and kissed him on the lips. She pulled him close to her but he wriggled loose, an awkward grin on his face.

"Let me go and look," he said.

Logan opened the front door and walked out on the porch to listen. It was hard to hear anything out of the ordinary with a howling wind and the surf breaking below. He walked over to the stairway leading to the driveway without turning on the flashlight so he wouldn't give himself away. Then he looked over the edge and didn't see anything out of the ordinary. He shined the flashlight down but still saw nothing.

Out of the corner of his eye he thought he saw something move and spun around. It was too late. Logan felt a sharp blow to the top of his head and the world went black.

It seemed to take forever, but he slowly drifted back to consciousness, loud voices and Elina's screams finally bringing him back to the light. He had no idea how long he had been out. Something wet was in his eyes and his vision was blurred. He couldn't make out what was happening but instinctively knew she was in danger. He used the porch railing to pull himself upright and staggered towards the front door. It was wide open.

"Elina," he hollered as he blindly made his way back into the house and found the living room. Logan heard muffled cries and made out her shape lying on the couch, but she was bound with tape around her ankles and wrists and across her mouth. Her eyes were huge with terror as she struggled to get free.

Startlingly, a strong smell of gasoline wafted into the house. He shook his head, desperately trying to clear his vision. The noxious odor actually helped. He worked feverishly to tear the tape binding Elina, knowing what was coming. Then he heard a loud voice. It was Charles.

"I could have been something, you bitch!" Anderson yelled. Then the front door slammed shut.

An instant later, there was an eruption of flames outside the windows that bathed the living room in a flickering, orange light. Logan saw Anderson run across the porch past the dancing tongues of fire and down the stairs. An instant later, smoke began seeping through the windows.

"Elina! He's set fire to the house!" he screamed as he finally tore the last of the tape from her body. "Go to the kitchen and call the police. Tell them to send the fire department and then go out the back staircase. I'll wake Doris and get her out. I'll meet you by the pool. Go, Elina, go!" he instructed her.

"Danny, you're covered in blood," she cried.

"Don't worry about that, just go, there's no time to waste!"

She ran to the kitchen and Logan raced up the steps to Doris' room.

"Doris," he screamed and banged on her door with his fists. "The house is on fire, throw on a robe and get out. Go down the back staircase!"

Doris appeared at the door, struggling with a robe, terrified. She caught her breath at the sight of Logan's bloody face.

"Mr. Logan, are..."

"I'm alright, just go, now!"

She ran down the hallway to the back staircase while Logan retraced his steps and flung open the front door. The shingles on the house were burning and sections of the porch were in flames. He ran to turn on a hose that Elina used to water her flowers and plants in the warm months but it had been shut off for the winter.

The wind was feeding the fire and he thought desperately of a way to knock down the flames climbing up the side of the house. He ran back inside and grabbed a denim Mack that he wore when they walked on the beach off a hook near the door. Then he remembered a fire extinguisher in the front hall closet, grabbed it and raced back outside. He used it to smother the aggressive fire that had charred the back of the house and was already climbing toward the roof. He just managed to kill the flames when the extinguisher emptied.

He looked around. Most of the porch was aflame and burning its way toward the house, the creosote-injected wooden planks fueling the flames. He began swinging the denim coat against the fire, shielding his face from the intense heat. He felt his hands burning but continued to whip the heavy coat against the blazing decking.

"You all right?" a loud voice yelled to him. It was a neighbor who had spotted the flames and had run over with a couple of small fire extinguishers.

The denim coat was nothing but a flaming rag by now and Logan's hands were badly burned. There was steam rising off his skin as the neighbor hit the remaining flames with an extinguisher. He heard the siren of a fire truck pulling up the driveway and knew that help had arrived. Finally, the blow to the head, his burns and the heavy smoke combined to bring him to his knees, and an exhausted Danny Logan passed out again on the porch.

The last thing he heard was the sound of the ocean. Elina was right. It was beautiful.

The strong arms of two firemen picked up his limp body and dragged him off the deck. Elina and Doris were waiting at the bottom of the steps as they carried his body to a stretcher. Both women screamed as they saw his burned hands and the blood and soot covering his face.

"Oh, my God, no Danny, you can't leave me now..." Elina cried. Doris wrapped her arms around her and let the medics work.

The firemen placed him on a gurney and a medic placed an oxygen mask over his face. Almost immediately he began coming around. Logan felt someone applying ointment to his hands and arms. Someone else was tending to the gash in his head.

"He's going to need stiches, but I suspect a concussion at a minimum. Let's hope his skull wasn't fractured," Logan heard. The words seemed to come from some distance away. He was going into shock.

"Call it in, tell the hospital we have a male, six foot, 175 pounds, severe laceration to the head, possible cranial concussion or fracture, both hands have second to third degree burns. Patient is in shock."

He felt the gurney move as he was lifted into the air and a jolt as it was pushed into the back of an ambulance. Elina climbed aboard and a medic slammed the doors. Almost immediately, it raced off toward Middlesex Hospital.

Elina looked back at her house. Firemen were dousing the last dying embers of the fire. Damage was limited to the front of the mansion. Danny Logan had saved her precious home.

And her life.

Thirty-Five

~~~ ❧ ~~~

Charles Anderson was on the run, but he had no idea where to run to.

When he decided to burn the Fenwick house down in a moment of complete panic and insanity, his logic was that it would frighten Elina's neighbors into selling him their properties. The rest would follow and within weeks he would have a nice, tidy parcel of land to present to Stephano Vaccaro who would be only too happy to present him with a check for $10 million. Vaccaro and Anderson would go their separate ways, he to build his bridge, Charles to live the life of a rich man.

It was only after awakening the next morning, still in his car hidden behind a vacant cottage in the North Cove, that he remembered he was already living the life of a rich man, and that he had tried to murder his wife, Dan Logan and Doris and committed arson.

462

Little by little, it all came back to him.

The decision to burn the house. Hitting Logan in the head with the heavy flashlight. Struggling with Elina and taping her hands and feet. Looking back at her as he left, feeling no remorse for what he was about to do. Dousing the porch with gasoline. Lighting the match. Watching in elation as the flames grew. And finally, fleeing.

In the childlike state to which his mind had been reduced by his fear of Vaccaro and the violence to which he had been driven, Anderson was confused now. He wondered if he should call Elina and Dan and apologize. But then, without regret, he remembered they were probably dead.

He recalled the scream of sirens, lots of sirens and imagined there were fire trucks, police and... oh, dear, ambulances. Yes, Elina and Dan were surely dead. And Doris, too. She was probably asleep upstairs in her room. That made him sad.

He suddenly felt very tired again, and not being able to think of what he should do next or where he should go, he allowed himself to go back to sleep. His last thought was that it was a shame that the Fenwick house had to burn. It really was quite homey.

While Charles Anderson was sleeping, every police officer in the State of Connecticut was looking for him and Danny Logan was in a critical care unit at Middlesex Hospital. Logan was in no danger, but his burns were severe enough that he'd have to endure excruciatingly painful treatments for some time. The morphine drip was keeping him well-sedated and thankfully unable to fret about his newspaper.

Elina sat by him through the long night, resting her head on his legs when the need to sleep overcame

463

her. A uniformed police officer, courtesy of Chief Sullivan, stood guard outside Logan's room.

Dick McGrath arrived about noon, just as Logan was beginning to come around. He introduced himself to Elina and asked her to step out into the hall.

"Mrs. Anderson, we're going with a story this afternoon identifying Charles Anderson as the person who attempted to murder three people, including you and my boss, and arson last night. We are connecting the incident to the ongoing investigation into 'Sound Crossings,' the proposed Long Island Bridge project, and pressure on Old Saybrook, Fenwick, Cornfield Point and other property owners to sell to him.

"I don't think I have to tell you that this will ruin your husband," McGrath said. "But everything we're going with has been corroborated by multiple sources and witnesses."

Elina looked into McGrath's eyes. There wasn't an ounce of pity to be found there.

"I understand, Dick," she answered. "I mean... I understand what you have to do. I don't have any idea what motivated Charles."

"Actually, I think it's very clear, Mrs. Anderson," McGrath answered bluntly. "First, greed. Second, he's got himself involved with some very bad people. The kind of people who will scare you into doing very crazy things. Anderson's actions last night were the act of an insane man."

She tried one more half-hearted plea.

"You do know that he was severely injured in an automobile accident several years ago and suffered a traumatic brain injury," Elina explained, still loyally trying to save her husband.

"Yes, I'm aware of that. I also know that he was blind drunk at the time of the accident, nearly killed a lot

464

of people and that the charges were swept under the rug probably because of the influence of your late father," he replied. "I don't think we want to go there, Mrs. Anderson. He also was healthy enough to pass the real estate exam, get his license and run his own business. It will be up to a judge and jury to decide if his actions last night were the result of insanity or criminal intent. It is my obligation to report the facts as they happened."

There was nothing else she could say to defend him.

"What Charles Anderson needs right now is a good lawyer, Mrs. Anderson. You might think about getting some legal counsel yourself," McGrath said.

"Whatever for?" she asked.

"I'm probably sticking my nose where it doesn't belong, but I'd sure be having second thoughts about my spouse if she tried to kill me," he said, again being painfully blunt.

Have the police interviewed you yet?" he asked.

"No, they're coming in this afternoon. We were hoping Danny would be awake by then."

"Good, we'll be able to get a statement from the police, as well. I want to talk to Danny if he's awake."

Logan was cleared headed enough to recognize his old friend.

"Jesus, Dan, that was too close. We're going to bury this guy, I swear..." McGrath said.

"No, Dick, just the facts. That will be sufficient, believe me. Get it right, please, that's the important thing," Logan responded.

McGrath shook his head. "Guess there's no other way, boss. How are the hands?"

"I won't be taking any notes for a while, but the doctors said I'll regain complete use of both of them. Not much scar tissue."

"The head?"

"Too hard to dent. They think I have a concussion. Nothing worse," Logan replied, making light of Anderson's attempt to cave in his skull.

"You were lucky, Dan. The newsroom was in shock this morning when the night desk guy sent out an announcement. This is one day when the managing editor is not only reporting the news, he's making it."

Logan laughed, then winced.

"Sorry, boss. Newsroom humor," McGrath said.

"I'm fine, it only hurts when I laugh," he smiled. "Dick, I'm appointing you acting managing editor. I'll call Lou White this afternoon and fill him in. I don't know how long it's going to be until I'm up and around, but I suspect more than a few days. As Greaves used to tell me, you've got the helm. The ship is in good hands."

"Dan..." McGrath was moved. "This is not the way I wanted a promotion.

"Don't let it go to your head. I'll be back," he smiled again. "You're a good man, Dick. And you've got good people. Take care of 'em and they'll take care of you."

"Right, boss."

"You know the paper's under some pressure on the circulation side, right?" Logan asked.

"It's the worst kept secret in the building, Dan. Yah. I know it's bad," he answered.

"Fighting the 'Bishops' hurt us, but there are bigger reasons than that. A lot of things we couldn't control have had a hand in this. But we're not ready to abandon ship yet and Lou has promised me there will be no layoffs. So you don't have to worry about that."

"That's good news. We'll sail her till she runs out of wind, boss," McGrath said, a pragmatist at heart.

"And if I know our team, the last edition will be as good as the first."

Logan grinned, remembering Lou White's similar conclusion.

"Ok, get out of here and get the Bulldog out on time. And Dick..."

"Yah, boss?" McGrath responded.

"It doesn't matter that I'm involved. Get it right, stick to the facts. Make sure you share that with Lynch. I'm counting on you."

"Loud and clear, Dan," McGrath responded soberly. "Rest. I'll see to it that this afternoon's edition is delivered to you personally. Mrs. Anderson can turn the pages for you."

"Shit," Logan said, looking down at his heavily bandaged hands. "I forgot about that."

Elina came back to him as soon as McGrath left. She kissed him on the lips and caressed his cheek. Tears were rolling down her face.

"Danny, thank God you're all right...I am so sorry... I had no idea he was capable of..."

"Stop. What Charles has become is not your fault, Elina. The accident, getting involved in this bridge thing and with the mob... he made those decisions, not you."

"But he's not right, he's not thinking clearly..."

"The understatement of the year," he answered, holding up his bandaged hands as evidence. "Even if that's true, there is nothing you can do. Charles has no one to blame but himself."

He held her, as best he could, as she cried.

"I've made such bad choices, too, Danny. Letting you go was the worst. Can you ever forgive me?" she asked, looking into his eyes.

He took a moment before answering.

467

" I did, Elina, a long time ago."

"This Boy?" she asked, apprehensively.

"Loves you...'will always feel the same'..." he answered without hesitation. She climbed up onto the bed alongside him, careful to avoid his injured hands, and kissed him. It was the kind of kiss that took away the need to say more.

Years of loneliness and wanting evaporated in Danny Logan's heart in just those few minutes.

But 30 miles away, Charles Anderson was also wide-awake and in need of reassurance. He had to talk with someone and figure out what to do.

He pulled out of his hiding spot and drove to the Dock 'n Dine Restaurant just a few blocks away at the mouth of the Connecticut River. He parked the car behind the restaurant to keep it from view, and then went inside to make a phone call.

A waitress changed a few dollar bills for him and he dialed a New York number.

The phone rang and someone picked up but didn't answer. It was what he expected.

"It's Anderson. I need to speak to Mr. Vaccaro," he said into the receiver.

No more than two minutes passed. Then a soft, almost soothing voice came on the line.

"Charles," he heard. It was Vaccaro.

"Mr. Vaccaro, I..."

"Don't say anymore," Vaccaro interrupted without a hint of emotion. "I know all about it, Charles. It's not something we should discuss on the telephone. You should come and visit. I appreciate initiative. Where are you? I'll send a car."

"Thank you, 'Big Steve,' Anderson said with relief and some pride. "I know I can make this right."

"Say no more, just give me the address."

A little more than an hour later, a black Cadillac sedan pulled up outside the restaurant. Anderson was waiting. He expected Vaccaro to get out or open a window and beckon to him. Instead, the driver, a tall, burly man wearing dark sunglasses and driving gloves got out and waved him over, then opened the back door of the car.

"Mr. Anderson, Mr. Vaccaro sent me," the driver said. "If we hurry, we can beat the afternoon traffic back to Manhattan."

"Excellent," Charles replied and climbed in to the back seat.

They pulled out of the parking lot, drove quickly down Main Street and took the entrance ramp on to I-95 south.

"Nice day for a drive," Charles commented to the driver. He didn't respond.

Just outside of Guilford, the driver abruptly took an exit. Charles was confused.

"Why didn't you stay on the highway?" he asked. "Are you going to take back roads all the way into New York?" Again the driver didn't respond but continued driving south on Boston Post Road. After several miles, the car slowed and the driver turned the car on to a dirt road that was barely visible from the street.

"What the hell? What are you doing?" Anderson demanded of the driver. There was only silence. Panicking, Charles tried to open the door to jump out of the moving car. The door was locked. So was the window.

"Hey, let me out! What the hell is this? Vaccaro is waiting for me, he's going to be pissed when I'm late," Anderson yelled. The driver ignored him. A moment later they came to the edge of a large pond. The car

469

stopped and the door locks opened. The driver got out and came around to Anderson's side. He had a gun in his hand.

"No," Anderson said. "Don't you know who I am?" he screamed. He swung the door open trying to hit the driver with it but missed. Jumping out of the car, he pushed the driver out of the way and began to run back up the dirt road. The driver patiently let him run while he took careful aim and fired.

Charles Anderson felt the bullet hit him in the back and fell face forward. There was intense pain for a moment, then nothing. He listened as the driver's footsteps approached, then felt the sensation of being picked up and turned over. He found himself lying flat on his back staring up at the sky. The area was heavily treed, but there were no leaves on the branches that crisscrossed above him. He remembered it was winter. For a moment he thought that was why he was so cold.

Charles Anderson was remarkably calm as he suddenly realized that the only thing he could feel was the cold air on his face. The bullet had severed his spine and he was completely paralyzed. He was going to die, he thought. Then the driver came into view and he straddled Anderson's body. Charles watched as the stranger aimed his gun at his face and again took careful aim.

In the few seconds before the driver put a .45 caliber bullet into his brain, finally putting an end to his warped quest for wealth and recognition, Charles Anderson thought about the people he had screwed over in his young life. The list was long. But the two faces that leapt before his eyes in the last second before he died were Elina and Dan Logan. They had been kind to him. He had returned their affection with ruthless disloyalty. It occurred to him that he deserved to die this way. The driver summed up his epitaph succinctly:

"Do I know who you are?" he mocked Anderson's question.

"Yah, I know who you are. You ain't shit," he said, and pulled the trigger. Three days later, an older couple out for a walk in the woods came upon Anderson's bloated corpse floating at the edge of the pond.

The next afternoon, Charlie Holcombe showed up at the hospital right on schedule with the Bulldog edition of The Hartford Times, the first paper off the press, to deliver it to Dan Logan.

"Punctual as ever, Charlie," Dan said to Holcombe as he entered the room. "I could set my watch by your visit. Let's take a look at the new baby," he laughed, holding out his hand for the newspaper with anticipation.

Elina smiled. She knew how deeply Logan respected his old friend. But she was first to notice that Charlie wasn't smiling today. "What is it Charlie? What's wrong?" she asked. He handed her the paper.

"It's on page one, below the fold," he said, handing her the paper. She took it from him. He handed Logan another copy.

"Sound Crossings" Agent
Found Murdered in Guilford

Elina screamed.

Logan shook his head and sighed.

"Just the facts, Charlie?" he asked. There was no sense of surprise in his voice.

"Just the facts, Danny. Dick McGrath had Tom Lynch triple check the identification. I'm sorry to say the boys got it right.

"It was Charles Anderson. One in the back, one between the eyes.

"A classic mob hit."

Thirty-Six

~~~ ҩ ~~~

January, 1977

"You look like a man who can't wait for the rest of his life to begin," said Charlie Holcombe, Danny Logan's best man at his marriage to Elina Hanson Anderson.

"It shows, huh?" Logan asked with a grin that lit up the dining room of the Fenwick house where he waited with Holcombe and the rest of his bridal party, Jim Greaves and Dan McGrath.

"I honestly didn't know you were capable of looking so happy, Logan," Greaves said, smiling.

"I remember the day you came in to The Times with your tail between your legs begging for a job," Holcombe laughed. "You looked about as whipped as

473

any kid I'd ever seen. It's amazing what a broad can do for your life."

"Now wait a minute, Holcombe," Logan responded. "Wasn't it you who told me, I quote: 'Let go of the broad.'"

"Look..." Holcombe laughed. "Every man deserves one mistake in life. I'm proud to say that was the only one I ever made."

The room was filled with laughter.

How ironic it was that the four friends really had only one thing in common, Logan thought. They were all out of work.

Their beloved Hartford Times had finally printed its last newspaper on October 20, 1976 on one of the saddest days of their lives. Each of them had shed a tear that night when they toasted the paper at a farewell party at the Travelers Spa. The Hartford Times had a 159-year run as one of the great American afternoon papers, but had simply run out of gas. It was a sad day for the city as well, and now the proud building at 10 Prospect Street, with its imposing massive green granite columns stood empty.

When he drove to Fenwick that night he knew that he had lost a great love in his life. But he had made up his mind that he was about to devote the rest of his days to an even greater love.

He walked slowly up the stairs to the porch of the Fenwick mansion and looked out over the Sound. The crashing sea and the smell of the salt air had become part of him now. It was where he belonged.

The front door opened, and Elina stood waiting expecting him to be sad and disheartened. Instead, despite the frigid air but with Long Island Sound as a backdrop and music provided by a choir of ever-present seagulls, he dropped to one knee and said the words he had been dreaming of since they were teenagers.

"Elina, after I find a good job," he began, a deadly serious look on his face that slowly evolved into a mischievous grin, "will you marry me?" He savored every word because he knew what her answer would be.

She sucked in her breath and raised a hand to her mouth. Her eyes filled with tears of happiness in an instant.

"When?" she asked as if he might be teasing her.

"Now."

"Oh, Danny…yes, yes, yes…" she said and ran to him, jumping into his arms with the joy of a schoolgirl who'd just been asked to the prom by the love of her life. They kissed with even more passion than that first furtive night in his old Chevy parked at the New Haven Train Station.

In the nearly two years since the murder of Charles Anderson, they had consciously worked to build the real and lasting relationship that Logan had waited for so long. He wanted to be sure that when the time came for them to make a commitment it would be founded purely on their love for each other. Nothing was more important. Not The Hartford Times, not Fenwick mansion, not fortune or fame. The only thing they couldn't live without was their undying love for each other.

And so, on a cold winter's day at Fenwick, but against a breathtaking backdrop of a cloudless azure blue sky and the deep green waters of Long Island Sound framed by the living room picture window, they became Mr. and Mrs. Daniel Logan.

Staring into each other's eyes, they shared a single vow:

"I promise that every time I look up at the stars, I will think of you."

It seemed that fairy tales could come true. The penniless boy from the South End of Hartford had fought off the devils and dragons and won the heart of the wealthy princess in the castle. They were destined to live happily ever after.

But then came chapter two.

In the spring of the second year of their marriage, Elina asked her husband if he ever dreamed of being a father.

The question exposed a long held fear that surprised her.

"My father hated me so much, Elina," he explained. "I've never known why. But I've always worried that I wouldn't be any better to my children."

"You have the chance to break the mold, Danny. To be a good father. A loving father. The kind of father your children will worship," she said. "I know that because that's the kind of husband you are."

He put his arms around her and kissed her on the forehead.

"There are so many reasons I love you, Elina. One of them is that you fill me with hope," he answered.

"Well, you better 'hope' I'm right," she laughed out loud, "because, 'Daddy,' I'm pregnant!"

Danny Logan let out a 'whoop' that was probably heard across the Sound in Greenport, Long Island. Doris came running from the kitchen fearing the worst but was soon dancing with the couple in celebration. They could not have been happier.

But after the first month of her pregnancy, Elina complained of feeling tired all the time.

"You seem to sleep well at night," Danny remarked when she talked to him about it. "Maybe you just need to get out in the sun more, you look a little pale. We could go to Florida for a while, or it will warm up here soon and you can spend your days soaking up the sun on the Fenwick beach. What'll it be, pal?" he asked. "Your wish is my command."

She laughed. "I'll be ok. Maybe I'll try to take a nap during the day. It's May. Another couple of weeks and the sun will be blazing. Thank you for being so understanding, Danny," she replied.

"Elina, I'll take you to the moon if it will help," he laughed, "but I have to admit, there is very little that I understand about what's going inside your body right now!"

Soon, he would know too much.

Elina's fatigue grew worse, and she noticed swelling in the lymph nodes in her neck and under her arms. Logan insisted she see her doctor.

"I agree, it's probably nothing, but we need to be sure," he said to her in the waiting room."

"I'm fine, I know I am," Elina argued, but she was worried.

When she was finished with her examination, Dr. James Wellsworth invited the couple to join him in his office.

"First of all, the baby's heartbeat is strong, a good sign so early in the pregnancy. But Elina's blood pressure is low and I'm a bit concerned that she is suffering from anemia. We can treat that, but we need to understand why. The lymph nodes are swollen as you suspected, so I've drawn some blood to be tested and we'll see what that shows by tomorrow. In the meantime, don't worry. I'll call you as soon as I see the results. The blood test will also tell us if it's a boy or girl so you'll want to think about whether or not you want me to spill the beans," he said, ending on a positive note.

"Do we want to know?" Elina asked when they got in the car."

Logan laughed. "Up to you darling. What I want him to tell me is that you're healthy."

"You worry to much, but I love you for it," she said and kissed him on the cheek.

"You know, we each own sports cars. One of us is going to have to..." she teased.

"No way!" Logan protested and blipped the throttle of his TR4.

That night as they lay in bed together, Elina's head tucked into the crook of his arm, Danny Logan stared at the ceiling and prayed for the first time since he was a little boy.

The call came just after noon the next day.

"Elina," Dr. Wellsworth said, "your blood work came back and you are definitely anemic. That means the reproduction of your red blood cells is decreasing for some reason. I could just give you some iron pills to help the symptoms, but I would prefer that you see a specialist who can have a look at your lymph nodes as well.

She was startled. "What kind of specialist?" she asked. "Where?"

"I want you to see a hematologist at Yale New Haven Hospital," he said. "Her name is Dr. Brenda Raycraft. She is excellent and has quite a bit of experience with blood disorders during pregnancy."

"A hematologist?" she blurted out in fright. "You mean I have a blood disease?" Logan was standing next to her and watched the color drain from her face.

"It's just a place to begin, Elina. I wouldn't push the panic button, we just need to be certain, ok?" Logan took the phone from her.

"Doctor, Dan Logan. I don't know what you told Elina, but I did hear her say 'hematologist.' When can we get her in to see Doctor…"

"Brenda Raycraft," Wellsworth repeated. "There's no urgency, Dan but neither would I waste any time. I'll call her now and set up an appointment. My assistant will call you back this afternoon. I'm assuming Dr. Raycraft will want to admit her for a couple of days to run some tests. We'll work closely on this. Ok? It's easy for me to say, but try not to worry."

"Thanks Doc. We'll wait to hear from you," Logan replied shakily.

"By the way, do you want to know the child's sex?"

Logan hesitated.

"No. I think we'll wait on that until we can celebrate that Elina's ok."

"That's the spirit, son."

The next morning, Logan drove her to Yale New Haven Hospital for a consultation with Dr. Raycraft. They were quiet in the car, neither having slept very much.

"Hey, favorite Beatles song of all time," he asked her cheerily.

She looked over at him and smiled, knowing exactly what he was doing.

"'This Boy.' I liked the song so much I married him," she said.

He reached over and grabbed her hand, squeezing it.

"I'll be here for you every step of the way," he said, his eyes watering.

"That's the one thing I'm sure of right now, Mr. Logan."

Dr. Raycraft saw them immediately and explained the few procedures Elina would undergo during the day. She was a pleasant woman who spoke with a calming voice and went to great lengths to ensure they both understood everything she said. Logan couldn't help but notice her impressive array of degrees framed on the wall of her office. All from Yale Medical School.

"We'll begin with a complete blood count, called a CBC and blood cell exam and then we'll take some bone marrow samples. You will receive a local anesthetic for the test, so there will be minimal discomfort. We shouldn't need to biopsy the lymph nodes as the blood tests will almost certainly tell us what we need to know." She stopped, letting the young couple absorb what she was saying.

"I know how anxious you both must feel, but please, know that you are in good hands at what I believe is the best hospital in the world. Just hold hands whenever you get the chance and this will be over before you know it."

A short time later, Elina was admitted to the hospital and wheeled away from her husband. Logan kissed her and promised he'd be waiting for her the minute the tests had been completed.

"I love you," she answered. "Always."

He watched as an orderly pushed her wheelchair down a long hall and stood staring for several minutes after she was out of sight. His whole world had disappeared from view.

Logan dropped numbly into a chair in the waiting room and didn't move for the next four hours. He was beside himself with worry and the nagging thought that he had no control over anything that was happening to the woman he loved more than life.

Finally, Dr. Raycraft came out to see him.

"She's resting comfortably," Raycraft assured him. "Come join her. We'll have some results before the end of the day and I'll stop by to talk to you."

Elina was sleeping when he entered her room. As gently as he could, he maneuvered his six-foot frame alongside her on the bed and held her. He fell asleep with his head resting on her shoulder.

Just before seven that evening, Raycraft, Wellsworth and another doctor they hadn't met before came into the room and closed the door behind them. Danny stood up to greet them. He noticed at once how somber they appeared. Raycraft came to Elina and reached for her wrist, checking her pulse out of habit as she began to speak. "Elina, the blood tests and the bone marrow samples tell us that all is not well..."

Logan felt Elina's hand grip his arm as Dr. Raycraft said the words "acute lymphocytic leukemia" and "incurable." He felt lightheaded and his chest tightened when Elina asked about the baby. He didn't hear Wellsworth's response, only saw him shake his head and touch her shoulder in compassion. There was more talk about chemotherapy and the new doctor, an Oncologist, was introduced. But there was only one question that demanded every ounce of courage he could summon to simply ask.

"How long do we have?" he asked staring into Elina's ocean green eyes. They had never looked brighter or more beautiful, even now, filled with tears. He reached across the bed and brought her hands to his face, kissing them.

The answer was vague, "dependent on so many variables," he heard in the distance, never taking his eyes away from her.

Three weeks later, Elina lost the baby. A little girl.

Fenwick
~~~ ૭ ~~~

August 16, 1980

It was almost midnight now, and when I looked down at her head tucked into the crook of my arm, I saw that she was sleeping. I hoped that she had dozed off before the end of my story, so painful to share, even more so to hear. I pulled the blanket up closer to her chin and held her tightly. Her breathing was ragged and her fever was worse.

There was nothing to be done.

I thought back to the last two years of desperate efforts to save her. Chemotherapy, radiation, bone marrow transplants, wonder drug after wonder drug. Nothing had stopped the progression of the hideous disease, only perhaps slowed it. Through it all, she held a smile on her face for me, even as her body withered, her blonde hair turned grey and her eyes, her stunningly beautiful ocean green eyes, turned cloudy.

Amazingly, Elina had spent her last days fretting over me being left alone. Despite my constant demands for her to stop such nonsense talk, she lectured me about taking care of my health, being happy, and most painfully, finding another woman to love.

"Another woman?" I would ask her in feigned disbelief. "What am I possibly going to do with two women in my life? Besides, there was only one girl 'This Boy' ever wanted."

"Who? Tell me!" she would demand, playing the game.

"Why you, of course, you incorrigible little brat," I would answer and she would giggle and laugh until it exhausted her. Then we would hold each other for hours, staring out at the Sound and listening to the waves lapping at the shore.

Now, we had finally reached the end of our story.

I slid my body down behind her on the couch and reached inside her blouse, cupping her breasts with my hands the way she liked when we cuddled in bed at night. I could feel her heart beating in the palm of my hand. Kissing her lovely neck, I said goodbye to the only person in my life that had ever touched my soul.

Gradually, her heartbeat slowed until it finally stopped. I pulled the blanket around her even tighter to keep her warm but it was a fight I couldn't win. She grew cold in my arms. I held her all night, reliving the story of us, over and over again.

When Charlie Holcombe came with our morning coffee, as he did every day, I buried my face in Elina's hair one last time, capturing forever her exquisite fragrance. Then I reluctantly relinquished her lifeless body to my dear friend who tearfully carried her to our bed.

It took me a few moments to get off the couch, knowing that we would never share it again. I finally pulled myself up, walked out to the porch and rested against the railing. The sun was low over the horizon, it's deep morning yellow reflecting off the whitecaps that laced the waves coming ashore.

Eventually I sat in one of the two weathered Adirondack chairs where Elina and I would sip our coffee each morning. I stayed there all day, remembering her and all that she had brought to my life.

She was the beautiful rich girl who had overcome the blind selfishness of affluence to which she had been born to become a compassionate and giving woman. Together we had discovered the real meaning of love, and she had helped me to understand where I belonged and to find my place among the stars.

I waited for the sun to set and the heavens to rise so that I could keep my vow. When the darkness came, I walked down the staircase, across the beach and to the water's edge. And then I raised my eyes into the void and spoke to her.

"Goodbye, my love. But know that you will always live in my heart."

A sudden breeze whipped across the shoreline, kicking up a salty spray against my face. It was if she was prodding me to say the words. I laughed aloud at her typical playfulness.

"You win," I shouted with joy at feeling her presence and screamed into the wind:

"I promise that every time I look up at the stars, I will think of you."

##

Acknowledgements

As I reflect on a career begun late in life, I know that I would never have written a word without the support and encouragement of my wife, Bobbie. There is much I owe her, but nothing so important as my sons Jack and Jay. She has been my partner for nearly 40 years, and I thank God for that late summers day when as a 14-year old teenager, I first laid eyes on her and fell instantly and totally in love. To Jack and my beautiful daughter-in-law Andrea, thank you for your unconditional love, for not allowing distance to separate us, and for giving me two of life's greatest treasures: my Grandsons Charlie and Jackson who fill me with joy and inspiration. To Jay, my buddy down the street, thank you for always being there for your mom and I, who cherish your love and loyalty. May all your dreams come true, my son.

When I began writing "This Boy," I was blessed to have the encouragement of four old friends who sadly passed early in 2016. To Bob, Cathy and Ag King and Eileen McCarthy, I will forever miss your love and friendship and I hope you are raising hell together wherever the party is. And to my great furry pal, Groban, the words came harder this time without you sleeping under my desk as I wrote. I miss you, faithful friend.

To my Grandfather, William J. McGrath, a man who epitomized love and humility, instilled in me a passion for history and filled my imagination, thank you for being there for me. I hope to see you someday to swap a few more stories. I'll bring the Ritz crackers.

Special thanks also to my friend Lisa Orchen, whose remarkable insights and sensitivities make her the consummate editor and author's friend; to Joyce Rossignol, my very first editor who taught me to love the art of writing; to Julie Follett, who opened my eyes; and to my age old friends Bill and Debbie Bartlett, Genevieve Allen Hall, Steve Bazzano, Diane Dustin Lord, Steve Zerio, Carol Russo, Jan Smith, Gail Donahue, Carla Unwin, Michael Jordan-Reilly, Peter Larkin, Cheryl Zajack Barlow, Sharon Tomany Marone, Lisa Rivero Jankowski, Patty Curcio and Earl Flowers, my everlasting thanks for your friendship and endless support.

And finally, my thanks to a few new friends who have accompanied me in my writing career and whose friendship and support I sincerely value: Captain (Ret.) Timothy J. Kelliher and Firefighters Frank Droney and Frank Zazzaro of the Hartford Fire Department; Hartford Hospital Fire Marshall and Chief of the Rocky Hill CT Volunteer Fire Department Michael Garrahy; Jeff Mainville of the Hartford Public Library; Michelle Royer of the Lucy Robbins Welles Library; and Sandy and Marshall Rulnick.

F. Mark Granato, November 2016

About The Author

F. Mark Granato's long career as a writer, journalist, novelist and communication executive in a US based, multi-national Fortune 50 corporation has provided him with extensive international experience on nearly every continent. Today he is finally fulfilling a lifetime desire to write and especially to explore the "What if?" questions of history. In addition to *This Boy*, he has published UNLEASHED, the story of one man's fight against a ruthless corporation, *Out Of Reach: The Day Hartford Hospital Burned*, an historical fiction account of the tragic 1961 fire, the acclaimed novel, *Finding David*, a love story chronicling the anguish of Vietnam era PTSD victims and their families, *The Barn Find*, chronicling the saga of a Connecticut family brought to its knees by tragedy that fights to find redemption, *Of Winds and Rage*, a suspense novel based on the 1938 Great New England Hurricane, *Beneath His Wings: The Plot to Murder Lindbergh*, and *Titanic: The Final Voyage*. Readers are encouraged to visit with Mark on his Facebook page at Author F. Mark Granato, e-mail at fmgranato@aol.com or on his website at Fmarkgranato.com.

F. MARK GRANATO

In memory of my faithful friend
and writing partner,
Sir Groban
2006-2016

Made in the USA
Middletown, DE
19 December 2016